THE MF

Gill Alderman was born in D... with two daughters and five grandchildren. She lives with her second husband (a research scientist), two lurchers and two cats in Cobh, County Cork, Eire. Until 1984 she worked in microelectronics research. This is her third novel.

Voyager

GILL ALDERMAN

The Memory Palace

'Each page a promise that all
shall be well'

HarperCollins*Publishers*

Voyager
An Imprint of HarperCollins*Publishers*
77–85 Fulham Palace Road,
Hammersmith, London W6 8JB

A Paperback Original 1996
1 3 5 7 9 8 6 4 2

First published in Great Britain by
HarperCollins*Publishers* 1996

ISBN 0 00 649773 X

Set in Linotron Sabon by
Rowland Phototypesetting Limited
Bury St Edmunds, Suffolk

Printed in Great Britain by
HarperCollinsManufacturing Glasgow

For H b J

ACKNOWLEDGEMENTS

Special thanks to Sue and Ian, Anne et Hervé and grateful thanks to Ray. Also grateful, and sadly post-humous thanks to Seán Dunne for permission to use the quotation from his poem *Message Home* (published in his collection *Against the Storm*, Dolmen Press, Mountrath, Portlaoise, Ireland, 1985) on the title page.

AUTHOR'S NOTE

The history and geography in this novel are (mainly) fiction.

The quotations which head the four sections of the book are from *The Haunter* by Thomas Hardy; *A Shropshire Lad* by A. E. Housman; *Proverbs of Hell* by William Blake and *The Crusader Returns From Captivity* by G. K. Chesterton. The quotation on the title page is from *Message Home* by Seán Dunne and the verse on page 347 after *For A Gentlewoman*, by Humfrey Giffard (fl. 1580).

PART ONE

JOURNEY SOUTH

How shall I let him know
That whither his fancy sets him wandering
I, too, alertly go?

THOMAS HARDY

His hands ached badly, as they often did at the end of a long keyboard session. He flexed his fingers while he looked out, beyond the screen, into the twilit garden of the old rectory. It was a little cooler; he thought the rosebushes trembled slightly. There might be a breeze, one zephyr only: just a breath of air to end the stifling day. The lawns merged with churchyard and field and, in Humfrey's Close, the Norman castle mound looked bigger than it was, worn down by nine hundred years of weather, rabbits and grazing sheep. A mile or so away, Karemarn's dark slopes were beginning to merge with the night sky.

The sun had set. The only light in the room came from the screen of the computer before the window, a luminescent shield which occulted the world outside as effectively as the steep hill hid the rising moon. It was covered with words, the conclusion of his newest novel and – as necessary an adjunct to his storytelling as the hallowed and familiar phrase 'Once upon a time' – with his authorial adieu to the reader, that essential phrase with which he always signed off at the finish of the task: 'THE END'. Then, his last words, his hand upon the creation: 'Guy Kester Parados, The Old Rectory, Maidford Halse, June 24th 1990'.

He stretched, reaching high, yawned wide. A grisaille light as glamorous as that cast by his mind-mirroring screen filled the garden and the small field beyond it. It was time to be gone. He clicked the mouse under his right hand and saw his work vanish into the machine. He would leave it now, to settle and sift out of his mind; when he returned after the break, he would come to it refreshed. Then, one or two readings, a little tweaking (especially of the unsatisfactory last chapter) and a punctuation check should suffice and he could be rid of it for ever, in the future seeing it only as an entity given public birth by others, separate from him, one more title on the shelf – He made a copy and, reaching up, hid the floppy disk in the customary place in the cracked mullion.

'You may now switch off safely.' He read the prompt and, reaching for the switch, said 'I shall, I shall.' It had been a long haul, this one, through the fifteenth. The landscape of the novels was so familiar that he no longer had to consciously invent it, only travel the road with his chosen company, as used to his fictional country of Malthassa as to the hedged and crop-marked fields of the rural Midlands outside his study window. It was an old picture, this place outside the house; he no longer needed to look at it to remember it, but only inwards, into his mind, where those more perilous places, the dangerous rocks, the wild steppes and untameable floods he had created called him persistently.

If I had gone in for the Church, he thought, would it have made me any happier? Would that honest life have felt more just, more true, than this of spinning the thread, weaving the cloth, cutting and stitching the garment of the storyteller? Would Helen have avoided me, or seen me as a greater challenge? I was a pushover for her after all, most eager to co-operate.

Maybe Dominic will prove to be my truest throw. I'd better take his card with me, and the letter.

He tucked them inside the road map of France and left his study with its confusion of books, papers and ideas; shut the door on it. In the bedroom, he rummaged, flinging socks, pants, shirts on the bed. Bliss it was to be alone, each member of his family far from home engaged in pursuits he could ignore, each task complete, all the bills paid with the monotony of forging sentence after sentence down the years: twelve volumes of his New Mythologies, the Koschei sequence; two other novels; three collections of short stories. And all the ghosts accounted for.

When he had packed his canvas grip he went downstairs. In the hall the ivy girl, the dryad his wife had carved a dozen years ago, bore her containment with grace. She was but half a girl, the remainder a contorted and leafy stem from which she stretched up, always reaching for the moon – his children called her, simply, 'Ivy' and hung their hats and coats upon her limbs. Just now, she wore a cricketer's sunhat on her tangled head and a silky Indian scarf about her slender waist. He took the keys to the Audi from her outstretched hand.

'Goodbye, Alice, I'll soon be back,' he said softly, speaking to the household ghost; but she did not answer him. Instead, the tawny owl called from his roost in the cedar tree, 'Who-o-o-o?'

Dark now, enough for stars. He walked on the lawn and looked up at them. They used to shine more brightly; he had forgotten the names of their constellations. He looked at the fantastic bulk of the house with its turrets, machicolations and flying buttresses. A fancy place for a man of the cloth – but a good home for a writer of Fantasy. He had already paid off the mortgage.

The car was still on the drive – he hadn't bothered to garage it the night before. He had paid for that too. Any top-of-the range car would have done but he had always had an Audi of one kind or another, since his first successes. He moaned about the cost of it, and enjoyed it.

The red car was his escape vehicle, deliverance from jail. He laid the map on the passenger seat and flung his grip into the back. Perhaps he would stop in Christminster, see Sandy; perhaps not – and, for once, decisions did not matter. Nothing mattered, except one fact: that he was now on holiday.

5

On the road, he sat alert in his speeding chair, in control. The car filled the quiet, starlit lanes with noise and rushing lights but, within, cushioned from the world, he found and felt a new intensity, a rebirth of the spirit, free of its monetary and marital chains. That was the illusion. He cherished it.

On Ottermoor he turned aside from the A-road, braked gently and stopped the car beside a gateway. He stretched the ache from his hands, unbent himself and got out. The shire lay before him, silent, dark; it might have been a haven of hope, a place to nurse – what? Not ambition: he had had enough. Dreams? There were too many. Those big fields and the marshy thickets which were all that was left of the old moor were spoiled, despoiled: by today's constellations, the clusters of orange lights above a roundabout; by the whisper of tyres which had replaced the song of the wind; by the small size of the modern world, forever shrinking, caving in upon itself. He could hardly see the moon for manufactured light. There were no otters.

The morning blazed upon him. Another scorcher. He adjusted the air conditioning and the sun visors, put his sunglasses on, flipped through the CDs, selected – ah, the old favourite, *Layla*. It flung him straight back, into 1973; and yet was just sound, a pop song; he felt none of the despair – no, the anguish with which he used to experience the song. 'Darling! Won't you, please?' In those days he had not known what to expect of the next day, much less the future undefined and, while he wondered how (and where) he might seduce Helen Lacey, wailed internally with the music, wrote short stories, went to parties, danced with a variety of women, even with his wife – what was a party in the seventies if it was not a long dalliance to music, truly a series of sexual overtures? 'You've got me on my knees.' No more. He was mature, old to some, and he knew how the world wagged. He turned the volume up and felt return also, as he passed a string of company cars, the sense of adventure and urgency which had set him going; he forgot his painful hands. They, the suited men with order books and briefcases, must be thinking (for they had seen him coming up, a red dot in their mirrors), 'There the bastard goes.'

Here on the motorway time and motion, art and science, were united. On the endless ribbon flowed, grey lanes merging and parting, pale bridge-arches springing nimbly, artfully, over the traffic, gone to be forgotten as the music played. He ought to slow down but the fast car's marque was a logo and an advertisement of his abandonment to the luxury of speed. The four linked circles on the bonnet were symbols of the diverse worlds he had set out to pass through, but not linger in. He had become a gypsy with no goal but the next horizon.

Names and numbers flicked by. The names of the service stations were more relevant than those of places, directionally astray, for the new geography of the motorway had obscure rules where north, south, east and west were always left. The traffic moved frenetically, dancing down the shimmering lanes. He was a part of the cavalcade, held safely in the steel and upholstery of his car, passing from lane to lane, putting his foot down, overtaking with all the energy and dynamics of the vehicle at his command. Outside the ever-changing constant life of the road, the blue lamps glimpsed ahead and the smooth deceleration to a steady seventy; fellow-travellers gliding by, black, white or Indian, once a Dormobile full of red-necked Australians. Lorries were a species apart on high: Norbert Dentressangle, Christiaan Salvesen, Geest and Reem Lysaght. A transporter bore yet more cars to fill the M25, a fleet of new Renault space wagons with the iridescent colours of beetles' wings, metallic green, bronze, amaranth, blue.

'Bloody caravans,' he muttered as he passed a swaying line of them. Caravan of caravans? Caravans of dreams? Squat wagons, like him in going south pursuit of lost ideals;

lightly and impossibly named: the Sprite, the Lapwing, the Pageant, the Corniche, their destinations uncorrupted birds, whispering salt marshes and the sea, the easy hedonism of topless beaches in the South of France, castles (in Spain perhaps) or moated chateaux lapped by vineyards where wine could be tasted and bought.

Helen's painted caravan had been the gateway to ecstasy.

The aching sensation returned again on the M26. He flexed his hands against the wheel. Sod it. But he wasn't going back. Some aspirin or paracetamol would settle it or that new stuff, what was it, Nurofen? Check with a doctor – in Dover maybe? No. He would leave all that behind him, with Sandy, Jilly and the family stuff, and the completed *The Making of Koschei.*

He pulled off the glaring tarmac into a service station. It was called The Clover Patch, and he laughed cynically. He felt tired and persecuted. A group of lorry drivers stared at him, and at the 20V: envy. He paid for his coffee, drank it quickly and, on the way out, bought a paper.

Ten minutes later, he stopped a second time to pick up a hitch-hiker, a young blonde. She did not appreciate his car nor the acceleration it was capable of; he could see one of her hands, tightly gripping the material of her loose, art student's smock, and she sat silent, utterly without small talk. On the busy motorway he had no chance to turn his head and be polite, smile at her.

'Going far? Dover?' he asked.

'I dunno,' she returned and he, the writer, the man whose business was with language, was immediately struck by the earthiness of her accent. 'I' was almost 'Oi'. He negotiated a way past a coach and glanced at her, about to ask: Was she born in his shire? She returned his look, a sprite of ancient mischief capering in her speedwell eyes; and yet there was a deadness on them, a dull glaze of the kind he had seen when he drowned the blue-eyed kittens. She could not be, she was – very like the hanged girl, Alice Naylor. It was luck, some whim of a guardian demon, that he did not steer into the crash barrier, and the girl lurched forward in her seat.

'For God's sake, do up your seat belt,' he said, took one hand from the wheel and passed it over his face.

He overtook a pair of lorries, trembling with the effort, and had to tuck himself in smartly behind a minibus. The leading driver leaned on his horn. The fast lane was empty. He veered out to a chorus of horns, and accelerated. 85, 90, 100, 110 – what was the engine capable of? He glanced to his left: the girl had gone, vanished just as Alice Naylor used, without a goodbye or a smile, to leave him in turmoil, bereft and aching to touch her beautiful, insubstantial body. Could Alice have followed him? Was this an omen or merely a sign of his mental exhaustion? He could not answer his own questions and concentrated on the indisputable reality of his fast and powerful car.

He stopped at the next service station and, in the gents, dashed water across his face and drank huge quantities from his cupped hands. His face, in the mirror above the basin, looked perfectly normal. It was the weather; too much hard work, this last week, his imagination fired up and unable to rest. In France he would shake off these dangerous fancies; and the aching hands. The phantom hitch-hiker! People did not, of course, hitch-hike on motorways. He laughed, and bit off the sound immediately as the door opened and a half-unzipped hulk of a lorry captain walked in and casually showered the urinal with pungent golden rain.

In the car, he first switched on the radio: normality, sound bites of news and chat; next bathed his shattered ego in tacky Queen: amazing how they had kept on going, changing style and image, yet turning out the same old reliable performance. 'Another one,' they sang, 'Another one BIT THE DUST' He was in Dover, automatically had slowed to a sedate street pace. A woman with a buggy standing still to watch him, some boys on bikes. What a fool he'd been back there, driving so dangerously. Lucky no police. The player switched moods for him: Bach, clear and refreshing as water, a quality fugue; anyone could play Queen.

A long sleep somewhere south of Paris, he thought – in a small country hotel with a good restaurant. He handed his ticket to a taciturn collector and was given a boarding card. No need for the passport here, though despite the Community some officials were – officious; but I'll need it for the bloody bank, in France. That poster: 'Prelude', the perfume Sandy wants. Does she see herself like that, stretched on a grand piano at dawn, waiting, naked under a dinner jacket, a conductor's baton in her hand?

A man was waving him on. He drove across the tarmac acreages of the port into a moving queue, bumped up the ramp.

Once upon a time he had been a poor storyteller, one of those who lived in a figurative garret and strove away at his art. He no longer thought of it as Art, that was too presumptuous, too precious a name for his hacking; yet it was still an art and something he had always been guilty of practising, the telling of stories – since early childhood: 'Mummy, Mummy! There's a wolf in the wardrobe!' 'Mu-um! I saw three monkeys up the apple tree!' Unaided, he had turned this facility for imagining the worst and the most bizarre into a career.

Guy settled into the reclining chair but did not open the newspaper he had bought on the road. His eyes ran with tiredness and his hands needed to be bent, stretched and massaged one upon the other. It was hard to break off, be free. He had left the two communications from his unknown son in the car, the postcard with the picture of the hairy Lascaux horse and the brief letter, and so must rely on memory to peruse – the letter, one in a pile from his fans, had dropped into the placid pool of his existence and stirred it up – he had known nothing of this child, Helen's boy; heard nothing – she had left him in December '73. He had not even known she was pregnant! Then, less than a fortnight ago: 'Dear Father –'

Dominic skied and played rugby, 'not cricket like you.' He had been born in Lyon – born fully grown into his father's consciousness, nearly seventeen, to take fourth place in the hierarchy of his children between Phoebe and Ellen. There was no photograph; he must imagine what a handsome lad (or bulky prop-forward) resulted from his union with Helen. Dominic was also a reader. The card referred to the alternative world of the *New Mythologies*: 'This reminds me of the Red Horse of the Plains' – and, indeed, the sturdy Neolithic animal, if it were caparisoned in catamount skins and bridled with leather cut from the hide of a forest ape, would pass for one of the Imandi's herd, a durable mount for one of the Brothers of the Green Wolf.

A wave of guilt passed through him, winding the tension up: he exercised his taut hands once more. He had said nothing to Jilly. No need.

His son's final sentences were the most arresting, the ones he had been fed: 'I am to tell you that Mother knows you are a handsome and successful storyteller who has learned all the skills of life and loving. She longs to confirm in the flesh what she has read.' Then, the clincher, the reiteration of the announcement which had driven him to finish his book and set off for the unknown: 'Your son, Dominic'.

Yesterday. All was yesterday.

Yesterday, when the painters had at last gone home and left the stinging smell of gloss paint behind them, evening had enveloped the stuffy house, wrapping it in a pause, an interval of quiet. For a while no vehicle had passed on the road beyond the wide lawn with its twin cedars and monkey-puzzle. The heat was Capricornian, tropical: a bath in which

11

he was immersed to be boiled gently, to be done to a turn. It summoned unlikely longings to lie with ice-maidens or with the cruel Snow Queen; to plunge into the eternal cold, there forever to die; to have no identity, to be himself no longer.

To be, he had thought, to be nothing, nil, no more man but flesh, dead meat decaying to the bone and then to earth, all one with what was and will be.

The smell of paint and turps had been pervasive and perhaps accounted for the light-headedness he had felt; he was mildly poisoned, a middle-aged solvent-sniffer. He had sat by the open study window and watched the shadows gather beneath the rose bushes. The house remembered, its garden a notebook on whose pages many had sketched their designs. The gold and white pillar-rose marked the place where he had first seen Alice Naylor, knowing who she was, and the memory of it to this day lingered with him, a corrupt but sweet odour which counterpointed his memories of her whose brief life had been brought abruptly to a premature close by the hangman's noose. He had lost count of the times he had seen Alice as she walked about the Old Rectory, or sat quietly on an invisible stool in the very heart of her enemy, the Church Victorious's camp. Her face – which death had drained of all colour – always wore an expression of profound terror and about her neck was a purple scar, where the hangman's rope had bitten her.

He had turned quickly from these painful memories to the other story, the fiction on the computer screen. One or two paragraphs were needed before the final lines he had already composed. He had forced his hands to type.

The frenetic mood, which had overtaken him at the start of the summer and remained with him, had subsided. He leaned back in the chair and took deep lungfuls of the hot and stale air. The ship vibrated as her engines turned; she stirred and trembled as no car ever could, almost alive, wanting to be under way – this most ordinary cross-Channel ferry. Sunlight slanted into his eyes and he masked them with his sunglasses.

How is it that I let myself be troubled by the past? He sank once more into yesterday, physically conscious of his hands. He remembered his initial panic at the intermittent ache: Is it a symptom of the advancing years? Must I learn to live with this neural gnawing, toothache of the tendons; appreciate it for what it is, my particular and personal infirmity, my own mnemonic for mortality – a pocket vanitas or portable skull-surmounted tomb. The escapement shudders, the sands run faster through the glass isthmus – Is it arthritis? Something worse? Incurable? The shadow that stalks us all.

Sandy's explanation was small comfort. Three initials, RSI, encompassed and explained his ills.

In the car last night his hands had kept troubling him. He had tried to forget the pain on the motorway; to lose it in speed – always being ready for the police in their unmarked cars. It was a short stretch before 'Christminster' flashed up its exit number and he fled around the intersection roundabouts and drove more sedately along the Badbury Road.

That way, you missed the dreaming spires. Unless? God damn his habit of turning every thought inside out to discover its psychic symbolism. But fucking Sandy was easy: she gave as good as she got; and he had been in need. He parked the Audi behind her Escort and opened the garden gate. There were shadows on the kitchen blind and he was about to put his key in the lock when a peal of female laughter from the open window made him cautious. He rang the bell: Dr A.F. Mayhew – my literate sex therapist, my sensual D Litt, he thought, and smiled.

His mistress, merry and flushed, opened the door.

13

'Guy! Good heavens!' she said. 'It isn't Tuesday is it?'

'Jesus Christ, Sandy,' he said, irritably. 'I'm not a dental appointment. And it's Monday.'

'Well, what do you want to do? I've a kitchen full of summer students – my American ladies. We've just opened a few bottles.'

'I want to come in,' he said, and did so. 'Next, I want –' He kissed her.

'I don't suppose they'll miss me for a while,' she said. 'Mary's showing them the video.'

'Not blue movies in the suburbs!'

'Really, Guy. It's a record of their stay. They leave tomorrow.'

Sandy's waspish mood began to fail her. Guy was stroking as much of her as he could reach, in the narrow hall.

They went up to the bedroom. The worn teddy which Sandy kept on her pillow annoyed him: a dumb and idiotic rival – which had been in bed with her many more times than he. He shoved it and it fell on the floor.

'You brute,' said Sandy. 'Aah, mmm.' Afterwards, he told her he was on his way to Dover, to the ferry. '"Prelude",' she said, 'That's what I like – as if you didn't know.' She got up and he slept. In the morning, she was there again beside him, ready to hit the button of the alarm before it shrilled.

'Six fifteen, my God,' she said, yawning. 'I didn't get rid of them until two. You've had a fine sleep, anyway.'

'I needed it. I've been working hard. Ow!'

He massaged his hands.

'What is it?'

'They ache. It's worst when I wake.'

'Poor chap! Have you been using your PC a lot?'

'I don't write in longhand!'

'That's what it is, then. RSI, Repetitive Strain Injury – like a sports injury. You've over-strained the tendons. The holiday will help – unless you start using the laptop.'

'I didn't bring it, just paper and pens. I might do some real writing, in my own hand.'

'Instead of Times?'

'New York actually. In the early days I did write everything in longhand. Then I typed it. It was the only way I could make sense of myself.'

'Unbelievable,' she said. She was a lot younger than he and knew him only as a best-selling phenomenon, comfortably placed, and comfortably off – once, he had driven her through Maidford Halse, the Hantonshire village he had lived in for nearly thirty years, and she had glimpsed his house, bulky and solid with accrued respectability, across shady lawns.

'I won the Christminster Prize for my first novel, *Jack's Tank* – the story of a National Service recruit. It's out of print now –'

'I didn't know – never guessed. What happened? What turned you into a Fantasist?'

'Sex,' he said, and she laughed, but with some puzzlement. 'A mortgage and a growing family – as you'll find out yourself one day, when I'm history – or experience.'

Telling this white lie was easier than attempting the convoluted tale of his past misdemeanours and haunting loves.

'Couldn't you have gone on with the serious stuff as well as the *Mythologies*?'

'Authors of Eng Lit are supremely selfish,' he told her. 'Successful pulp novelists can afford to be generous to their families, and their mistresses into the bargain. Look at you: what paid for your abortion and the weekend at Le Manoir afterwards?'

'*Koschei's Envy*, I suppose. That was the last, wasn't it?'

'I finished *The Making of Koschei* before I drove here last night.'

Sandy looked into his face.

'Does it matter what tale you tell,' she said, 'as long as

you have the power to overwhelm your reader's senses and hold him in your grip – for as long as the story lasts?'

'In theory, no; in terms of monetary reward, yes. Tell me, Sandy, do you give your students in-bed tutorials? Must I write a dissertation before I get my oats?'

He embraced and fucked her vigorously, quite certain that he demonstrated much more ardour and skill than a younger man; lay relaxed and satisfied across her and played with wisps of her titian hair (the colour was natural, unlike his wife's).

'You should get some Chinese balls,' she said, dreamily.

'I beg your pardon?' Her comment startled him. He was not sure if she was joking, or criticizing his performance in some obscure female way.

'Chain of thought,' said Sandy. 'Like these, look.' She leaned from the bed and took from the bookshelf a small, cloth-covered box which she opened to disclose two silver balls resting on red velvet. 'They keep your fingers supple, a kind of physiotherapy. Like this: roll them about on the flats of your hands. Might help your aches. Avis Dane swears by them. She's a pianist and she uses hers every day to exercise her hands.'

The balls rang softly as they travelled round her out-stretched palms.

'Bells too!' said Guy. 'Very dubious, one of these pseudo-scientific cures. I bet it has its origins in magic – or is an urban myth, like the Child Who Was Kidnapped At Disneyland, or the Phantom Hitch-hiker.'

He tried to imitate her, bending and tilting his hands so that the balls rotated. It was hopeless. One after the other they slid off and landed with dull chimes on the bed.

'There's a lot of alternative medicine about – it works, too,' said Sandy doggedly. 'I take evening primrose oil for PMT. I suppose it's a New Age thing – but real enough, not gypsy stuff.'

'I used to know a gypsy well,' he said, half to himself.

'Mm?'

Unwise to tell; and again, too complicated. Besides, he was sleepy.

'Oh, nothing, thinking ahead,' he said, pulling Sandy down beside him. She was warm; she was short and tucked neatly inside his embrace, like his wife – but was without Jilly's middle-aged creases and sags, smooth, taut-limbed. Poor Jilly, away in the States being mauled by art-lovers. Her carvings were more exciting than she, these days – shouldn't have had another child, so late. Could he remember Helen's body? She had been – what? Years ago. Perfection, exact of proportion, well-endowed by Dame Nature or by one of those dead mother-goddesses she'd revered. He was on his way to see her. Possibly. And Dominic, their son. He slept and dreamed of a boy and a man, who both looked like himself; they fished in a bran tub and caught Christmas tree baubles and silver bells. Then he had to run: something huge and clanking rushed past him – he had to catch a train! He had to catch up with someone! 'Helen! Wait for meeee!' he cried, but his mouth was sewn shut with black thread. He jumped awake.

'– time?' he asked.

'Seven.'

'I'll never catch that ferry now.'

'Yes you will. You still have four hours.'

Sandy, in her dressing gown, made breakfast for them. It was her kind of breakfast with yoghurt, muesli and freshly squeezed juice; usually, he delighted in the differences between her way of life and his own. Today, they irritated him. That Garfield poster above the fridge. Why on earth? – she was a bright girl. They had said goodbye lightly, and left a great deal unsaid.

Coming to, he saw his fellow passengers about him, heard their incessant chatter and the magnified voices booming from the television overhead. He sat upright to massage his hands, imagining the strained tendons chafing in their narrow sockets. RSI. What a bugger, what a hollow laugh: he had a fashionable complaint. Last night he had needed sex; now he needed a drink.

Guy Kester Parados, author (BA Christminster, Caster Cathedral School and Fawley College, born Alfrick-on-Severn 1941, married Jillian Meddowes, sculptor, 1962, six legitimate children and four illegitimate excluding two abortions and one miscarriage), went to the Camargue Lounge. Under his left arm he carried a copy of the *Independent* and two books, *A Year in Provence* and the first volume of *A la recherche du temps perdu*. He wore jeans and an Armani tee-shirt. A linen jacket was slung across his shoulder. He was about six feet tall, with thick grey hair, grey or blue eyes, and was clean-shaven. He might have been any age between forty and fifty, although he was two months short of his forty-ninth birthday. He had no peculiar distinguishing marks and kept himself fit by playing cricket and by taking long country walks; had, in any case, no hereditary tendency to fat.

He experienced some difficulty with the number of objects he carried and resolved his problem by stacking the books and paper on the bar while he removed his RayBan sunglasses. He ordered a pint of Theakston's Ale. When it was served, he took it to a table by a window and nursed his glass. After putting on a pair of horn-rimmed spectacles, which gave him a bookish air and made him look suddenly older, he opened the paper and read steadily, scanning the headlines first before turning back to peruse the articles in detail. Occasionally, he took a drink from his glass. He looked up once to stare at a blonde girl who sat at a nearby table, shook his head and read on; again looked up, at the mural on the opposite wall of ibis making piebald patterns against a landscape of fluid sky and marshland.

* * *

18

'I began building the year the Sacred Ibis left the marsh. The foundations were soon dug and the footings laid. It was, after all, a small building. Many years passed before my spiritual troubles began, coinciding with the first extensions.

'A new building for a new decade (my third). I was full of hope and my plans for the future excited me almost as much as the architectural drawings themselves; and far more than the white hands which, joined in prayer and resting on the sill of the confessional, were all I could see of Nemione Sophronia Baldwin, the youngest daughter of the reeve.

'I had almost resolved to leave the Order. Strict observance of the Rule was very hard for a young man of twenty who could control neither himself nor his dreams, which were of an explicitly sexual nature. Yet Nemione's self-sacrificing patience was an object lesson to me. Though I was tempted to abjure my vows and join myself to a battalion of the Brotherhood of the Green Wolf, I resolved to remain at Espmoss for two more years of study and then take what came. My courage was not of a high order. My disordered infancy followed by a childhood spent learning the Rule had made fear a close companion. I had often been whipped, at school by the proctor, Baptist Olburn, and in the cloister by Brother Fox, the Disciplinarian. The contemplation of freedom seemed sin enough.

'We were free in all other respects. That I was allowed to begin this building (now such a remarkable edifice, as you see!) demonstrates how liberal was the Rule toward ambition. I had successfully completed my years as altar boy and novice: my building and the beautiful drawings of it were a kind of reward. The lodge (it was too small in those days to be called a palace) would contain both past and present, that much was obvious but, before I laid one stone, I had a tantalizing decision to make: should I now commence to erect the walls – they were to be of the finest white marble – or should I forsake the dark footings while I designed and planted the gardens?

19

'The reeve's daughter wore a gold chain about her slender neck. A small gold cross hung from it, one of the symbols of our faith. The four arms of the cross represent the points of the compass, north, south, east and west, and thus, our world, both material and spiritual. The device also represents the many cross-roads which we will find ourselves paused at, during life, while we ponder a vital decision: which direction to take now?

'I had come to such a node myself or, if the metaphor may be laboured a little more, stood simultaneously at two. I had chosen to ignore the one; the dilemma of the other, smaller problem, lodge or garden, I solved in an ingenious way: I would attempt both tasks at once, devoting the cool mornings to the garden and the afternoons, which the sun made warm and pleasant, to the building. I determined to plant the equivalent of Nemione's cross, our life, in my garden, and make it the basis of my design. This was difficult. Perhaps if I sited the building at the centre of the cross . . . but that precluded all additions. I might construct the cross-design in one quarter of the whole – such exquisite and nice considerations! The extensive gardens should both begin and complete my pleasure. The forbidden word again; it haunted me. A Green Wolf has every opportunity – is master of himself and of all the worldly delights I forbade myself. A Wolf would not linger in the cloister, hoping to catch a glimpse of Nemione. He would stride out to look for her.

'I wanted to make nothing less than a shrine in which every object, animate or not, made spiritual sense. This is the reason for the incompleteness of the "wilderness" walks. They should be creations of artifice but I could not exclude such intruders as the wild rose and the coconut-scented gorse, nor these fine thistles and docks – and why waste genuine sports? I am even now too ambitious; and still too lazy to achieve all my ambitions.

'Notwithstanding these outside imperfections, the interior

of the building is, as you will see, in perfect order. We will climb the staircase (genuine porphyry – but mind the broken step!) and enter by the brazen doors which, yes, resemble more than a little the Gates of Paradise.'

The old man took a key from the leather wallet he wore on his sword belt, fitted it to the lock and turned it.

'I love to entertain my visitors (few enough) with such speeches,' he said. 'They are props to the ailing structures of my mind. As for the palace – here it is. I cannot escape from it. It has swallowed me whole, mind and body, hates and loves, possessions, beliefs, gold – that which glisters and is my fool's reward and grail attained.

'Since I am the one you never forget, it will be easier if I show you round. I'll make you regret your memories of me! The grand tour I think, the one that takes in all the sights, leaves not a stone unturned. I do not have the resilience of some, not now. I lack the boldness of those outside.

'Here we are. I'll close the door – it lets in too much light, and also dirt, from outside. This is the chamber in which I was born. You must begin at the beginning, you see, if you are to make sense of my memory palace.'

His guest craned his head forward as he tried to distinguish from the general gloom the heavy pieces of furniture with which the room was furnished.

'Could we have a little light?' he asked.

'A glimmer!' His guide struck a match and lit a small bull's-eye lantern. But even with this it was hard to make anything out – the furniture seemed very big and also far away, the sort of dim and massive wooden giants he remembered from early childhood, of bottomless chests, cavernous wardrobes and tables as big as houses. He stepped gingerly forward.

There was a bed. The covers were partly thrown back, white sheets, blue blankets and a patchwork quilt. He might just about manage to climb up. His teddy bear lay on the quilt; the smell was right – Castile soap and eau de Cologne, a faint overlay of sweat.

'Mummy?' he said and heard the dry laugh of the old man with the lantern.

'Sorry, young man. I cannot preserve *your* memories.'

'But this is my mother's bed; where I was born, not you.'

The old man laughed again.

'That remains to be seen,' he said. 'The case as yet is unproven.'

Guy read the book review in the centre pages of his newspaper. It spoke highly of a new biography of the Jesuit priest and scholar of Chinese, Matteo Ricci, who in the sixteenth century had invented a mnemonic system which used an imaginary building, such as a palace, and its furnishings as an aid to memorizing (for example) tenets of the Catholic faith. When published for his Chinese patron, Ricci's method attracted many converts: the memory palace was open to guests, who used its courts and statuary to understand the new faith. Guy shivered. This kind of thing happened all too often: he devised a fictional description or idea and, a few days later, read of it in the newspaper or heard someone describe it on the radio.

He re-read the article, his imagination caught and held by his parallel idea of a building full of memories, a cenotaph of reality as phantom-like as memory itself, and then, remembering he was on holiday, he turned to the sports pages. He read the breakdown of the cricket scores and forgot them immediately. The last lines of an old story came to mind: '"Damn you,"' she scrawled across the parchment, "you sucking incubus, you salivating fiend from the abyss, you who have stolen my voice and left me with shadows; left me nothing but a dark palace peopled with ghosts and my fantasies."'

The words sank beneath the troubled surface of his mind.

He looked out of the windows: these huge sheets of glass could not be described as portholes, nor anything nautical, and belonged to the holiday fantasy. The sea was calm and sunlit; the busy Channel, on which the traffic moved as steadily as on the motorway, had a peaceful, purposeful air. He enjoyed being at sea and let his gaze wander over the other holidaymakers in the room. The girl had gone, it was mostly families – someone had left a hat on a nearby chair, a familiar, frayed straw with a wide brim and a loose band of white chiffon. He remembered where he had seen it: by the Congo, the Amazon, the Nile, the Ganges – all on TV; and by the Thames when its owner, Etta Travis, had leaned on the Embankment wall beside him. After somebody's party. They had talked about the river below them; what treasures, such as the Battersea Shield, it had given up; what might remain concealed beneath the succulent mud. Then Etta had run suddenly after a taxi, hailing it with her hat; and she and the famous hat had been whisked away into the summer night.

Etta was approaching him from the bar, a glass of wine in her hand.

'Guy!' She had a pleasant voice, was pleasant altogether and feminine, always dressed in skirts, never trousers, even in the remotest outback, jungle or prairie, her habitat so much more than the streets of London. They were long skirts of gauzy Indian material; indigenous peoples respected her because of them, she maintained. Yet, if her style had not been so well-known, such dress would have been anachronistic here amongst the garish shorts and jingoistic tee-shirts of the other passengers.

She retrieved her hat and sat down beside him.

'This is a prosaic way to begin an adventure,' he said.

She smiled. 'I'm on holiday – on my way to a cousin in Tuscany. Yourself?'

'Likewise. Just drifting. Jilly's in New York – exhibition.'

'I saw it in *The Times*. What beautiful work! I must buy

23

some for myself before it all disappears into the mansions of the seriously rich!'

They continued to make small talk. He was disappointed in her: an anthropologist who travelled the world as she did should be incapable of such chit-chat. He wanted her to tell him tales of centaurs, mermen and sirens, long yarns of her perils amongst the anthropophagi; to fulfil the fantasies he, and her viewing and reading public, had of her wading through crocodile-infested rivers, smoking with head-hunters, chewing coca high in the Andes – and always commentating, telling everyone what, why and wherefore. In exchange he wanted to tell her of the places he knew well, those way beyond her wide experience, those she – however determined she was, however much she desired to explore them – might only visit by proxy in his storyteller's magic shoes: the eternal forests, endless plains and everlasting cities of Malthassa. She met extraordinary characters, he created them; he explored an internal world, but hers was external and bounded by space and time, by the present and only time she could experience: this crowded bar, these inane, sentimental, holiday-making Brits.

'If you don't mind me saying so, this is a slow old way to reach Italy,' he remarked. 'I should fly.'

'My car's down below. I shall take a few days over it, drive south, maybe east into Switzerland, drop down Europe that way –'

'No undiscovered peoples?'

'Europe gave up her secrets long ago. Excuse me now –' She drained her glass. 'Or will you join me for lunch?'

'I'll wait until I can get some French cooking.'

'It's habit with me: eat what's available in case there isn't any more. Goodbye, Guy – nice to see you again. *Bonne chance!*'

'*Bonne route!*'

*   *   *

24

The interlude with Etta Travis had made him restless. He gathered his books together: perhaps he should buy something for his son – but what kind of boy was Dominic? What were his tastes? Should he buy some small gift for Helen? He made his way through the crowds, towards the duty-free shop.

The reception area near the shop was thronged; he had not realized before how busy the ship was. Lots of people, mostly young backpackers, sitting on the floor; some seasickness cases lying flat. Someone should clear a passage: what if there was an emergency? He was stepping over and amongst the bodies when his gaze, always quick to interpret the printed word, was arrested. One of the poor sailors had fallen asleep with a book open in her hand. He could just about make out five words at the page-heads: *Lèni la Soie* and *Evil Life*. He knew something of Lèni, Silk Lèni, poor French silk worker, prostitute and accomplice of a psychopathic priest beheaded (for that, call it what you will, 'guillotined' or, dully, 'executed', was what had been done to him) in Lyon in 1884. Helen Lacey had kept the original of Lèni's diary in her gaudy gypsy van; presumably had it still, unless it had been consumed in the fire. The acrid smell had filled his lungs and filtered into every one of his garments, remaining there for weeks, a distillation which evoked the heap of smouldering ash which was all that remained of the van and its ornate fittings.

The sleeper stirred. Now he must notice her whom he, on holiday to escape his personal Furies, had tried to ignore: the blonde girl in baggy-kneed leggings and loose shirt; the girl, of no more than sixteen or seventeen years, who was so naively beautiful.

The book – the god-forsaken book! It had slithered to the floor and closed. He could read the words, printed over the drawing of a guillotine blade, on the cover:

THE EVIL LIFE OF SILK LENI
CURSED BY HER BEAUTY,
CONDEMNED BY HER APPETITES,
LENI WAS DAMNED

There was a conspiracy. Some devilish conjunction of memories and events was following after him, was there before he had time to think or act. This girl, whom he had noticed drinking lager in the bar, was like the one he'd given a lift to, or thought he had: the mute (for she still slept) expression of some kind of prevision or hallucination, a being he had brought into life by *thinking*. She looked like ghostly Alice Naylor.

Nonsense! A daydream, a girl, a book he should have known about. These added up to nothing more sinister than coincidence – and perhaps it was stupid to try to combine a restful holiday with a visit to his one-time lover and their son.

A little regretful because he wanted to steal the girl's book and read it at once, he made a mental note to buy a copy when he got home, stepped clear and paused to look back. The girl was stretching, her regular Quattrecento angel's lips drawn back, her mouth open in a wide yawn. He reached into his pocket and extracted his sunglasses; put them on. Now invisible in his disguise as an older but fashion-conscious and confident man he entered the duty-free perfumery, where he was again confronted by the *id*-Sandy, black jacket open, scarlet, lacquered nails closed eloquently about her conductor's baton: a symbolic prelude indeed! Now Helen's favourite perfume – would he find that here? He remembered its name perfectly: 'Sortilège' – Spell.

* * *

26

The car ferry *Spirit of Adventure* passed easily through the crowded waters of English Channel. Her wide decks were dazzling in the sunlight, her red, white and blue logo and liveries placed and labelled her; she came to Calais, if not precisely in peace, at least in the certainty of commerce.

Most of the vehicles that clanged off her car decks were family conveyances, big, new, shiny – but crammed with luggage, children and their toys. Henrietta Travis drove a small Peugot and was alone. She glimpsed Guy's flash red car behind her and smiled. He would be taking the *autoroute*, eating up kilometres and fuel while she, on *routes nationales* and by-ways, headed for Alsace – or the Franche-Comté. She would take the road for Reims, make no firm decision yet. The sun still shone, hours before dark – but now, there was a delay, one of those inexplicable stoppages common to all traffic queues. After ten or fifteen minutes, they began to move again and soon were rolling past the barriers. No one stopped Etta.

At the ferryport gate the usual cluster of hitch-hikers waited. Etta stopped her car beside a pale-faced girl whose choker of black velvet only emphasised her pallor. She looked sick and bewildered.

'Are you all right?'

'It's just the sea: I travel better by air.'

'Want a lift?'

'Paris? The A1?'

'I'm going to Reims, but I can drop you near Cambrai. There's an intersection: you ought to get a lift south there.'

'OK.'

The girl got into the car. She was very slim and very young, Etta noticed; but clearly an experienced traveller. Etta had started travelling in such a way herself, made no judgements and asked no questions. They talked about holidays and clothes.

*　　*　　*

Guy was relieved to be back in the Audi. While he waited in the queue, he re-read Dominic's letter to verify his destination: 'Coeurville, Burgundy', that was all. When he reached the town – or village – he would have to ask. He hoped it was a small place.

The official at the passport control barrier, who had been busily waving cars on, signalled him to stop. He took a cursory glance at both versions of Guy's face, grinned and said,

'My wife reads your books, Monsieur Parados, the translations. There is money in books? I shall tell her you come to France in your beautiful Audi – "*Vorsprung durch Technik*", Monsieur! Good holidays!'

Guy smiled vaguely, and drove on. Even the grey bypasses of Calais looked welcoming in the sun, which shone as fiercely as it had on the English side of the Channel; but he did not linger. Calais must always be a place to leave.

The car went faster in kilometres, 180; reading this speed and its mph equivalent on the dial, he had to remind himself that both were illegal. At three o'clock he pulled into a service station and bought coffee and *pain au chocolat* – a childish pleasure this. Though you could buy the stuff at home these days it was a quintessentially French delight. Who else would think of enfolding dark chocolate in flaky yeast pastry and serving it as a snack?

He walked back to the parking area. He was clear-headed now and relaxed, the pain had left his hands: it had been a result of tension, nothing more – and damn Sandy's theories and her odd Chinese therapy. After a bad start, the holiday had begun. Before he started the car, he made sure of his route, A1, Périphérique, A6, and chose a CD to begin with. *Phaedra* was suggestive of continuous speed and a longed-for destination.

He turned the key, signalled, glanced in the right-hand mirror, began to drive away and glanced again: a girl, the girl, was there, a little way behind him, walking on the grassed reservation in the centre of the car park. Ghosts did not behave like that. He stopped the car and touched a button: the window beside him glided down and he looked out.

She was exquisite, striding out; untouched like a painted icon or a very young child. An orange backpack hung from her right shoulder. He, to her, was old; but he would presume, confident now that he was sure of his priorities and certain that the holiday had begun.

'Do you need a lift?' he called.

That was all he was offering, for God's sake.

She looked up, located him. Her voice came clearly to him.

'Please!'

She was running, her breasts lifting her shirt as she moved, her backpack bumping against her shoulder; she was beside him. Her face, as she looked at him, was innocent and he was relieved to see that it differed from that other in his memory, the sly and shy face of the dead witch, Alice Naylor; and disturbed again to see that she wore a black velvet choker fastened tight around her long, white neck.

'Get in, then,' he said, committed. 'Here, let me take that.'

She was there, in his car; seated beside him. Her leggings were marked with dust and her shirt had a coffee stain on it, but she had recently combed out her hair and smelled of the soap in the restaurant toilets.

'Hi,' she said.

'Hello. Which way do you want to go?'

'Oh, quickly, quickly: what a lovely car. Are you famous or something? It's called "GUY 5"'

'I am Guy. It's my fifth Audi. I am going past Paris and down the A6 toward Auxerre. Is that any good?'

'Who cares? – yes. I have to be in Lyon by Friday: Dad's picking me up.'

'He's already on holiday?'

'He lives in France. He and Mum are divorced – she's in Eilat with her toy boy.'

29

'I see.' A prematurely old, wise child; and made so by the behaviour of her parents, he thought.

He drove, and she talked. She made this journey several times a year, she said, from her Kent school to her father's house near Lyon. Of course, she was meant to fly (Dad sent the air fare every time) but she, although hopeless on a ship, preferred to take the ferry and hitch. No one ever checked, neither the school nor her father – and it would be easy to invent a likely story. She spent the money on clothes and CDs.

'What CDs have you got?' she asked. 'Here?' and rummaged through the stack.

'You're an old hippy, like Dad,' she remarked. 'Did you know that Phaedra hanged herself?'

'Yes,' he said, but he was thinking, the association no doubt triggered by the music and her remark, that she was about the age of his eldest daughter, Phoebe.

'She fell in love with her stepson, who rejected her. Then she hanged herself,' he said.

'Do you have any children?' the girl asked.

'Yes.' He thought, Gregory is twenty-two and married, with a baby daughter; Daniel is seventeen; Phoebe sixteen; Ellen fourteen; Grace eleven; Ben six. 'They're on holiday.'

'They?'

' 'Fraid so.'

Dominic was sixteen too.

'I'm going to visit one of them,' he offered.

'Don't worry about it,' she said and suddenly and lightly touched his knee. 'I have – um – four half-brothers. One of them is black.'

'Oh?' She had removed her hand but left a sweet and subtle disturbance with him, of both body and mind.

'Who are you, then?' she enquired. 'Guy – ? '

'I write,' he told her. 'I expect you've seen my books – the *Malthassa* series, the *New Mythologies*.'

'Really? You're *Guy Parados*. We did *Malthassa* for GCSE.'

'Jesus Christ! That's recommended reading? I'd no idea.'

'You should be pleased: all those teenagers reading about sex and magic, though they cut most of the sex out of the school version. I bought my own copy and read the whole thing.'

He felt his past experience propelling him, as surely as the car. His right foot, sympathetic, bore down and the car's acceleration blurred the green fields of France. The girl drew in her breath and, expelling it gustily in the word, exclaimed 'Wow!'

'And your name?' he asked, lightly holding the car on course.

'Alice, Alice Tyler.'

He misheard her, wilfully or by that psychic trick which turns what is heard into what is desired. Distant memories called him with soft and echoing voices.

'Alice,' he said, 'Alice Naylor?'

'Not "Naylor": "Tyler" – T for Tommy. And I'm usually Allie.'

The bright world of the *autoroute*, its unfolding, motionless ribbon and his speed held him in their turn.

'Oh, no,' he said, and grimaced; then smiled. 'You are not an Allie, you are most definitely an Alice.'

'Who's Alice Naylor? Your girlfriend?'

'Alice,' he told her, 'is someone I read about.' (He could not say 'know') 'She died a long time ago, in 1705. She is buried in my village.'

He drove on through the Vallée de l'Oise while the girl chattered. Sometimes he had the illusion that he was driving his eldest daughter; Phoebe had picked up the same vapid talk and culture from her friends. He watched the road, as he must, and noticed the traffic on it which, lighter than that of England though it was, had still a good variety of vehicles. There were obvious differences, more Mercedes and

31

Renaults, no Vauxhalls, and, while he wondered what had become of the motorists from the ferry, they passed a little clutch of British cars. No salaried holidaymakers in these, a Rolls and a new Jag, two big Rovers. Then came three British lorries, giant kith and kin of the European trucks he had passed on the M25. The road signs looked international. How long, he wondered, before the cultures merge? This is Europe, not France. Individuality is disappearing.

Alice spoke,

'The secret places have gone – the deep tree-filled coigns, the lazy rivers and grassy banks, the unexpected flower-studded meadows,' she said. 'This is all there is – motorway, bridge after bridge after bridge. Europe has shrunk.'

'What?' He was annoyed – no, just mildly disturbed – to hear her speaking in such an adult and authoritative voice.

'You were thinking how much things have changed, weren't you?' she replied. 'Don't worry. The perilous places still exist – they've just moved over a bit. In a sense, they are even further from ordinary people than they were before, they are so hard to reach. But a storyteller can find them.'

He glanced at her and while he thought, so briefly, that her mix of semi-adult profundity and teenage chat would be odd if it were not so engaging, noticed only that her expression was demure and that her hands were folded, not in her lap as they would be if she wore a skirt, but because of the encasing leggings, against her groin.

Rain surprised them as they passed through a national park. He read its name aloud, from the sign: 'Parc Jean-Jacques Rousseau.'

'I wonder where the noble savages live now,' he said, half to himself. 'Perhaps Etta knows.'

'There?' he wondered, as Alice waved to a group of bikers.

'They're giving us the V-sign,' she said.

'We're going faster than they can.'

'No. Like Churchill not "up yours" – aren't there noble savages in Malthassa?'

He frowned. The world he had created in his mind had grown so vast, he sometimes had trouble remembering all of it. It had got away from him, he felt, and was trying to live on its own. The frown helped him grasp and hold it.

'No,' he said. 'There are only the Ima and they are neither noble nor savage.'

Then they were entering the choked sprawl that is outer Paris and were caught in a crowd of traffic as dense and wild as any London jam. It moved erratically but always at high speed and he had neither time nor attention for Rousseau's philosophy.

'Look out for the signs which say "Lyon",' he snapped. 'No, don't talk.'

'OK, OK.'

His hands involuntarily tightened on the wheel and a painful spasm passed through them. He felt a waterfall of sweat run down his back, despite the air conditioning. No wonder: the heat. The signs above the road shimmered with it and he read the ambient temperature on one, 28C; checked it against the readout in the car. As he looked at it, the 8 became a 9. Alice had found the bottle of water he kept in the car and she undid and passed it him without comment.

Nemione Baldwin knelt to dip water from the river. She lowered the brass cup into the current and held it steady there, so that the water which filled it flowed with the stream.

'Thank you, nivasha,' she said, and spilled a few drops of water on the ground. I leaned forward anxiously to look into the water but could see nothing there except the stones of the river bed. Should I have seen the nivasha lying on her underwater bed of green weed or, worse, swimming towards me, I would have been mortally afraid – and eternally curious, filled with the same desire for change and danger that makes men climb mountains or trek into the forest's infinity.

33

Nemione handed me the brimming cup and I drank gratefully.

She had changed a great deal; but no more, I suppose, than I. Her loose, maiden tresses were gone. The fair, almost white hair was braided and looped about her ears and pinned in elaborate merlons high on her head – that was how it looked to a military man. She wore a long gown of green stuff, open from the waist down to show white petticoats. There were rings on her fingers and jewels at her throat and in her ears.

But in all this elaborate show there was no hint of seduction or carnality. The gold cross of our Order hung chastely amongst her trinkets.

As for myself, the reflection in the slower water at the riverbank showed a dark and travel-weary face above a dented cuirass from which the embossed wolf's head had all but worn away.

'So you became a licensed outlaw,' said Nemione.

'And you a lovely and fashionable lady!'

She laughed – the sound was richer than it had been when it echoed in the cloister – but it suggested wit and a keen mind, rather than woman's art.

'What gallantry! Who would have thought that silent Koschei Corbillion would grow into such a cavalier?'

She drew a fan from her pocket and flicked it open; put it to her face and looked at me over its rim. Her eyes were the colour of male sapphires, or the Septrential Ocean, and they matched the blue eyes painted on the fan. She flicked the fan which subtly and rapidly was changed, becoming a thing of grey estridge feathers, then a froth of rose and white blossom; again, and it was as green as her skirts, a simple chusan leaf.

'Perhaps not "My Lady", but Prestidigitator,' I said.

Nemione shook her head.

'That is for gypsies and mountebanks.'

'Then . . . Sorceress?'

'For the time being let us agree on Prentice.'

She touched the leaf and folded it away like a fan.

'You, Sir Koschei, Wolf's Brother,' she continued, teasing me. 'Are you in search of your fortune, or a pretty wife perhaps?'

'I have left one war to journey to another,' I told her. 'That's the truth of it. My apprenticeship will be as long and as hard as yours.'

'But fighting only lays waste to the body!'

'Not true. It saps the spirit just as well.'

'But you are young, and strong enough for it. How long is it since you left our Order?'

'Two years this day week.'

'Then I left it only days after you.'

A breeze came rustling through the forest and stirred her fortress of hair and her finery. She sighed and tapped one foot on the stones by the river.

'I would travel more simply,' she said, 'but I thought this frippery a good disguise – the peasants will do anything for a high-born lady. Did you see my dwarf as you came along the track?'

'I saw nothing but the birch trees and the birds in them – and a hind in the shadows.'

'He is an idle knave! I sent him forward to spy out the way.'

'Surely it is dangerous to be here, alone. What if I were more Wolf than Brother? What if I were the Duschma with her sharp nails full of poison and her ulcers festering with the pox?'

Nemione stood up straight. 'I am in no danger,' she said, with more than a hint of pride. 'I may be an apprentice but –' With a dextrous twist of her fingers she made the folded fan disappear and, in its place, a narrow tongue of flame grow. She held out her hand and invited me to touch the flame which, notwithstanding my fears, I did. It was cold.

35

'Now watch!'

She tipped her hand and the flame slid down it, dropped to the ground and burned there. Soon it was licking through the grass and leaves, rapidly growing into a hazard.

'Stop!' I cried.

'You are afraid, Koschei. Of a little fire? See!'

The fire collected itself together in one place and Nemione, gathering her yards of silk about her, sat down beside it and held both hands up to the blaze. At that moment also, a short and stalwart figure stepped forward out of the bushes.

'Bravo, Mistress,' the dwarf said, applauding her. She smiled a welcome. I realized that her abuse of him was, like her costume, an affectation, and that they were as fond of each other as mistress and servant may be.

The little fellow looked somewhat like an eft or newt in the breeding season, or like a scorpion perhaps, with a sting in his rapier. He wore a breastplate and cuisses of silvery scales, and his skin had a silvery cast too. I remembered what my mother had told me when I was a child at her knee: that a dwarf of the Altaish, though he leave his mountain home for ever, must always retain this ingrained livery, tincture of the metal he had dug and abandoned.

'This is Erchon,' said Nemione.

The dwarf bowed low.

'And you, sir,' he said, 'do not need your armour to be recognized as a Brother.'

'Good day, Master Scantling,' I returned, and he bowed again, with a flourish, and walked on down the little stony beach and into the river, where he waded thigh-deep.

'Take care!' I shouted.

'Peace, Wolf's Head,' said Erchon. 'The nivashi cannot smell a dwarf.' From close beneath the riverbank he lifted a fish-trap which he opened and emptied on to the bank. A mass of writhing fish, as scaly and argent as himself, fell out and the dwarf in his turn fell on them, banging their heads

36

against a stone. Soon he had spitted them and was roasting them at the fire.

'The trouble with this pretence,' said Nemione, as her dwarf offered her a portion of the fish, 'is that silks are not practical for the wayfaring life. I had better give up being a lady and turn myself into a gypsy. It will be easier that way.

'Eat your fish, Erchon, Koschei. Do not look at me.'

The dwarf obediently turned his back on her and began to devour his fish, not bothering to separate them, flesh from bone, but eating them whole, heads, bones, tails: all. I bowed my head and used my knife on my fish, trying hard to concentrate on the food.

Yet I could not help peeping at Nemione. I saw her prepare herself for conjury with a whispered charm. Then she closed her eyes and started to strip off her jewellery. I do not mean that she unclasped and unpinned the many pieces she wore but that she touched each one and, at her touch, it vanished. I had to bite hard on a piece of fish to stop myself exclaiming. She stroked her embattled hair. At once it began to writhe, twisting about her head like a nest of vipers as it freed itself from its confinement and settled about her shoulders like some errant and lusty cloud. I had to bite my hand to stop myself crying out in fear.

Next, she began on her garments.

Perhaps the spell was a primitive one; or, more likely, she did not know enough to transform her dress with one pass. Her garments melted successively from her and left her sitting there in nothing more than a thin, white shift.

I thought, I am a Brother and I should take what is offered me. I moved my hands, putting down the fish.

'Cheat!' cried Nemione, opening her eyes. She glared at me.

'You are very lucky, Brother Koschei, that I did not slay you where you sit!'

Judgement had the upper hand. I was quiet. If she could not make the unclothing spell more elegantly, I reasoned,

37

she was unlikely to have the powers of life and death. After a moment or two had passed, when we were both calm, 'Forgive me, Mistress Baldwin,' I said, and bowed my head.

So I did not see what Nemione did to clothe herself again but only that, when I was allowed to look at her, she wore the red and orange garb of a Rom and a burden of brassy necklaces around her neck.

'No more lady,' she said.

'You look as well in this gallimaufry,' I said.

'Oh, empty compliment! Now I am a dirty hedge-drab.'

'You have the same angel's hair.'

'I can't change that,' she confessed. 'Help me, Koschei, for old times' sake; help me to darken my hair.'

By good fortune I had with me a bottle of the dye with which we Green Wolves used to darken our faces on moonlit nights. I took the stuff from my wallet and showed it her.

'This may help. You must dilute it in water. Then rub it on.'

'Perhaps if I use my comb – oh, fie! It is gone with the gown.'

It was my turn to laugh; but I only smiled gently.

'I have a comb.'

We worked together, Erchon and I, he fetching water from the river in the brass cup, which fortunately had been left on the bank and so had not packed itself away in whatever ethereal trunk or closet the fine clothes were laid; I mixing a proportion of the dye into each cupful and combing it into Nemione's hair with my soldier's comb of steel. It was hard to do – not the dyeing, which worked admirably – but the combing of her gossamer hair. Never before had I stood so close to her. The only women I had touched were rough camp followers and country girls who, knowing their business with men, were greedy and sharp-tongued. Nor did their skins smell sweet as a damask rose and feel like one petal of that rose, fallen in the dewy morn.

'Spare me,' I whispered in her ear, so that the dwarf would not hear. 'I am a man.'

'Pretend we are sister and brother,' she said. 'As once we were, in the Cloister.'

So I finished the task. Nemione, looking into the dye-bottle exclaimed,

'It is all gone!'

'I shall easily get more,' I lied. I knew that the penalty for losing any part of my kit was three month's duty without leave and possibly a flogging at the end of a rope.

The stuff was drying in her hair, turning it as black as a night-crow's wing. She looked as bewitching as the Queen of Spades.

'You will soon get a gypsy lover, Mistress,' said Erchon the dwarf.

'Look in the river,' I said. 'You will see yourself how much you look the part.'

She stood there a long time, on the river's edge, gazing at the rippling simulacrum of herself.

'I shall journey safer when I have found a band of Rom,' she said. She turned and looked at me.

'What can I give you Koschei, for your patience and your dye?'

'A little piece of yourself – to meditate on and to love.'

'I will give you some strands of this counterfeit hair. But that is not enough. I have a long and perilous journey ahead – but I do not need Erchon any more. What gypsy lass has her own dwarf? I will lend him to you and, when I send, you must discharge him from your service.'

'Very well.'

She pulled some long hairs from her head and gave them to me; I coiled them up and put them, wrapped in my neck-cloth, in my wallet. Then she gave me Erchon, telling him to march smartly to my side and there remain, until she called.

'Goodbye,' she said, and turned and walked away along

the track, her brave gypsy clothing bright in the shadows of the overhanging trees. She did not look back but Erchon and I watched until we could see her no more. Then, facing each other, we exchanged smart salutes before we shook hands.

'Will she soon find company?' I asked the dwarf. 'Do gypsies travel in this locality?'

'Yes, Master – and many of them at this time of the year. There is a horse fair in Vonta, fine trotters, proud pacers, sumpter horses, palfreys, vanners, destriers, barbs – what you will. And the mountain men bring their cast-off slaves to sell.'

'Yet there is danger for Nemione.'

'She will survive it, more than half nivasha as she is,' the dwarf said.

'She is the daughter of the reeve at Espmoss.'

'But who was his mother? And who is her mother?'

'Why does she journey?'

'Ours not to ask, Master; nor to reason why.' As he talked, Erchon busied himself in tidying our temporary caravan-serai, and trod upon the ashes of the fire. He heard the rumble before I did, and the jingle of harness.

'Hark!'

'Into the trees!'

'Too late, Brother Wolf. There is the caravan-master and he has seen us. Smile as they pass and pray they will soon overtake my lady.'

We stood aside to watch the procession of gypsies pass.

'Look, gypsies!' Alice exclaimed.

'I can't. Tell me.'

'You can see the ripe corn. They are camped on the edge of the field. The chrome on their vans glitters in the sunlight and they have a lorry – two – and a car; there's some washing on a line – gone now. Out of sight. What a pity gypsies gave up horses and painted vans.'

40

'I knew one who lived in a *vardo* black as coal, and every line and carved curlicue upon it was picked out in gold and red – and a great hairy-heeled mare pulled it.'

'Dominic's mother?'

She must have guessed it.

'How do you know?'

'I read your letter when you went for a pee.'

It was the sort of thing Helen herself would have done; that this Alice had pried in his guilt did not make him angry, but irrationally fearful. She was cheeky and unpredictable, that was all, he reasoned, the child of a broken home; and he had left the letter and the postcard on the dashboard.

'Why did Dominic send you the picture of a horse?' Alice continued.

'Thought you'd read my books.'

'Not all. I suppose there is a horse like that in one of them.'

'Right! The Ima, who live in the Plains of Malthassa, herd horses – we were talking about them earlier, when we passed the sign that said "J-J Rousseau". The best ones belong to the Imandi, their leader, and the best one of all is the Red Horse.'

'What colour was Helen's horse? I can't remember.'

Again he was disturbed. He was sure he had not revealed Helen's name; and Dominic had not written it down. He had not told her what colour the horse was either: he was certain of that.

'I didn't tell you,' he said. 'She was brown and white – skewbald, or "coloured" in gypsy parlance. They prize pied animals highly.'

'Half and half, like good and evil; neither one thing or another, like me,' Alice said and then, before he could respond to this new slant upon her puzzling character, reached forward and reinforced his unsettled mood with a fresh CD.

'You don't have to do that each time,' he said. 'Put in a stack.'

'I want this one.'

Clapton again; and the album was called *Backtrackin'* – what he was at, to drive half way down France on this fool's errand; doubly a fool for picking up this precocious waif? Well, it wasn't so far to Auxerre, where he would drop her. She would easily find another lift there, or a room if she intended to stay overnight. He listened to the music and felt the morass of nostalgia stir and individual memories rise up like wraiths.

They had reached Burgundy and were passing a sign to Sens. The landscape was rich and rolling: you could see how lords and princes had prospered here, he thought, and built their *chateaux forts* and later on, when there was a kind of peace, their tree-embowered, swan-encircled chateaux set like still islands in a motionless sea, so formal were the pleasure gardens. As if to echo these thoughts, a brown road sign with a formalized chateau, turreted and neat, came into view and, beyond it, the edge of the forest which covered the hills on either side of the road. Other signs warned of deer, though a high deer fence marched with the margins of the wood.

'They used to hunt all the time here,' he said. 'In the Middle Ages. In fact, Saint Thibaud loved the hunt so much that in his church, ahead of us in Joigny, he is shown on horseback, off to the chase with his dog. And Archbishop Sanglier was of course known only as "The Boar". I wonder, was he a thickset, muscular man, a grasping priest who loved the riches which gave him the freedom to hunt? – the riches of Mother Church. There is a famous Treasury in the abbey at Sens.'

'Wasn't it in Sens,' the girl said, 'that Abélard was condemned?'

How could she know that – a history lesson at school?

'Not for loving Héloise,' he said, 'but for an intellectual

sin: for refusing to set limits to the activity of human reason.'

'Reason? Peter Abélard?'

'He was a great churchman as well as a lover. A formidable intellect! Though, it is remarkable that he did not lose his reason after he was set upon.'

'Thinking was all he had left,' she said. 'Thinking of Héloise and praying.'

'Excuse me – but you've studied the period in class?'

'Oh, no. They don't tell us young wenches about castration. 'Taint a fit subject for a liddle gal.'

Phoebe spoke like this sometimes, putting on the accents of a yokel.

'Oh, ah,' he replied in kind, looked full at her and caught her watching him. He knew then he had won that joust – this time she had not fooled him into a delusion – and continued casually,

'Burgundy is famous for happier things as well.'

'I bet you wouldn't say that if you lived in the Middle Ages!'

'I don't suppose I would. But look, here's another reminder of hunting: a service station called L'Aire de la Biche – the Hind's Place. Would you like a coffee?'

'Please!'

They sat opposite each other at the table. She drank her black coffee and eagerly devoured a large slice of *gâteau*. This is the first time she has eaten today, he thought and asked her 'Would you like a proper meal?'

'Later?' she said, the question mark riding high in her voice.

A woman was watching them with unconcealed curiosity; he had seen several men glance and he leaned back and looked at the girl as if to confirm that he saw what the others saw. She had the kind of beauty many men divorced good wives to gain, that unknown and conjectured many who would envy him, escorting her – if that was the correct term for his role in this surreal interlude.

43

'Later?' she had said. Although an interval of time had passed, he decided to reply.

'OK. Later on.'

He saw the shape of her clearly now, both intellectual and physical, and in that moment knew that he would try to seduce her, though his conscience would attempt to save them from this pleasurable and questionable conclusion. Sandy was well into her thirties; this girl was little more than a child. He calculated. Thirty-two years separated them, at least.; but he wouldn't be the first – there was that Stone. OK. And several Country singers. He opened the sun-roof when they were back in the car and again drove fast, breaking the speed limit. He knew, without looking, that Alice was smiling with pleasure, heard her laugh as she held down her slip-streaming hair. It was about fifty miles to Auxerre. Soon the town rose up in the hills on their right-hand side and 'There's the cathedral,' Alice said.

He remembered Saint Edward's, where he had been choirboy and chorister; another time, another country, almost another religion, his, pared down from the excesses of Catholicism. His conscience gave a feeble flutter. Polanski, it said.

'I'll drop you in Auxerre,' he offered.

'I'd rather come with you!'

She had said it, condemning him. He felt his lust recognized and justified.

'All right,' he said. 'If you are absolutely sure.'

'Oh, absolutely!'

A little later, when they were paused at the tollbooth, the girl laughed softly and said, 'My father is always telling me not to accept lifts from strangers.' He gave his daughters the same advice.

'What can I say to that,' he asked her, 'without being totally flippant?'

'You could say – "Soon, I won't *be* a stranger"!' She laughed again.

They left the *autoroute* and took a lesser road which

followed the course of the Yonne. The signposts said 'Avallon'. While intelligence and education told him that the name must be derived from that of a long-dead Celt, the chieftain in these wooded lands, an older and intuitive sense recalled Avalon, the island vale Arthur was carried to in death. Dusk inhabited the roadsides and waited in the trees. They passed through Lucy-le-bois. He felt heavy with fatigue and unwanted symbolism.

In Avallon, he was pleased to see, the houses were tall with open shutters laid back against stone walls; trees in the squares, flowers in troughs. A civilized place. The town was quiet, as if its citizens had already retired to bed. No one about to witness the betrayal of his conscience. Yet he drove past the big Hotel d'Etoile and parked in a narrow street. The silence of the town invaded the car. He sat still and the girl beside him did not move.

While the car, as its expanded metals cooled, made the only noises to be heard, he unfastened his seat belt and twisted in his seat until he faced her. He felt that he should make some overture or heartfelt confession which would sanctify what he proposed.

But Alice's unfathomed sensibilities moved faster.

'Avallon,' she said, pronouncing the word in the English fashion.

'Av-eye-yon.'

'I know.'

'Or Arcadia?' he asked her. 'Paradise?'

'Paradise? Not yet – look, there's a hotel. At the end of the street.'

He held her face in both hands and kissed her, at once wanting all of her – but 'wait' his noisy conscience said and he released her. She laughed loudly and, putting on a new accent, said,

' 'Ow romantic!' She laid her head against his chest and laughed again. They both laughed, rocking in their seats, releasing their tension into the stuffy air.

45

'Come on, Miss Essex,' he said. 'Let's go.'

The dusty footpath was only wide enough for one. They walked in the road, hand-in-hand. He looked at his watch.

'We'll eat. First,' he said.

The hotel restaurant was papered in red, and shabby. He read the menu quickly and, while Alice studied it, looked about him, embarrassed. He had erred. It looked the kind of place to which commercial travellers brought their pick-ups. The red paper made him think of hell, not paradise (though, conceptually, what was the difference, both asylums for different breeds of ecstatics?). The fires burned low for want of heretics and adulterers to incinerate. He peered into the gloom and made out a waitress lingering by the kitchen door. Near her, a bizarre group sat at dinner – French, a family – and he recognized the hotel proprietor who had booked them in. Perhaps the waitress was his wife? Who, then was the other middle-aged woman; who were the other women? Two sons and an idiot – correction, a boy with learning difficulties: three sons?

The waitress saw him staring and began ferociously to cut bread. She laid a long loaf on the board and brought down the guillotine blade, bang! bang! bang! He winced. She brought the bread to them and he watched it reforming its squashed self while he gave the order. Alice was mute. He chose a salad for her, lamb, *pommes Lyonnaises*; the wine. How bad would it be?

'Monsieur,' the waitress said, in mangled English. ''As good flavour.'

'"Taste", Madame,' he corrected stiffly.

Alice yelped and stuffed her table napkin in her mouth – but the food, despite the odd family, the wallpaper, the dust he could see griming the dado rail, after all was good. He poured a young Beaujolais. It waited in his glass, a toast to Fortune, Life and Youth. He lifted the glass. She was waiting, too, red-blooded adolescence, reciprocal sensation imprisoned in her pretty cage of flesh. She smiled at him and, from the tail of his eye, he saw the family file silently from the room.

'Now we're alone,' said Alice.

'Near enough.'

She drank.

'Hello,' she said.

The time came. They mounted the stairs. The same red wallpaper enhanced the gloom. A low-wattage bulb lighted the turning of the stair; they went higher and there, nearly opposite the lavatory, was their room: 18. The age of reason and responsibility.

'How old *are* you?' he said abruptly as he opened the door.

She affected not to hear. It was not a question he could repeat – not without seeming a total fool – and they passed into the room. The stark central light was on. Her rucksack stood beside his grip on a little luggage stand. The bed was turned down.

Alice spoke: 'What a place! Wow!' and ran to open the window.

'It's all right. The linen's clean,' he said, while realizing he had misinterpreted her words and actions. She was leaning out of the window. The light curtains billowed about her and a hot breeze shoved the musty air of the room aside.

'We're in the roof! It's miles down to the street – I can see your car dozing there as if it was in its own comfy garage, not forced to spend the night outside the police station.'

'At least no one will try to nick it.'

He too crossed the room; stood behind her. So close, he did not know what to make – of himself, nor her who continued to lean out and report on what she saw with the enthusiasm and fresh vision of minority. Questions marshalled in his mind: Why? Shall I leave – before it's too late? Is this a legitimate adventure? A sordid romp? While he pondered, he caressed her shoulder, at last permitting his hand to journey down her supple back and gently touch her clefted buttocks in their absurdly thick tights – leggings. No pants. No bra. She must have removed those two surplus (for their purposes) garments when she went to the loo. Her breasts. Against the windowsill.

He could not think. He was entranced. But the girl left the window, brushing past him as if he was already old news. He watched her explore the room, the wardrobe with its extra blanket and pillows for those too soft to sleep comfortably on the French-style bolster, rolled in the end of the sheet; the curtained enclosure which hid the washbasin and eccentric plumbing; the two religious pictures. She undid her backpack; took out washbag, underclothes, a hairbrush, her book.

He hung his jacket on a chair and sat on the bed, his resolution fading; rolled over and looked in the bedside cabinet where, on a shelf above a chamber pot, he found a Gideon bible. That these expressions of human spirituality and grossness should be displayed in such close proximity amused him, and he laughed out loud.

'What have you found?'

'The bible and the *pot de chambre*.'

'Is that *funny*?'

'Only if we need either.'

'I'm quite godless,' she said, 'and I bet you are too.'

'I –' he said, hesitating over the sentence ('used to be a choirboy'? 'was married in church'? 'am married to a rather devout Christian'?) 'I am undecided –'

It was an expression of his state, now, here. He stood up and switched off the light. At once, the context dissolved, the absurd conversation, the prevarication. Night was a better landscape for an amorous conjunction. There must be a moon. Her garments were luminous in the pallid light: her

48

body would have the same lucent quality. He began to be excited: no more words. He approached her swiftly, conscious of the sweat and grime on him, the wine on his breath.

This was not what he'd imagined – champagne, a better room. Beside her he was a rampant giant and for an instant wondered: will she protest? The texture of her unshent skin made him delirious. He bent to take her offered kisses and, as he felt her warm, dry hands upon him, it occurred to him – a new horizon, a fresh Darien – that

the white beer I had consumed, following on the three ritual glasses of kumiz, was doubtless to blame – but there was no time to think further, blaming mere beverages. I had chosen carefully, deliberately; had won the only girl of the year to bear faint resemblance to Nemione Baldwin, a scrawny witch of a creature with a sweep of hair as yellow as the sheaved corn. The contest, to a renegade Wolf, had been simplicity, a matter of judgement rather than ability, some skill in aiming at the narrow target.

I waited, the corn stalks pricking my bare thighs. That I should sit here at all was accident. Tired of my journey and the prospect of more fighting, I had remained on the itinerant smith's wagon; so, arrived in this village, a poor rat-haunted place on the very hem of the Plains, where a rash of small cornfields competed for bare unattractiveness with scorched pastures where grazed a few horses the Ima had outworn. I had known nothing of the summer festival I walked into, combined propitiation and celebration. Strangers were scarce. The old women had pounced on me and, in truth, they were like corn rats themselves, bright eyed and chattering, nipping at my arms and shoulders with little snatches and tugs. The young women had been driven (mirthful though they were) into a ruinous barn on the edge of the field. I contested with the village youths and one other unfortunate stray, a fat itinerant horse-butcher, upon a shooting-ground which resembled the Green Wolves' butts as little as my prize did the fair novice-turned-thaumaturge.

Here she came, walking delicately in bare feet across the stubble, veiled in dirty white. As she drew nearer I saw that her bridal veil was an old flour sack.

Well, I had got myself into these curious circumstances.

It was a long time since I had had a woman.

I felt pity rather than desire; also an absurd shame which quickened when I thought that these ignoble deeds must, when they had become memories, be kept with the jewels in the memory palace. I moved the sacking aside and looked into her thin face, averting my eyes from the rest of her wasted body.

'You need not, mistress, if I do not please you,' I said. It was a poor attempt at the courtesies I had been taught in boyhood. But that, too, was past.

'I must,' she whispered. I had difficulty in understanding her dialect: 'I want,' was what she seemed to say.

'Then where is our bed?'

'Here, on the dry ground,' she said; or was it: 'On the fruitful earth'? – and, without more ado, she flung the sack from her and eagerly knelt upon it where it fell. I hastened to kneel with her; but I wondered, were we about to pray?

'One thing,' she said. 'Before – why me?'

This, I understood, looking askance on my lower body which, independent of my intellect, had begun to prepare itself for the lovers' contest. Was I to be kind, or cruel?

'You remind me of the woman I love,' I said.

'That is a good omen,' the girl said.

'Is she a good woman?' the girl said.

I lay down in a confusion of body and mind, the myriad facets of my existence dancing in the air and crowding close about me on the rough sacking. The girl also lay down. For ten beats of my heart nothing happened, but the sun beat down; then she was there, covering me, and I thought that Famine rode till she kissed me and I remembered the unsurpassed smoothness of the beer they had given me. After this, her breasts might make milk as sweet as the thick, fermented kumiz.

That was the meaning of it all: a harvest, a child.

Or a simple adventure.

Was this the real meaning behind my voluntary diversion from the journey?

Of course! A simple – and delightful – adventure of a common kind, Guy assured himself. The quarry and reward of men down the centuries. If unlike his affairs with Helen, Susan, Diana, Sandy –

Alice Naylor, her character uncovered by his researches and by her final, unremitting presence in his house, had ingenuity and invention, most alive and most alluring in his dreams where her miserable expression was transformed to laughter; where she always refused him, closed and cold at the last moment even as he tried in vain to enter her.

This other Alice had known very well what she did, where to touch and how, so that, at last expiring in her he came to the summit of the highest pass, the zenith of his ambition; after which her involuted, tender succulence was his.

He watched her sleeping with no sense of guilt. The warm night enfolded him. France herself cradled him. He hardly knew her either: a few jaunts here and there, some holidays in various situations – there was a vastness, and also an unpredictability, about her which England did not have. In a bed, in a house, in a street, in a town, in a green province, in a wide country, lies my love – He grinned to himself in the dark.

In all the building, no sound. He thought of the weary proprietor and his family; wondered where they slept. Close by? In a separate wing?

He lay and sweated, cooling as the fluids dried. A door banged. Someone passed the door – perhaps. A car, long way away. Suddenly he was in the car, driving furiously; and instantly awake. Christ, how his body ached; hard to know which bit to stretch. Must remember – more petrol, postcards, pay the bills – no, on holiday. Now he was wide awake. He stretched out and switched on the lamp beside the bed; rolled slowly back to look again at the marvellous girl.

She lay on her right side, facing away, all white, the blonde hair like straw in a sunny field or the thin filaments of flax Rumplestiltskin span into gold for the king's daughter. Her legs and arms were graceful, long; everything, breasts, belly, buttocks, neat and under-used. He looked again at those small breasts with their pale pink nipples, touched her shoulder gently, lifted her hair. Her face in repose was delicate; did have, indeed, the features of one of Sassetta's angels. She still wore her ribbon. The black band tight around so long and white a neck disturbed him; he was not sure if his unease was spiritual or sexual; but 'I'm quite godless,' she had said. Curse the inaccuracies of the English vernacular! Did she mean 'moderately' or 'totally'?

He touched the velvet ribbon gently, noticing how its silken edge bit into her neck.

The curious book she'd been reading on the ferry lay there, with her bits and pieces on the chair. He got up softly to fetch it; lay down and opened its lurid cover.

'*The Evil Life of Lèni la Soie.*' Inside was a frontispiece taken from a contemporary sketch; it showed a dishevelled beauty kneeling in prayer before a crucifix. Curious, he thought, how ready we are to accuse every whore and make of her a repentant Magdalen at once attractive and repellent. He turned the pages and found a short introduction.

'France,' it began, 'called La Belle. Imagine two wide rivers and a city of tall stone houses, great squares where people walk, art galleries, churches, gardens, a ruined Gallo-Roman theatre high above the city. This is Lyon today.

'Now let us imagine another scene. It is the latter half of

the nineteenth century and the houses which cover the hilly quarter of Fourvière are falling down. This is the oldest quarter and those who live here, above the city but below the site of the new basilica, are also decaying from the harshness of life, from drink, from hunger. There is so little that even the rats have moved out, away to the Croix Rousse with the whores. Some of these evil-living women are thin, some fat; some even, to cater for all tastes, very old, wrinkled, dry; some are pregnant and some are as beautiful as Aphrodite. Lèni was such a one –'

Guy stopped reading, irritated by the present tense, drama-documentary style; plagued by recollections which streamed up as unstoppably as mist from wet ground in the sun. He had never known Lèni – how could he? She was dead – like the first Alice. He had not known Lèni, but he had read her diary, all the closely written confidential pages of it and could visualize her neat letters exactly and the brown limp-covered book itself, soft leather binding worn bald. It used to live, a landmark amongst the paperbacks, on the little shelf above the bed-place in the gypsy *vardo* and Helen, rising from him in her resplendent nakedness, had brought it down and shown it him, revealing at the same time her inmost thoughts, for she kept her own diary in it, and also in French. Somewhat bewildered he had read there that he, Guy Parados, was *un trésor* and also *mon amant très fort et infatigable*. Schoolgirl stuff on reflection, these days. He had grinned at her and said 'Thanks! I hope I am,' and had asked her why she wrote in French, not Romany.

'It's the language of lovers, isn't it?' she had replied.

He remembered some of Lèni's entries. She had, he thought, compared her priestly lover to a stallion and herself she had personified as his breakfast. She had also implied that he was stupid: *quel imbécile, quel désastre!* Nothing else could be retrieved – except – yes, a homily as vapid as every cliché: 'Fortune favours fools', in Helen's translation; but the French was *Aux innocents les mains pleines* which, translated literally, meant 'To simpletons, filled hands'. The innocent, the idiot son of the family downstairs certainly had those, clasping tight his bread and biting into its crust. Guy leaned back against the headboard and closed his eyes.

'*Pleine*' had another meaning, probably several, for sense in French was, as in English, governed by context. Ah! It meant 'complete' or 'whole'.

Complete hands to fools. A good hand, a complete flush. No! Nonsense. He was dozing when there was work to do. He skimmed the short introduction, noting the facts: Lèni's lover, Father Paon (absurd name! – but how it characterized him) was the nutter, a slave to every vice and luxury and deeply involved with other Satanists of the time, in particular Olivia des Mousseaux and a second priest, Henri Renard. They were famous at the time: the decadent novelist, Huysmans, had interviewed them and it was said that their erotic practices had inspired both the Marquis de Guaita and Aleister Crowley. Paon took Lèni to live with him and abused her – yet she remained with him, loyal as a spaniel, and more, she watched him bloodily murder the girls they lured to his Black Masses. *Petites rosses insaissisables*, Elusive little nags: that was what she had written about the girls! Guilt and revulsion kept Guy fascinated: that this obscure Lyon seamstress whose diary he had held ... But the place to which they were brought, that had not sounded like a maniac's lair. It had another, haunting, name, *un paradis inconnu*.

An unknown Paradise. Death, he supposed, and the Otherworld: Heaven, Hades, Hell, Avalon, Elysium and the Land of Youth. The Isles of the Blessed. It had many names, as many as man's fears. He read the dénouement of the extraordinary tale:

'Their own over-confidence betrays Lèni and Paon. They kidnap the daughter of a consul, a dark Mexican lovely. Respectable Lyon and the *demi-monde* are equally horrified but, even so, it is necessary for the arresting civil guard officers to bribe the militant *Canuts* or silk workers and to have their protection in order to enter the district, find and arrest the couple, and discover the horrors they have perpetrated. This is what they found:

'The door of the apartment wide open and Paon, dressed like a dandy in silks, reclining on his ornate bed of shame, his new telephone receiver in his hand and the noise from a disconnected call the only sound. He wore a blank look and offered no resistance. In the kitchen, Paloma Diaz del Castillo lay in a welter of blood on the scrubbed deal table, horribly maimed and quite dead.

'Paon was guillotined in Lyon in 1884 but his mistress, the beautiful devil Lèni la Soie, was never brought to justice. Helped by her silk worker friends, she had fled into her native territory, the local warren of alleyways or *traboules*, and there disappeared.'

He wondered how Paon had defended himself at his trial. Historic Lyon was a depository of hatred, a place in which many had been brought to book. He had visited it three years ago with his wife: for a day and a night, time enough for Jilly to spend an afternoon in the Silk Museum, for him to find and choose the best restaurant. They had left the children in England with Thérèse and were trying hard to live harmoniously together. It wasn't a second honeymoon but they had a good holiday and went on to the Alps. In Fourvière he had explored some of the alleys or *traboules* with a sense of trespass, for many were gated, others obscure and damp and all along them stairways and doors led to inhabited apartments. He had found a likely restaurant and was standing contentedly in the warm afternoon sun reading the menu when, further down the narrow street, there was a flurry of cars and heavy motorbikes ridden by helmeted men.

A wide façade, cramped up against the pavement, was the back of the Palais de Justice. He had witnessed the departure from it of Klaus Barbie whom the Lyonnais were trying for his crimes against Jews and gypsies in the War. They had even found a lawyer who would defend him.

Who would, or could, defend Lèni? He began to read the narrative which was couched in her words and taken from her *journal intime*:

'You, man or woman of the future time, you my Reader and my Judge, will observe that my spirit, like the *traboules* of the Croix Rousse, goes in as many directions as the compass needle. As for my heart, that too has its yearnings, for my father, for my lover, but most of all for the unknown paradise. I liken it to the hills beyond Fourvière in whose long shadows we lived happily before these centuries of revolution . . .'

And I am in Arcadia, he thought suddenly. What have I to do with this miserable stuff? He looked at the girl asleep beside him. *Et in Arcadia ego* – where, in a perfect, sylvan paradise, Death intrudes. He would wake her and comfort himself with her body.

The black ribbon was tight. He wondered, fingering its soft surface, how she could bear such tightness and he felt under her hair for a fastening. There was a bow, which he untied, and the ribbon slipped off and fell upon the bed while he, recoiling, saw the mark it had concealed, a dark ring of blemishes about her neck. Ghostly Alice wore such an ineradicable necklace, her hangman's keepsake.

Alice Tyler opened her eyes, blinked pale lids across the blue and put both hands up to her throat.

'You beast,' she said.

He was not able to respond. Alice sat up. She switched on the bedside light and retrieved the ribbon. With electric light to illuminate it, the mark diminished. It was not very big.

Alice tied the ribbon and covered the mark.

'What is it?' he asked.

'What does it look like?'

'Horrible – I'm sorry. It reminds me –'

'Of something nasty in one of your books – in your imagination! It's a birthmark, stupid. Usually I cover it with make-up, but sometimes I wear the choker instead.'

'I see.'

The girl switched off the light and lay down.

'Go to sleep,' she said and then, more kindly, 'Save your energy till I wake – properly.'

A blighted angel, child of Hell scarred by the woodcarver's chisel – but he was asleep and dreaming, miraculously able to walk on air amid the wooden seraphim which held up the roof of St Edward's Cathedral.

Guy stood at the mirror in the curtained enclosure which held the washbasin. He lathered his face. They had 'made love' again though it had felt like war. Alice had clawed and bitten him, arousing him to a brutal response. He had not tried to please her, only himself. When he had finished he had looked down at her and found her gritting her teeth.

'Hell,' she'd said.

He had apologized and found then that he had opened a door, the way which led to her. She had wriggled and twined herself about him. More sex followed and now it was eleven o'clock. He was exhausted. He was too old.

He looked into the reflection of his own blue eyes. There were shadows there, a dark cast in each eye; his eyelids had a cynical and oriental droop. The white lather made a substantial beard and the gloom behind the curtain had taken the English pallor from his face and replaced it with darkness. Christ, he almost looked like Satwinder staring balefully across the bridge table. He blinked rapidly and shaved away stubble and the foam. The familiar wide-open eyes gazed steadily back at him.

'Aren't you ready yet?' Alice, beyond the curtain, asked.

'Almost.' He dried his face, came out.

'You've read some of the *Malthassa* books,' he said. 'What

does Koschei look like – the Mage, the chief male character?'

'Well, if you don't know –' she began.

'I do. I just want you to describe him for me.'

'OK. Um – he is very dark, hair I mean and skin. A bit Arabian, I suppose. His eyelids droop, to make him look really sinister – and he has a big scratchy beard. Yuck!'

'You wouldn't like to be in bed with him?'

'No way! He's a nasty piece of work.'

'Is he? Is that how you read him? He began as a noble man, although a questioner. At first, he was a simple adventurer.'

Pleased by the manner in which my adventure away from the route between Tanter and the battle at Myrah Pits had ended, I sat beside the horse-butcher on his flat cart. It was our raft of oblivion and good will, both conditions induced by our astonishing sojourn in the village and by the stupendous quantities of alcohol administered to us at the end of the midsummer fest.

The cart belonged to the butcher. It had been commandeered by the villagers and used to transport the summer brides in their procession about the fields. An arch of withies had been nailed to it and this, still hung with wilted grasses and small field flowers, remained. The butcher said he might fix a tarpaulin to it, to keep off the sun. He was a slack fellow. He had promised to buy me a meal, but we never stopped at an inn.

In addition to the withered garlands and we two men, the cart carried two dead horses. These, a red and a red roan, lay quiet but nodded their heads – which hung over the tail of the cart – to the jolt of the ruts. The live horse which pulled them snorted and tossed his head to keep the flies in motion.

'You're a good horse,' the butcher said and wrenched on the reins. When the cart stopped he leaped from it through the gathering cloud of flies and into the ditch, where he pissed copiously and plucked a large bunch of herbs. These, he carried to the horse's head where, standing with legs akimbo and shirt and breeches gaping, he tucked the leafy stems into and under the straps of the bridle. He made a noise, Waahorhorhor! to the horse or in relief, scratched his belly, fastened his buttons and mounted to the driver's seat.

'Perhaps *they* would also like to be decorated,' I dryly said.

'Naw.' The butcher was emphatic. 'One bunch should do for the lot of us, dead and alive. Strong stuff.'

The flies which had made a sortie to examine the effect of the herbs rejoined their companions and helped them annoy me. But the butcher seemed impervious and soon began to sing in time with the jolting of the cart,

> When I — was a lad
> I ——— loved a lass
> But she loved another
> MAN
> Oh
> When I —

I took off my hat and beat the air with it. The flies rose up like a whirlwind, and descended again. I, too, sang.

In this manner, we travelled some eight or ten miles. The Plains and their mean margins were behind us and I was cheered; but the forest lay before and this knowledge was death to the brief springtime of my heart. I looked at the butcher, whose flushed face was covered in beads of sweat and flies.

'Do you not fear the forest?' I said.

'It is but trees. I have trees in my garden. In the forest there are many more, but they are the same things of trunks and branches.'

'Then, do you not fear the Beautiful Ones?'

'I have never seen a puvush.'

'Hush! There may be one nearby. I think you are a city man who knows the stone street better then the forest track.'

'All but a few leagues of the forest is trackless, so I have heard. But you are correct. I am a man of Pargur.'

'Pargur!'

'It is not quite as marvellous as they say; perhaps only half as much – perhaps half equal to your wildest dreams.'

The forest closed in as we talked. It seemed to me that puvushi might well be hiding under the forest's canopy, green and brown as the shadows and, beside, that each rill and boggy place was the home of a nivasha. As well as these spirits, I feared the Om Ren, the Wild Man, which might lie in ambush awaiting unwary travellers; and the Duschma, she of plague and agony. I had seen her twice, once in a sleepy village where she watched our column pass and smiled horribly and, again, stalking the battlefield in search of fresh young men to feed on. My sword was blunt against such and, from past and recent experience, I knew I would not be proof against the allure (false though it is) of the earth and water spirits. Soon, I must leave this gross but, nevertheless, human horse-butcher. Ahead, the dwarf Erchon had told me, the ways parted in a wide Y and the left-hand fork went towards the town of Myrah, while the right-hand veered across a tract of forest fringe. Somewhere beyond this, the battle raged. A mighty chestnut tree grew in the cleft of the Y and under this Erchon had promised me he would wait. I should not be alone in the forest; but a dwarf is not a man. They keep their own customs. Erchon, disregarding the duty Nemione had impressed upon him, had left me for three weeks to meet his fellows at one of these arbitrary gatherings.

The chestnut trailed its leafy skirt upon the ground. Erchon was nowhere to be seen; in hiding, no doubt. He fears the forest folk as much as I, despite his boast that the nivashi cannot scent dwarves, I thought. I said goodbye to the butcher, his raggedy, weed-bedizened cart, his dead horses and the flies.

'Goodbye, Master Wolf,' he replied, screwing one of his eyes into a hideous wink and confounding me with his words. I had been careful to reveal neither identity nor allegiances; I wore an old shirt and jacket over my cuirass and, further, had tied a dirty length of cloth I'd bought for a farthing in Tanter slantwise about my body to suggest to any bold jack that I was a brigand. My beard was growing fast.

'I see it in your eyes,' the butcher explained. 'A look of confidence – nay, arrogance – under the dirt.'

'I suppose it's useless to ask you to hold your tongue,' I said.

'I'm not such a gossip as you suppose, not even in my cups. I leave that to my wife.'

I gave him more than he deserved, a silver threepenny bit, and wondered what kind of woman would allow him to bed her. The butcher tested the coin on his teeth.

'A good one,' he said. 'Thank ye. I'll keep it in case I meet a werewolf.'

I watched him drive off, watched him till he was out of sight. Then I called softly,

'Erchon, Master Scantling.' He liked his nickname and usually answered it at once; but there was no response. I called again and, pushing the pendant branches of the chestnut tree aside, crept into its shadow. All I found was a dappled green shade, empty. I circumnavigated the tree. Nothing.

I cursed Erchon. The universal reputation dwarves have for carousing is fully justified. I supposed the wretch lay drunk in some alley or fleet. I wished he would awake with the father and mother of sore heads and a sick stomach as well.

I did not know what to do. Soon, it would be dusk; then, dark. I had planned to set up temporary home with his help, a camp where we might rest safe by the light of a good fire with one to watch while the other slept. The track looked quiet enough, striking off amongst the trees, a band of late sunlight illuminating it and picking out the colours of the summer flowers which grew beside it. I resolved to walk along it until the sunlight gave out, or I reached a corner.

It was a pleasant walk. The birds sang and the shade under the trees tempered the heat. I could see a herd of deer a little way off, all of them lying calmly at rest. A family of rabbits grazed; I walked so softly I did not disturb them. I walked with such unwary joy, and a deeper feeling of peace, that I did not notice the corner till I had rounded it, nor that the light had fled and given the forest back to Night. I must hasten back to the chestnut tree. That stood by the road, at least. I might even chance upon a late-travelling waggoner who would carry me to Myrah. I turned in my tracks and was confronted by the terrible marriage of oncoming night and the forest's own shadows. The tranquil animals were gone with the sun.

Soon I came to a parting of ways, one I did not remember. Surely I had walked along the only track? I took the left fork, certain that it led in the direction of the tree at the Y. I walked fast and held my head high. I did not look behind me nor to right or left. The track led me on but I never found the chestnut tree, only another division of roads. This time, in near-panic, I took the right-hand fork. And so continued, faster, left then right, alternately cursing myself for a fool and praying for my own safety

because soon there must be a junction at which the girl could safely be set down to continue her journey. Then, free of her, he would also be released from his unlovely desires. Men found themselves in court for less.

The road was sunlit and empty. It wound below steep vineyards and above a little stream buried in dusty summer boskage: he should be enjoying this, not behaving like a guilty fugitive. But she – he glanced – looked happy enough.

The morning, which was almost afternoon, had continued difficult. Leaving behind them the shabby hotel and the simpleton taking the air on its steps, he had explored Avallon with Alice. They came to a busy café, sat at a pavement table and ordered pastries and lemon *tisanes*. He did his duty, and bought a picture postcard of Avallon to send his wife.

'What's the date?' he asked Alice.

'June 25th – Wednesday, all day.'

'Of course. Yesterday went on for ever.'

A red currant from the *barquette* she had eaten was stuck to Alice's upper lip. It looked like a glistening drop of blood. He leaned across the table and wiped it away with his handkerchief.

'I'll go and 'phone Dad.'

'Do you know how – in French?'

'I do, Guy. Yes,' she said confidently. She left him and went into the café. In her absence he contemplated her, the little he knew: When he'd asked her the date a faint frown had appeared, and quickly cleared from her brow. He could imagine that frown in class as she worked at her lessons; he could visualize inky fingers, the rows of girls, the uniforms.

Quickly, untidily, he wrote bland platitudes on the postcard and addressed it.

He was startled from a second reverie when Alice swung out of the café. The first thing he noticed was the length of her legs, brown in the daylight against the white of her shorts. Perhaps she wore these briefest of coverings on the tennis courts at school?

She sat down opposite him and played with the packets of sugar in the bowl.

'Have you finished your postcard?'

'Yes – I'll post it now, before I forget.'

'Poor old man!'

'Alice?' Now he would ask the question. 'Alice, how old, exactly, are you?'

63

She smiled, not innocently.

'Fifteen,' she said.

'Come on! You must be seventeen – at least. Don't tease.'

'I was born on April the first, nineteen seventy-five.'

'Come on!' he'd said again, angrily.

So now they were driving, nearly parallel with the *auto-route* it was true, but seemingly deeper and further into the French countryside.

'Where does this road go?' he asked. 'Look at the map.'

'Yes, Mr Parados.'

It took her moments. She was very quick – both to start a hare or follow one up.

'It goes to your village, the one you're looking for – Coeurville.'

'But I was going to drop you somewhere – where you could get another lift!'

'It's OK. It's only Wednesday.'

'I *am* going to visit an old friend.'

'It's OK, I said. I'll stay in the car.'

'Fuck!'

'Yes, Mr Parados.'

He ignored her.

'Fuck, my bloody hands are hurting like buggery.'

They were there, had arrived in Coeurville. Automatically, he had slowed the car when they passed the sign. He drove sedately into the square. His sudden blast of irritation was gone with the bad language, though the tendons still ached. He was purged and limp.

'I'm sorry, Alice.'

''S all right. Temperamental writer!'

He parked. The place was deserted, the shops and the café shut, though a battered table, under which an old dog slept at full stretch, seemed to await visitors. Guy got out of the car and prowled the square, conscious that he was the anomaly; he and the red machine. Alice too had got out

64

of it and was wandering on the far side of the square, peering into dark windows and the openings of shady passage-ways. She looked as though she belonged, a composed French girl dreaming out the heat. He sighed. Her hair shone in the sun, all the long length of it. She needs a boy, he thought, one of those tawny young lions one sees prowling at the sea-side, someone who won't be irritated by her silliness.

In the centre of the square, a war memorial rose out of a bright bed of magenta and scarlet petunias. He went closer to it. It was unusual. Three figures, Victory, Hope and Liberty lay one upon the other, and Victory, who flourished a sword, pressed Hope (to death it seemed) beneath him, while the figure of Liberty, far from being the usual resplendent Marianne, lay at the bottom of the heap and was angular and distressed. He glanced again at Alice, paused now outside the shuttered café. He saw a blind fly up, and the glass door opening. Alice disappeared inside.

Then he was alone in the silent square. He looked around him once more and willed the village to awake, but nothing stirred except the dog which got to its feet and also disappeared inside the café. The shop next to it was a general ironmonger's and then came the bakery and *patisserie*. That was all, except for the butcher's shop on his left, where a small horse's head sign indicated that this particular butcher killed and cut up horses. He went to find Alice.

She was speaking in French to a woman, something about a gypsy, *'la romanicelle'*, the Romany woman: she was asking the way to Helen's house. In Avallon, apart from one hesitant *'Merci'*, she had let him do all the talking and to hear her now, with laughter and complicity in her voice, fluently conversing, shocked him more than had her precocious sexuality. Of course she would, with a father resident in the country. A cup of black coffee stood on the counter in front of her and, as he came in, she turned to him and smiled and the French woman began to prepare another coffee.

'You haven't far to go,' said Alice in English. 'It's the old presbytery and it's just by the church.'

'Helen's house?'

'Yes. The fortune-teller's house. She is well-known here – ask Madame.'

He spoke to the woman: 'Good day, Madame,' he said in French. 'She tells me you know Helen Lacey – *la voyante*?'

The woman, who had a broad, strong face, turned and looked him in the eye. 'Hélène, Mme Dinard, yes,' she said. 'The girl is correct. Yes, the fortune-teller. A suitable profession for a gypsy, but – she owes everything to that man.' She put his cup of coffee on the counter.

He lifted the cup and drank gratefully, feeling the warmth of the liquid flowing through him and the ache ebbing from his hands.

'She is married?'

'You can call it marriage.'

'To Georges Dinard?'

'Yes. The butcher, there – the horse butcher.'

Alice gently touched him. 'You go,' she said, 'and I'll wait here. It will be better.'

'Wait in the car if you have to. It isn't locked. Here –' He gave her a two hundred franc note. She suddenly hugged him and kissed him on the lips.

'Thank you,' she said. 'And, by the way, I am seventeen – last April.'

He left her in the café and walked swiftly across the square and along the dappled street, where lime trees grew in dry beds between the pavement and the road, until he came to the church. That 'Thank you' of hers – it had been like a farewell, a kind of 'Thanks for everything'. He had no idea if she were now telling the truth about her age.

The church looked abandoned. It was neglected and weeds grew on the roof. There was absolutely no sound, no notices, no indication that it was ever used. The door was shut and locked. He'd forgotten this was usual. The key would be lodged in some obscure house miles away. He thought of entering the church. Not to pray, God no, but as an interval, a break in the journey between Alice and Helen.

Beyond the church, a pair of scarred stone pillars marked the entrance to the Old Presbytery. He wondered where the priest lived now; perhaps, as in his own village, in a new house.

The gates were open; sagged, in fact, on lax hinges against dark evergreens. He walked up the short pathway to the front door and lifted his hand to the bell, noticing as he rang it how the paint lay flaked and twisted on the wood, weathered into many shades of green. He felt a hot quietude swell and billow towards him from inside the house, a silence made absolute by the noise of the bell. If, after all this, there was no one at home! He listened. He waited; glanced to right and left. Like those in the square, these tall windows were closely shuttered.

Treading carefully, like an animal which wishes to hide, he crept to the nearest pair of shutters and pulled on one of them. The window behind it was open and, as he peered in, the smell of the house came to meet him, a blend of dusty warmth, stale incense, roses and her perfume, 'Sortilège'. The dusky room was crowded with large pieces of furniture and he felt a child's dread: some other place that he remembered intervened between the room before him and his present intentions. His mother's house had also been crammed with massive pieces of oak and mahogany; but here were also statues, two gilded and oddly decadent humaniform lamp-bearers, an Ethiopian dwarf and an Egyptian hawk-headed god; and a bronze nude who concealed her pudendum with a caressing hand. The rose-scent came from a bowl of spent and faded beauties whose petals lay scattered on the floor.

He withdrew; pushed the shutter to. Perhaps at the back of the house –

There was no one in the garden at the rear. A mulberry

tree filled up most of the yellowed lawn; the flowers in the long beds drooped in the heat and roses scrambled, overtopping a wall. He saw that a part of the area he had first taken for scorched grass was a yellow towel, and walked up to it. Someone had been sunbathing there: a tube of sun cream lay by the towel and the towel itself was spotted with what at first he took for blood, the juice of the mulberries. For a moment he considered the pleasures of eating ripe mulberries in such an advantageous position – they might drop into a waiting mouth – then, looking up into the tree, saw that the mulberries were still green. The stains, then? He shrugged inwardly, turned and walked toward the house.

A porch with benches in it shaded the back door and on one of them stood a red-splashed mixing-bowl. The door itself was open; beyond it a shadowy hall with the inside of the front door at the far end, stairs, open doors to left and right. Guy raised his hand to knock.

He saw Daniel, his second son, walking towards him and was bewildered. Reality intervened; comprehension.

'Dominic,' he said. 'You are Dominic?'

(What would he say, the tall fair-headed boy – Helen's son – his son – the true love child?)

'Hi, Dad!'

Guy was shocked: the accent was American. But now the boy was close. What should he have said: 'My son, my son!' with tears – of joy? He held his arms out in a gesture of welcome. This boy was taller than Daniel – already. And two years younger? His brain made frantic calculations and Dominic, smiling from Helen's fathomless brown eyes, walked into his embrace. Kisses, one, two, three – he was almost French. Dominic smiled properly, his teeth virginal and even against his year-round skier's tan.

'Mom said you'd be here today,' he said. 'She was in the yard, in the garden.'

Guy, overcome at last and assailed by the lost legions of the past, spoke carefully.

'I am very glad to see you.'

(He has my nose and build, he thought. The rest is Helen.)

'Great. No problem.' At least he sounded like a normal teenager. 'Would you like a drink?'

'Er, no. I don't think so.'

'Later then? You want to see Mom.'

'I do want to see your mother. Very much.'

'And you're worried. I'm what you hoped for, but I'm not. I learned my spoken English from Georges. He was in Chicago for a while.'

'Georges?'

'Ma's Lilo.'

'What?'

'Live-in-lover. You know.'

'Oh. Yes. The butcher.'

'That's him, the horse-butcher. *She's* in the *vardo*. You can go there if you like. It's in the orchard, there's a gate in the garden wall. See you later!'

A fleeting memory of Alice Tyler jumped at him, and was gone. He forgot her. He was wholly lost, as helpless as he had been years ago, when he had first seen Helen on a country bus and, dismounting at her stop, had followed her – home, as he thought, but actually down a long and winding lane which led eventually into the secretive valley of the little river Char. She had stopped on the pack-horse bridge and waited for him –

Soon afterwards the worst and best ten months of his life had begun.

Now, seventeen years later, he was walking to her through a sunlit afternoon garden in France.

He had wanted to fuck her there and then, in the February snows beside the river, but she, taking him by the hand, had led him to the black-painted *vardo* in the old cattle-drift, had made him her apprentice. Had made him her slave. It wasn't till June –

He opened the door in the garden wall. A skewbald horse

was grazing in the orchard. The sleeping van, the *vardo*, stood a little way away, close beside a cherry tree. Ripe fruit brushed its curving roof. It was identical with the original, the one which had burned; an exact copy, down to the golden suns and moons around the door. He panicked. The van was so much like.

Her face, as dark and perfect as it had been that first time, rose up in the doorway. She still had her incredible cataract of hair. It fell straight down from a centre parting and then curled upon her shoulders like water rebounding: the sign of a gypsy sorceress. She leaned upon the half-doors and watched him approach. She said nothing. He trembled in his expensive canvas shoes. She is still dressed, he thought, in that crazily beautiful mix of antique clothes: she is the epitome of a gypsy-woman.

Helen looked down at him.

'You always come when I call,' she said.

'Don't mock me. I came to see Dominic.'

'Yes! You came to see the boy.'

Her voice had deepened a little, against his memory.

'Come in,' she said, and opened the doors. He stepped up into the van. The interior was dim and heavily perfumed. Her crystal ball and tarot cards lay on the folding table and her lucky chank shell stood on the shelf above the bed; the paperbacks were there as well and, incredibly, a soft leather-covered manuscript book which looked very like the diary of Lèni la Soie. He admired the turned and carved woodwork, the shiny stove and the patterned china; the lace edgings on the sheets and the crocheted bedspread.

'It's wonderful,' he said. 'It looks the same –'

'It *is* the same.' She gave no explanation but seated herself on the bed and waved a hand toward her chair. He sat down.

'Now, welcome, Guy. The years between us have vanished today. Our son has brought us both here.'

'He is a fine young man.'

'He was born of a sorceress and fathered by a story-teller. Would he be ordinary?'

'I suppose not.'

Helen stood up to light the oil lamp upon the cupboard. She lifted the lit lamp down and held it by its heavy base; the yellow light illuminated her dark skin and made it glow like burnished bronze. Guy could not see a mark or a line upon her face. Her lips were as softly full as they had been when she was only twenty-two.

'I am thirty-nine, Guy. Am I still beautiful?' she asked him.

He breathed in and held the breath a long moment.

'Yes,' he said, eventually, when he had studied her as if she were the Mona Lisa or one of Titian's heavenly nudes. 'Yes. The only thing which has changed is your voice. It has become melodious, a contralto holding your every experience.'

'Good. Do you love me, Guy?'

He could not find a ready answer to this question, and hesitated. She intervened.

'Oh, I know you have "loved" a lot of women.'

He still could not find an answer but, groping in his mind for words, found one he thought might do.

'I certainly love my memory of you – but when the *vardo* was burned: at first, I thought you had died in it.'

'The police did not discover my remains!'

'But you had gone. I had to reconstruct my life. There was a void in it.'

'I am glad you no longer love me, Guy, for I have lived with Georges Dinard for nearly ten years and it seems like eternity.'

'You brought me all the way to France to tell me that?'

'As you said, you have come to visit Dominic.'

Helen set the lamp on the table and sat close by him on the locker top. He stared at her face, and its shadow which the lamplight threw high up the wall. Her beauty was supernatural; he had never seen another woman close on forty

71

with a face like that. There was no artifice about it, no cutting or stretching, no clever making-up. It was the face of a young woman, and as such puzzled him. She divined his thoughts.

'If you had come to the house ten minutes earlier, you would have surprised me lying naked in the sun,' she said, 'and you would have seen that nothing has changed. You would also have embarrassed me. As you know, Romany women are modest and do not show themselves to strangers.'

'Helen! You are cruel.'

'And you are an old philanderer; but you are the father of my son. We will drink a toast to the past at dinner this evening. You'll stay in the house.'

'I must fetch my car from the square and I have a – er – companion.'

'Of course you have. Think of the old days, Guy. You were an adulterer then. I made you one.'

He closed his eyes to avoid her, but could not avoid the things she spoke of and roamed the gallery of his mind, pausing now and then before portraits and pastoral scenes. He saw the dished summit of Karemarn Hill, the craggy circle of hawthorns extending their ragged shadows under the stars; snow, and himself cold, alone. He saw the same trees bright with blossom and a full Spring moon, the twelve naked witch-women dancing round him, backs turned, legs leaping, buttocks muscular, flat, rounded, heavy –

Helen spoke into his echoing mind. 'Those were the days – of youthful adventures!' she said. 'But now you see clearer visions than I do. Why not show me your power? Tell me a story!'

'Very well.'

His eyes remained closed. It was easier thus to invent, and it prevented him from seeing her burning beauty. He began to tell her a story:

*   *   *

'Once upon a time, as they say in Malthassa and other unmapped countries of the mind – once, then, upon a fine midsummer's evening, Koschei came upon Brother Fox perambulating the cloister. He was young and still without discipline and the Brother, whose profession was to instil self- and other disciplines in the novices, was of middle age; but both men felt the lightness and cheer which the warm evening induced. Brother Fox paused so that Koschei could come up with him.

'"Look, Corbillion," he said. "Even the moths are hungry – see the fat moon moth feeding on the honesty flowers in the garth, and the night-hawk on the woodbine."

'"I," Koschei responded dreamily, "Do not hunger in that way. Neither marchpane nor sugar, not tender veal nor a bloody beefsteak would satisfy me. I am in love."

'The sly Brother held his long sleeve up against his mouth and laughed quietly into it. At length, recovering, he said,

'"With whom, my Cavalier Corbillion – or am I bold to ask?"

'"With Woman, with every She, with the Female and the Feminine – the Sex itself," answered Koschei.

'"And none of these in particular?"

'"There is –" Koschei began and, stifling the sentence and the thought that provoked it before they were fully born, began again,

'"Any," he said, "would satisfy me tonight – young, old, fair or foul, in her prime or past it."

'Brother Fox looked sideways at the young novice and admired the white teeth which gently bit into the fleshy, lower lip, the dark, jutting nose and the black curling hair which, against every rule of the Order, had been teased into ringlets and dressed with perfumed oil. Indeed, the heavy perfume dizzied the monk.

'"You are an agreeable sight yourself," he murmured and, speaking more loudly, said,

'"I know where to find a pretty something which will

73

quench your fire and satisfy your pride. Return secretly to your cell and wait there. When I return with the prize, she shall knock three times."

'The newly risen moon shone into the cloister garth and Koschei marvelled as he looked at its unwavering light and at the pallor it lent the bright flowers. Everything, the stones, the plants, the arches of the cloister and their two faces, his and Brother Fox's, had been turned silver or black. Brother Fox winked lewdly at him, half dispelling the magical mood, and padded off in the direction of the town. Koschei returned silently to his cell.

'In Espmoss, at the sign of the Rampant Lion in Grope Lane, Brother Fox concluded his negotiations. The midsummer madness was full on him and the moon shone bright in the street outside; or else why did he spend his own coin and risk his reputation for sternness and severity to please his favourite Novice? He had chosen the woman as one might a peach, for colour and ripeness and for the complex odours which assailed his keen nose when he bent his head and applied that huge organ to her silk-shrouded bosom. He pinched Ysera carefully on the buttocks, paid over his silver to the bawd, and brought the wench home to the cloister.

'Koschei sat quietly on his mattress of straw and thought about Woman, soft where he was hard, tender where he was vigorous, submissive where he was masterful. The moon shone on his windowsill and a narrow ray of its light penetrated the cell and lit a square of flagstones by the door. At length, that door was thrice tapped and a scented, warm and breathing bundle of silks propelled into the room by the plump hand of Brother Fox. The door closed. Koschei did not hear Brother Fox's footsteps as he walked away; the monk might still be eaves- or, rather, hinge-dropping, peering through the crack with a hot and beady eye. Koschei did not care: Ysera stood before him, packed in her silks like a surprise parcel. She had on a veil, and a wrapper of silver, but her face was dark like his and her veilings shrouded her upper body only for her lower was encased in tight trousers which shimmered as she gently moved, eyeing him. He had never before seen a woman trousered. The sight was almost too much for him. Her curves, her differences, her fascinating sex, all were revealed as the garment writhed and glittered with her movements which, every second, became bolder and more seductive.

'"I dance for you," she whispered.

'Koschei reached out and took her in his arms. He untied her first veil, and her second, and kissed her on the lips. Then, turning his head the better to kiss her tiny, right ear, he saw a shadow tremble and settle itself across the square of moonlight on the floor. The Fox! But wait – it was no man's shadow, being female and at once sinuous and slender. For a moment he thought it must belong to Ysera but, no, her shadow and his were twined together at the edge of the room. His ardour faded, his desire fell away; he did not kiss the ear of the pretty whore in his embrace but pushed her from him and stared into the night beyond the window, where stood the owner of the intrusive shadow –

'A woman, leaning casually against the tracery. She was naked and her long hair fell down her back in a great cascade and was as white and pallid as the moon's light; she had her back to him and her hands were upraised to her head, one holding a brush and the other a comb. All Koschei's passion and his firm resolve deserted him. He did not want Ysera nor any other woman, kind or cruel, but this one, this enigma who stood so carelessly outside his window, and he concentrated on the splendour of her hair. He wished to kneel down and worship this Unknown and felt his heart and soul dance merrily together in his chest.

'"You must go,' he told Ysera and threw her silks back at her. "Go!"

'"But, lord," she said entreatingly, "Oh new Beloved, Best of Men – Bright Youth, how can I leave such a one as you before I have seen the manner of your make?"

'"Go to the Brother who brought you here. His appetite surely exceeds mine now; he will satisfy you lickerishness."

'"Very well." Ysera bowed her head. "Yet – be blessed, young Novice, and enjoy whatever life brings henceforward – even your pain and your longing which, I see, is for the unattainable and not for common women like myself. Farewell."

'"Good bye,' said Koschei, hardly aware of her going.

'Now the door was shut and he alone again; but with this dream, this vision, at his window. Should he call out to it, approach it – touch it through the unglazed window-arch? He knelt on his mattress and held up his hands in prayer. The Unknown stirred and, as she turned toward him, let down her hair to cover her nakedness. He recognized her, his sister-neophyte, Nemione Sophronia, chaste star and lodestone of the novice-class, daughter of the town's chief magistrate, Ninian Baldwin.

'Koschei shivered on trembling knees and felt his whole body shake. For an instant she was there, solid, tangible – but he would never be able to prove that now – and then she was gone. No one was there in the cloister outside the window, nothing but the arabesques of stone and the empty roundels carved by chaste monks long ago; nothing but the moonlight setting the cloister garden ablaze with its consuming, dazzling white light. He looked down and saw that, although Nemione had disappeared, her shadow still lay on the floor of his cell. Marvelling, exhausted, he stretched himself out beside it, laid one hand on the shadow's empty breast and slept the heavy, sweat-exuding sleep of the damned. But, in her own cell, the false Novice of the Order and true of the magic Arts woke still and –'

Guy faltered and stopped speaking. Opening his eyes, he saw the dimly lit interior of the *vardo* and the gypsy, Helen Lacey, who touched his lips with a cold forefinger and said,

'Amen! But softly now; be still.'

His head swam. She, as enigmatic and beautiful as his creation, Nemione, smiled with a dozen curved and lovely sets of lips. The mirrorwork on her bodice reflected his myriad dazed faces.

'I'll be all right in a minute,' he said. 'It's nerves.'

'You are all right now.'

He felt steady, back at the reins. She, he realized, had willed him calm.

'Shall I go on?'

'No. I have enough – it is old stuff, that.'

'Yes, from *Koschei's First Pilgrimage*.'

'Old matter,' Helen mused, 'ancient and far-off, full of the magic of your fantasies, Nemione and Koschei compounded of my dreams and yours. Us. We, as we were but are no more. You and I as we might be if – if all the world were paper and every tree had golden leaves and every flower a pearl at its heart. If. But. To no purpose. Besides, Koschei is not in the Cloister. He is in the Forest.'

He did not understand and continued to stare at her, mesmerized by her dark eyes. He used to call them 'snake's eyes'. They were still that, bottomless pools in which he saw the tiny twin images of himself.

'My Love,' he whispered. 'My one Truth.'

Helen's breathing changed: the even gusts became deep snatching breaths.

'Don't!' she cried. 'Is it not enough to have possessed my body a hundred times, and my soul with your words?'

He looked away, at her velvet skirt, her rings, her soft, mirrored breast to which, he noticed, was pinned a small, gold cross. It looked gimcrack and poor amongst the finery; but such, he thought, was once my talisman too. He should ask her why she wore it there, beside the pagan glories, but something else distracted him: a thin sliver of light had pierced the darkness of her bed beside him. It was moonlight, the moonlight he had conjured in his tale and so, since the

77

curtains which covered the window over the bed were only half-drawn, it had crept into and enchanted the small, close room, touching the many crystals there, the looking glasses, the glossy china and Helen's agonized face.

'Leave my *vardo* now,' she commanded. 'Before it is too late.'

She folded her hands in her lap and bowed her head. He thought, I cannot bear to go; but I must. The intimacy of mind is over, she has some other task and does not want me here, a distraction – at least I am that. Should I return to Dominic? – and Alice. The remembrance of Alice's youth flowed into and tantalized him. He had abandoned her in the afternoon; hours had passed.

He stood up, unfolding his body with care.

'You feel your age,' said Helen. 'Never mind: those aches and pains will pass. *She* helps.' Though he looked at her when she spoke, she kept her eyes downcast. Perhaps she was able to see him, all the same? And who did she mean by 'she'? – herself, Nemione, or the bright moon?

'Dominic will show you your room,' she said.

She did not speak again nor seem inclined to speak, though he waited. He sighed and left her, descending the three wooden steps of the *vardo* into an orchard bewitched by night and by the scents of honeysuckle and tobacco flowers. The other perfume, 'Sortilège', the distillation of their vanished hours together was in his pocket. He took it out and left it on the top step. The house, too, was quiet and shadow-haunted. He found his way along the hall and opened the door on the left, the one which had first disgorged and brought him Dominic.

The bright light startled him. A nocturnal creature, an old badger caught in headlights, he stood still and blinked rapidly. Alice and Dominic were sitting side by side on a big sofa, cans of beer and Coke on a coffee table in front of them. The television was on. Dominic turned lazily and smiled at him; Alice was also smiling.

'She kept you ages!' Alice said. 'There must have been a lot to talk about.'

'Seventeen years' worth,' he said. He could not begin to tell what had really taken place.

'And now you are tired?' his son said. The innocent remark pressed a trigger in him, resentment at their sparkling, hopeful youth.

'Where did you find *her*?' he testily asked Dominic.

'In the square. She was guarding your mean machine. You should have brought them both with you, up to the house, Dad –' (Guy winced at the familiarity) '–You'd left the keys in her. It was too much: I drove her round for you – she's on the drive.' He rolled sideways in his seat and extracted Guy's keys from his pocket. 'There you go – Dad.'

'Thank you.' Guy took the keys and stowed them deep and safe, in his own pocket. 'I suppose you can drive – surely you're not old enough?'

'Oh, I'm old enough. I'm not old enough to be on the road by myself, that's all.'

Guy perceived that he was frowning. Alice looked up at him, such a melting look of pure azure tenderness. If she went on with it, he would be embarrassed in front of his own son.

'I'll go and see what damage you've done,' he said. 'I'll take a walk before I crawl into my bed – you won't mind amusing Alice for a little longer.'

'*Oui, Papa!*' The boy was still grinning. No one should have such perfect teeth, Guy thought. He could not help grinning back and so retreated, disturbed, abashed. He let himself out by the front door. How stupid to let his exuberance irritate me, he thought, and felt a new surge of annoyance when he saw the Audi, perfectly parked with all its windows closed and its doors locked. He peered through the windscreen. Nothing was damaged. He walked round the car gently kicking its tyres.

At least the absurd confrontation, if that was what it had

been, had put his refreshed desire for Alice back to sleep.

– But he had forgotten to ask where he was to sleep. And she?

He walked past the church and on, beyond the confines of the village. The road led to St Just and the Burgundy Canal. Maybe he would go as far as the water, see what a French cut looked like by night. He was walking roughly north-east, away from the *route nationale*, away from the *autoroute*. He passed beneath some evergreens. Their clean scent was unavoidable and he inhaled it pleasurably. The trees hung low over the road and, looking at them against the dark backdrop of the sky, he puzzled at their shape and wondered were they cedars? cypresses? The moon must have set, already. Then what time was it? He consulted his watch, pulling back his sleeve and holding the small dial on his wrist close to his face. Without his glasses he was blind, in this respect. Yet this quiet was what he needed, an interval to stroll in, a period of time alone between Helen and Alice, before bed, before the question of Alice's bed came up. He was still staring into the additional night of the trees when a soft noise behind him made him turn his head. The noise was scarcely audible, like someone trying to move silently and avoid breathing.

'Hello!' he said.

He could make out nothing certain, no animal or passer-by against the darkest shade; but he was sure he was no longer alone. Another man waited – there, where the branches dipped down; more, this man, whom he could barely see, wore a ragged beard. Guy walked toward him, one fist raised; walked through him: indeed, there was no other there beside the dark, the shadows and his imagination. He smiled to himself and shrugged, turning his pensive gaze once more upon the trees, for surely they did not deceive him. They were a pair of arbor vitae, one much taller than the other.

* * *

I thought: if I climb the biggest tree I shall be safe from the beasts of the night and can rest, if not sleep, till morning. I had a second thought: in Ayan I had heard one market woman tell another that every ring of earth round every tree has its guardian puvush, and I visualized a legion of them ranged out all over the world. I stood still in my fear and someone spoke,

'Helloo! Master Corbillion.'

Erchon, the slippery truant, come into the forest on my trail to save me!

It was not Erchon. A creature greater and blacker than any nightmare or sea monster stood beside me. I tried to make it out in the darkness, but all my diminished senses could tell me was that it loomed, huge, and smelled rank as a sewer after a feast day.

'What are you?' I cried. 'Why have you come to pester me in my trouble?'

'You might strike a light; then, you could see me,' the creature said.

At once, I began to fumble in my pockets for my tinder-box.

'Not like that. Try Nemione's way. I believe in you.'

I think it strange, to this day – a portentous action – that I obeyed this unknown of the forest and the night. I knew then neither incantation nor pass, but I tried (despite my fear of the unseen creature) to empty my mind of all distractions and concentrate on the idea of fire, of heat, of flame, of matter consumed by searing brands. I bent my consciousness inside myself and searched in all the far reaches of my being for the strength to make the first spark. I journeyed in the deep recesses of my mind and, when I had gathered hope, need and momentum and they threatened to burst from me and destroy everything before them, myself also, I enclosed these inchoate forces in the iron channel of my reason and sent them forth with a softly breathed 'Go!'

81

A spark sprang out of the darkness at my feet and from it a tall yellow flame arose.

'Excellent!' said my companion, laid his hand upon my shoulder and gave it a clumsy pat which felt like the shaking a terrier gives a rat. My new-born light showed me that his hand was a mighty paw and that the rest of him matched the hairy appendage for strength and hideousness. The mouth from which his scholarly voice issued was a red maw, lipped with thick folds of leather, toothed like a tiger.

I cried his name fearfully, 'Om Ren!' and, losing all my new-found power, began to mutter a woman's charm to placate and appease him.

'Peace, master,' the wild man said. 'If you were a mere soldier, albeit a Green Wolf and one of the best – if, as I say, you were a common man, I would have let you continue your hopeless wandering. You would have died.

'But I have stepped into your path because I wish to speak to you. Look upon my intervention as happy – but also as the beginning.'

Here, he paused to scratch his genitals, outdoing the butcher in lewdity and grossness. He gave me a terrible grin.

'I am a beast in body,' he said. 'Filthy as any hermit, disgusting of habit as a pariah dog; and cursed with a mind as pure as snow-water. Listen to me:

'You, Koschei Corbillion, have demonstrated your undiscovered powers to me. Will you continue on your way to join battle with the Myran forces and perhaps meet death as certainly as if I let you wander into the wilderness? You have twenty-five years only but you are an adept, of both praying and fighting; in your short life you have already been two men, a priest and a soldier, yet you are the same Koschei. Few are given the ability to pass through successive transformations and remain themselves.

'Do I speak riddles?' Here, the Om Ren smiled his ghastly smile again.

'I follow you,' I said.

82

'Then, to continue: this chameleon quality of yours is one the Archmage himself would give a sight of his soul for. It is searched for and sought after; a man must be born with it, of course: it cannot be bestowed. You possess it. Will you waste it?'

'Do you mean that I might practise magic?'

'"Practise magic" indeed! Magic is not Medicine. You *are* Magic. It surrounds, inhabits and becomes you – you must learn its particular language, that is all.'

It was my turn to mock:

'All?' I said. 'To learn that "language", as you call it, takes a lifetime.'

'Best begin!'

'How do I know you are not a false spirit of the forest, a dissembling will o'the wisp or jack o'lantern sent to lead me astray?'

The great beast laughed, or howled rather.

'Do I look like the *ignis fatuus*?'

'Why should I believe your words?' I countered.

'It was you who made the fire.'

We both looked down at the flames, which burned in contained fashion between us.

'And you also,' said the Om Ren, 'who has begun to build the Memory Palace by the cloister at Espmoss.'

'That is just a small house, a hut, filled with certain objects which hold associations for me.'

'Is it? When you walk in there, it fills with the ghosts of your past, does it not? – with the presences of your mother and father, the little dog you had when you were a boy. You have made love to Nemione Baldwin there, have you not?'

'Alas, only to her doppelganger.'

'But you remember doing so, do you not? Can you distinguish between memory, imagination and clairvoyance?'

'Yes!'

'We will make trial of that assertion. Look into your fire! What do you see there?'

I crouched over the fire involuntarily and looked into its red heart. I suppose the Om Ren made me, with his crystal, matchless mind.

For a moment or two, I saw nothing beside the glowing coals; but soon I saw them divide and fall away as if they were the stones of a breached city wall and I looked through the doorway thus made. I saw a tower, absolute in its loneliness. It stood, tall, grey, and topped by a small turret with a conical roof, on a promontory above the ocean. Its sole door was twenty feet up the wall, and there was no ladder or stair. High above that was a slit window. I looked into it. What I saw filled me with disquiet.

I saw Manderel Valdine, Prince of Pargur and Archmage of Malthassa, in all his solitary glory. Cloaked (against the cold) in furs and robed (against any suspicion that he might be an ordinary mortal) in cloth-of-gold studded with brilliants, he was conjuring before a great map stitched together from many parchments. The curve of the wall repeated itself in the curve of the map fixed to it. It seemed leagues across that wall of map.

Valdine made arcane gestures with his staff.

'Show me!' he cried. 'Show me the place of safety!' Sweat stood in dewdrops on his broad forehead. The bald dome of his scalp glistened. He groaned with the effort of his spell, like a man in torment, like a man in ecstasy.

'Valdine casts a spell,' I told the Om Ren. 'A terrible spell, surely of plague or destruction, his face is so white and red.'

'Then listen carefully!'

The Archmage in my fire bent down, slowly lowering himself to the floor. He abased himself before his magic map, making desperate plea to Urthamma: he, the blessed, cursed demon, is the god of magicians. A column of light arose from the body of the Archmage, a twisting column composed perhaps of his golden robe or of the very essence of his manhood. I saw Urthamma standing twined within

84

it, great and glorious, glowing like a lighted brand above the crouched figure of Valdine.

'You try me!' said the god.

The man on the floor mumbled wordlessly.

'I tell you, Valdine,' the god said from a mouth like a broken crossbow. 'Your desire for immortality is an embarrassment on Mount Cedros. I am a laughing stock.

'However –' Here, he yawned and clawed his fiery tresses into some sort of order. 'Look at your map when I am gone. The fair province of SanZu is as good a place as many.'

The god yawned again and, turning widdershins gracefully, disentangled himself from the oriflamme of silken matter and disappeared. Valdine leapt to his feet and I peered hard through the insubstantial window, disappointed because I was too far away to see any detail of the map other than a wedge of lines which seemed to represent a rocky promontory as cruel and precipitous as that on which the Archmage's spytower stood. I heard Valdine cry 'Λah, salvation!!'

The vision faded and the magical fire dimmed as if I had exhausted it. I stood in a murky twilight with the hideous man of the forest, who tapped my chest with a horny forefinger.

'Well?' he demanded.

'Valdine deserves his position as Archmage. A formidable show!'

'But what did you see?'

'He was using his powers to find a place of absolute safety. He summoned Urthamma!'

'No such thing – as a place of absolute safety. But what was it that you saw?'

'I told you. I told you everything I saw, as it happened.'

'But did it happen? Was it an episode from your imagination, projected into the fire? Was it precognition? Was it memory? Was it mere prestidigitation?'

'It was a vision.'

'Ah! Most deceitful of mental processes; most desired. You saw them when you were a religious, did you not – and not always spiritual in content?'

'They were invariably sacred. I saw the blessed Martyrs at Actinidion and the Saints in Glory; Nemione Baldwin undressed twice only – more holy and more lovely than any Martyr or Saint.'

'You remember all these visitations, or visions?'

'I think so.'

'Then what is the difference between the original and its copy?'

I began to protest. My memories were surely most precious, most detailed, each nuance lovingly built up – embroidered – dwelt upon. I wasn't sure. If the vision had been less than the memory, would I have remembered it at all? At last,

'I don't know,' I confessed. 'I'm not sure if I know the difference between memory and imagination. As for clairvoyance –'

'Huzzah!' the beast thundered. 'Bravo! Now, as you have satisfactorily proved my point, I will take you to my house and there you will get a meal and a good night's rest before I set you on the way you should have taken.'

The Wild Man led me by the hand through the dark forest. I was glad he held my hand in his huge paw, content as a child to be led by his nurse for all that my hand was the broad and sinewy gripping instrument of a swordsman. A puvush danced. Nivashi sang to me, leaning up from the streams and marshy places with sad and seductive expressions on their pale faces.

'Look,' said the Om Ren. 'Look and learn from looking; but never touch one. She would burn you instantly to death with her icy touch or, if she felt playful, drag you down to her streambed, lie and let you mount her as you drowned. The puvushi are little better. Their toys are ivy stems and rotting wood. You would have one chance of escape rather than none – if you were lucky.'

He squeezed my hand until it ached.

The Om Ren's house was a shambling affair as squalid and dishevelled as himself. It did not look like a house but like a great faggot of branches someone had thrown against a tree.

'The puvush of this tree's earth is saintly,' he told me. 'Peace now, Iron Glance, it is only myself.'

I heard something scratching in the earth. Inside the ramshackle house lay a heap of straw and a long coil of straw rope.

'My bed and my weapon,' said the Om Ren proudly. He showed me his larder, a hollow in the tree, and took seeds and nuts from it.

'Eat!'

I managed to swallow a few dry walnuts and a handful of green wheat. Noticing a big red nut amongst the remaining grains, I stretched out my hand.

'No!' the Om Ren suddenly cried. 'Not that one. It should not be amongst these wholesome fruits. Let me put it away.' He picked the red nut up himself and tucked it away under the long hairs which covered his belly. 'That nut could kill you.'

'I have never seen its like before,' I said. 'What is it?'

'It is called the Ripe Nut of Wisdom. It is nothing of the kind of course, but the peasants tell stories about it. It looks so appetizing.'

'It does indeed. Is it a deadly poison?'

'A good one would bring on an attack of the megrims. The one you saw is addled: it is full of the eggs of the black worm and they are fatal if consumed.'

'It is fortunate that you saw it in time.'

'Oh, I am a careless fellow. Cankers, toadstools and belladonna are my daily companions. Have the rotten nut if you will. It may help you. It will bring catastrophic changes if you use it well.' He retrieved the nut from his body hair. 'There! Here's to a fresh intelligence and new wisdom in the world – if you discover how to use the nut!'

I tried, of course, to question him further, but he would not respond and diverted all my queries with uproarious laughter or with his vile bodily habits of scratching his private parts (not at all private in him but hanging there for all to see), his belly and his armpits. His body was obviously a pasture to herds of fleas and lice; for my safety I had to remain with him while the darkness lasted and sleep in his musty bed, where he snored and scratched all night. Yet I thought him a kindly creature, more bark than bite. What use as a weapon was a rope of straw? – and his house was like an unlit bonfire. The wolf in the children's tale could easily have blown it away and any wildfire which coursed through the forest after a storm would burn it down.

We woke at dawn and breakfasted on the last of the seeds. The Om Ren shambled out to relieve himself against his house and, after a decent interval, I followed him. He glanced in my direction as I urinated and, leavening his words with one of his fearful smiles, said,

'If I may say so without offence, you Wise Men are poorly endowed. How do your women pleasure themselves on such a tiny thing?'

'They are very inventive,' I said.

He laughed and offered me a drink of rainwater from his cupped hands. It was good water, he told me, collected from another hollow in his tree. Treading carefully, that we did not disturb Iron Glance's slumbers, we left his home. We walked for a while, not long, and soon came to a broad track, which we followed. Though it was lined with tall bents and foxgloves, I did not recognize it.

'Are you sure this is the way?' I said.

The Om Ren replied with a wave of his arm. He pointed to a tree in the middle distance and this, I recognized: the chestnut which spread its branches low to the ground, like a woman's skirt.

'The Silver Dwarf waits there,' he said. 'In hiding. His kind are happier when they cannot see the sky. Listen! A woodbird sings. It is a good omen. Go safe on your way.'

What should I say? Not feebly 'thank you' nor yet suggest some temporal reward.

'I hope you never find yourself the master of the Red Horse,' I said, intending, by this obscure and convoluted compliment, to wish him a long life.

He laughed, or roared, through his hand – I think he hoped to mute his voice.

'You mean to say "I hope your skin is never made into a bridle for the mightiest stallion," I think. It is an honour, Master Corbillion, and I will be already dead, you know. The Ima have access to the power of my kind, even when the wielder of that power is dead.'

'Well, I hope they have all they need, for a long while yet.'

He gently thumped me. It felt like one of the well-aimed blows of my sparring partner. 'You won't get to the battle,' he said confidently. I protested:

'I will. You have put me on my road!'

'You will go to Pargur. I think you have a desire to see the city and a greater desire to interview its prince, the Archmage Valdine.'

'Have I? I must follow my duty first, wherever it leads me.'

The Wild Man took my hand in his and squeezed it, much harder than he had before.

'Does that hurt?'

'Aagh!'

He let me go.

'You are a self-deceiver, Koschei,' he said. 'You are already more than half way to abandoning your life as a Green Wolf, just as you abandoned your life in the cloister.'

89

'Perhaps.'

'Certainly. But the dwarf waits under the chestnut tree. He is anxious. You forget how sharp his hearing is.'

I set off along the path, intending to turn and wave. When I looked back, the Om Ren had gone, camouflaged by the forest greenery like a puvush or a deer. I pushed my way under the branches of the chestnut. Erchon was sitting there on the ground, his back against the trunk of the tree and his goods spread out around him, rapier on top.

'Who were you talking to, Master?' he asked. 'A gypsy was it, or an apparition? The Om Ren himself!'

'Hush, you fool! It was he.'

'You don't say?'

'It was the Wild Man indeed. I was lost in the forest – I have a tale to tell.'

'It will sound better over breakfast.' The dwarf got up and rummaged in a woven basket. He fetched out a length of smoked sausage, bread, mustard and beer.

We sat down to eat, safe enough beneath the chestnut tree. I told him as much of my tale as I judged fit, gratified to impress him at last.

'Perhaps we should go to Pargur before we turn toward the battle and possible death?' I suggested finally.

'Perhaps we ought, Sir Green Onetime-Wolf. I should like to see my Lady. She journeys to Pargur.'

'I should also like to see Nemione!'

'Then we are agreed?' said Erchon, and I felt that he had taken hold of my uncertain scheme and made it into a reality.

'To Pargur!' I said. 'But where were you, Erchon, till now? What delayed you on the road?'

'Oh that is another tale – not so grand perhaps as yours. I was detained in Tanter by a – hold, master. Be still.' He leaned forward quickly and pressed his ear against the ground.

'Hooves, wheels,' he whispered. 'The Romanies – no, it is a timber waggon. Rest easy. I'll continue my tale.'

Guy heard the lorry changing gear before he saw it, one of those continental juggernauts sensibly barred from his own country, which now with lights blazing and engine growling threatened to engulf and crush him under its wheels as comprehensively as might any Hindu god-waggon. He jumped back into the hedge, only there was none, and found himself floundering in a dry ditch, strands of barbed wire clutching at his clothes.

When the lorry had gone and he had extricated himself from his predicament – lucky it was a dry night! – he turned back towards the village, comforted by the few lights still showing there, small yellow, homely stars.

'I bet the bugger never even saw me,' he muttered, '– another careful French driver.'

One of the yellow stars shone out of the downstairs room at the Old Presbytery, the comfortable living-room in which he had left his son and Alice Tyler. The curtains had been drawn back, and the lamplight illuminated a stretch of gravel and his car. A second car, a big saloon, was parked beside it – Georges Dinard's, he supposed. He heard Alice calling softly, 'Guy! Guy?' She was standing outside the open front door, her white shirt gleaming almost as much as her hair.

'There you are! You missed dinner.'

He went swiftly up to her and put his arms round her. 'I'm sorry,' he said, 'I'm always abandoning you. Where's Dominic? Inside?'

'He went to bed, ages ago. We are to sleep in that room.' She pointed to a pair of open casements above the dining room into which he had peered in the afternoon; long ago in terms of new experiences: before he had met his son, before he had re-encountered Helen.

'And Helen?' he asked Alice. 'Have you met her?'

'Oh yes. She cooked for us and there was Bordeaux *and* a Pouilly Fumée. Georges came back from Lyon.'

They, he thought, are now in bed together. Jealousy crept up and snapped at his heels; he wanted to run into the house, upstairs, to throw the usurper out.

'She left you some food,' said Alice.

'I'd rather go to bed!'

'OK – this is the way.' They walked, still joined in their embrace, up the staircase which turned near the top to repeat the layout of the wide passage below. The moonlight, he saw delightedly, had returned to light the passage and to coat Alice with its glamour. A crowd of statues stood elbow to elbow before him.

'My God!'

'They belong to Georges. Dominic showed me. There are others in the dining room,' the girl said innocently. 'Each one is connected with a death.'

'That's sick.'

'Every artefact is connected with death, isn't it? Everything passed on when someone dies.'

'The gypsies burn all the possessions when one of them dies, even the sleeping-waggon.'

'The *vardo*, yes. There's a figure of the god Horus down-stairs. Dominic told me it belonged to a man called Paon – who was guillotined for serial murder. In Lyon. In 1884 –'

He touched the cold figure of a woodland nymph. 'I know,' he said. 'I looked at your book in Avallon, while you slept. Strange to find something of Paon's here.'

The whispered conversation, or the moonlight, was affect-ing him with a nervous agitation. He thought Alice relished her revelations too much, though her shoulder felt pleasantly warm under his hand.

'Just coincidence,' she said. 'Come on.'

Their room had bare, polished boards and a wide bed, its white linen inviting. There were no curtains.

'I'll close the shutters,' he said.

Alice caught his arm. 'Leave them. I want to see you.' She unbuttoned her shirt. 'Look! Wouldn't you prefer her?'

The soft finger of the moonlight reached right across the room and touched the statue of a second nymph, surely the sister of the first. Instead of wild fruits and leaves, this one wore a garland of kingcups and water lilies. The white marble she was carved from had been so highly polished it seemed as though her skin was wet, and they both went up to her and laid exploring fingertips upon her, Guy upon her left breast and Alice upon her right thigh.

'Magic!' he whispered. 'She is you.'

'No, she isn't me; not now. She's a nivasha – like you put in your books.'

'You know,' he turned away from the statue to Alice. 'I don't think I have ever described one. I imagine them much more deadly, sinister attenuated creatures.'

When he turned to look at the statue again it seemed dead and prosaic, a heavy piece of Victorian sentimentality standing guard over a cupboard door. In the moment of conversation with Alice he had glimpsed her moonlit body under her open shirt. He picked her up and laid her on the bed.

'We are fortunate,' he said. 'Two nights of love under the moon. I want to see you in daylight too, at midday when the sun is hottest.'

'In a hayfield – in an orchard in the shade of an old tree.'

But moonlight, he thought, best becomes her. He knelt over her. 'Wait,' she said and sat up to unfasten the ribbon which concealed the blemish on her neck. The mark looked darker, almost livid. He touched it.

'It doesn't spoil you,' he said.

'No. How could it? It is a mark of courage.'

'I don't understand.'

'Because I survived hanging. They imprisoned and tortured me, they tore off my nails one by one. They strung me up on the gibbet outside the town gates, but I did not die –

93

not for another sixty years. I hung till evening and when they cut me down, I had not died.' Her voice rose triumphantly.

'You are Alice Naylor,' he whispered.

'I am Alice Naylor, Roszi, and Alice Tyler.'

'Roszi?'

'Ah, Roszi.' She gave no further explanation, but held his fingers against the scar on her neck. He could feel slight ridges and troughs, the negative cast of the twisted hemp.

'Your survival of the hanging has rewarded you, given you a kind of eternity?' he said but, no doctor or mortician accustomed to horrors, he shivered involuntarily. In the old days, such reverential touching was reserved for ghastly relics, feet of dead saints, dirty bones, crucified hands – which still took place in some holy fanes like Mediterranean churches, temples of the Far East; and this, the guest bedroom of Helen Lacey's house in Coeurville, the town where he had lost his senses to this odd schoolgirl. She moved his hand away from her neck and held it between her breasts.

'You understand, Guy Parados,' she said, 'because you are yourself abnormal, a storyteller obsessed by his inventions – so much so that you write them down and get them made into books which obsess others. Yes, I am Alice and Roszi and Alice again.'

'My Roszi?'

'Go to the top of the class, Mister Author! – but the real nivasha, not the paper one!' She laughed, almost maliciously. 'She lives in me alongside the others – just as you are both Guy Kester Parados and Christopher Guy Young.'

It was true, what she said. In a way, he was possessed of many identities and these were only two, the ordinary self he had been born with and to and his hard-won, writer's persona.

'Yes, I've almost forgotten my real name,' he admitted.

'Christopher Guy is a law-abiding Christian husband and father.'

'Who is Guy Kester?'

'The writer, the storyteller. My lover!'

'Winter to cover your Spring!'

'Autumn perhaps, but hard as frost!'

'Warm me! Soften me!'

Inside her – Arcadia? Paradise? – he moved slowly and deliberately. He was, as his son had intimated, a man learned in all the skills of life and loving. Alice accepted him now, whatever her first intentions had been, as he accepted her – whoever she was. One of his chief delights was to touch her softly, as if she were his precious, mortal soul, a living talisman which might easily break or melt in his hands.

They rested and slept a little, lightly, lying close. He woke, kissed her and rolled her over so that she fitted him exactly, tucked between his thighs and his chin. He began to kiss her neck, lifting her long skein of hair aside to reveal the skin. The mark of the rope went all the way round, a weird necklace.

'We might almost be married, newly wed,' she said drowsily.

'We are, for tonight at least.'

'I feel goodness in you, but deeply buried. You could be one of the kristniki, a Twelver – one of the twelve sons of Stanko who fight the witch-host on St John's Eve.'

'Christopher probably is. Guy is quite a different other. Once he played the black dog, cold Master Robin to a coven of witches.'

'Many years ago.'

'I am here because of it. And Dominic.' He opened his eyes. They focused lazily, adjusting to the twilit distance between Alice's neck and the marble nymph. Her sylvan sister stood beside her now, frozen in an attitude of suspense. He blinked and closed his eyes again, too involved with Alice's body to make sense of what he saw, if it had any sense in this illogical night. Women in childbirth took notice of neither bombs nor portents; he, held more securely than a child deep in Alice's birth-canal, had no interest in the world beyond it. He abandoned himself to the sensation their conjoined movement produced.

Lying still, exhausted; dead within her, he succumbed to the curiosity which awoke in his mind now that his body was satisfied. He opened his eyes wide. The second nymph, who still stood on tiptoe, surprised in her prurient, lustful eavesdropping, was Helen. The door behind her was open. He could make out the dark shapes of furniture in another room. Perhaps she wants to begin again, bring me another dozen lusty women to serve? he thought.

Helen knelt beside the bed and laid a hand on each of them, himself and Alice.

'Good,' she said. 'I knew you were still an adept. Roszi – Alice, you were always a sublime minx.'

'It is better, far, far better,' Alice murmured, 'than my icy spring, or school, or imprisonment – oh far, far more than my golden torture.'

Guy, listening to them, half believed he dreamed; but, no, this body-warmed sheet was real, this golden hair, this small, aroused breast.

'Love is close to torture, is it not?' Helen inquired.

'Ah – yes!' he said, and Alice echoed him, 'Yes – ah! – yes.'

To lie with them both, as once he thought he had, sometime, in the witches' dreaming long ago: inwardly he rehearsed an invitation: Will you join us? – No – Helen, come a little closer – lie down on this side. As if she heard him, Helen drew back and stood by the statue of the nymph.

'Look,' she said. 'But you must not touch!' He studied her, marble-distant beyond Alice's warmth and the smell of her pleasure, far away. The body was as perfect as the face. Dawn, which he suspected of trespass in the room, bringing parting, bringing day, made a goddess of her. Here was no slender woodland seducer; no maid of chill waters. She had heavy breasts, a small waist, swelling hips; all of these no older, no less alluring than they had been when she left him at the age of twenty-two. She had the dangerous look of Herodias, the cunning of Jezebel, the beckoning come-hither blatant sexuality of a Salome cast in metal, heated in the fire, poured into an unimpeachable mould.

The pain of desire, which Alice had likened to torture, returned to torment him as he lay looking at her untouchable nakedness, feeling Alice's pliant flesh and will against him.

'Why deny me?' he said. 'Georges must enjoy you!'

'Georges. Ah Georges, who slumbers soundly! He understands my predicament – I must go back to him. Sleep!' Swiftly, she turned away and passed through the doorway. He heard her turn the key. The door was made impregnable and Georges slept with her behind it, behind the thin shield of its panels. Guy lay quiet, entirely limp and relaxed, every part still except his mind. Alice slept. He rehearsed the unquiet night, going over and over its many and intimate details until his imagination was sated. He remembered Alice's uncalloused feet, her straight toes and her tender earlobes, her waist, her lips, her tongue, her navel: all these asleep beside him. He remembered the bracelet Helen used to wear about her left ankle, her painted toe-nails, the many rings which pierced her neat ears, how he could almost span her waist with his two hands and how her tongue met his; the jewel he had removed with his lips from the deep pit of her navel: all these asleep beside his successor, Georges Dinard.

He remembered the serious young man he once had been and the insatiable rake who still woke in him; the Christian he was and the pagan, the husband and the philanderer. He remembered his books standing in a line at home, all with crimson covers and the distinctive lettering of the legend beneath each title: A Book in the Malthassa Series, by Guy Kester Parados – or Christopher Guy Young whose unremarkable name he had let drop as carelessly as a lost handkerchief. He signed everything now, books, contracts, cheques, with Parados's name.

The early birds were waking. Words from the first line of *The Making of Koschei* haunted him: 'I began building the year the . . .' He chased the troublesome ghosts from his mind – he was on holiday, enjoying such a vacation! He fell asleep as the sun came up and turned the cold white statue gold.

Guy woke again because his left hand was aching. The struggle to come fully awake was aggravated by troublesome thoughts of typing and driving. Maybe Sandy's Chinese balls! He grinned, half asleep. Of course, not Sandy. Alice. And it was Thursday, the third day in France. Alice was lying on his hand. He freed it. The ache continued and his right hand gave a sympathetic twinge.

'Blast!' he said. He would get up, walk for a while. Relax and forget it.

The sun was well up. He leaned out of the window, the sill covering his nakedness. Georges Dinard's car, he was glad to see, was a plain four-door Citroën. It sat like a lumpen ox beside his shiny predator. Vineyards crowded the village and their bright uniformity stretched into the distance, over hill and through valley, meeting whatever tracts of forest stretched out to meet them in a blur of dull and biting greens. When he turned from the window and saw Alice sleeping under the watchful eye of her tutelary nymph he felt at least twenty-five and, simultaneously, as old as a biblical patriarch. David, wasn't it, who needed a virgin to warm him in his dotage? Alice slept, but maybe Helen was awake, about. He stretched and massaged his hands before collecting the scattered garments which, when they were assembled to clothe him, made up the image the world perceived as Guy Parados.

* * *

In the kitchen a cooling pot of coffee was the only sign of life. Guy found a cup and drank some of it black. Outside, the garden was in shade and, suddenly needing the sunlight which had warmed him at the bedroom window, he went out and walked swiftly across the grass until the shadows were behind him. He opened the door which led into the orchard.

The black *vardo* was closed up. He glanced at and avoided it, striking out for the far side of the orchard where, instead of the vines he expected, a small stand of hazels and other scrubby trees hid a plantation of conifers. An indeterminate but regular noise drew him: it sounded for all the world like a giant drumming deep in the heart of the wood. There was no hedge or other boundary and he walked amongst the trees until he found a ride where tall grasses and a few foxgloves struggled upwards in the dim light. The ground was dry and strewn with old pine needles and cones. He followed the ride and the sound until he came upon a clearing. Here stood a group of ruinous wooden buildings that looked as if they had been old before the wood was planted. Some letters were chalked upon the nearest. When he was close enough to see them properly he made out the single word 'Arcadie' and the memories and associations it woke confused him. Someone had written it there as a joke, he supposed.

Ivy made the place picturesque and the early morning sun reached with long fingers into the clearing. The puzzling noise had resolved itself into a regular beat. He stood in the warmth and willed his seething mind blank for precious, restful moments. Relax! On holiday! Then he walked quickly to the barn and looked into it. A man was sawing wood at a small saw-bench powered by a compact little engine. The brassy shine of the engine and the smell of hot oil attracted him. He took a step forward and the man, who was turning to reach for a fresh branch, looked round and gave him Dominic's insolent grin.

The shock of recognition and of disparity which coursed through Guy's body made him shout,

'What on earth are you doing here?'

'Calm down, Dad. This is my place. My saw mill.'

'Saw mill?' Guy noticed spreading continents of oil stains on his son's hands and clothing as he repeated the words in bewilderment.

'Mine, Dad. Wake up! *Attention!* Where I cut up wood. Some of the trees are big enough for sale now – but I mostly deal with the dead stuff. We burn it in the winter – you must've noticed the wood-burners in the house.'

'Why have you written "Arcadia" on the wall?'

'It's always been called that. It's on the old maps, too. Want a go? That looks a likely branch.'

Guy was grateful for the boy's invitation. It muted the dismay he felt at this young prodigy's invasion of his life. He smiled at his son and picked up a sweet-smelling pine bough, heavier than it looked. They would work together at a task, for the first time – no matter that the land and probably the buildings belonged to the unseen, undefined Georges Dinard. He laid the branch across the saw bench.

'Hold it steady!' Dominic said. 'The bench will bring it to the saw.'

Guy hung on, pressing against the branch and feeling the stroke of the engine throbbing through metal and timber. The blade spun on its mount, its teeth reduced by the rotation to a blur. In a moment it would slice into the yellow heart-wood and send fine sawdust flying. He would breathe the pungent scent of the cut. He felt the blade hit and bite. Dominic was staring at him with eyes as dark as Helen's, the fascinating eyes of the gypsy, swallowing him, drawing him into a fathomless pit. Struggling with his son for mastery, he forgot to watch the wood. It was only when he had wrested his gaze from Dominic's that he saw the blood on the saw-bench and the divided branch and realized it was his own; that the spinning blade had cut as neatly through his wrists. He saw his son's shocked face. He saw his two hands lying on the floor and then there was an interval of utter quiet and total darkness. Someone was lifting him, carrying him towards the light. He blinked and closed his eyelids against the brightness. It was night again. The forest surrounded him. A deer fled before him into the silence.

Did Erchon also see the white hart, I wondered. It was a phantom deer, not one of the spotted kind I had seen near the last road. We journeyed separately again, the dwarf and I, not this time because of wayside adventures but because Erchon (so he claimed) had heard his mistress, Nemione, calling him.

'In daylight?' I had jestingly asked, 'or in your dreams?'

'In bold daylight, Master,' he had answered. 'I am only amazed that you cannot hear that lilting voice. It comes clearly to me through the trees.'

Next day he left me, riding high on the withers of a stray woodsman's horse which he had waylaid. I laughed at him.

'I shall get there faster,' I called after him. 'That runaway will take you to some remote logger's camp.'

Erchon laughed at me: 'Not it, Master!' He clapped his heels against the neck of the horse which flung itself into a gallop and, so, they departed, the little man a flash of quicksilver, the horse shock-maned and wild.

I was tired of the forest, utterly weary of the infinite close ranks of the trees. There is no end to the forest in Malthassa just as the country itself — if that is what it is — has no boundaries. These exist far away, rumour tells, but certainly no one has dared draw them (even with dotted lines) on the map, or seen them — And so, in a sense, I was glad of the deer's company for the little while it ran ahead of me. They are dire straits when a man is glad of the companionship of a ghost.

I came to Pargur. It appeared suddenly before me when I

stepped out between the last of the trees. There is no road to it; each one must find his own way through the forest. True, I once heard that there was a road, a broad highway paved with mottled skarn, but it must have been another rumour or some tale begun in an inn; and if once there was a road, it disappeared under the forest long ago. One leaves the forest, and the city is there, immediate. Its towers of crystal and its quartz revetments dazzle the eye: the multiple refraction makes it hard to see exactly where they stand, sisters to the prismatic mists which cloak the city's southern flank.

I came to Pargur. It was winter and fifty yards of virgin snow lay between me and the city walls. Behind me, the eternal forest spread its green without a trace of snow. I had been a long time on my journey and was still more travel-stained, as tattered as a beggar or one of those travelling mountebanks who carry a whole world of enchantment in their packs. I came exhausted to Pargur, the Mutable City, and struck out gladly across the carpet of snow. As I reached its narrow gates, which shone like a sea-breach in an iceberg, I looked up and saw above me the most amazing sight of my journey. Moving imperceptibly, as if it hung aloft in perpetual stasis, drifted a giant balloon of purest white. Ice-crystals glittered on its curving sides and red fire roared at its base, a little above a frail basket which hung down on ropes. There were people in the basket. I could see a tall head-dress of some kind and, more, folds of silver fox fur from which a hand reached out, and waved. A wan face appeared above it, glacial as the moon's, and the lovely, lilting voice which had called Erchon floated down to me.

'Hiy, Koschei, hiy-yi! Koschei!'

The guard, who had turned to me to ask my business in the city, straightened stiffly. He clicked his heels together and grounded his pike with a mighty thud.

'Archmage Valdine,' he said, 'and the Lady Nemione.' He looked me up and down. '*She* called *you*,' he muttered.

'Yes.' I looked him in the eye. His eyes were a muddy, peasant colour: I felt as though I held my face in dung, willingly. I saw his gaze waver and his pike did also.

'I have business with the lady,' I said.

He stood aside and I walked into Pargur.

The first thing I saw when I had passed the city gates was a palace standing upon a lake of ice. People, slipping, sliding, walking, gliding upon steel blades, riding in sleighs, thronged about it and I heard music, which seemed to come from within the palace. A juggler tossed coloured sticks into the air. A fire eater blew tongues of flames from his throat; I wondered, was he the warmer for it? The cold had a hold on my very bones. I pulled my jacket closer about me and wiped away the frost crystals which were forming on my eyelashes. A woman who was passing looked at me and touched her head, which was covered with a huge fur hat. At first I thought she meant to insult me but then I understood that I should cover my own head. I untied the sash from Tanter and wrapped it round my ears and face; now, I did look like a beggar. I stepped out on to the ice.

As I went, slowly and carefully and not at all at a pace befitting a soldier, I blinked hard to keep the crystals from re-forming about my eyes. I could see a second palace, identical to the first, a little to the left, a short distance behind it. I looked about me and saw a third palace and a fourth; a fifth. Eventually I came to a halt, bemused. The people who surrounded me did not seem at all discomfited by this plague of palaces, but continued with their merrymaking and conversations. I spun on my heels.

Now a man came up to me, a seller of hot chestnuts which he carried on a sort of portable gridiron over a tray of glowing coals. He offered a bag of them to me and, when he heard I was a stranger in Pargur, laughed and said,

'What do you think of our capital city?'

'I have seen very little of it,' I cautiously answered, 'but it seems to be a fine place, though suffering perhaps from an excess of palaces.'

'Take no notice,' the chestnut seller said, 'or, if you will visit one, take that one, there.' He pointed. 'They are made of ice, you see. We build one every year.'

He walked off, leaving me more mystified than before. I resolved to see the inside of at least one palace and hurried, as fast as I was able, to the one he had indicated.

It was a marvel, clear and cold, its inner walls covered with a layer of misty frost through which the crowds outside could faintly be discerned. There were no rooms in it, apart from the one great cavern and this was filled to bursting with dancers who whirled deliriously to the music of an organ. Its pipes were made of ice and they towered against the wall in a gamut of gleaming stalagmites and stalactites. I tried to get closer, curious about its workings, but this was impossible. Instead, I was dragged into the dance. The women, in their wraps and furs, smelled like stoats and they had small, even teeth which glistened between parted lips. Their upper lips all had the shape of tiny bows and their lower lips were thin. The men were tall, bearded like myself and muscular, but they tolerated me and I was flung from hand to outstretched hand until I reached the door again. The music never ceased and the dancers whirled on. I was afraid. I suspected that if I entered one of the other palaces I would find the same dancers, the same music and the same organ; that I might even encounter myself.

I crossed the ice. It was darker now, the sun gone and the first deep blues of evening paraded one after another across the sky. Back on solid earth, albeit frozen and coated with snow, I turned into the first street I came to and found myself upon a wide avenue which led towards a hill. All at once, the bells of the city rang out from every tower and campanile and their echoes stayed a long time in the frosty air and in my head as I stood looking at the hill. A great white castle stood there, overspreading the slopes of the hill and littering its rocky escarpments with crenellated towers and bastions. I frowned. I should have been able to see the castle from the city gate. When I looked behind me, I could see that gate and the sentry who guarded it; this, despite the fact that I had turned a corner. There was no trace of the lake nor its array of pleasure-palaces. I stopped a passing boy. He looked real enough.

'What is that place on the hill?' I asked him.

'That?' He looked at me as if I were a cretin. 'That is Castle Sehol.'

I gave him a sixpenny piece. 'And who lives there?'

'The Archmage, sir. The Lady Nemione is there as well, his guest. She holds court, Queen of Winter and Love. It's the Winter Fest, sir. That's why everyone makes holiday.'

'Can I get up there?'

'No sir, oh no – not unless you are the devil himself, or a winged angel.'

'But this road leads to the castle gate?'

'Sometimes, sir; sometimes it does.'

I turned away from him. My jacket, I realized, had fallen open. The boy must have seen the wolf's head on my cuirass, the insignia of the Brotherhood. The sight of it and not the sixpence was the reason for his deference. So. Maybe I carried my passport on my chest.

'Koschei! Koschei Corbillion!' The voice was mellifluous, seductive; it was Nemione's voice, teasing me as she used at school and afterwards, in the cloister. 'Koschei, you are getting warmer!' It rang in the street and in my head; the stones echoed it, the towers threw its chiming back at me, but only I could hear Nemione's magical tongue.

I continued on my way, if a way it was, following the unearthly voice and the kerbstones which bordered the road until I found myself near the castle. Here I paused, unwound the cloth from my head, shook out my hair and combed my beard with my fingers. My comb was lost long ago, left behind at one of my camp sites in the forest. I found the lock of hair Nemione had given me in the summer and twisted it between my fingers as a talisman. The wolf's head visible and my face stern, I advanced and shouted for the guard.

I was at once shown every courtesy. The battered wolf's head, though I had deserted it, did not fail me, and admitted me unquestioned and unsearched to Castle Sehol. Two men-at-arms escorted me through the gate. Unlike the old wooden gates of Tanter or Actinidion; not like the narrow gate of Pargur and very different from the new bronze doors of my memory palace back in Espmoss, the entrance to Castle Sehol was no solid barrier but a flood of light so dense and tangible it seemed almost to be water. The passages through were mere wormholes in the prism and I guessed that there was only one correct way. The first man told me to grasp his belt and the second held the skirt of my jacket.

'Your pardon, sir,' they courteously said.

I believe I could have passed the gate without their aid for, all the while, Nemione instructed me, her voice much clearer than those of the two men walking with me. They had learned the way by rote, that was obvious, for they walked along it chanting 'Left and left and right and straight and up –' and so on. I interrupted them:

'Can you hear another voice?'

'Quiet, sir; excuse me, but you'll lose us.'

We emerged from the elaborate defences and I saw a perfectly normal castle yard with a disused quintain pushed into a corner, a well, a couple of cannon, a dog kennel and a chained mastiff which barked loudly at me. Towers dominated each corner.

'Where are the Lady Nemione's quarters?' I asked, looking up at the great bulk of the inner bailey higher on the hill and the curtain walls enclosing other towers and a monstrous keep.

'In the White Tower there,' the first man replied. 'That is the doorway sir, a plain and honest old-fashioned hinged one with a lock and key. Estragon has the key today, on his belt.'

His comrade found and flourished a large key, unlocked the door and stood back to let me pass. I thanked them both.

'Tell me, before you return to your other duties,' I said. 'Is the Lady locked inside this tower – and will you lock the door after me and make me a prisoner?'

'Oh yes, sir; but she is no prisoner, nor are you. There is no keeping the Lady Nemione behind locked doors.'

I climbed a twisting stair. Nemione called more loudly, nearer: 'Very warm, Koschei. Hot – hotter. Climb! Faster!'

I came to the stairhead and stepped into a room. All white inside it was, as chill and icy as the day. A golden head confronted me, the cast head of a woman mounted on a pillar. It looked a little like Nemione, but less charitable, and its mouth had the same chiselled and perfect bow shape as the mouths of the dancers in the ice palace. Even as I stared at them, they parted and the voice of Nemione came forth,

'Koschei! You have arrived – at last and after so much travail. Welcome!'

I looked beneath and behind the head, to see how it worked.

'Now, Koschei,' it said. 'Curiosity killed the cat. Don't you remember Master Praxis telling us so, after Catechism?'

I looked about me, round the room. Clearly, it was Nemione's for the green gown she had worn when I met her by the brook lay across a tapestried bed and jewels, brushes, bottles of scent and other female things were littered about. I touched her gown and unravelled her hair from my fingers, stroking it smooth in the palm of my hand.

'Will you compare that gypsy's mane with these tresses?' the head asked and I swung round. Nemione was there, come silently into the room and splendid, indeed the Queen of Love.

'Enough talk, Roszi,' she said, addressing the head which

at once closed its eyes and clamped its lips together in a thin and cruel line.

My being, soul, heart and body, sighed for Nemione. Her hair was her own again, fair silk floss which hung down her back and covered her shoulders. She wore a white gown cut low, no jewels except her own sapphire eyes and a frost of minute diamonds on her embroidered gloves. She carried a small golden bow and trailed her coat of silver fox behind her.

I bowed, moved instantly to courtesy.

'A beggar-gallant!' Nemione cried. 'The queen and the gaberlunzie-man!' I struggled vainly for a compliment to pay her, though many lewd associations came to mind. 'And what do you think of my Head?' she continued.

'High magic, no illusion?'

'Oh, Koschei. You are a child.'

I thought of the magical skills the Om Ren had called out of me, and said nothing. Nemione dragged her fur across the floor in my direction.

'Help me then, Green Wolf. Arrange the robe about my shoulders.'

It was harder for me to comply with this request and still be calm than it had been six months ago, dyeing her hair in the forest.

'My hands – I am stained from my travels,' I said.

'You are filthy! No matter, you look just as a strong man should after a journey and your beard has grown very well. Now help me.'

I lifted the heavy coat. A hundred foxes must have died to make it. Draping it to best effect about her was tricky and several times my hands brushed her skin. Asmodée! How I wanted deliberately to touch it, to hold her in my arms, to kiss her! Her bed was less than a yard away.

At last, Nemione was arrayed. The silver fur stood up in a silky crest about her neck and I compared it in my mind to a column of white marble rising out of mist. I dared not look lower. The fur became her. She picked up a mirror, looked at her face in it and threw it on the bed.

'Come Koschei. I will show you my Court of Love.'

I followed her willingly, looking down with pleasure as the slippery fur draped its weight around her shoulders and revealed her narrow back; taking care not to tread on the stuff, which swept each stair as she descended. The stair led into a red-painted antechamber: no sign of the door the men-at-arms had locked. She saw my frown.

'You are puzzling over the topography of this place,' she said. 'A geography without laws. It should not trouble you long.'

She opened a door, beckoned me.

'There!'

The chamber was pentangular. It represented a five-pointed, lucky star and in each of the five angles stood a statue. I had no time, walking swiftly after Nemione, to examine them closely but I could see that they were personifications of the several states of Love. A white throne stood in the exact centre of the room, on a dais. Nemione stepped up and sat on her throne. I stood below.

'Now Koschei,' she lectured me. 'This is the room in which I try all the sad cases which are brought before me and judge whether the plaintiffs mean what they say. Love, as you know, is blind. He is foolish as well. If you were a plaintiff, I wonder what you would say?'

'I would say nothing, Madam,' I said, entering her game. 'I would be on trial for my life – for daring to love the judge.'

'Very pretty! Yes, you would argue your case well and have no need of a lawyer. But what if you were – a rude country boy who loved a highborn lady?'

'I would rely upon my well-built labourer's physique to speak for me.'

'Or a thin clerk from a crowded town – in love with a pretty actress?'

'I would study the language of love by night and practise it by day!'

'Or a mage who loved a sorceress?'

'I would forgo my Art and learn another to surprise her – such as the carving of toys, the painting of miniatures, or the writing of poetry: all in honour of my mistress.'

'That is my case, Koschei. Valdine is in love with me and I, as Queen of Love, must judge his verse. Of course he expects it to win, without contest.'

She handed me a little book of manuscripts bound in ivory and gold.

'Read there.'

Aflame with love and jealousy equally, I opened the book at hazard and read what I found there:

> My lady is a pure white rose
> Whose sharp and deadly thorn,
> Lodging in my bosom,
> Draws forth drops of scarlet blood
>
> My lady is a silver knife
> Whose blade of truest steel,
> Cutting deep the tissue,
> Wounds my tender, weeping heart.
>
> The cure, Madonna –

Etcetera. 'It is mannered,' I offered.

'True – but that does not bar it. It may be mannered and still good verse.' She leaned forward on her throne, her chin resting on her gloved hands; she looked as pensive as she used long ago, when we were children and her great-aunt told us stories by the fire. 'What would you do, Koschei? Is it possible to oppose the Archmage? How could I rid myself of him? I tell you Koschei, old friend, I am afraid that he will win the contest. Then I shall lose everything.'

'Why not kill him?' I said.

'You do not know what you say!'

'I am a soldier.'

'You are mad. Go away! Leave me alone before *you* destroy me.'

Obedient, even to her anger, I left the Court of Love. I found myself in an empty, vaulted corridor somewhere deep in the castle. Had Nemione called me only to spurn me? A rat scurried by. I did not care where I was and walked blindly, my head in a whirl.

He did not know where he was, though he thought he might be dead. There was a sensation of movement, others of numbness, dizziness, sickness. He coughed and began to vomit. Someone held a cloth to his mouth. His eyelids fluttered. Yellow daylight deafened him, voices dazzled.

'*Le soleil l'aveugle!*'

'*Oui ! D'accord!*'

The darkness returned.

When he next woke, he felt warmth at either side of him. He could not grasp it; could not grasp what caused it, what it *was*; but he could smell. He felt his nose tickle, lifted a hand to it, felt a cool finger gently rub. The smell: soap, soapy smell, clean, young, Alice? This side. Who the other? He opened his eyes. He was in a car. He was in the back seat of a car with Alice on his left and – trousers, hairy hands – a man on his right. Tobacco smell.

His hands were aching. RSI. Repetitive strain injury. Sandy. His hands ached and he was being driven in his own car. No Sandy. He raised his head a little – driven in his own car by a chauffeur – by Dominic! Alice sat beside him and the man on the other side. Clean-shaven, dark, big; another man sat by him in the car, the Audi, a man he did not know. The butcher? Georges? Georges Dinard!

'Georges?' he said.

He heard the man speak: '*Oui, mon ami*. It's OK. Take your ease. Relax.'

He heard Alice speak:

'Take courage, Guy. Be calm. There has been an accident.'

Dominic: 'A little accident. It's all right.'

He would stretch his aching hands. He looked down. Two bulky bandages rested on his knees. One of them was bloodstained. He screamed.

'You must hold him, Georges! He is mad with it.' French. But he understood. 'Dominic, stop!'

'No. No. Give him the medicine.'

'Stupid! He had a full dose.'

'Give it!'

A foul taste filled his mouth. He tried to spit it out. He choked and swallowed.

He floated, safe in his comfortable seat. He knew that Alice was there. She touched his cheek. He floated and looked out of the window. A lovely green landscape was rushing past. Little fields. Planted. Vines: wine. A taste of wine would be a very good thing. Especially now.

'Can I hold your hand, Alice?' he said.

'Not now, Guy. Not just now. Look out of the window. We shall soon be there.'

'There?'

'Lyon.'

Dominic drove fast. It was all right. He could drive. It was OK. Dominic was driving. Dominic was speaking.

'We'd better try Mother's remedy on him. A light application of blood.'

'Shh! Shut up, you fool!'

'He's asleep.'

'He isn't.'

Not his problem. Others. He could kill Koschei. His fault. He should kill him. It was an impossible task to set yourself. He remembered how his hands had flown away like white birds in a dusty dawn. He remembered some of it. The

112

sawdust. The barn. Hands. The wood. Sunlight. Hands in the night. Hands on Alice. Never again.

I could push him off a rock.

'What's that?' he said. The land was steeper, away from the road, rock piling itself upon rock in petrified imitation of the greens and browns of the vineyards below it.

'La Roche de Solutré,' said Georges. '*Préhistorique*.'

Natural battlements; ancient stone: a sheer and perilous stronghold. Bushes and stunted trees clung to precipitous rockfaces.

'That's the Rock of Solutré,' said Alice. 'It's a Stone Age site – they used to drive horses off it to kill them. Oh, sorry.'

'My ancestors!' Georges laughed.

'Nearly five hundred metres high,' said Dominic. 'I have climbed there.'

'That's high.' He was managing to speak, through the fog; conversing. 'High. Weren't you afraid of falling?'

The cliff upon which Pargur stands is of such height, it is a nonpareil. No human mind, unless housed in a brain as superior to man's as his is to an ant's, could have conceived such a marvel. I stood upon its narrow brink and felt spray from the void hit my face. The land fell away so violently and so far that seabirds disappeared into the vapours below and rainbows sprung, curved, recurved and plunged back to extinguish their refracted light in the mists. I watched the gulls becoming luminescent shape-shifters, now red, now yellow, now a drifting combination of blue, indigo and violet.

The situation and the view were stupendous. I was wet, despite the waterproof I had bought that afternoon. I stood on the slippery ledge and thought of another height, the rocky bluff I had glimpsed upon the Archmage's map. The place existed; it was no trick of mind or fancy. I had found and visited the library in Pargur's Midday Plaza and in its

113

fiction collection discovered and examined a map of northern Malthassa. Although it was overprinted many times with those two spell-binding words, 'terra incognita', I found 'the Plains and – at their heart – the valley of SanZu. A series of angular lines were marked in silverpoint, "High ground".'

I likened the peril in which Nemione had placed herself to the uncertain state of someone without a head for heights forced to stand on this ledge where I, with my strong head, was giddy. Or caught in the proverbial cleft stick, between two stools, the hard ground and a rocky place &c. The Archmage had tutored her and given her title, money and position; now he asked for his reward, nothing less than Nemione's body and, with it, her heart and soul. She would not give those up. I was not then ready to contemplate another scenario, one in which Valdine was dead and I, occupying his place, was confronted with her adamantine obduracy. I believed I could win her; worse, because of our nearness in childhood and our common novitiate in the Cloister, I believed that she was already half mine.

Besides I had my memories of her stored away for reference in my little Memory Palace, and many more to add to them. When I was – what? More powerful? A prince? If ever I could, I should move the Memory Palace to Pargur. This city and no other must become my home. I recognized it and it knew me; it was the place to which I wished always to return, however and wherever I travelled.

A watery sun shone on my face. It had sufficient heat to disperse the vapours for a second or two and I glimpsed a turquoise ocean at ultimate distance between the projecting toes of my boots. Convinced that there was a way, be it long and hard, to all my desires, I turned to leave the precipice. Another marveller had joined me on the narrow path, a thin midnight candle of a scholar clad in blue velvet hood and gown. He blinked at me from eyes half-blinded by study, orbs as pink-rimmed as a ferret's.

'You must be aware that we have no sea-going ships,' he said.

'I am,' I said, and wondered if he wanted to debate the nullity. 'There are small boats in Malthassa, barges, rafts and the like, but no ships capable of venturing on that deep. Yet every one of our country's male citizens is familiar with tall ships – grain-clippers, barques, schooners, barquentines – and with the special words which belong to them. Why do we not build one and go to sea?'

'It is a paradox. They must exist elsewhere. They are in our books: I tell you this only to explain the precipice. Pargur is built upon the edge of the land and you may picture what you have been vouchsafed a glimpse of moments ago, the vasty deep, the rolling main, the mighty and boundless ocean entirely *without* ships. The upper layers of this cliff are composed not of stone strata as elsewhere, but of the city's occupation layers, every one in use, not lost to all but archaeologists (though the number of archaeologists who have attempted to determine the date of Pargur's first foundation is legion) but functioning as units of the Mutable City.'

'This is why it is so hard for a newcomer to find his way about?'

'Quite so. And why we fly above the confusion in our balloons. Yet you have got out of Castle Sehol unaided and found your way here. I see you have bought a waterproof from Comyn. Wise, eminently wise. He is the best in town; far better than his father or his son.'

'Synchronal family members?'

'In synchronal Pargurs.'

'Why is there only one Lady Nemione?'

'Obvious, my dear sir. Because there is only one Manderel Valdine – and one Koschei Corbillion. Come, Master Corbillion, let me lead you to the Archmage before my grandson or my grandfather appear and steal my job – it is hard to avoid one's family or one's obligations to them, though the concurrent existence of so many makes the city strong.

115

Indeed it has always had the reputation of an unslightable stronghold, such fame that no force dares try the boast. Long may it continue to occupy the principal place in the military, merchant and occult life of our country.'

'. . . merchant and occult life of our country,' said Georges. 'It has a long enough history, a terrible history. You are not the first, monsieur, to be brought here in unhappy circumstances. What a city is Lyon!'

Guy smiled lazily. He watched the traffic passing by. He was relaxed, remote from all effort and sensation. Not long ago, his discomfort had been acute and Dominic had stopped the car. Then Georges had assisted him from it and, by the roadside, helped him piss as if he were an invalid or some mad old king with his retainer.

When he was settled in the car again, Alice put a comforter between his lips; he was her baby. He had no cares. He sucked and drew the sweet smoke into his lungs. Past Alice, beyond the window, trees and suburbs crowded against a high wall. The road ran steeply down, as if it needed to hide. It became the bottom of a trench and then they rushed into a tunnel and lights blazed about them.

This stuff about his hands. It was all a nonsense, it was inexplicable. He was too far away to understand.

'Lyon is very old,' Georges was saying. 'First the Romans, then the Franks and after them the Holy Roman Emperor. Rabelais, puppets, silk, the Resistance – how are you feeling?'

'Not myself.'

'Ah, very good!' He laughed, as if Guy had made a joke. 'Never mind: we will soon have you safe.'

When the car stopped again, he would die. He must have lost a gallon of blood. He could remember it spattered on the sawdust; the barn had looked like a butcher's shop. He could remember Helen's excitement at the sight. She had

116

touched one of the bloodstains with the tip of her forefinger, put the bloodied finger in her mouth and sucked, as he was sucking now, on the cool joint. That was before they had treated him. They must be driving him to a hospital. Why hadn't they called an ambulance?

The blood-coloured car was good enough. Fast.

Where was Helen? Never mind; no problem. Alice sat beside him.

'Kiss me,' he said. 'Please kiss me, Alice.' The girl turned awkwardly to him and gave him a cold kiss on the cheek.

They were out of the tunnel. There was a river. Red roofs. Hills. Churches high. He had been here independently. He knew where he was: was that the Saône or Rhône? Where was Vieux Lyon, the old quarter? He did not know this area where new glass buildings were slotted in between old houses. The car began to climb. Narrow streets. Shabby facades. The car stopped outside a high building.

'We have arrived,' Alice said. 'We are here!'

'The hospital?' He looked at her in desperation and caught agony in her eyes.

'Why, yes,' she said.

Georges helped him from the car. He turned again to Alice, but she avoided him, walked round the car and opened up the back. She took out his jacket and a plastic bag and gave them to Georges. Then, without a word, without a second look, she slammed the door down; got into the front seat beside Dominic. The engine purred. He watched his car slide away, his last sight of it a flash of red at the corner of the street. The lighter flash in the driver's seat was the blond head of his son. His legs were weak. He stumbled against Georges.

'Courage, my friend!' the man said, supporting him. 'It is not far.' He leaned heavily on Georges and the butcher led him along an alleyway, down one flight of stairs and up another. They entered a dark doorway. A dirty blanket lay on the floor and Georges kicked it aside. The passageway was short and more stairs lay ahead, turning in an empty hallway, high, stone, steep. The walls were dank and the paint upon them had faded to a memory. The damp air smelled of urine, guilt and decay. They climbed.

Doors on the left were closed and dark. They passed one which was blocked by heavy timber cross-pieces. They mounted higher. One door remained, heavy and scarred, with six panels lined with dust. If it had been possible, Guy would have put out a hand and marked the dust with his fingerprints. Georges knocked.

It was still; as quiet as a court of law in the afternoon. He listened to his panting body. From the other side of the door came the faint sound of footsteps and keys. The door opened a crack. Georges spoke into it.

'*Bonjour Lèni. Il est là.*'

No one answered but the door was opened a little wider, enough to admit them, and a small hand clutched at his sleeve.

PART TWO

EXCURSIONS IN PURGATORY

Horror and scorn and hate and fear and indignation –
Oh why did I awake?

A. E. HOUSMAN

'Monsieur! Here you are at last.' She spoke in French, a small, middle-aged woman with tiny hands like a child's and a firm and exact mouth. She held his sleeve and guided him. In her other hand she held a lighted candle in a spiral-shaped candlestick. Beyond her he could see the dim shapes of large pieces of furniture.

'Where is he to go?' said Georges, whispering as if he had entered a theatre after curtain up.

'In the salon, beast! You have the intelligence of a herd of dead pigs.'

The shutters were closed and the light of the candle feeble. Nevertheless, he could see a table and side tables, numerous couches, a large cupboard or sideboard, and the bed. The woman put the candle down and she and Georges lifted him on to the bed. He lay on his back and looked up. The bed had its own painted ceiling on which damaged cupids were playing. Half of them were torn to pieces, as if by gunfire. He heard the woman dusting her hands, one against the other, and Georges gave a grunt.

'There!' he said. 'It is done.'

Guy rested his bandaged arms on the coverlet. The pillow tickled his face. He sneezed and the woman flourished a handkerchief and wiped his nose.

'Thank you,' he said.

'It is nothing. I have often done the same for the holy

Father. Now does Monsieur wish for anything? Some water, a cognac perhaps? To ease himself?'

'No. Thank you.'

She and Georges walked away from him. He could hear them talking softly on the far side of the room. Then they went out and left him, desolate as a sick child, locked in like a convict when he was innocent and they guilty. He heard the key turn in the lock with a sound like stones falling on a coffin lid. Presently, he rolled on his side and tried to make sense of the gloom.

Soon, the woman came back.

'Now,' she said, 'I will help you. I will undress you and put you properly to bed. You can sleep.' She came close and untied his shoes. She took them off and began to unfasten his jeans. 'We will leave the vest.' She fingered it. 'This is a vest?'

'Tee-shirt,' he said. 'You know.'

She pulled down his jeans, removed his underpants. Her hand, in passing, brushed against him. 'At least,' she said, 'you have not lost that!' She folded the jeans and laid them on a chair. 'I will help with the bedclothes.'

He lay in the antique bed, still as a corpse. He listened, hearing her moving about the room. Then it was quieter. She had gone again; again he heard the cold click of the doorlock. He listened for cars, and people talking in the streets of Lyon, but no sound reached him from outside. He thought about running away but, when he sat up, was dizzy and weak. The door was locked anyway and the woman had the key. How would he take and turn a key?

Later, he awoke. Several more candles burned in the room. The woman was sitting beside him.

'Good evening,' she said. 'I am Lèni and you are Guy, isn't it so? I have some soup for you.'

He wanted to protest but he was still weak, and he was hungry. Lèni helped him sit up and, perching close beside him on the bed, fed him potato soup with a large spoon.

When he had finished she said, 'Now you need the pot.' He shook his head, but she threw the bedclothes aside and held an earthenware jug to his limp penis. 'Let it go!' He turned his head aside in embarrassment.

'It is nothing,' Lèni said. 'I have often done the same for the reverend Father. Do you need to make the other?'

'No!'

'Now take your medicine.' She held a small glass to his lips and tilted it. The liquid was not bitter like the stuff they had forced down him in the car: it tasted of wine. 'You must take it or you won't sleep!' He swallowed it.

When she had settled him, she blew out all the candles but one and left him alone. He stared at it. It was the one she had carried when she met them at the door, a long candle of yellow wax in the holder called a cellar rat. A tail of metal could be wound up a metal spiral, lifting the candle as it burned down. He concentrated on it, operating the primitive mechanism in his mind. The burning candle smelled of animal fat. He watched the blue heart of the flame until it grew as large as he was and expanded about him as he lost consciousness. He slept.

He slept for days, waking in blurred candlelight: sometimes myriad flames danced before him, sometimes one flame burned alone; once a ray of daylight found a way into the shuttered room. His taste buds revived to successive flavours: meat, potatoes, carrots, fish: all liquid; slept again. He tasted water and the spiritous medicine. He slept and woke, called for the jug or else was helped to balance on the cold and narrow rim of a chamber pot. Lèni bathed his face and washed his body. She sang to him, *Fais ton dodo, mon p'tit frère*, 'Go to bye-byes, little brother.' He did not dream and, waking suddenly after sleep as dark and dead as a closed vault, was terrified. He thought he had lost his imagination, all his story-telling abilities. He used to write, didn't he? Waking one day with wet cheeks, he turned to Lèni and said, 'I have written many books.' 'You can talk to me

123

instead,' she replied. 'I, too, used to write. In my diary; but
– it is lost and I continue without it.' Sometimes he opened
his eyes and saw Georges watching him from the doorway.
Sometimes he saw Lèni sleeping on the sofa across the room,
covered only by a ragged piece of cloth, still wearing her
rusty black dress.

'I am in mourning,' she said once.

'I make my penance,' she said another time.

The dressings on his arms were smaller. He began to
dream, at first of the cathedral where he had sung in the
choir and alone at Christmas, standing before the altar in a
blaze of candlelight, not Guy Parados but Chris Young, a
small, blond boy with the voice of an angel. The great church
was full of gloomy spaces, greys and browns relieved by
glorious windows made of light. In his dreams he performed
exacting tasks: dismantling a watch and piecing it back
together, every minute wheel and cog, each separate jewel;
painting a doll's house with a fine sable hair brush. He carved
an intricate and perfect castle out of an ice cube; then took
it up, held it in a candle flame and watched it melt. His
fingers burned. Each tendon ached and hot wires pierced his
wrists. He spent longer periods awake, staring at the ceiling
of the bed. The severed limbs of the damaged amoretti
circled above him and the complete ones smiled, touching
each other's wings with chubby pink fingers. His groin itched
and he rubbed himself against the sheets. He thought of
horses rolling in summer meadows. He thought of chimpan-
zees and the higher apes, dextrous with fleas and sticks. He
thought of his lost identity, his disappearance and his lack
of fingerprints. All right, he would be a horse. When next
he settled to sleep he ran out into a field of clean grass.

There was a smell of sewers and rotting meat, of maggot-
ridden offal. At first he thought it came from himself and
feared for his undoctored wounds. He saw, when Lèni
changed the bandages, that his stumps were covered in a
dirty green paste with a smell of ditch bottoms. 'All the

herbs of St Jean,' she said. 'You are ready for anything.'

She was combing his hair which, like his beard, had grown into an untidy thicket. He looked closely at her, noticing upon her face lumps and pits which the candlelight had hidden from him. Her skin was sallow and slack and her breath sour. The shadows under her eyes were craters and she had lost two of her front teeth. The bed and the room were in the same state of decay, the sheets and silken bedspread full of holes, the bed hangings tattered. At night he heard mice running on the furniture, leaving their dirt and their footprints scattered over the dust. The smell was part of the room, a manifestation of its antiquity, and its essence. An antique telephone stood with the candlestick on the bedside table and he manoeuvred it closer with his arms and, putting his ear to the fallen receiver, listened to silence. He stared into the murk. The statues of two deities flanked a huge credenza. They looked Egyptian, sinister. One had the mild head of a heifer and was crowned with a crescent moon. He knew that one: Isis, the moon goddess, in her animal manifestation, Hathor. The second was male, stiff-legged, carried a staff to which a glass lamp-shade was incongruously attached, and wore the head of a hawk. He had seen its like before but he could not remember where, nor could he remember the god's name. He felt the mild-eyed heifer to be friendly and was fascinated by the hawk. He did not know why, but his interest in it troubled him, as did his forgetfulness.

The food was still soup, but it was thicker and full of pieces of meat and vegetables. Lèni picked up the spoon to feed him.

'I can feed myself!' he said vehemently.

'How? You cannot hold the spoon.'

'Hold up the bowl.' He bent his head and grasped the rim of the bowl with his lips. He sucked and lapped, burning his mouth and sending hot dribbles of soup down his chin and chest. 'Bravo!' said Lèni. He ate bread in the same animalistic way. Next time, she brought him a piece of veal and he bent his head and took it up in his teeth like a dog. Lèni fed him pieces of peach as a reward. He was pleased with himself. His strength was returning. When it had come back he might think constructively. He did not know how long he had been a prisoner and, when he asked Lèni, she would only say 'Some days.'

'How many?'

'Some.'

He ate another meal and slept another sleep: day or night, it was all the same. Lèni carried in a bowl of warm water and washed him. Then, delving in her pocket, she pulled out a crumpled piece of newspaper which she spread beside him on the bed. What was she up to now? He looked at the piece of paper and started when he saw the heading, *Weekend Times*. Lèni answered his unspoken question.

'Dominic brought it me,' she said. 'He is not all self.'

The date! That was the crucial information. Guy read it carefully: 'Thursday, October 10th 1990' – almost four months since he was – since he was in Coeurville – with Helen. With Alice, yes.

'This is today's paper?' he asked Lèni.

'Oh, no. A little while ago.'

Guy, reading on, saw his name in heavy, black type. He thought he was reading an obituary, his own; but the article was impudent and slangy. The headline detained him and he frowned over it:

FANTASTIC TRIP?

Guy Kester Parados, fantasy author or paradox? No one has seen him since June, no one in his home village, Maidford Halse, Hantons., will speak out. He left few clues behind him, and the pages of his newly published novel

126

The Making of Koschei give nothing away, save the dark deeds and motives of Parados's evil hero, the magician Koschei, enigmatic hellish entity and manipulator of guilty and innocent alike.

Koschei's creator, born Christopher Guy Young, Alfrick-on-Severn, 1941, was himself enigmatic, in ambition, in life-style. He went to the Cathedral School in Caster but wrote of black magic and beastliness, sometimes of bestiality. He did not use his Christminster First as a stepping-stone to the soft beds of academe but dwelt in rural obscurity writing, at first, indifferent verse and later (in 1973), after resurrecting himself as Guy Kester Parados, a fantastic and Fantastic first novel, *The Magician Koschei*, the first in his wholly successful *New Mythologies* sequence. His books have attracted the praise of both Valentine Vernon of *The Face* and Trevor Nursling of the *TLS*.

He lived quietly with his wife, the sculptor Jillian Meddowes, at the Old Rectory where they raised a family of six children and a 'torpid' Labrador named Pyewacket after a 17th Century witch's cat.

Maidford Halse is quiet, sleepy. The beer is warm, the village team was playing cricket and I passed three elderly spinsters on bicycles. As did Guy Parados most likely. His car was an expression of his personality, the ultimate hot saloon, a tornado red Audi Quattro 20v (see Motoring Section) with a distinctive, egoblaze of a number-plate, GUY5.

The disappearance has its own set of paradoxes. Guy Parados was seen leaving home about 9.00 p.m. on June 24th, and was not seen again until 11.00 a.m. next day, boarding the Calais ferry at Dover. Three of his readers who did not want to 'spoil his holiday' by speaking to their hero refrained. But in the Camargue Lounge Etta Travis, TV traveller and tribal diarist, enjoyed a drink with him. At Calais, Pierre Roger, a passport official, stopped GUY5 to admire both car and driver, who was seen later near Senlis picking up a girl hitch-hiker young enough to be a friend of his 16-year old daughter, Phoebe. They headed for Paris on the A1 but were next glimpsed on the A6, at the Nitry *péage* 190 km south. And were not seen again, though Jillian Meddowes later received a card posted in Avallon, Yonne *département*, on June 26th.

'Hi darling, here I am in the sun. Hope it is shining on you. See you soon, love Guy.' A husband's cheerful greeting? A deceitful ruse?

When he disappeared, Guy Parados was dressed as usual and as seen in his publicity photographs. Faded jeans, cream linen jacket, black Armani tee-shirt with the words 'make it' in grey lettering. But clothes do not entirely make a man. Guy Parados is 6'1", lean and fit, blue eyes, thicket of iron grey hair, 49 going on 40. He cannot magic-

ally vanish like his chief character,
Koschei, and anyone spotting him is
asked to contact New Scotland Yard
or a local police station.

Not an obituary, quite. A tribute perhaps and news, old
news. Guy looked up from the page and caught Lèni's eye.

'They are looking for you then,' she said.

'You have read it?'

'*Oui*. I have some English. You are a famous man.'

'I might as well be dead.'

'*Pas de tout!* You are alive. I see that you are, and I will
care for you until –'

'Until?'

'The time comes.'

'Turn the paper over!'

She complied. The reverse of the sheet was, he saw, completely taken up with an advertisement for a computer. I
had one of those, he thought. I wrote my stories on it.

Lèni sewed long cuffs of blue silk to his jacket, washed
and dressed him and helped him walk about the room. His
legs were stiff. She sat him on a dusty chaise longue, set a
row of candles on the marble mantel shelf and, on a table
inlaid with ormulu and mother-of-pearl, laid out the imple-
ments for smoking: pipes, multi-coloured Egyptian ciga-
rettes, tobacco, matches, knife, and a scarlet, lacquered box.
She carried in a tarnished silver-gilt tray with a queer glass,
two bottles and a dish of sugar cubes on it.

'Let us be comfortable,' she said, and sat beside him. She
cut a slice from the block of tobacco and began to prepare
a pipe. It was, he saw, no conventional pipe but a strange,
thin metal object with a bulbous bowl.

'Opium,' she said. 'You have been drinking laudanum.'

He watched her take powdered opium from the red box, mix it with the tobacco and prime the pipe. Then, turning to the bottles, she made her other drugs ready: sugar, clear water and yellow-green absinthe. The water slowly dripped into the liquor, turning it cloudy and bringing with it the sugar it leached from the cube.

'Yours,' she said, 'and mine. A woman's thighs are softer than horsehair. Take your ease.'

He stretched out on the couch: there was room for him to lie at full length, if he rested his head on her lap. When he was comfortable, she gently put the narrow stem of the opium pipe between his lips. He sucked at it while she held the pipe close by her breasts and bending over him, kept it steady. The first taste made him cough and she moved the pipe a little in his mouth, bending lower.

'It will relax you, bring you pleasant dreams,' she whispered. 'Let me take a sip of my Lethe-water. Ah, it is good!'

He smelled the mould in her clothing and felt her sagging breasts close against his cheek, comforters as near, but for the decayed silk, as the pipe and more familiar to him than his vanished hands. He sucked again and felt his head invaded by the awful ghosts wakefulness held back. He was in the cathedral again, walking in the nave. But, he paused in his tracks, someone was speaking, a she-someone, Lèni la Soie herself, standing up before him at an eagle-headed lectern and reading to him from a leather-covered book. He was content, in his confusion, to recognize and know her as the original of the *Evil Life* which he had read sometime – in Avallon was it? – and the author of the diary Helen kept in her *vardo* – but wasn't that burnt and Helen and the diary with it? Helen, ah Helen who had such a slender waist –

'Listen to *me*!' Silk Lèni was speaking again.

'I shall never find peace until I have told my true story!' she thundered, so he lay down on the nearest pew and rested his head on the black hassock someone had left there. He listened to the silk worker's tale:

Father Paon was an idiot, *un imbécile*, but fortune favours fools, does it not? Sometimes he was like a stallion who devoured me as a mettlesome horse does its oats; and what a stallion, what a lover – at first.

I am before myself.

A fine fellow, my sinful priest, as exquisite as the peacock which gave his family its name. A dandy – truly! His family were wealthy landowners, farmers and then winegrowers, ambitious as the old Burgundian kings, and Paon, who had no more interest in agriculture and viticulture than *confit* of turkey itself except when the results of both were presented at table – he, poor fellow, was made to study and turn himself into a holy Father. For a time he served the church, in one small village or another, but then, seeing how the hierarchy of the church favoured some at the expense of others, made application for a change – So he came eventually to Lyon.

Lyon, my city: she is old and filled with centuries of magic filtered through the dusty summer air, swept along her two rivers; deep in her earth. I am of Lyon like my mother and my mother's mother, like my father a silkworker. I am the daughter and the descendant of Lyonnais, one myself. Paon met me here, in the Croix Rousse district. That was the start of it. It was on a Sunday, after Mass. I was walking on the Boulevard at the top of the hill, a gay place then and bustling with families, lovers, Sunday strollers; I had a new gown, I remember, and my lovebird. Paon took my arm when he saw me, like a good Father with his daughter in religion; we went to drink wine and, when we had drunk and talked and were saying our goodbyes, he told me how much he wished to become my confessor. I should find him at St Michael's, he said, in the fourth confessional on the right.

We complemented each other, Paon and I, like the pricking of lust and blind will. He had strange ways, and an odd way of speaking, for a man of God.

'I see a woman with the smile of Circe,' he said, when I was seated in his confessional. 'The loveliest of my penitents. She might be the most refined of tender maidens – who could guess she is a common silk worker, a clever seamstress and a prostitute as well? The little perching bird she wears in her hat crowns her as regally as gold or diamonds – it is as pink as her lips. Now, Silk Lèni. I want you to visit me in my house: I have a devil for you to exorcise.'

'What kind of a devil, Father?' I asked.

'A carnal imp, daughter. It interrupts my meditations and my sleep; it rises up when I pray and when I look at you.'

'Will you forgive me, Father? I may be about to sin,' I said and listened as he prayed for me, which he did rapidly and also guiltily, I judged, though I could not of course see him. He left the confessional and I waited in the church a few moments, pretending to pray, and then followed after him at a discreet distance, my parasol up to conceal my face, though the sky was cloudy. I knocked at the door of his house, a little fearful for I knew he shared it with another priest and that they had a housekeeper who, for aught I knew, was a dragon.

Father Paon was standing in the parlour. The sweat ran down his face but he raised his biretta – for all the world as if it were a silk opera hat – and bowed to me. I looked about me. Though Mother Church is so rich the parlour was poorly furnished and I noticed at once, it was so strange – it did not accord with what I expected in a priest's dwelling – that there were no holy pictures, not even one of the Blessed Virgin. Then I saw a statue in a niche by the chimney and was lifting my hand to cross myself when I realized that the statue was naked, and black.

'Oh!' I cried out before I could stop myself. 'Oh, Father – she is just like the Negress, Lisette, at Mother Jupon's!'

132

Father Paon's mouth twitched but I could not tell if he was amused or angry. I made haste to correct myself.

'I mean, Father,' I said, 'that she is like the Black Sara who rescued Our Lady from the sea; she the gypsies still worship in the Camargue. Perhaps not such a strange lady to find in the parlour of a priest.'

He stared at me as if I mesmerized him – waiting, I daresay, to see what stupidity should next fall from my lips.

'It is a curiosity, an antique, my child,' he said. 'You admire her? Come, you may touch her. She does not bite.'

I went up to the statue and touched it cautiously. I could see, now I was close to her, that the black lady looked more like a demon than a woman for she had an ugly face, very badly carved in my opinion, and as for her hands, her legs and feet – they were mere suggestions because the sculptor had concentrated all his skill and attention on her female parts which were rendered exact, only much larger than is normal. Clearly, too, she liked her food – or was pregnant, since her belly was big and round. It made me think of the fate of all women and I stroked it with my fingertip, the priest watching my every move. Such close attention made me uncomfortable: the meeting of a priest and a prostitute is usually not prolonged by a lesson in aesthetics! I turned about to stare back at him and saw that the sweat still poured off him and, more, that he looked red and troubled.

'You are not well, Father,' I said. 'Let me call the house-keeper.'

'No, no,' he answered. 'It is not her I want, not today – it is you.'

So the time had come. I was quite calm; it was business after all. I remembered his words in the confessional.

'Ah!' I said. 'It is the imp of course. It is bad today, I can see that, but I am quite sure, Father, that you have made a friend of someone well able to deal with it.'

He had the nerve then to argue about my fee but eventually we agreed a price which satisfied us both, so I went swiftly

133

to him and lifted his soutane. It was not the first time I had helped a priest. Afterwards, when I was washing my hands in his kitchen and his sense had come back to him, he gave me my money and a pretty hat pin, not at all the kind of object you would expect a priest to know of. He had chosen well; it wasn't a cheap affair but one from the jeweller's on the Boulevard.

'When will you return?' he asked. 'I should like to tell you more about the Lady in my parlour.'

'Whenever you like,' I told him; his gift had pleased me that much.

'This evening then,' he said eagerly. 'Father Renard will have returned and I know he will find you as charming and as – skilful as I do. The statue belongs to him in any case and he should be the one to instruct you in its use.'

I left laughing: coin and an amethyst set in gold on the end of a good gold pin – for half a minute! And, I thought, what a pair; what a couple, those two priests, Father Peacock and Father Fox! Soon I was laughing on the other side of my face. All that had passed between Paon and myself was an overture to the main drama; a test, if you like, of my mettle.

Guy, drained of the priest's lust, lay still.

'I have been dreaming,' he said. 'Is it the opium?'

Lèni laughed. It was a richer sound than he expected from such a dusty, worn body.

'I amuse you,' he said, ' – at least I can do that.'

'It is your innocence which delights me,' she said. 'Here, I have prepared a new pipe. Breathe the smoke in deeply. I shall drink another absinthe.'

Her eyes were bright with the alcohol already, he saw; two shining pits. He remembered something.

'I have read your diary,' he said.

'Indeed? How is that possible? – it is lost.'

'No,' he insisted. 'I have seen it and I have read it; and there must be other copies of it because someone has made it into a book.'

'A book! Then I am famous, like you?' She laughed. 'Where did you read my diary, Guy Parados – in your fevered dreams was it, or have you the power to creep inside my mind?'

'Your diary is on a shelf in a gypsy caravan not a hundred kilometres from Lyon. You have no need to worry: it is quite safe.'

His statements seemed to strike her as absurd because she laughed again and eventually, putting one hand to her head, said,

'Yes . . . naturally, that is where it should be. How could I forget? – but the diary does not tell the whole truth. Lie still and do not hinder me with irrelevancies; I must confess all:

I went back to Paon's house the same evening, hungry for the baits he had dangled, the possibility of more money and more gifts of gold from both priests in return for what I was mistress and professor of!

It was a beautiful evening – the two rivers were like ribbons of gold. I looked at Lyon and the Lyonnais enjoying the warm air and believed myself fortunate. As I crossed the footbridge over the Saône I noticed that the priest who crossed in front of me was talking to himself. I guessed he must be Father Renard and hurried to get as close to him as I dared.

'I am Joseph Antoine Renard, Priest, Magician and Exorcist,' he said, as the other people on the bridge stared after him. 'I am potent tonight, filled with the majesty of the new gods I have abused and rejected and of the old gods who call out to me from the earth.' He looked up at the church on the hill above him and at the huge statue of St Michael which tops it. 'Ah!' he cried. 'You too are dressed in cloth-of-gold, but all that glisters . . . Is it fire, Michael? Do you burn in anger or because you know your god is false?' He laughed. 'Crush me if you dare!' he shouted. 'What are you but a leaden statue. Fly! Take wing!'

He was a tall, severe-looking man, so I had no difficulty in following him in the crowd. He went into the Old Quarter. The way home took him past the house where the Mourguets made their Guignol puppets and old Guignol himself, the chief puppet, was staring down at him from the sign above the door. 'Crush me then, cloth man,' he cried. 'You'll find my body is steel!'

He was either mad or what he said he was. His blaspheming did not upset me. I found it as thrilling as the taste of absinthe. The front door of the house was open and Renard walked straight in. I followed after and surprised him in the hall: my foot caught on a hole in the mat and I stumbled. He swung round and prevented me from falling by grasping me with both his long arms.

'A little coquette, scarcely one-and-a-half metres tall, her hair up to add height, a silly hat pinned to it, a silk gown every bit as good as anything the divine Sarah might wear – and cut with style and dash,' he said. 'Who are you, my dear?'

'Father Paon bade me come,' I said. 'And I am Lèni, called la Soie, Father – sir.'

'A pretty lady,' he said, half to himself. 'And a true daughter of Lyon: are you interested in the history of your city?' he asked me and bent to kiss my cheeks.

'Yes, sir. I am very interested, especially after seeing the statue in the parlour.'

'The Blessed Virgin?'

'Another lady, sir – ready for her bath perhaps.'

'Ah – she has a name of her own. It is Cyllène.'

He smiled at me. (I was still in his embrace.)

'Seelen?' I echoed.

136

'Indeed. A word from far away; long ago also. The lady has many names and was worshipped once – like Mary. She is far older of course, an antique goddess of Life and Death.'

'I am a good Catholic.'

'I am sure you are; but do you go to Mass?'

'I went to Confession this afternoon. Father Paon absolved me of my sins.'

'Then you are ready to hear Mass! I shall tell you a secret, my dear. We will celebrate Mass here this evening and you may attend if you so wish.'

'I like adventure; I will stay, yes,' I said. 'But, surely, Monsieur,' I looked directly at him. 'Surely you are far too worldly a man to be a good priest?'

'It will be a special Mass,' said Renard.

Father Paon came into the hall at that moment. He did not seem disturbed to find me in the arms of his brother-priest and after patting Renard affectionately on the shoulder, extracted me from his embrace and himself embraced me! Then they both led me into the parlour. I say 'the parlour' though it looked very different; in the afternoon it had been a poor, gloomy room but now it was hung with red draperies and the window-blinds were down. A single candle burned in front of the Black Lady – and she had been moved on to a little table covered with a black cloth. A woman knelt there praying. She was quite naked – without a stitch to cover her.

Paon gripped my arm.

'Our Lady on the altar is the key to Paradise,' he said, 'but if you wish to rid yourself of ignorance and understand what that is, you must dress like Olivia there.'

'She is wearing nothing at all!' I exclaimed.

Renard began to laugh.

'We have shocked the harlot,' he said. 'Come, Lèni, you are always taking off your drawers.'

'Not in church.'

The kneeling woman turned her head then and gave me

such a look of love that I lost my fear and began to undress, dropping my garments where I stood – and Paon and Renard left the room! When I was undressed I only hesitated a moment; then I threw away all the virtue I had left and knelt down beside the other woman and the idol. She looked up again and whispered,

'Who are you?'

'And who are you?' I returned, staring at her. She was very young, much more than I.

'I am Olivia des Mousseux,' she said haughtily and spoiled her airs and graces by adding, 'The Fathers' housekeeper.'

'Such a child as you?'

'Father Paon brought me out of the orphanage to work here.'

'Well, maybe you are better off,' I said and fell quiet because the two of them had come back into the room – changed out of their black clothes into rich garments like you see in church on high days. Paon had on a golden stole and an embroidered mitre and nothing else and Renard wore a red and gold chasuble and, again, nothing else. He carried a chalice. They stood on either side of the altar and Renard, raising the cup, began to speak. Such mumbo-jumbo as you hear from a beggar in the gutter!

It was Greek, Paon told me later, and Hebrew and Persian and the chalice too, another antique like the statue, that was from Persia and had belonged to a king. Such a beautiful thing, that cup, enamelled sky-blue and covered in engravings like tiny flames and the strange letters of an alphabet unknown to me.

I found myself able to understand Renard after a while,

'Come, Cyllène,' he chanted, 'Come Asmodeus and Babylon, Urthamma, Moloch Sinistrus and Bel. Come Abrahel! Come Lucifer!'

He raised the cup in the air, lowered and drank from it. I heard a noise like the rush of wings and felt Paon pushing his body in between mine and Olivia's. Renard leaned down

138

and offered me the cup to drink. There was blood in it and I drank. Renard, high above me as it seemed, had grown leathery wings and I could feel the feathers which were growing from Paon's back push against me. He drank next and then Olivia. We were all so young after that, younger than Olivia; like children at play, and with the energy of children except that we had the feelings, the organs and the appetites of grown men and woman. Renard grew a red tail, which pleased me mightily, and we played together all night long in that red-hung room – until the bells of St Michael's reminded us of the good citizens of Lyon we must be by day.

My life was yet my own, at that time. Paon's ascendancy was not complete until the warp and weft of our secret desires were woven together into strong cloth. He knew nothing of what I did when I was away from him; when I carried on my two trades. One night, about a month after the first Black Mass, I brought him back to my rooms and we re-enacted some of that night's rituals. Also, he took out his pocket-knife and made a small cut on my right breast. He licked the blood from it.

'This is strong and spicy blood, Lèni,' he said. 'It is easy to understand how you found your true vocation.'

Soon, he had my measure and asked me to give up other men and my sewing too. He rented this apartment from my father and furnished it as you see – to keep me in comfort and luxury. He divided himself and his time between his two lives and dressed accordingly in his black or in the latest fashion of the *beau monde*. We lived quietly when he was here. We would lie on the couch, as you and I are doing (that is his opium pipe), or we would go out to dine and afterwards dance and drink. In bed he was ingenious and voracious and I worshipped him.

We liked to drink our coffee together in the morning – just like a real, wedded couple. He would not touch stale bread, not even dipped in the coffee, and I had to go out for it before he was awake. He ate it with slices of liver – raw liver, you understand; I must always have some in the meat-safe. Knives too, a fine selection such as a good cook has – all to be laid out in proper order in the kitchen drawer. 'In case of need,' he said. And the best cognac. He would drink half a bottle of that after his breakfast. Then he would take me out walking on the fashionable streets, observe the women promenading there and make his selection. He was most particular.

'No,' he might say, as a group of girls walked past us. 'Your smile is not so sweet; your skin is more like sacking than silk; you are no coquette – and you, mademoiselle, though your hair shines and your glance is bold, cannot be compared with Lèni. But you, pretty brunette with the exquisite profile –'

An incorrigable womanizer, you think? All is not what it seems. Apart from me and the little Olivia, he would have no mistresses. Sometimes he stopped and persuaded a blonde, sometimes a brunette – he did not care as long as they were 'ladies', the daughters of the *bourgeoisie*, for such were certain to be virgins and he wanted their purity to mutilate, not to debauch. He lusted after their blood which, he often said, was sure to be better stuff than the horses' blood he got for our Masses. It was not long before he made me play the bawd while he waited at home, impatient for what I would bring. Poor fools! They thought I was a go-between, an intermediary for some diplomat or visiting prince and they preened themselves to think they were so distinguished – the insatiable little nags! They expected to be ridden! Barbara, one was called, an Englishwoman, the daughter of a lord; and Berthe – she was a doctor's daughter. God rest them. We drank their blood and poured offerings of it over the Black Cyllène.

Soon Paon needed more than knives to enforce his will. He bought a butcher's cleaver and one of the new guns, a

Colt revolver. As for me, I was his sketch-book and model; after a few weeks of sitting to him, my neck and breasts were covered in a fine network of cuts and scabs. Opium is a wonderful sedative! And he was an artist, my Paon. In 1884 – soon after Easter when the park is full of daffodils – that spring, Paon noticed a newcomer at Mass in St. Michael's, an elegant gentleman, the new Mexican consul. Next time he came there, he brought his daughter and when Paon told me of her beauty I feared he would conquer her in the same way he had me, and then desert me. He took me out to dine at La Mouette and then to the theatre where he pointed out *la Mexicaine* and praised her dusky skin, her clear eyes, her curls, her nose, her tiny hands and feet. (He had taken his opportunity to study her well from the confessional.) We went on to the celebrated Restaurant Phèdre for a late supper of oysters and champagne – he knew what pleased me. The consul's party was seated at the next table and Paon made me drop an earring and so we fell into conversation with them. I complimented Madame on her hat and she admired mine.

She asked me who was my milliner and I told her 'Lèni la Soie!'

The girl was wearing Paris fashions: a gown of ruched tussore, ostrich feathers in her hat – a picture. Her stole – white fox – hung over the back of her chair. I thought her good enough to supplant me and I admired Paon's taste, and his ambition. They were easy prey. I offered to conduct Madame to view the paintings in the Musée des Beaux-Arts and made friends with her daughter. Soon we were meeting to drink coffee and eat pastries and I was trusted to chaperone Paloma, the pretty *ingénue*! I brought her home with me: she sat over there, on the Empire chair by the chimney, and ate bonbons from a lace-trimmed box. This place was not as it is now with a hundred and more years of grime and wear on it: everything was new, you understand, and the house itself was a fine and elegant building where a master silk-weaver carried on his trade and his daughter lived with her rich lover!

I introduced Paloma to Paon. Though he had been morose for a week, he was instantly gay and cheerful; he opened a bottle of champagne and poured it into three shining glasses. We lifted our glasses for the toast.

'To you, Paloma, my sweet, my dove,' he said. 'To the most beautiful of all!'

The girl, whose French was indifferent, found no difficulty in understanding him and laughed and smiled at him with the eyes of a sheep. We got her drunk – it only took two glasses; and now, I thought, he will seduce her in our bed, beneath the cupids which have watched our play. Jealous Lèni! He did nothing of the kind, but put his arm round her waist and led her into the kitchen.

'There is more champagne,' he said.

I followed them.

'Tie up her hair. Quickly!' he told me and I pulled a ribbon out of my sleeve and gathered all the black tresses in a great bunch. The girl only laughed and kept on laughing as we fastened her arms to her body with the rope he had used on the others. Then she began to scream. It was a work-day and the looms were busy in the *ateliers* below. No one could hear. In any case, I muffled her screams with a cushion. She hardly made a noise when he produced the knife and cut her throat.

'Another angel for Paradise,' he said. 'Where shall we hide the body?'

'The Rhône?' I suggested.

'Interment is better. A grave for each limb.'

We had been able to dispose of the others, some to the water and some to the earth. Usually we had to carry their remains many kilometres out of town in a closed carriage. The head of the doctor's daughter is buried in the wood behind the village presbytery in Coeurville where Paon had once been priest. I remember the place well, because the locals called it 'Arcadie' and it was a pretty little wood with foxgloves growing in it.

Paon kissed the hands of the dead girl, left and right; right and left. He was like an automaton. He panted as he kissed the white fingers and talked to me,

'She was a Mexican – the daughter of a powerful man – they make magic in Mexico – in Zacatecas – Oaxaca – in Tehuantepec. Her blood – will be – the best. Bring immortality – beauty.'

He stopped worshipping the girl and told me to get the axe, while he untied her dead body and heaved it on to the table. He made the first cuts, through her clothing to the bone and then, saying 'You will need the knife as well,' left me to collect the blood and carve the meat. I had not needed to feel jealousy. Paon was faithful after his fashion.

I heard him go into the salon and lie down on the bed. A loud gunshot startled me and my knife slipped as I was cutting open the front of the girl's gown. There were several more shots. But nothing was amiss. Paon had simply fired his revolver into the canopy of the bed as he liked to do when he was tired or full of ennui. Then the telephone rang and I heard him speaking into it,

'Paon here.'

In the same moment there came a thundering on the apartment door. How could I answer? I jumped up on a chair and looked out of the window. The courtyard below was filled with a surging crowd of people and, on the other side when I ran there, the same. There were riders on horses and our men, the silkworkers, with staves and rifles; and police. I ran shouting into the salon,

'Quickly, quickly. Help me with the girl. There are *gendarmes* in the street below.'

Paon dropped the telephone.

That is all. They took him away but, when the crowd saw me, they surged forward up the stairs and overwhelmed the police. I was hidden amongst them and passed from house to house along the *traboules* until I was safe. Like me, Renard was never discovered; he drowned himself, jumping from the footbridge where I first saw him, in the winter of 1906. The river was high and he was swept fifty kilometres downstream. As for Olivia, she died of the pox before she was twenty.

'And Paon – he *was* condemned to death?' said Guy, twisting his head to look up at Lèni.

'Yes,' she said. 'After his trial. What other verdict could there be?'

He thought he should be shocked into flight from her comfortable lap, or should in some way (but how, without hands?) attack her to punish her in kind for her weak and enthusiastic complicity in Paon's crimes. He was too warm and relaxed to care. He counted the candles, seven on the mantelpiece and three on the little table, he thought. It was light enough to see how much her long life and the telling of her tale had hurt Lèni.

'Are you sick, my friend? Will you drink?' she said. 'Turn yourself a little more: there is a cup of water for your thirst.'

He turned his head again. It was true, he did feel queasy, like a man all at sea, floating . . . The cup, which had no handles, was more like a deep, footed bowl. It seemed to rest on nothing but a shaft of candle-light like a shadow or a phantom itself and its dark blue surface was glossy and covered in tongues of flame.

'That is the chalice!' he said. 'The cup Renard used at the Black Masses. Let me see it!'

'Will you drink?'

Lèni held up the cup and he looked into it. He expected blood to make him whole once more, but there was only a little clear water which Lèni tipped into his mouth. She did not put the cup down only held it there, beneath his chin.

'The King's Cup. It shows What is Gone,' said Lèni. 'Look

144

well.' As in a deep pit, he saw the room he lay in; but the furniture and furnishings were new and dustless; brightly-coloured. His own reflection was superimposed on that of the room. It wavered in the drop of water which remained and he stared at it and mourned his ugliness, the long hair and beard, the frowning brow, the new lines etched –

Another man was staring up, out of the bottom of the cup, directly at him; very close. He was thirty-five or forty maybe, his features strong and his coarse brown hair rumpled. Guy recognized him.

'Georges!' he exclaimed, the single word leaping from his lips.

'Paon,' corrected Lèni. 'It is Father Paon.'

'No, it is Helen's lover, Georges Dinard. True, he looks younger but it is the same man.'

'Georges Dinard, Father Paon: what's in a name?' said Lèni. 'Pay attention!'

The man in the cup spoke. 'This is justice,' he said. 'My final reward. I shall soon be with them, the beautiful dead.' A thunderous noise rushed from the bowl of the cup and it trembled and shook in Lèni's hands. The face moved suddenly forward and fell out of sight. Guy recoiled. He could see past Georges Paon's bloody neck and headless trunk into a huge and crowded square. The people there were silent and motionless and then a great murmur swept through the crowd as a group of clouds, so suffused with rose and gold they looked like distant palaces, floated across the sky and three white doves flew down and perched on Paon's body.

'When he opened his eyes, he was in Paradise,' whispered Lèni. 'A whole man once more.'

Guy lay back. 'Give me justice,' he said. 'A reward for my endurance.'

He closed his eyes and, surrendering to the opium, walked on down the nave of the cathedral until he came to the altar steps. The sun shone in all its glory through the east window above him. Beyond was a kingdom of light which, when he floated out into it, overwhelmed the mighty building and pulled him into a vortex. He spun there unprotesting for an age.

A small light glowed. Guy saw that it was the flame of Koschei's lantern and that the old man himself was in the room with him, an unfamiliar room which was neither Lèni's silk-lined purgatory nor the first room in the Memory Palace. Koschei was intent on his task of arranging some objects on a table and Guy, peering over his shoulder, was able to distinguish them, one from another: a school exercise book lay next to a dark red ball, and a long necklace of cowry shells snaked between the two.

'Hah!' said the magician suddenly, 'I felt your presence with me some time ago. Age and experience does not moderate your curiosity.'

'Those are my things.'

'Prove it.'

'Open the book.'

Koschei held up the book and turned its pages with fingers whose nails had grown so long that those which were not filed into sharp bodkins were twisted in upon themselves and curled like ram's horns.

'Well?'

'It says "Chemistry" on the cover but there is a story inside, my first. It is about a boy and an eagle.'

'It says "Alchemy" and the story inside is my first. It is about a fair young girl who bears more than a passing resemblance to the Lady Nemione.'

'The ball then. It is a cricket ball and it was given me by my father.'

'Nonsense. It is not a ball but a pomander, look. Smell it! As for the shells, I stole them from Nemione (she used them when she was learning to divide and multiply) and strung them myself.'

146

'That is a necklace I bought in Fiji for my wife.'

Koschei held up his lantern. They stared at each other. The magician combed his beard with his nails and Guy pushed back the lock of hair which always fell into his eyes when he was annoyed. He was surprised when Koschei smiled.

'A truce,' he said. 'It looks as though we must agree to share these mnemonic devices.'

Guy nodded, but his sense of honour was not satisfied.

'Is this the second room?' he asked.

'The second in the sequence, although the first to be built. I constructed a new shell about the original building when I moved it to Pargur.'

'You did not move it! How could you? The Memory Palace stands in the Virtue Garden behind the Cloister of Espmoss.'

'No. I moved it – though I left the garden. It was no easy task: a challenge to my powers. Because a thing is difficult and terrifying, neither I nor you avoid it. If you look behind the door there, you will find something which challenges you.'

The door was low and narrow, but when Guy stood in front of it, it seemed large. It was like the cellar door in his father's house and like the door of the cupboard where the suitcases were kept, and like that door at school before which the choirboy Chris Young had stood in fear. The latch, however, was made of iron. It was stiff, but he pressed it hard. The catch yielded. He did not like the way the door swung out towards him.

There was nothing behind it but a flat, empty space like a painting of the inside of a cupboard. He challenged it to tell him something. Then he saw the stairs, a steep wooden flight of them ascending into darkness, and he was afraid.

'You must go up,' said Koschei, behind him.

'Will you make me?'

'You will force yourself.'

Guy set his foot on the first stair and lifted the second after it. There was no handrail and as he went higher, he feared the drop; but this was a minor emotion compared with his fear of the staircase itself. Above him he saw a turn. A sourceless light illuminated it and nothing else. The space around the stair was completely dark. He came to the turn and climbed again. A door confronted him. It was a door like the one below, exactly alike, and he opened it with sweating hands. The gale that was his own breathing surged about him. He climbed. When he reached the top he would find the answer. He climbed until he came to the turning. He climbed to the door and opened it. He climbed the stairs and woke.

He was in the cupid bed. The amoretti flew lazily, grinning down at him and making obscene gestures with their fat fingers. Even the damaged ones were in the air, flailing their amputated legs. He begged them to be still and the biggest, which wore a garland of rosebuds, hovered over him.

'What is at the top of the stairs?' he asked it.

The cherub covered its mouth with the tip of one of its wings and laughed lewdly.

'If you don't know,' it said, 'no one does. Excuse me now. It is about to rain and I would rather keep dry.' It kicked out vigorously with all its limbs, like a strong baby in a cradle, and flew away.

Guy heard the rain falling and turned over in the bed. Lèni was approaching, the silver tray in her hands. She put it down beside him and laughed, deep in her throat.

'I have brought you a gift.'

His two hands lay on the tray, resting there like gangling spiders. He looked at them, lovingly. They were beautiful. He recognized the ridged nail of his left thumb and the old scar from the chisel on the right little finger. His father had forbidden him to use it but, knowing better, he had taken it and, out in the garden, tried to cut the all-important groove in the deck of his toy boat. Otherwise the gun slipped off.

His hands. Of course, he could not move them; but he could contemplate. The wrists had not healed but the skin and flesh had settled into a damp boss. The bone was rough and splintered where the saw had torn through. There was no pain, just the cold. He could feel the smooth surface of the tray and then the catchy texture of the silk bedspread under his fingers. The hands were moving, all on their own, and Lèni smiled at him. She sat on the bed. He wanted to touch her: a thank-you. In amazement; in wonder and delight, he watched his hands walk to her and climb on to her skirt. The old black dress was also made of silk. He stroked the stuff. His severed hands took hold of hers. He smiled.

'Everything is smooth,' he said. 'The silk, your fingers, but the rough skin of my hands catches it like sandpaper.'

'We had to look after our hands,' she said. 'So that we did not damage the silk.'

'Did you weave it?'

'No, I used to parcel it up for the buyers from Worth and the other Paris *couturiers*. Then I became a seamstress myself and sewed the wonderful stuff. Do you know how many silkworms die to make a kilometre of yarn? A thousand, ten thousand? – *one*, monsieur! It is because of my trade that Paon brought so much *soieries* in here: the bedclothes, the hangings, the upholstery, my clothes, his – even his drawers!'

'You really are Lèni la Soie?'

She did not answer his question directly. 'I have been a long time fading here,' she said, 'but I daresay I will last the course. I have given up the blood, though Georges might bring it even now. Who wants eternal youth? All I desire is rest and now that I have told you my tale it may come. Yes, monsieur, I have aged as you can see, and lost my *joie de vivre*.'

'Tell me more about the blood. How can it preserve the flesh when it is a fleshly thing itself?'

149

'Are you Paon? You do not need such a thing. For you, there will be another way.'

'Then tell me: have you seen Paradise?'

'One glimpse as he died. I stood at the back of the crowd, afraid to be discovered, and I saw what passed over him when the doves flew down from the sky. I saw a garden with a little house in it, a house of marble and gilded tiles, though when I questioned my neighbours in the crowd, they had seen nothing but poor Paon dying.'

'That is Koschei's Memory Palace. In Malthassa.'

'Have you been to Malthassa?'

'In a sense. In so many words, tens of thousands of words.'

He had expected her body to give some of its warmth to his hands but they stayed cool. She had been beautiful. Now her beauty was of the same kind as his hands', of life denied and a past preserved like a lovely moth in formalin. The absinthe had destroyed her face and dulled her eyes and her expression. Her mouth remained unravaged, and her small hands. He gripped them tightly with his mind and his hands did what he asked of them.

'This is my reward,' he said. 'For endurance. Why did Paon mutilate you?'

'He put his mark on me. He wanted to preserve me for himself. My scars are his. Let go!'

He freed her hands. Instead, he gripped the silk of her skirt. She unfastened the high neck of her dress: white stuff beneath, lace and laces, the stiffness of a corset. His severed hands followed after hers. He felt them all, successive layers, her disintegrating shrouds, until the ridged flesh of her breasts was underneath his fingers. In between the scars, the skin was smooth. The contrast and the ecstasy of touch, of restored touch, aroused him. The hands squeezed the woman's breasts while he watched them perform, as might a voyeur.

'*Aux innocents les mains pleines,*' he said, laughing at his macabre joke. He expected Lèni to move now, closer to him.

150

He wanted sex; with his dead hands moving as he willed them, he had become a necromancer.

'You are no fool,' she said. 'You are a wise man and a magician as well – But too much power is not good for you.' She looked down at her exposed breasts and at the puckered hands which clung to them. 'Come, fetishes, it is time to sleep.' She stood and gently detached the hands, which offered no resistance. They lay passive in her small grip; indeed, he had lost all the sensation their independent activity had given him. She carried them from the room and he, rising quickly to follow her, found the door shut in his face. The brass knob looked slippery and stiff. In vain he tried to hold and turn it with his teeth.

Nothing had changed despite the weird interlude of touch and feeling which had just passed. He did not know which frightened him most, her words or her control over him. He lay down once more on the bed, in his prison, and closed his eyes in despair.

He could hear thunder rolling, soft and menacing, far away. He imagined the iron clouds gathering over the vineyards to the north which, he thought, was somewhere on the far side of the room, beyond the wall and beyond other unknown walls.

Lèni lit the candles.

'This place of shadows,' she said, 'this afternoon is truly the anteroom to hell.'

The thunder was scarcely louder but it waited outside, a ravenous beast. Lèni took up her mending.

'Paon's holiday shirt,' she said. 'I cannot keep up with the decay.' Guy watched her thread her needle with a fine, blue thread and fit a silver thimble on the middle finger of her right hand. The needle was so small; but she held it confidently and pushed it in and out of the shirt collar.

'How can you do that?' he said.

151

'It is not so difficult – if one has hands.'

'Shall I tell you a story?'

'Yes. Why not? It is your trade after all, as this is one of mine.'

The Archmage spat into the golden cuspidor. The nut I had given him was infested with the eggs of the black worm and now, after swallowing it, he was bringing up tiny gobbets of blood which stained his sputum and convinced me that he would soon die. He coughed loudly and said,

'This is not the Ripe Nut of Wisdom. You have been tricked.'

'No, Archmage, I am not deceived. What the nut is, or was since you have greedily swallowed it whole, surely depends on how it is received: how it is used. If you had bitten into it, you would have seen what it contains – poison.'

I had not believed what the Om Ren told me when he picked the nut for me and pressed it into my reluctant hand, 'A fresh intelligence and new wisdom in the world – if you discover how to use the nut!' but, seeing now before me the pain my act of acceptance was causing the Archmage, I silently praised the wisdom of the Man of the Woods. In a little while, the splendid robes, the castle, the pele tower of Peklo, the infallibility and intellect of Manderel Valdine would be mine.

He coughed again and spat out more blood.

'You are trying to kill me, Koschei,' he groaned. 'You are both dissembler and assassin, as it is written.'

'I would prefer to be remembered as the instrument of your foretold death.'

'It is time,' Valdine groaned. 'It is five o'clock on the fifth day of the eleventh month, and this is my seventieth year. The lady Nemione is taking tea with her dwarf in the White Tower and, in the Tower of Silence, Olburn is pressing my faithless son to death.' His dying eyes glittered and he clutched his stomach and bent forward in agony. 'Release me!' He tried to draw deep breaths of the fetid, perfumed air.

'I must help you succeed,' he gasped. 'You know the old jingle: "In a bed, in a house, in a street, in a town, in a green province, in a wide country, lies my love". Think on it. You will know that you have found my soul: that you can at last slay me when you hold in your hand the alabaster box on which is written *Prospero's Book*. Open it and burn what you find inside.'

I leaned eagerly over him.

'I must begin with the "wide country"?'

'Yes, yes.'

'The widest lands I know in Malthassa are the Plains.'

'Good, good. How you torture me. Go!'

But I had not finished with him. It pleased me to see him writhe.

'May I take Frostfeather?'

'Why not? You will take my life. Take whatever you need. Only, make haste.'

I looked about me, at the stone walls and the tapestries, the chests and the blood-red carpet on which the Archmage's carved chair was set. His Book lay open on a lectern, its covers of human skin held firm in the fingers of a carved monkey, and a long marker of tasselled silk upon it.

'I think – I will take your bookmark!' I said.

'Spare me that!'

'I will certainly take it.' I folded the thing with care and laid it in my wallet next to the dyed lock of Nemione's hair. Then I left the room and strode to the head of the winding stair. The Archmage called me back.

'Against my will, I must advise you,' he said. 'Make a secure place in which to hide your own soul. You stand there, brave in your new clothes, strong in body and mind – so *young* – and ridiculously mortal.'

✦   ✦   ✦

The white balloon Frostfeather rose above the city and I, though experiencing still the novice's sensations of nausea and of time cut off, leaned against the basketwork and looked down. Pargur was already far below. It looked like a diamond pinned to a mantle of green velvet. A margin of blue, the beginning of the ocean, ran along one edge of it; the rest was lost in mist. But we, rising above these lowly visual delights, came out upon a sunlit plain where the great illusions of nature, her ever-changing, insubstantial towers and palaces made an immense city many times more fascinating than Pargur.

Peder turned from his work with furnace and sandbags.

'We shall rise another ten thousand feet,' he said. 'You must put on your furs and strap your air-cowl to your head.'

I was already clad in woollen breeches, stout boots and a leather overcoat. He passed me a long fur robe which was lined with the soft skins of unborn lambs, a warm stole for my neck, and gloves. I put them all on and he handed me the cowl or breathing apparatus. I pulled it over my head and secured its straps. They were narrow and they fastened with several small brass buckles. The front of the cowl was a mask with a window of clear mica to see through and an ugly muzzle like the jaw of the Om Ren himself. Inside it were contained the materials which enabled one to breathe in a rarefied atmosphere, a quantity of dried sholgirse and seven pulverized geodes mined from the great asteroid which fell on Pargur in the Year of the Warrior. When mixed together these exuded air. A small lever broke the membrane which separated the two components and this, I operated. The device was then good for two hours. Peder donned his own protective clothing and we stared at each other, two fur-clad apes in a flying basket thirty thousand feet above the friendly ground.

I breathed easily and surveyed my aerial realm. To step from the balloon and walk away across those golden fields

154

would not have been a difficult feat. They looked as solid as the pavements outside Espmoss.

All at once the clouds parted and revealed the measureless forest. The clouds dissolved. Ahead of us the forest gave way to bastions of snow-encrusted rock, and, on the basket-rim next to my fur-covered hands, crystals of frost built themselves into miniature battlements. The stays from which the basket hung turned silver, but Frostfeather's silk envelope was unaffected, warmed by the fire which drove her and which made a pleasant play of red shadows on her snowy sides.

'The frost is pretty,' remarked Peder, 'and deadly. We must risk it to cross the Altaish mountains. Overland, the journey would take a year.'

'I know it!' I said fervently. 'You forget, I travelled to Pargur from Espmoss.'

'Perhaps the journey would take you only eleven months, sir,' Peder said. It seemed to me that he sneered, but I dismissed the notion from my mind. It was irrelevant in our lofty situation.

The erratic motion of the balloon, as Peder steered her from one uprising draught to the next, made me light-headed. I breathed deeply to counteract its effect. The frosty wires which held us up became cylinders of light and a black cone floated before me. I tried to catch it between my clumsy gloves. I heard the ocean pounding in my ears. The russet ape which was the Navigator, Peder Drum, stepped away from his fire and stood close.

'Aren't you well. sir?' he asked. His voice boomed and faded. 'Not too comfortable in that cowl?'

I lifted my hands slowly, labouring to make them obey me. I held the muzzle of the mask and shook it. Peder laughed. It took all my Green Wolf's will and schooling to kick out and disable him. He fell against the basket's side and while he struggled to get up, I pulled off my gloves and picked at the buckles of my hood until I was free of it. It did me no

155

good. The airless kingdom of the frost was stifling me. We struggled, Peder and I, on the yielding osier floor. His familiarity with balloons was pitched against my soldier's skills. He pulled a long-barrelled pistol from his sleeve. It was a primitive weapon, but I despaired. One shot would kill Frostfeather and we would plunge with her into the mountains below. I got a purchase on his arm, and forced the pistol to discharge harmlessly into the withies. I took it from him and threw it over the side. Then, with all my remaining strength (the inhuman strength of one at death's door) I wrested his cowl from him and held it to my face. I breathed air. It was good. Peder panted hard and his brown eyes begged silently like a dog's.

He deserved to die. Without him, I could not fly the balloon.

'Is there another cowl?' I said.

'No. Yours has no geodes. Give me –' His voice faded. I took a deep breath and held the mask to his face. When he was sufficiently recovered, I made a bargain with him: he must transfer his allegiance to me, or die as soon as we landed in a safe place. I reminded him of my past career. I told him the truth: that I had killed twenty men.

'We have one cowl between us,' he said. 'It will last another forty minutes perhaps. That is not enough time to cross the Altaish.'

'Then we must land in the mountains.'

'No Navigator has risked it.'

'We have no choice.'

We worked together at the furnace, he instructing me. He was superbly skilled. When he began to damp down the fire to reduce our height, I prayed to the gods of the Altaish.

'That will not help us,' Peder said. 'Save your breath.'

The rocks closed in about us; we followed a canyon which bored into the Altaish. Snowy plateaux and hideous crevasses, the whistling of the wind in high places and the leaden roar of avalanches were our only companions there. The canyon led us on. No man, surely, had ever ventured there before. There were no colours save grey and the white of death. The roaring of some troll or giant of the mountains pursued us. It was a while before we realized that what we heard was no supra-natural phenomenon, but thunder hurling itself at the rocks. The void heaved beneath us, tossing Frostfeather about as if she were a cork in a rough sea.

'But I can breathe,' Peder shouted, moving the mask aside.

'Yes?' I did not trust him: he would have to win my regard. I reached for the mask. 'I trust you breathed deeply?'

'There is real air, sir.'

I took a lungful, expecting it to choke me. It was sweet and cold, the gift of the Altaish, and I was glad that I had prayed.

'Thank you,' I said aloud. Frostfeather bucked. We held her landing cords and rode her through the storm. Forked lightning crackled from her wires and made arcs about us. The rocks above were smashed and came tumbling down. We watched them hurtle past; we marvelled at the lightning's blinding yellow flashes and the audacity of the storm, which had no regard for us. We were toys, mere fleshly automata, to be destroyed. I prayed again and, as I spoke the last word of my last prayer, the rain fell in a great cataract which extinguished both the lightning and the fire at Frostfeather's heart. The rain swept us downwards, drenching and draggling the silk of the balloon and twisting it into a rope.

We came to rest in a reed-bed. The enraged waters of a river rushed past us and we sat still amongst the remains of Frostfeather until we felt calm enough to move. The storm passed over and vanished down the canyon; the sun came out. We were close by a shingle beach and crayfish crawled about in the shallows. A rainbow sprang out above us.

157

I was the first to wake. The night had passed. We had spent it dry, in a low cave under a rock. We had made a fire and roasted on hot stones the crayfish we had caught. I crept out, bending myself double in the narrow mouth of the cave. Outside, the sun shone in a clear sky. The unforgiving mountains towered all around, the river ran serenely, and a flock of goats grazed the sparse weeds on its far bank. A boy-child, the goatherd, was turning over the wreckage of Frostfeather. He saw me and leaped away over the boulders in the river, pausing only when he was half way across and out of reach.

'Look!' I said. I held my hands out and, by an effort of intense concentration, made them appear to contain a bunch of grapes. The boy was curious, and greedy. He came quickly to me.

'Now!' I said. Once more, I applied my mind. The grapes turned silver and flowed away in a molten stream which vanished before it hit the ground. Now I held the attention and the spirit of the boy. He looked up at me as if he expected to be destroyed on the spot or, at the very least, transformed into a brute creature.

'Are you hungry?' I said.

'Always.' He spoke a dialect of the Altaish. It was something like Erchon's native tongue, and I could understand him. I found, and unlocked, our box of iron rations and gave him a disc of dark chocolate. Though he had clearly never seen or tasted the like, he ate it with relish.

'My friend sleeps in the cave,' I said. 'We are envoys of the great Archmage of Pargur but the storm caught us and deposited us here.'

'This is Vondar Gorge,' the boy said, 'and that is the young Von flowing past us. My village lies upstream and, upstream of that, is Vonta and the road.'

I cheered and huzzaed, waking Peder who came out of the cave.

'We are close to civilization,' I told him. 'Vonta, where they hold the Summer horse fair, is not far away.'

Frostfeather was not as badly damaged as we first supposed and, with the help of the men of the village, we got her up to Vonta, where a basket maker repaired the holes in her wickerwork and a seamstress the rents in her silk. Peder rigged her carefully and lit the furnace. She began to swell proudly and to tug at her lines. Next day we left the little town, which was pleasant enough, with its painted houses and dwarven silver shops, but dull out of the fair season. We followed the Von to its source and crossed the watershed with the last of our air, again sharing the breathing-cowl. Frostfeather sailed on steadily by day and night. When the stars came out, Peder steered by the seven jewels of Bail's Sword. We were nearing the Septrential Ocean, which we must cross before we saw the first dun hillocks of the Plain or encountered the first herd of horses.

It is beyond the wit of man to explain or to elucidate the inconsistencies of Malthassa's topography. Enough to say: it, like the gods and snows eternal, is. As mutable Pargur is and Espmoss, the nivashi and puvushi, Roszi in her coat of gold, and my metastatic Memory Palace.

Peder, as we travelled, made himself my faithful servant. He gave me good advice but never again argued with me, nor questioned my decisions or showed with words or facial expression any quality other than profound regard. He spoke of 'we' – 'when we have reached our goal', 'when we have overcome', 'when we return to Pargur and [here dropping the plural and collective for the singular and remarkable] Koschei rules the city'. Also, he flew the balloon.

The blue waters of the Septrential Ocean passed beneath us, vast and naked of all human influence. Its fifty-foot waves were ripples to us. I saw from the balloon, or thought I saw, all its encircling shores; but, when we reached the first plains town of Ma, I was unsure; it was possible that the ocean, like the one at Pargur, continued beyond man's ken; it was possible that the two seas met to girdle the land in a gigantic watery zone.

The citizens of Ma were taciturn, half plainsmen and half townsfolk. They kept their horses corralled in enclosures fenced with brushwood and rode them on tight reins. I longed to see the true horses and riders of the Plain and the great Red Horse himself (he who is bridled with the skin of the last Om Ren) and I asked an elder to take me out of the town. Peder intervened.

'You will see them soon enough,' he said. 'The obstacles which lie ahead are not physical. We must leave Frostfeather here and borrow Plains horses to carry us to SanZu.' He went out of our lodging and I heard his voice in the street outside and another, answering it. Half a day later he returned. A second man followed him into the room, a small fellow whose hair was tied back and smeared with red grease. He was hardly taller than a dwarf but he carried a full-sized naked sword across his equally naked back. Two lengths of striped cloth hanging from a belt made of silver discs were all the clothes he wore, except for a pair of tall, soft boots.

'This is our guide, The Rider Who Bestrides the Bay Horse from the Marches of SanZu, Nandje the son of Nandje.'

I stood up and bowed to the little man. The Ima, in my imagination, were a race of tall and graceful men, whose nobility showed in both their faces and their deeds. I was not prepared for greasy savages. This one did not return my greeting; nor did he smile or speak.

'He is listening to your soul,' said Peder.

The man, when several more silent minutes had passed, stepped up to me and laid his hands on my stomach.

'That is their greeting. Now he will speak.'

(I have not yet explained that all languages in Malthassa have a common root and that communication between the races is therefore comparatively easy. The exceptions – there must be at least one, must there not? – are the dwarven language of the Altaish and its dialects.)

'You are Koschei; I am Nandje,' said the Ima and continued with great fluency to address me: 'I have listened and I have heard. You are an ambitious man, Koschei Corbillion, and your soul, though it is always restless, has the strength and tenacity of a hunting lioness. Welcome to the Plains.

'I know SanZu Province well. It is close by the place of my birth. I have brought you the horse you will ride there. If you come to the door you will see him standing next to mine. His name is Winter and he is one of the lesser stallions. To ride a master of mares like my Bay or the noble Red is the privilege of kings and the Ima.'

Nandje's measured speech was his only noble quality.

We looked out. A group of horses stood quietly in the centre of the street and it was easy to identify the Bay, Nandje's horse, amongst them, a stallion clearly and the most richly decorated with pendant tassels of dyed horse-hair and with strings of silver discs like those his master wore. My horse, Winter, was iron grey and the mount selected for Peder was a stolid brown. Other horses waited to be loaded with packs.

'Speak to your horse,' Nandje said.

I had always considered horses to be beasts of burden and of small intelligence. What one said to them might be defined as 'speech' only because words were used but, like the butcher's loud 'Waahorhorhor!', these words degenerated in the utterance into sounds as bestial as a neigh. I did not want to offend Nandje, the Plains horseman, at this early stage so 'Winter!' I called, 'is your name given for your dusky and speckled coat, as harsh as the frozen ground, or for the time of your birth?'

The horse turned his head and looked, over his shoulder as it were, at me. His large dark eyes were rimmed with sweeping black lashes. They reminded me of the eyes of a gypsy witch and disquiet grew in me as the horse continued to survey me, behaving in this exactly like Nandje when he listened to my soul. Soon, I thought (and trembled), he will speak. Winter walked slowly up to me and pushed his bony nose against me. His nostrils widened and he sniffed at my coat. In its left hand pocket was a piece of hard biscuit and I took it out and fed it to him. Thanks be, he did not speak; but Nandje did, answering my question.

'He is named Winter in anticipation of your destiny,' he said.

'It is an ominous name.'

'Winter has its delights, does it not? Come, Koschei: let us go into the inn and drink to our departure while your servant loads the horses.'

I fell sick when we had ridden two days of long and hard hours' traverse on the sunlit Plain where nothing but hillock succeeding brown hillock showed that we made progress toward our goal in SanZu. For another two days I lay on the ground, weak and in a melancholic humour, while Peder tended me and Nandje silently smoked his clay pipe at my side. On the third day I rose, well enough; but Peder fell ill. So, we lost five days in all.

'Something pursues you out of Pargur,' Nandje said, puffing on his pipe. 'Some ill will.'

'It is a weakening ambition,' I told him. 'It does not have sufficient strength to do us permanent harm.'

Valdine, with his magic map and his mirrors, could have followed my progress all the way to SanZu; but wracked by the poison, his vitals consumed and gnawed at by the vitriolic worm out of the nut, had insufficient strength to pursue or wound us. Incapable of working up the passion and perverted carnality from which he drew his genius, he had thrown the worst hex of which he was still capable over us and visited us with a plague so destitute of vigour that these lost days of fever and discomfort were all the damage he could wreak. I prayed again, to my old God of the Cloister and to the Lady herself, that he was too great a heretic to call on the Duschma and her fatal infections.

162

We rode on. Occasionally we saw herds of horses grazing the dry and withered grasses or parties of Ima horseman riding by. They did not greet us nor attempt to come near. Nandje carried a kind of standard, a long pole topped with a bunch of grass which, he said, told them we were intent upon a pilgrimage and would not welcome distractions. On the fifteenth day we saw the curves of greater hills before us, still a long way off. Nandje gestured at them with his staff.

'SanZu,' he said.

As I rode, I had ample time for reflection. Sometimes I thought of my home in Espmoss and of my quiet, cloistered youth – which Nemione took from me. I had run from the Religion and turned soldier that I might return one day and impress her. Then I had turned in dissatisfaction from that false destiny to magic, Pargur and ambition. I was that rare thing: priest, soldier and mage. The Om Ren had shown me myself; what Nandje told me had confirmed I was the man I desired most to be.

I thought of Nemione: of her beauty and her coldness; of her desire to use me. Because of this, I rode to SanZu; I rode in response to a few kisses. She had come to me after I had poisoned the Archmage, flaunting her chaste presence in my bachelor chambers. This time she wore a gown fastened as high as her chin and long, hanging sleeves. It was white, symbolic like the other of her virginity, but buttoned from chin to toe with coral cupids and these, I knew, were all sewn on to tempt me to unfasten them and also to forbid me any such familiarity. Nemione gave me nothing for my journey, no gift and no advice, but paced about my rooms admiring the new furnishings and poked her lovely nose into all my books and drawers. Then, as she turned to go, 'Come here Koschei,' she said imperiously and, when I was close enough, put her veiled arms about my neck and kissed me three times, teasingly, fleetingly, on the lips. 'You have done well, for a cloister mouse,' she said, and ran away down the stairs.

At least, I thought mournfully, I have saved her from Valdine. The worst he could summon now was a mild fever, a bout of vomiting and a headache. His agony made him impotent.

'"In a bed, in a house, in a street, in a town, in a green province, in a wide country, lies my love." Think on it,' Manderel Valdine had instructed me. In this jingle, this commonplace peasant triviality, the key to his soul's hiding place was concealed. I tried to construe it, but my pictures of Nemione made constant interruption and I imagined her lying in her tapestried bed amongst her female gewgaws, conversing with golden Roszi, her watchdog. I imagined her nakedness and warmth in the night and, my lust awoken by these phantoms, moved uncomfortably in the saddle and fixed my gaze upon the hills and the unknown. A green shadow crept beside and about us, the new grass growing. Spring had come.

'Look, Winter,' I said. 'See what was concealed in the cold ground.' We paused, to let the horses taste the fresh shoots.

At long-desired and hoped-for last, we rode into SanZu, halting at the border so that Nandje could bid us good-bye. This he refused to do, saying it would bring us bad luck. 'Only trust in yourselves,' he said, wheeled the Bay suddenly about on its haunches, and galloped off in a cloud of dust and good will. Peder and I rode on, following a high road for we were, once again, in civilized country. We saw the low buildings of farmsteads crowding around their stackyards and, in the fields which stretched to the roadside, the young flax plants were poking tender heads out of the fertile ground, while the mulberry trees which grew in groves around each house were in fresh and tender leaf. Small birds sang and old men sat outside the wayside inns, enjoying the warmth and the promise of the land and, in the foothills beyond the farmlands, a great brown rock breasted the sky. There was my sign: the rock whose steep contours had been marked on the Archmage's magic map and on the map I had seen in Pargur! The sun shone on it with as much fervour as on the cultivated valley but the rock, I thought, was a barren and unkind thing to find overshadowing such fecundity. On the far side of a shallow river, which we forded gladly, we saw the town of Flaxberry and, riding along its cool streets, found ourselves pressed on all sides by curious citizens who asked us where we were going. It was expedient to conceal the reason for our arrival.

'We need sleep,' I said, feigning weariness. 'Good beds, hot water and food.'

Thinking we must be pilgrims, they led us to the nunnery.

I walked in the cloister with the abbess. It was very like my old refuge of Espmoss, pervaded with order, calm and quiet purpose: I felt at home. Polnisha, the deity they worshipped there, was once, the abbess told me, a foreign goddess from beyond the forest.

'Then it has an end?' I asked, excited by my thoughts of trees thinning out and the needle-strewn ground giving way to meadows or to an empty strand on which the sea dropped its bounteous waves.

'Our books tell us that it is not boundless,' she replied. 'I, myself, believe that the forest is a fog which fills the mind and not a wood at all.'

'I have walked in it!'

'Have you?' She smiled.

'It moves!'

'Does it? Did not you?'

'It appears to be both beyond and on the near side of the Plains,' I ventured.

'Appearances can be deceptive,' she returned.

After supper, I entertained the nuns. They were not nuns

165

in the strict sense of my old order but hand maidens or lay sisters. Those are better descriptions. They were less devout than true nuns but no less merry. I stood up before a crowd of them and went through my repertoire of tricks with sunbeams, moonbeams, silver doves and golden cockerels. I extracted yards of ivy from Peder's ear and conjured a worthless, sparkling necklace (which I told her to keep) into the bosom of the prettiest nun. How they all laughed when she felt it lying cold and slippery between her breasts!

'Asmodée!' I said to Peder, 'If only I dare offend the abbess and let that trinket be my herald and not my ambassador! – but I must play the harmless fellow, a travelling prestidigitator who has no vices.'

I cultivated the abbess, attending on her assiduously. So, though I never asked her name, I wormed out all her secrets until I knew the routine of the nunnery as well as she. She showed me the abbey's extensive mulberry groves and its wide acres planted with flax in rows as neat as partings. She conducted me on a tour of the retting-pits and the cool barns where the silkworm caterpillars and, later, their cocoons, were reared.

'This place, she said, 'is now Polnisha's home. She watches over the sowing of the flax, its growth and its reaping. It is she who taught our ancestors what to do with the silk caterpillars they found in the mulberry trees.' She showed me the goddess's reaping hook and her bobbin of pure silk thread, which were kept in a shrine upon whose wooden doors was carved the grinning, fleshless face of Death, and she showed me the doors of Polnisha's house. I walked around the outside of this building, a large and elegant house lit by arched windows too high above the ground to spy through. I spent time in the abbess's private library where I read about the goddess and also about women's deepest desires, knowledge I kept in my heart to use. In truth, I was lost. I did not understand Valdine's jingle. It seemed no more to me than a silly love poem or a child's skipping song and

I told Peder to prepare the horses so that we might ride out to the Rock. The prettiest nun pursued me, continually finding herself wherever I was. Polnisha, she said, was sometimes a goddess of love, especially by night. Then the goddess rose from her bed to bathe.

'I expect you will watch her from the window of your cell,' I said.

'Oh, no. Polnisha stays in her house. I shall look out, in case I see you.'

'Look well,' I said, and kissed her hands.

I had no intention of visiting her cell. Nemione was my love. Whatever dreams and desires she sent me, I must bear. I sat in my own cell and pondered the nun's words. She meant the moon, of course: the moon rose from her daytime bed. Unless, in Polnisha's house some vision or manifestation was displayed, a revelation germane to my purpose – I went hastily out and walked about until I saw the nun.

'Walk with me,' I said.

We strolled in the cloister and the cloister garth and I led her out into the nunnery garden. We walked beneath the walls of the goddess's house.

'The abbess tells me that this wonderful building is the holy of holies,' I said. 'She showed me the doors – what labour, what art went into the making of them! Would a mere man, a traveller such as myself, be allowed a peep at what he supposes must be finer work within?'

'No!'

'I must tell you: I am not really a conjuror but an architect in the service of Manderel Valdine, Prince of Pargur and Archmage of Malthassa. Could you accommodate such a man?'

My double meaning was intended – an unsubtle weapon. I drew her into the lee of a buttress and kissed her. I found the cheap necklace I had summoned tucked inside the neck of her habit and played with it while I paid her worthless compliments.

'I know where the key is kept,' she suddenly said. 'I will show it you –'

'If,' said I, 'I promise to come to you in your cell? Very well. A bargain, then!'

We sealed it, naturally, with more kisses. One might kiss an aunt, or a friend. Therefore I did not lose faith with Nemione.

Petrified, or turned to stone: the furnishings and artefacts, even the food laid out in baskets, the baskets themselves, seemed sculpted from marble. Polnisha's house contained everything she might require from agate books to a deep, onyx bath. Her mirror had been fashioned from a sheet of red-veined porphyry. The goddess herself, the guardian of the flax crop and the silent cocoons of silk, lay grey-faced in a granite bed and was covered over with a length of cloth whose warp was linen and whose weft was silk. It was the only flexible, organic thing in the House beside the dancing flames in the lamps and myself, who knelt in the shadows and was petrified, suspecting magic but unable to sense it.

'You must not stay there,' the nun had whispered as she took the key from its simple hiding place in a barrel of flour. 'One glance to satisfy your curiosity before – oh, Koschei! – you return to me. And replace the key.'

I had already determined to wait in the House until daylight came to dispel any lingering evil or enchantment I might behold. I knelt on the cold floor, as motionless as the sleeping goddess, my hand on the hilt of my sword. Outside, the world waited for the moon: I saw her light grow gradually until it filled the windows and moved in bright shafts over the floor. The lamps burned low. In a moment I should fall asleep, a false knight keeping failed vigil. I heard a pin drop and, following on its tinny echo, the voice of a girl:

'God rot!'

Putting her stately mask and her coverlet aside, the god-

168

dess climbed from her bed and stood beside it, yawning. She had long, brown hair and was dressed like the peasants of the region in colourful weaves. She rubbed the sleep from her eyes and began to walk about her house, examining the various stone objects until, coming to a table laden with a counterfeit feast, she snapped her fingers and picked up a carven loaf. I saw the loaf turn soft and brown in her hand. The girl bit into it hungrily. Crumbs fell upon the floor; I smelled new-baked bread. Then, with a muted gasp, the girl dropped the loaf and rushed back to the bed. From some recess in its rigid pillows she took out a box made of pale, luminescent alabaster. Now that she had it safe again, she again walked about her house until she stood beside the bath where, after placing the box on the rim of the bath, she snapped her fingers twice. Water flowed out of the empty air, and filled the bath. She undressed swiftly and stepped into the tub. I, straining out of the shadows to see, was far more interested in her box than in her body, wanting love and in need of lust though I was.

'Now!' I said to myself, 'here is a fine opportunity.'

Water streamed from Polnisha's face and hair. She looked up at me and said,

'Who are you?'

'Koschei the Pretender.'

'That's a meaningless title! I am the Living Goddess.' She lay back and floated in the water. 'You can touch me if you like, but I won't promise to cure you.'

'I am not ill. Besides, another woman waits for me.'

'One of those stupid nuns? They must be as bored as I am – but you are a handsome young man. You are not a farmer.'

'I am a magician.'

'Who borrows his skills from Urthamma. Watch me!'

Three times she snapped her fingers. Immediately, a cockatrice appeared on the rim of the bath. It hissed at me and set its foot on the alabaster box. Her ridiculous trick

169

annoyed me but it was a clear sign that the box, or its content, was valuable.

'Watch me!' I said. I made the water in her bath turn red and, while she splashed it contemptuously at me and prepared a fresh insult in her mind, I drew my sword and spitted her conjuration. Having no corporeal body, it disappeared at once. Before she could snap her fingers again, I served her in the same swift way. Her blood was the same colour as my illusory dye. I wiped the blade of my sword clean on her discarded dress, picked up the box and fled with it.

Peder had the horses ready in a trice. We left the place without disturbing anyone: women who pray and who have, therefore, clear consciences, sleep as soundly as the dead.

This adventure of mine was the cause of a war. When the dead goddess (a paradoxical impossibility) was discovered, the men of Flaxberry pursued us. We observed their rage in safety, from the vantage point of Frostfeather's basket, and I made a spell which dropped hail on them. They fired a few arrows at us, but we were out of reach of their feathered sticks and sailed on, unharmed. They had falsely concluded that I was an agent of the Imandi, the Rider of the Red Horse, chief of the Ima, and careered furiously back to Flaxberry to make their preparations for the first assault. A few thousands died. It was a small war, a long time ago.

Isolated from such dangers and passive in Frostfeather's floating basket, I was at leisure to examine the box. Hideous octupi and other denizens of the ocean were carved upon it in cameo and, within a garland of kelp, the words the Archmage had told me I should find: *Prospero's Book*. Other words were traced beneath this inscription,

> Deeper than did ever plummet sound
> I'll drown my book.

170

'What does it mean, Peder?' I said, without expecting a reply. The Navigator was, as usual, occupied with keeping his fire burning at a steady rate. I waited a moment and opened the box – it had no catch or fastening.

There was a book inside. Manderel Valdine had instructed me to burn what I found there. Fortune had favoured me with the means, to hand, but first I opened the book, thinking it must be the journal or other secret writing of an ancient sage. I was disappointed. There had been writing in the book but it was all faded and illegible, worn away by the salt water into which the book had been cast. The pages had also suffered a sea-change and wavering marks like seaweed covered them, and the dried tracks of sea-snails, and fishes' scales. I closed the book and some grains of sand fell from it over my hands.

'Let us rise a little higher, Peder,' I said. 'Here is fresh fuel.'

I placed the old book in Frostfeather's furnace. Soon, it was consumed, and nothing of it except some ashy flakes which blew away in the wind, remained.

'Valdine is dead,' I told Peder.

I decided to keep the box. It was a pretty trophy and should go in my Memory Palace so that when I mused there in my dotage I would recall these long-ago events with perfect clarity. I turned to close its lid and saw, perched on the box's rim, a small yellow manikin about two inches high. It had neither face nor ears but seemed able to see and hear me easily for, as soon as I stretched out my hand to take it, it skipped away.

'Peder!'

My servant joined in the chase. We swung wildly about under the balloon. The manikin was nimble and ran three times about the basket while we, slow heavy creatures, turned to look for it. It danced on the top of the furnace and ran along my sword; but it could fly no more than we could and had no way of escaping to the ground. I caught it in my hands and felt it flutter hard against them like a trapped moth. I opened my hands a crack, enough to see it. This was the soul of the Archmage, not the book. Perhaps I could squeeze it to death.

Peder peered at it.

'It wears something round its neck,' he said. 'Can you not see it?'

'Ah, yes!' It was a length of wispy thread as fine as a hair. I parted my hands a fraction more and Peder managed to get hold of the thread. He held it between finger and thumb and the manikin dangled from it.

'Give it to me!' I swung the tiny creature about in its noose. A thin, high-pitched note came from it, the whine of a gnat. I swung it again; again, it screamed. When I had let it revolve twice more it hung limp. I held its slack body and pulled harder on the thread. It never moved and I dropped it into the fire.

'Now,' I said, 'the Archmage is dead.'

'Long live the Archmage!' Peder smiled at me.

'I think we have some way yet to go,' I cautioned him.

We flew over the forest at a height no greater than three thousand feet. We could not cross the Altaish without breathing cowls and resigned ourselves to a journey of many months. Sometimes, we landed in a wide clearing or on a river bank and picked, or killed, our food in the plenteous larder there. The journey was one of risk and tedium, but its slow passages and privations were too small to trouble a man of action like myself, or like the self I was then.

Some journeys end in meetings, the happy resolution of earlier partings. Some end in disappointment, others in death; but those we choose to remember, to the extent of keeping diaries of what passed or writing long meditations on, the better to recall every event – those are preludes to a better life thereafter and, sometimes, to fresh journeys. I have known men who spent their lives on journeys, whether abroad in the forest and mountain country, or at home amongst their books, and I have often thought that these peregrinations of the mind bring the greatest reward.

Traitors may journey, and the virtuous; soldiers, magicians, merchants, the Rom; favourite sons and prodigals: each has his goal. Mine, in that spring's latter days, was all I had ever desired – fame, wealth, position, name, a beginning to the rest of my life, Nemione – and this great goal and grail of mine waited for me in Pargur, a yellow diamond far below: Summer had come to melt the city's ice and turn her glittering roofs to pools which caught and held the sunshine. Peder and I were dazzled but, looking up, saw white streamers of cloud far above us, the heralds of continuing good weather. The ethereal wind drove them and, willy nilly, our fragile craft on toward the sea.

'It's an ill wind that blows nobody any good,' said Peder morosely. 'There is my house, and my garden with its pear tree and fountain. Now, if it *were* possible to row Frost-feather! – be of good cheer, Master: the updraught from the cliff will turn us back and we shall land safely in the castle courtyard.'

The current of warm air at the edge of the land threw us violently upward. Peder muffled his fires and we began slowly to descend. I saw Castle Sehol on the starboard side; already it towered above us and we heard the hubbub of city and castle as we sank. I glimpsed a scrap of golden cloth hanging limply from the flagstaff on the Devil's Bastion.

'Look, Peder, the Archmage's oriflamme flies,' I said. 'Surely a regent has been appointed?'

'I am not a mage,' he replied. 'Augury is a branch of your trade.'

So, coming light as thistledown to earth, we entered both Pargur and Castle Sehol unopposed. We were not enemies, or were not perceived as such: what connection could there be between the persons of the Archmage's Ambassador and his loyal Navigator and the death last winter of the Archmage? We mounted to his living quarters: these, I intended to secure before I made my verbal assault upon the Council and my intellectual assault upon the secrets of Manderel Valdine's pele tower upon the promontory.

The ante-rooms and staircases were deserted; no doubt the regent had a different suite. I discoursed on the paintings and the architecture as we walked and Peder, falling in with my mood, asked to be given one of the many portraits of the Queen of Love as a memento of our journey and our partnership.

'The Lady will welcome you with open arms!' he said.

'You think so?' I allowed myself to be persuaded, sketching in my mind new apparel for Nemione my bride.

There was a guard on the door, one young soldier whose air of boredom radiated tangibly from him. I greeted him,

'Hilloa! It is a tedious task to guard an empty room!'

'Sir?'

'I have come to survey and itemize Master Valdine's effects.'

'He said nothing, sir. I am not to admit anyone.'

'Come! Such devotion to duty is very well when the master lives but now that the Archmage is dead, what harm is there in admitting his friend to his old quarters?'

'Dead, Sir?' He became zealous and barred my way with his pike. Another moment and he would be shouting for his fellows.

'Was the Archmage's illness a long one?' I asked.

'He is in agony, Sir. We all pray for an end to it, but he will not give up. He writes the daily orders even now, Sir, sitting up in bed.'

I dared show nothing either of my alarm or of my amazement.

'May I not enter to pray with him?'

'No, Sir. Any who wish to speak with him must report to

174

the guard below. I do not understand how you walked past them.'

'In the same way I entered Pargur in the winter of last year. Like this,' I said, as I concentrated all the force of my remarkable mind upon his dull brain. He met me with an unscaleable, blank wall.

'You *will* admit me. I am Koschei.'

'Never, Sir.'

'Very well – but you will put down your pike and draw your sword. That's the way. Now, on guard.'

It took me three minutes to despatch him. The guards came running but the commotion was over and the stubborn guard dead at me feet. I did not know if I could quell four men but, fortunately, they were led by Baptist Olburn, their captain and the castle's torturer. I had not seen him since the old days, when he was Proctor in the Cloister, and a cruel ruffian to boot. Gathering my courage, I hailed him.

'Why, Olburn – you would not harm your old whipping-post, your little whining dog?' I put my bloodied hands up to my face and whimpered like a frightened child.

'Corbillion!' the torturer roared. 'Stand up and take your punishment like a man!' He thumped my chest and threw me off balance: it was a fond embrace to him.

'You used to terrify me,' I said.

'Whipping boys is tedious work. I longed to punish the girls,' he said.

'How does Nemione?'

'She has the men just – there!' He gestured lewdly with his thumb. 'Her beauty is a wondrous thing, Master Corbillion. It would weaken the knees and sap the will of a blind celibate.'

I pointed at the man I had killed.

'I must see the Archmage,' I said.

'Is that a request to the captain of the guard?'

'It is indeed. Will you let me in there, Olburn?'

He studied me, his green eyes (whose gaze used to terrify

me) seeming to glow with a concentration which made his bulk seem more terrible. He must have spent one of his lives as a bear.

'You have not lost the blood-lust and temper of a Green Wolf but you have acquired a new dimension. And you have survived the Archmage's orders, tamed Peder and brought him back with you. I think I shall – yes, I will,' he said. 'The time grows ever more disjointed.'

He called for the key and opened the door. I heard Manderel Valdine's agonized groans and his racking cough before I stepped up to the bed and roughly pulled its curtains aside.

'Koschei!'

'Peder failed his mission – though he tried well,' I said. 'I thought I had killed you, twice.'

Valdine laughed, as much as he was able. 'The book was worthless,' he said. 'It was once the grimoire of a noble magician, but five hundred years on the sea bed will destroy anything. The nuns of Polnisha of course believe otherwise.'

'The yellow manikin?'

'A soul, dolt! Someone's soul.'

'But whose?'

'Its loss is not your concern. Others exist to grieve over it. You are tightly held between the springing tines of a cleft stick, Koschei. Can you feel the pressure? Your sword – which I see is bloodied; I suppose poor Michael is your most recent victim – is of no use to you. You did not find my soul: you cannot kill me – oh, inflict further agony if you will.'

I pushed the blade into his bedding until the feathers spilled. I raged.

'You will have to retire, Koschei,' said Valdine, 'until you think of something better than this crude soldier's force.' He picked up his pen again. 'The orders, Baptist. Peder, pass me my book. I shall read of love as I cannot practise it.'

He read a few lines, put his pen in the book to mark his place and laid it down.

'I tire easily, Peder,' he said. 'Perhaps you would read to me.'

'I forbid it!'

'Oh? He is your creature now? Read to me, Peder.'

The man looked at me to gauge my temper. I nodded, and he opened the book and prepared to read.

'Such a pity, I used to have a charming little bookmark,' said Valdine. 'I wonder where I have mislaid it?'

'The red one, sir?'

'Yes, so pretty. Never mind, read.'

'"Any woman, as I have told you in Discourse I, may felicitously be played upon to produce a tune, but if you will play upon your Lady you must imagine the finest taut-stringed spinet. The wires represent her nerves and sinews. The outside of the instrument, inlaid with divers precious veneers as mother-of-pearl, silver, gold, malachite, or that stone which men call Goblin's Copper, you may bestrew with such gifts as you can get, as rosebuds, perfumes, neck-laces, as liberally as the housewife uses her unguents and polishes. But if you will make her sing sweet airs you must learn which of her Parts –"'

I went out, passing Olburn and his lieutenants, who did not spare me a glance. I would have preferred imprisonment or torture to this ignominy. Peder, Olburn and the guards surrounded Valdine like a pack of liverless spaniels.

I sat alone in my rooms, remembering how Nemione, standing by the chair I now sat in, had mocked me and, afterwards, kissed me in the door. I could not go to her and admit my failure in her cause. She would hear of it soon enough. The lamplighter came along the street; I heard his cry from far off. As the flame outside my window sprang into life and the room was filled with its diffuse glow, someone knocked on the door.

'Who's there?' I called. It was not locked.

'Peder Drum. I am coming in.'

'What can you want?' He stood before me looking glum.

'I am still your servant. It was politic to stay with Valdine and read him his erotica.'

'And now it is politic to come here and disturb me in my study?'

'I have folded Frostfeather and packed her away in her basket,' he said. 'I will prepare your supper.'

He made me a savoury dish of toasted cheese, and young chickens which he ran out to buy from my neighbour who kept a yard of cackling poultry. He washed the dishes and put clean linen on my bed.

'Rest, Master,' he said. 'It will all seem different in the morning.'

I slept deeply for several hours and woke to hear the clock on the Library tower strike four. Dawn had come and the lemon-coloured light in my room promised heat and sunshine. I looked at the ceiling, which I had caused to be painted with a design of planets. A mouse scratched somewhere in the room. Perhaps I would get a cat. The mouse was bold, looking for food. It would be disappointed. I looked across at the chair where I had left my clothes and saw Peder, no mouse, going through my pockets. I said nothing, only watched him and feigned sleep. He took out and opened my wallet – the same wallet I had carried on my first journey through the forest. Nemione's hair was in it.

Peder opened the various pockets carefully and, at last pulled out a bookmark, long, red and tasselled: the marker I had taken from Valdine's reading desk because it pleased me – and pleased me to steal a trifle from him.

'Is that you, Peder?' I said sleepily, as if I had just woken.

He laid my wallet softly down and slipped the marker into his pocket.

'It is, Master. I heard you cough and came to see if you were comfortable. I feared you might have taken a chill in Frostfeather yesterday.'

I did not know if he was armed.

178

'That is kind of you, Peder. I feel quite well and require nothing but sleep until eight.'

'Very well, Master.' He took a step forward. No weapon was visible; but he might have got a new pistol to replace the one I had thrown into the Altaish.

'Peder, perhaps you would tuck in my blankets more tightly?'

He came closer, near enough, and I, rearing up in the bed like a panther, leapt upon him. For the second time, we wrestled. My bed was firmer than the floor of the basket and I soon pinned him under me. He was only a Navigator and here, out of his element, he was subject and I king.

'Do you read – much – Peder?' I panted.

'Yes!' He was not afraid. I wished I had used magic on him and terrified him.

'And need a bookmark in case you fall asleep over your text?'

'It is a useful device.'

'So useful it becomes necessary to steal one from your master instead of buying your own?'

'If you will release me, I will tell you something,' he said.

'What can you tell me about a petty crime?'

'I can tell you the whereabouts of Manderel Valdine's soul.'

'I will not let you go, but I will permit you to take a less servile position.'

Peder moved in my grasp until he was upright.

'I am yours,' he said. 'There is no need to mistrust me –'

'– You have betrayed my trust –'

'– I am about to redeem it. The soul of the Archmage is hidden in the bookmark. Here.' He extracted it. 'Take it.'

'How can I believe you?' I asked him.

'Make a trial. Cut it up: you will soon hear of his death. Or better, destroy it in his presence. He is so sick that all his powers have deserted him, and Olburn only waits for the next move.'

179

'Why did you not steal it before?'

'You held the upper hand.'

'As I still do. What would you have done if you had restored his soul to the Archmage?'

'Served him. It is yours now and I will serve you.'

I made Peder responsible for the disposal of the corpse of his old master. I wanted to be sure he understood the finality of death in Malthassa, even for a mage, and I made certain stipulations: Manderel Valdine was not to buried, either in consecrated or unconsecrated ground, nor was his body to be cast away in any river or the sea. Nor was he to be burned, entombed above the ground or in a cave or cellar; his remains were not to be glorified upon a pillar, or with a cenotaph or other memorial in Pargur or any of its manifestations. The body was not to be taken out of Pargur.

Peder employed Olburn to cut the body up. He fed each neatly butchered section to the wild dogs which roam the streets in Nether-Pargur.

You ask why I did not serve Peder Drum in the same way? Yes, I was a fool; but the man's knowledge was useful to me and I admired him for his mastery over the air. Compared with Peder, the other navigators were mere perching birds.

I took care of the ashes of the bookmark. The memory they awoke was dear to me. I had held the tasselled marker over Valdine in his bed and cut it in ribbons, afterwards burning them in a censer. Their fumes smelt sweeter to me than the rarest musks or oil-of-cedar. When I reassembled my Memory Palace in Pargur, as I intended, I would keep the censer and its dry content in a specially-constructed reliquary; meanwhile, I kept them under lock, key and sigil. I was satisfied and content. Valdine had made wondrous music as he died.

* * *

I wore my soldier's garb to greet the civilian governors of Pargur. They acknowledged me as Usurper and invited me to prove my powers; meanwhile, they appointed Elzevir Tate, the furrier, Regent. I particularly remember, for I keep the flag in my Palace, the lowering of Valdine's oriflamme and the raising of the city standard in its place. Below it on the rope they flew the small multicoloured pennant which shows that the governaunce of the city is in jeopardy.

My preparations for dinner with Nemione I made with greater care. Peder had found a body servant for me, a slow but particular old fellow named Ivo. An orphan of the Septrentine wars, he had no other name. He was respectful and quiet and knew his discreet work.

Ivo shaved me and trimmed my beard and hair. He cut my nails, stood back and surveyed my naked body.

'Next, the bath,' he said. 'Master Koschei, if you would.'

I lay an hour in the bath, as Ivo instructed me. I would leave it much refreshed, he said, and himself renewed the cooling water with fresh jugs of hot. A lutanist he had engaged played to me as I bathed. When the hour was up Ivo brought me a glass of wine and dried me as carefully as if he were a mother, and I her babe. Then Ivo dressed me.

At seven by the Library clock I stood complete before the mirror and admired myself. I was then twenty-seven years and six months old and was healthy, eager and full of energy, no cloister mouse or crypt weasel but as fine a man as any gallant on the streets of Uppermost Pargur. My hidden and devious mind was that of a much older man, one of maturity and experience, although in hindsight I acknowledge the intemperate fits of pride and sheer rage which occasionally possessed me. I wore a suit (scarlet, white and black it was) of the sort the Lord Marshall favoured and carried three weapons: the one Nature gave me, a dagger in a gilded ivory case, and a posy tied up in lace to give the Lady Nemione.

Ivo fussed about me. He tucked a handkerchief in my breast pocket and pulled and teased it until its black-work edging was displayed to his satisfaction. He surveyed me once more, squinting at me with his watery old eyes as if he would compare the naked, unadorned foundation he had scoured clean with the finished man.

'A fine sight, Master Koschei, a goodly sight. You will dazzle her.'

'Let us drink to it, Ivo!'

I toasted him, but he would take no wine.

'I shall drink my ale later and think of you and the lady,' he said.

Nemione received me in one of the castle's day-rooms. I watched her carefully from the first and saw, as soon as I entered the room, that she appreciated my outside and the fashionable rags in which I had decked it. Must I describe her clothing again? Indeed, I must: her dress was so much a part of her, the set and scenery before which she played. The gown was dull gold, a figured brocade – I have a piece of it here. Let me look. There are Arcadian lovers who kiss, in the weave. There is a tomb also. I had not noticed that before, but now its significance is obvious. At the time I saw only the lovers and her amber jewellery, the largest beads of which lay on her breast above the kerchief she had tucked into the bosom of the gown. Its skirt was short enough to show her ankles, the clocks on her stockings and the red heels of her shoes. She smiled, but her speech was still barbed.

'The cloister mouse has become a popinjay!' she said.

I bowed and presented her with my posy.

'You will find that this particular popinjay is not stuffed with straw,' I said. Nemione buried her face in the posy and eyed me over its rim.

'With what, then?' she challenged. 'Is he puffed up with pride in his appearance, with empty boasts, or with pure lust?'

'With love, Nemione,' I said. 'I have carried my memory of you across the Altaish and beyond the Plains into SanZu. It has survived every peril.'

'Then we had better go into my Court of Love,' she said.

Her throne had been removed from the dais, and a table, a tall candelabrum and two chairs set there in its place. I helped Nemione to seat herself in one of these and took the other myself. She laid down her posy, rested her elbows on the table and her chin upon her hands and gave me a long, sapphire look. It made me giddy. I saw in it a future of endless intimate years. Nemione sat up and clapped her hands and Erchon ran in to answer her summons, a lighted taper in his hand. The very model of a house servant, he ignored me and bowed low before his mistress.

'Send in the food, Erchon,' Nemione bade him.

'Will you have music, my lady?'

'I will deal with that, Erchon; keep you to the duties I have given you.'

The dwarf bowed again and left us.

'You would enjoy a little music, Koschei?'

'If it also pleases you, my Lady.'

I did not see her move, nor speak or shift her gaze from me, but the five statues which stood in the five corners of the room took each a step forward and raised its hands. The first had a recorder, the second a little drum, the third a dulcimer, while the fourth and fifth held up chimes and bells. They began to play in such a lively manner that I could have believed them creatures of flesh and blood.

'Soft music!' Nemione cried.

Then came the food, brought in by a line of solemn little girls clad all alike in short white gowns with wreaths of summer flowers in their hair. These, too, looked mortal till they came close and the absolute perfection and regularity of their features showed them to be mutes fashioned out of Nemione's sweet energy and the spirits of the damned. The eyes of these childish creatures were cruel. The last in the line, which carried a flagon of wine, was different, its skin slippery and blue-green, its sparse black hair awry like waterweed in a flood and its swollen lips – a most hideous touch – borrowed from a pouting fish.

'Bring the wine to my guest,' Nemione instructed it and it came and stood beside me in a miasma of river-stench and marsh-gas. 'Now pour.' Meanwhile, its companions served up game and sauces, long stems of asparagus and blunt scales from the heads of girasoles all drenched in butter.

'Did you make all these creatures?' I asked my Lady.

'Yes. All. Do you think my taste too choice to allow deformity, Koschei?' She picked up her knife and began to shave thin slices of flesh from the breast of a fowl. 'Monstrosity is the north face of beauty and one cannot be properly appreciated without knowledge of the other – as the libertine must experience pain in order to come at a true understanding of pleasure.'

'The pretty ones, I might have expected,' I said, 'but this, this ganymede – it must be an experiment, a templet. No doubt you have fashioned it for another use and only bid it serve at table to teach it good manners.'

'It is an uncouth thing, certainly.' She dipped the tip her long forefinger in one of the dishes and licked the sauce from it. 'Ginger, Koschei, mustard, pepper! Taste them!' She poured a great pool of the sauce over my meat. It burned my mouth as I ate; she, who ate the same, did not appear to suffer.

'Is your blood hot enough now, Koschei?' Nemione said. 'Does your heart burn?'

I smiled: 'Only for you, my Lady.'

She pushed her empty plate away. At once, the sham maidens came to remove it and took away all the dishes. The fishy one, still by me, refilled my glass every time I put it down. The musicians sounded a tinkling fanfare, as if ice fell upon glass, and Erchon carried in ice indeed, a mermaid carved from a block of it.

'Something to cool your palate, Koschei,' Nemione said. 'Will you have breast or belly? A little tail perhaps?'

'I will have whatever you, yourself, have. You must guide me in the appreciation of this novel dish.'

'Oh, I will only take a finger or two. That is no kind of portion for a man.'

'Then,' I said, 'I will take her head.'

'May it bring you wisdom!' With the precision of a surgeon and one warm breath, Nemione divided the head from the body and in the same way, removed the little finger from the decapitated mermaid's right hand. She put it in her mouth and bit it in two. The ice in crunched in her mouth. I stared at the silent head in my dish. It had a face I recognized, that of her golden mouthpiece, Roszi.

'Break off her nose, Koschei! Why do you not taste her lips?'

Already, the head was melting. Tears streamed from its eyes and clear spittle from its mouth. I spooned up some of the liquor: it tasted salty. The disintegrating head continued to stare and I stared steadily back. It gave me a watery smile as its features dissolved into clear water.

'I mean to show you what a sham love is,' Nemione said.

Her gaze met mine; once more, those brilliant eyes unmanned me and I felt myself weak as water. I looked away and, in so avoiding her blue glance, caught sight of the guard in the corridor. His studded jesserant, pike and leather helmet made virile trespass in Nemione's world of gramarye and I thought of my hideous mentor of the forest, the Om Ren and, taking strength from the memory, I resolved to fight. I stirred the liquid which had been the ice-cold sea-maiden with my fingers and my mind. The ice began to reform.

'And I,' I said, 'will prove love's strength and infallibility.'

Time trod slowly but I had no idea of its passing. The head of the mermaid re-formed under my command, exactly as it had been before. I was pleased, not only with my power to make an image of Nemione's familiar, but also with my perseverance. I waved my hand to indicate that Nemione should take her turn. The icy surface of the mermaid's brow reflected her azure concentration and she blushed delightfully with her effort. Tiny beads of moisture grew upon her brow and her upper lip. I wished I might kiss them away.

In the dish, the mermaid's features leached slowly away until she was water. I took my turn once more: the mermaid's cold face returned. We struggled long, Nemione and I, the dish between us. At last, we were exhausted and there was neither ice nor water in the dish, but a mush which was not one nor the other, continually in flux. Nemione closed her eyes in weariness for an instant – a breath, a sigh – and I, through a mist of failed concentration and imminent megrim, willed the head into being. Patiently, it rose up from the freezing water and returned my gaze.

'Your try, Lady,' I said.

Nemione bowed her head. She sat unhappily in my dominion but did not attempt escape. On the contrary, she was so quiet and tearful that I stretched an errant hand across the table to hold hers and comfort her. She recoiled from me.

'The weird Child is mine,' she said sullenly. 'Come, my daughter.' She beckoned to the fishy imp which left my side to kneel at hers.

'It serves and obeys you, certainly, and the energy you used in fashioning it makes it your slave. It is obliged to you for its very existence.'

'All those, yes; but I gave birth to it – as other women do. It was born in the spring, while you were away.'

Fear and its companion, rage, alerted me but I tempered them.

'Who dared touch you?' I said quietly. 'What obscene incubus invaded the sanctuary of your room and your body to father it?'

'It is Manderel's Child, Koschei. I agreed to bear it for

him and, when it was a year old, to give it him for his sole use. Listen! I will tell you what passed between us. It is not as you think.

'Manderel wrote to me, no love letter this nor poem, but a heartfelt and servile request: if he found a way by which I might painlessly bear his Child without the customary intercourse, he would free me from all obligation, past and future, to him and let me go to Castle Lorne.

'One winter's day, when I was swimming in the hot baths in the castle gardens, my maidservant came to me. She brought me a legal parchment and a small bottle like a perfume vial. I stared at them both for a long while. The document was the agreement between Manderel Valdine and myself, to bear his Child under the conditions (which were specified) of his request. The bottle contained the last of his seed. I thought, it will be weak stuff given his case; most likely it is dead already. I called for a pen and signed; then, as the document instructed, I tipped the seed in its vile liquor into the pool with me. I felt nothing, though I swam and lay there for two hours. When I was dressed I went about my affairs as usual, continuing my studies in magic, music and philosophy. I held court over my lovelorn subjects in the afternoons. Soon I knew that Manderel's last vain mix of magic and matter had worked. I was with child and I sent him a note of one word, "Success."

'I carried the Child two months and felt it quicken. It was born after three months had passed, giving me no more pain than does a surfeit of good food on a feast-day: a little white slimy thing no bigger than your thumb which yet had the strength to crawl on to my leg and, thence, to my belly – nay, further. I gave it suck. It was my babe. I fed it every hour for two days; by then, it had grown a blue skin and was as long as your arm. It hurt me with its sharp teeth when I nursed it.

'"You must be fed meat," I said to it. "You grow apace and I can no longer support you with my milk." It spoke its

187

first word then: "Fish" and fish was brought for it, stewed in milk. It refused to eat, crying still for "Fish" and so I sent for carpling from the fishponds and these it devoured, starting at the head and working down the body of each fish until it had eaten five. It grew again, almost as big as it is now. It walked and ran about my room and sang with the voice of a young river.'

I stared at her as if she were a gorgon and had mesmerized me.

'Does it have a name?' I asked. I thought a good name bestowed upon it might mitigate its ugliness and turn it into something I could tolerate. Then I would disregard these loathsome matters, court Nemione until she deferred to me and, in wedding and possessing her, dispel the last vestige of Manderel Valdine.

'I was to call it Gaster in memory of his traitorous son. But it seems to be female and so, it is nameless. What should I call it? Destiny or Hope? Belle or Brute?'

'Why did you agree?'

'It was the better of my desperate choices and I reasoned that what Manderel asked for was neither marriage nor a lover's privilege, but something abstract – harmless.'

'Pretty one!' she called suddenly. The Fish-Child stood up and twirled upon its finny feet. It danced and sidled up to her and she let it climb into her lap and rest its ugly head upon her breast.

'There, there,' she said, and held its bloated face to her white bosom. I could not sit still opposite her and watch. I rose, jumped from the dais, and walked about the room. The statues, which long ago had stopped playing and retired to their places, eyed me cruelly. I turned about and went back to Nemione. Her savage Fish-Child still nestled in her lap.

'I think I have won, Koschei,' she said. 'Erchon!'

Her dwarf took the Child from her and hoisted it on his back. They left the room together, she towering over the silver dwarf who carried her misbegotten offspring pick-a-back as if it were the legitimate child of a lawful marriage made before God.

I could have smiled at my defeat if Erchon, pressing his suit, had overcome her maiden's pride to win her. Or raped her so that she bore his mongrel! Tragedy would have made her a heroine not this base conspirator. Her virgin body brought into being the vile miscegenation conceived in Valdine's corrupt mind; I could not bear to think of their perverted union in the pool.

I ran from the Court of Love to the castle gate, forcing the guide to hurry through the maze before me. The misleading reflections in the prism blinded me; without Estragon to lead me I would have been for ever lost. I hurled myself through the changeable streets, not caring where I went: there was some relief in action. Instinct alone brought me to my own door and I stumbled up the stairs, pushing past Ivo who came out to greet me. In the sanctuary of my room, I sat down and wept.

I sat in my room. Bereft. Shamed. It took two days for me to understand which was the worst condition. I called for food and fresh clothes. Then, with inner and outer man refreshed, I descended to the lowest and most vile level of Pargur's changeable territory. Here I wasted a week in debauchery.

In Nether Pargur, to which zealots liken Hell saying it cannot be more depraved, I swung with a harlot on a glass trapeze, swam in milk with another, and rogered a third while I watched a troupe of young men dance in travesty. I think I did these things although there is no record in the Memory Palace. I found lodgings in a house of ill-fame and there lay on a gilded sofa smoking the pipe of oblivion until I soared up out of Pargur and its mutabilities and entered the world of dreams and make-believe.

Erchon was waiting for me when at last I came home. He smiled wryly when he saw me.

'I am here for old times' sake,' he said.

'Those uncomplicated days are long gone,' I answered. 'What confronts me now is a maze of new ideas. I must live by my wits, Erchon, to win. My first task is to discover the way to the Archmage's pele tower.'

'Peklo,' he said. 'That conundrum is the reason for my visit. Here is my hand – in comradeship: I can only guide you part of the way.'

'My success is in your interest?'

'Your victory is of great interest to all dwarves and men.'

'And Nemione? Your loyal service?'

'You know that I, too, love her vainly, Master Usurper. But it is not wounded vanity or disappointed desire which prompt me. Pargur will vanish if the complex tides of its being are subject to wilful female magic alone. The city needs an Archmage.

'I will help you; but I will not swear allegiance nor shall I desert my Lady. When my short scene is done, I shall return to Castle Lorne.'

'How do you propose to help me, Erchon?'

'I am not an indifferent swordsman, when one is needed, and I have a good sense of direction. Also, I know the whereabouts of the map which shows the way to Peklo.'

'You *know* it? What good fortune!'

'As long as I give you my knowledge, Master – and telling brings its own problems. The map can only be in one place and that is in the matter that was the Archmage.'

'It no longer exists. Peder fed his butchered body to the pye-dogs.'

'Then, Master Koschei, you must indeed use your wits.'

Thus Erchon condemned me to many more inactive days of thought. Though Ivo went abroad on my errands, I did not move from my rooms until I had a scheme and then, I hesitated. Soon, it rained, light and successive summer showers which drove the citizens on the street below my window into the shelter of the shops and taverns. I went out to the fishmongers and, from thence, a parcel beneath my arm, to the water meadows beside the River Lytha where I sat beneath a willow tree and waited.

Ivo, my third eye, had every day observed Erchon strolling with a small companion beside the river. Soon, from my leafy shelter, I saw him coming. The other, who could have been his dwarf-wife or any comrade of his race, was muffled in a cloak. I stepped out into their path.

'Do you swim with it as well?' I said.

Erchon caught hold of the Child so that it should not take fright and run away.

'I see that you have reached your conclusion, Master Usurper,' he said.

'I mean to prove my suppositions at the least. Will it sit under the tree?'

'It is a shy thing but it loves to be entertained, and I think you have the best means of entertaining it in your parcel. Come, Sprat, let us sit down and talk with this gentleman.'

'Sprat?'

'My name only. My Lady, though she dotes on the Child, will not give it one.'

The Child watched apprehensively with open mouth and sharp teeth on view. Its thin hair had been dressed in plaits and it wore a sumptuous gown of the kind its mother loved. Its finned feet showed beneath the embroidered hem.

'Why does she not push it in the river?' I whispered to Erchon.

'Master, she is woman!'

'I suppose every mother loves her child.' I undid the string which tied my parcel and unfolded the several layers of paper to reveal a plump young smolt. Nemione's Child cried out at the sight, a strange and forlorn whistle like that of the lone otter I once heard on a moonlit stretch of the Esp at home. I offered it the fish and turned away, for I still could scarce endure to behold it and I knew that if I saw it eat the raw fish, I must leave. The noise of its gulpings and tearings was enough.

'She is satisfied,' Erchon said. 'Turn this way, or she will be offended. She is more sensitive than she looks.'

'She? It,' I said, but I turned about to see the creature baring its teeth at me.

'She smiles,' said Erchon.

I bared my own teeth in reply and, swallowing my disgust, spoke to the Child.

'You father was a noble man,' I told it, 'but he is dead. (Does it understand me, Erchon?) I am also a magician who, since he cannot talk with Manderel Valdine, must needs visit you – all that is left of the greatest mage.'

The teeth remained uncovered.

'Well, then, will you let me hold your hand in mine for a while so that I may get an impression of your father's greatness?'

The teeth were covered now, by the goldfish lips. The head moved up and down.

Erchon spoke for the creature: '"Yes."'

'Why doesn't it reply? It understands me.'

'Fish have no speech organs.'

'Then why did Valdine not get an articulate child?'

'Who knows the mind of an archmage? Perhaps, because he was so weak, he failed, and this unfinished creature was all he could engender. You must know that every man climbs the successive steps of creation in the womb.'

Willing courage into my veins, I held out my left hand and Nemione's ill-gotten scion extended a webbed mockery: I felt its cold, damp skin against mine and could not suppress a shudder. To my horror, it stroked my face with its other hand.

'She thinks you are warm and would comfort you,' said

Erchon. I closed my eyes. The fishy hand lay quietly in mine and I felt, faint as the heartbeat of a mouse, the shadow of Valdine's memory stir. I saw him from a great way off and as he was in the Otherworld, seated on a stone at the bottom of an echoing well.

'It works!' I whispered to Erchon and immediately cursed myself, for the vision disappeared at the eager sound of my voice.

Thereafter I met Erchon and the weird Child, for which Nemione had no name but which the dwarf called Sprat, each day, and each time I brought it a choice, whole fish. By night, I read in my books, seeking a precedent for what I had to do. A week passed. The Child remaining passive, I progressed (if the word will suffice to describe my disquiet) so that I was able to sit her on my knee and so receive a strong impression of her dead, once-potent sire.

On the eighth day I persuaded Erchon to leave me alone with the Child, which liked to play in the leafy tent beneath the willow tree. I gave him money for ale, and promises, and, while he drank in the nearest tavern, I sat with the Child in my arms and thought about what I must do next. On the ninth day Erchon left me as soon as my money was in his hand. The willow tree hid my base actions from the world but, to be the safer, I cast a pall of silence over the Child and myself.

The she-shaman, Katsura, once called up the spirit of an alraun which had been confined a thousand years in hell. She clothed his ash-root image in the simulacra of male garments, and fed it on bread and wine. The image woke and moved, but it would not speak to Katsura nor tell her the secrets she longed to know. Katsura laboured hard and cut a new image, man-sized, from a living ash. On this, she resolved to work her strongest magic, of carnal longing and the fulfilment of desire.

193

I took my last precautions, which were to tie its sash tight about the Child's mouth and bind its hands with the ribbons from its hair. Then, though I did not know what I should find beneath its long skirts, I lifted them, and forced it. There were orifices like those of a woman. This was the magic Katsura had used; to make it work in my needy case, I imagined that I had the Fish-Child's mother under me.

As I expended my virility, my understanding rose up in the weird Child's consciousness and, passing through a terrible chasm where demons were engaged in hideous games, soared until it rested in Valdine's mind. I read his past and knew his hopes and disappointments. I read his 'map' and learned the way to Peklo tower.

I looked down at the Fish-Child, which was weeping silently. Quickly, I covered it up and covered myself. My use of it was no worse than the employment of a whore: it would get its wages and besides, was cold-blooded. I unbound it and rewarded it with the tail of a silver salmon and with sturgeon's eggs. Its snivelling and whimpering ceased at once and it allowed me to tie the ribbons back in its hair while it fed. I kept the sash. (This is the very one, faded now. It was the colour of a ripe cherry when Nemione's Child wore it. I still believe my own sacrifice of taste, pleasure and discernment justified: the perverse union was but a small step on my way to Valdine's throne.)

When Erchon returned I gave him a purse of silver to use for the entertainment of the Child.

'Do not bring it to me any more,' I told him. 'I have what I need.'

If Erchon was not made purblind by my promises and coins, he never gave sign of it. He came to my rooms next day, all quickness and vitality, spoiling for adventure, armed cap à pie.

'You have seen the map, Master Usurper,' he said eagerly. 'When do we set off?'

To disappoint an accomplice is unwise.

'Tomorrow, Master Scantling,' I replied, using the old nickname. 'After dark. You will enjoy yourself: we must first assail the white hills and bosky mounts of Nether Pargur. When they are safely conquered we can proceed: there is a gate –'

'To a hidden way?'

'Something like. You shall see.'

The thought that I, a young man with hearty appetites, should have been surprised by the appetites of a dwarf astonishes me today. I intended to lose Erchon in the labyrinthine purlieus of Nether Pargur but never dreamed how easy it would be. He succumbed to the first temptation, the second. And the third – I left him in the arms of a lusty country girl who had come to Pargur to sell a parcel of her land and made a better profit out of selling her flesh (I paid Erchon's reckoning). I went into the jakes, which was untenanted, and, after relieving myself, spoke the formula I had found in Valdine's mind. There had never been a map. In a trice I was whisked away. A she-devil appeared in the void beneath my spinning body and bore me up in her arms. I saw the tower-top and the sharp rocks of the lonely promontory below and, while I wished I had stayed to enjoy the soft continents the dwarf was exploring, found myself descending rapidly. The demon had dropped me.

I screamed, but only once, for my speed halved, then quartered, and so by increments decreased until I stood safe, and still unbuttoned, on Peklo tower. Quickly, I fastened the buttons. The door of the little bartizan on the roof stood ajar. I pushed it open and ran down the spiral stair into the Archmage's sanctum. The magic map hung on the wall, just as I had seen it in the fire I conjured for the Om Ren. Alembics, glass retorts and bottles of poison lined the shelves and a painted globe stood in the centre of the room. I breathed deeply, a great lungful of the chymic air. It excited me, far more than anything I had ever experienced; this excitation was a thing of the mind, an intense cerebral frisson. I looked at the map. It was not the one I had seen before. This showed the web of narrow streets I had left behind me – there was Mistress Innocent's house of pleasure. I stared at the globe, puzzled: Malthassa – the letters were clear – was not a country nor a continent but the whole world. The globe began slowly to revolve. Pargur passed me, and Vonta, Ma and Flaxberry. Great areas of the forest were marked 'terra incognita'. I saw Myrah, Tanter and Espmoss and I thought: I can use this device to bring the Memory Palace from Espmoss to Pargur – where shall I site it? The gardens of Castle Sehol would be a fine place, already planted with box hedges and laid out in perfect symmetry, or upon a lake permanently frozen – but where to begin? The room was full of objects which demanded my investigation; there were the floors below. I went to view them.

Immediately below, the library, a small room full of choice volumes bound in many-coloured leathers and silks. I could see Valdine's Book lying on a table, unmistakable in its binding of human skin, but I dare not touch or read it; I did not even dare to enter the library at this stage. Below this floor I found luxurious living quarters, one room also it is true but so richly appointed that I made sums of their worth as I examined each item. One of Valdine's golden robes hung in a closet, and displayed upon an ebony bracket shaped like a heart I found an ivory statuette. Black and white, I mused, darkness and light: Manderel Valdine and Nemione Sophronia Baldwin, for it was her image. I took it up to examine, while I wondered, did she sit for the sculptor? Was it a work of the imagination? I, who in my remembered fancy had seen her naked, compared my dreams with those of the artist. They were the same. I held Nemione in my hands, touched her and turned her about, remembering her false kisses and her empty promises. My experiences with the whores and my studies in the library of the nunnery had shown me what women enjoy and I vowed that I would have her, whatever it cost me and, in token, kissed the cold breasts of the statuette.

A storeroom occupied the lowest floor. There was very little in it beside some cases of wine and a ladder. The door into the tower opened out of this room; but who could use it? I turned the key and opened the door. The rock below was bare and inhospitable. I could hear the roar of an angry sea.

The final secret to be discovered was underneath all this, accessible by a grating in the storeroom floor: a deep, dank oubliette, a cellar so strong and dark the liveliest demon might be shackled and confined inside it. I saw Nemione there, her fine clothes sodden and soiled, her lovely body pinioned. The intensity of my vision shocked me but I recognized it as the truth. My huge ambition brooked no failure.

I returned to the bedroom and drank a glass of water there; next unbuckled my weapons and cuirass and removed them; I undressed, knelt down, and made my first prayer to Urthamma. Then, rising determinedly up, I put on Valdine's robe; which my murdering of him made mine.

Will you learn my Art and painful Craft? Then I must fill a hundred pages with descriptions of occult style and technique and a hundred more with the fruits of a thousand years' study and yet more hundreds with summaries of libraries full of almanacs, demonologies, herbals, horoscopes, geometries, grimoires, pharmacopoeiae &c. I must make primers in the ancient languages, list quodlibets, rebuses, zodiacs, words of virtue such as Origo, Sol, Floy, Ischyros and so forth, and words of bane which cannot be written. I shall be obliged to become a teacher of necromancy, cartomancy, rhabdomancy, geomancy, zoomancy and the rest. After these, it will be necessary to teach the proper passes, the meditations and the incantations; the names of the demons, lesser and greater; the names of the gods and the angels; the ways of calling a familiar, a sooterkin, an imp, a sprite; the manner by which it is best to seduce a nivasha; the nine names of Zernebock – and there are those who say that magicians are born, not made, and those who prove the truth of the saying such as myself, the Archmage Koschei.

Let my Art remain Enigma and my appearance be at least as mutable as divine Pargur. The heart of the matter at present under consideration is the conveying of my Memory Palace entire from the Garden of the Virtues at Espmoss to the gardens of Castle Sehol. Though the exercise and effort brought me within sight of hell, I used my wits, the globe and the map.

When I had put off the robe, I slept in Valdine's bed until I was recovered and then, resuming my ordinary clothing and my arms and armour, spoke his formula in reverse and was whirled aloft.

The key to the Memory Palace was in my wallet. While I extracted it I stood before the little marble building marvelling at the symmetry of this folly built upon my sweat and grime. It stood in one of the beds of the knot garden, a low box hedge ringing it. In its old place the half-finished cruciform garden would remain. Without a reason for its existence it would be utterly debased, the void circle at the centre its only quiddity. It pleased me to imagine this cenotaph to the memory of my memories. I determined, after leaving space for the expansion of the Palace, to have a replica of the Virtue Garden (alike unfinished) constructed about its present site.

Admiring the pattern as I progressed, I walked up the steps of saurian porphyry and unlocked the bronze doors. Inside, all was quiet; indeed, the place had that air of melancholy mustiness which soon grows in an unused building. I crossed the first dark room and threw open the shutters. The warm light of Pargur fell into the room, illuminating the table on which I had set out the counting-shells I took from Nemione's desk in school, and the closed door. I stood a moment at the table, caressing one of the smooth shells, before going to the door, opening it and climbing the stair which led out of the cupboard. By a precipitous route about the galleries and vaulting, I climbed into a small room. From its window high above the crossing of the cathedral one can look down and see the cloister roof and Nemione's window. She is always there, a fleeting memory dressed in green and white, in her hands the flowers she has picked a-Maying. I looked, and sighed. The room was full of my past and future sighs. I heard the latest one echoing round the room – and I heard a heavy footstep on the stair. Quickly, I concealed myself: the shadow behind the door was the only hiding place. I rested my eager right hand on the hilt of my sword and gripped its scabbard.

There entered a shambling creature which blocked out the light. It sniffed deep and, scenting me, turned about. I saw that it carried a long rope which had a noose at one end.

'My friend,' I said urgently, 'It is I, Koschei the Magician. Do not strike!'

The Om Ren, the Wild Man, roared. His terrifying laugh smothered my redundant sighs.

'I see Koschei the Coward!' he said. 'Is that a spell in your hand?'

'How did you enter without a key?'

'Memories are not always bidden. I am an unexpected visitor, but no doubt this pleasant little palace is full of entertainments. I should like to see your library.'

'There is no library.'

'Are you certain? Let us pass through that door there, and see what we can find.'

A new door appeared in the wall as he spoke. I recognized

199

it: the door to Manderel Valdine's library at Peklo, standing ajar as I had seen it not half an hour before.

'It is yours now,' said the Om Ren. 'As I am sure you must remember.'

I stepped into my library. Valdine's Book lay on the table, unmistakable in its binding of human skin, and I touched it. I opened the Book, no longer afraid that a shadowy force would strike me because I was looking at a memory.

Inside the cover I found an inscription hand-written in angular and outlandish script, but I read it easily:

The Book of Baal

which contains the names

of all my subjects

Babylon, Asmodeus, Urthamma, Cyllene, Lucifer, Moloch, Bel, Sinistrus and Abrahel, or the City of Evil, the Angel of Darkness, the Daemon of Fire, the Crooked Queen, the Fallen Angel, the Golden Idol, the Leaden Idol, the Left Hand and the Incubus. These are the nine common names and identities of Zernebock and my name is Koschei Corbillion. I am Prince of Pargur and Archmage of Malthassa.

I was filled with joy. It rose up and brimmed out of me; I wanted to shout my name from the towertops. I turned the first page, which was black as sin and blank and, after that, the pages were alternately red and white. The list of names filled them, to the end of the book. I saw some I recognized: Baptist Olburn, Gaster Valdine, Ninian Baldwin, Brother Fox, Elzevir Tate, the name of my mother and that of the man she claimed to be my father (these upon the white pages) and others I did not: Alice Naylor, Alice Tyler, Lèni la Soie and Helen Lacey (these upon the red).

200

'It is a Book of Souls,' I said.

'It is what you sought,' said the Om Ren. 'Your face and body reveal your satisfaction.'

'Magic, though she is a hard mistress,' I said, 'well rewards a bold man.' I closed the Book. Its empty place was waiting for it, upon the back of a wooden eagle, and I laid it there, open at the first page on which my name was written. My forest friend sat down at the table.

'I will watch the Book and rest until you call,' he said. 'You say yourself that you are full of courage. Are you man enough to walk about the library alone?'

I did not answer him with words but walked away from him around the corner of the first shelf. The library was very small. I lifted volumes down from the shelves, examined and replaced them, one after another, and so wandered bodiless among the shelves, my mind engaged with the matter in the books. When I at last became conscious of a gripe of hunger in my belly and an itch caused by a flea making his dinner on my neck, I was startled to find myself in a different room. It was the library still, no doubt of that, but the colour of the ceiling, the light, the disposition of the shelves all differed. In case I was mistaken, I ran back to the first shelf and looked behind it: there was no table and no Om Ren.

I pressed my hand against my head, to clear it. This library (but who knows the Truth?) was a memory: how could I have remembered the future? Had I interfered so much with the matter of the Memory Palace and Pargur that they had coalesced, making this library as liable to sudden and confusing changes as the city? I thanked my new gods I was not exploring the real one at Peklo tower. I looked this way and that, seeking enlightenment, and saw Manderel Valdine standing by me, not a yard away. His eyes were bright and full of malice. He glared at me.

'In a bed, in a house, in a street, in a town, in a green province, in a wide country, lies my love,' he said.

201

'Not yours, but mine,' I angrily replied. 'I, Koschei, will be her only bridegroom.'

Valdine still glared.

'In a bed, in a house, in a street, in a town, in a green province, in a wide country, lies my love,' he said again.

'It may be true,' I said, 'that the dead cannot bleed, but I can still cut the head from your corrupt body!' I began to draw the sword at my side but he did not move, nor did he seem to notice my rage, only repeated once more, 'In a bed, in a house –' as he vanished slowly from my sight. I thrust back the sword into its scabbard. Who can terrify a ghost? Someone coughed behind me and, turning, I saw Valdine. This time, his eyes were afire with pain.

'Make a secure place in which to hide your own soul. You stand there, brave in your new clothes, strong in body and mind – so young – and ridiculously mortal,' he said.

'Begone! Do not torment me or I will have you exorcized!' I cried and, as the late Archmage again faded from my sight, I realized these spectral figures were tricks of my memory. I was the victim of my own remembrance. I walked on between the countless shelves and un-numberable books. The potent words, my former prince's admonitions, which my memory had disinterred took on new significance. I was now the prince; I was the mage. It was unthinkable that Nemione should still refuse me. As for my soul, the advice was timely. Once it was hidden, and in a closer place than Valdine's had been, I would be cousin to the immortals.

I encountered no one else, but the rooms were legion. Many of them had been Valdine's, but there were countless others, every book I possess, will possess and had possessed, and every one of which I had heard tell, both of Malthassa and of that other world which, my mother used to tell me, lay close beside it. Polus was there and Shakespeare, the Two-fold Scripture and the Bible. I saw a title which confounded me: *Koschei's First Pilgrimage*. I took it down and read of my adolescent adventures in the Cloister. One room contained a daybed and I lay on it, exhausted yet intending by a final feat of concentration to solve this matter of my soul's concealment. Perhaps I could hide it here, amongst these octavos and folios begotten by and given birth in my memory?

The music grew and twined about me. I was an oak, the music was ivy; I was the rock beneath the flowering plant; I was the man whom the woman embraced. I was alone. I sat up slowly, careful lest I scare the fragile notes to flight. The music was so melodic and so forlorn that my breast swelled with yearning and I felt an obstruction in my throat. I must open my mouth to let the sob come forth. I put my hand to my mouth and felt the emotion leave me. The Om Ren was singing *arioso* and my soul, a slim blue creature no bigger than my hand, stood rapt upon my palm.

Stealthily, I reached with my left hand for the neckcloth tucked inside my sark, loosed the knot and dropped the cloth over the inattentive creature. It hardly struggled and I spoke to it.

'I must conceal you in a place of ultimate safety,' I told it. 'Will you be content and not try to stay with me?'

I lifted the scarf a little. The soul nodded its head.

'If you die, so do I,' it said in my voice.

'That is very true. Come with me now, and you shall choose your own resting place.'

I carried it uncovered on my hand among the shelves. It looked about, as if it searched for something it had forgotten.

'That one,' it said, 'with the red cover. No, that is not the one. The calfskin binding? No. I have it! The book with the worn cover – was it once green?'

'This book?'

'Yes. The letters are faded: can you read the title?'

'No, but it is a book of poems.' I took it from the shelf and my soul walked to the edge of my right hand and, jumping to the left, knelt beside the book.

203

'Open it – steady!'

I turned the pages until it was satisfied. It read me some lines from the page it had chosen

> Forlorn! the very word is like a bell
> To toll me back from thee to my sole self.
> Adieu!

and, lying down upon the printed lines, motioned me to close the book upon it. Gently, I did as it bade me. It wriggled itself comfortable between the pages. The last I saw of it was a thin edging of blue, like a forgotten paper, before this too was withdrawn. I turned to the Om Ren who sang on, doubtless like an angel. His voice had changed for me, without a soul to interpret it, and had all the discordant charm of a nocturnal serenade by Pargur's tomcats. Wondering at it, for I did not then appreciate what losses a soul-less man must sustain, I shook his arm violently. He blinked his hooded ape's eyes and said,

'You have woken!'

'Unless I still dream?'

'Perhaps every life is dreamed by a sleeper of whom we are unaware. Go now, Koschei. Claim whatever your deeds make your own. Go – it is safe to leave your memory of me in the Memory Palace, is it not?'

I was relieved to shut the door on him and on the rest of the troublesome past; upon my essays into the future too. The castle garden was a place of peace and soft shadows where, although the sun was well past its zenith, flowers and insects enjoyed the warmth. I sat a while in an arbour, emptying my mind. When it, too, was quiet, I rose and walked the gravel paths in the knot garden. Here I saw Nemione, hurrying along a different path. I called to her,

'My Lady! Do you hurry past me so that you may not forget Valdine?'

'Koschei!' She turned, one slender hand lifted to shade her eyes. Then, miracle of miracles, she came to me, stepping over the low intervening hedges until she was in my shadow. She smiled.

'Unjust! You think I gave my heart away because I lent my womb to Manderel?'

'What other explanation can there be? You dote upon his brat.'

'Poor half-breed! I am compassionate, that is all.'

'Compassionate!'

Nemione blushed – I swear it. The blush began at her fair forehead and spread like a new dawn across her face and neck until it vanished underneath the bosom of her dress. The gold chain and pendant cross she always wore was scarcely less bright. She looked timidly at me.

'I am afraid, Koschei. What is there in the garden this afternoon to cause this unease?' Again, she stole a glance. 'It is you! I feel your will and your resolve – strong as a young lion. You have found the way to Peklo tower!'

'I have been in Peklo. My right to the principality and to Valdine's mantle is proven.'

'Will you kiss me, Koschei? I do not think I will resist.'

Who, offered paradise, refuses? Yet I hesitated, calling on the superior wit I knew was mine to smother the last glimmer of my disgust at her sophistry and its result, the stealthy, dispassionate impregnation and the birth of Valdine's Child. Nemione placed her hands on mine and tilted up her face; but she did not close her eyes and I saw, though it was almost obscured, a spark of her old spirit. I kissed her long and kissed her again, folding her absolute loveliness in my arms and cloaking her will with mine. Her eyelids fluttered and fell and her body grew lax. At last, after a storm of kisses, she opened her eyes (dull turquoises) and, a sleeper returned to the light, stared at me as I were a stranger.

'What have you done to me?' she cried.

'You gave yourself to me: to the Archmage.'

205

'No! I was entranced. Say you have not touched me, say I am whole still. Did I kiss you?'

'Sweetly, generously.'

'Alas – no!'

'And I kissed you, your face, your closed eyes, your lips, your neck –'

'Worse, worse.'

'That is all.'

Nemione's upper lip lifted once, in triumph and relief. Her eyes lost their submissive look and their intense colour returned. 'You are slow, Cloister Mouse,' she taunted. 'Only the tyro applauds the overture.' It was bliss to feel her body move, resisting my embrace. 'Tyche, Flax, Fortuna,' she whispered, and all sensation left my arms which dropped, numb, to my sides. 'Nemione!' I held my will against the weak force that pinned them there and felt it sway and bend. 'Nemione, you cannot prevail. Urthamma!' Warmth and motion flowed into my arms and I raised them. Nemione took to her heels, petticoats flying. I watched her run away from me, tempted to make her trip, or to turn her about in her flight so that she ran toward me. I laughed as I watched her go, combs flying from her head and her hair tumbling from its pins, her stockinged legs exposed to the gaze of gardener and sentry alike.

'War it is,' I called after her. 'I fight to win!'

It is impossible to tire of Castle Sehol. Like Pargur, the city over which it stands sentinel and guard, it is founded (the professors say) on the dreams and fancies of its first prince, Garzon, and is unstable and subject to constant change. Its inmates are used to its continual deceptions and treat them as pranks: if a kitchen is found to be fifty yards further from a dining hall, so be it. Later princes built on Garzon's whimsical footings, adding a tower here or a solar there. Fortunately, some of them also had the wit to pay attention to the castle's defences which are the finest in all Malthassa and less subject to sudden variation. Decimus Toricello, a stolid man of regular and modest habit and a clever engineer, was responsible for the re-siting of the curtain wall, the Devil's Bastion, the casemates which house the quarter-mile cannon and the fireproof magazine. He loved ferns and mosses, which he studied when he was not campaigning, and it is pleasant to find a hart's tongue fern or a yellow patch of reindeer moss high on the battlement walk, where there was none the day before. Pleasant also the fountains which appear and disappear in the inner courts, and the singing birds; even the bats which sometimes fly between the twin towers of Vanity and Probity, swooping through the music room as they go, may be viewed as nothing more than a nuisance.

The castle is also able to change its colour. In winter it is white or crystalline, in spring a green flush like the first grass in the water meadows steals over it, high summer warms it and it resonates with the nightlong merrymaking in the city streets below, its colours unpredictable but always clear; as the leaves fall, it grows sad and grey but, recovering itself on sunny days, exhibits the rugged gloss of a ripe pippin or a shining gourd. When I entered it as Archmage and prince, it welcomed me: its stones glowed tawny and appeared new-cut; its flags and banners stood proudly out, but the many-coloured pennon which had the Regent's badge upon it was limp. Still wearing cuirass and field-armour, I went into the Shield Hall. Elzevir Tate was sitting on the Archmage's throne. He looked at me, struck the gong at his side and shouted as loudly as he could, in his merchant's trembling flute,

'Who comes hither?'

There was a ceremony to be enacted and trials to undergo and I found the prospect tiresome. I held my left hand high and pointed at the wall behind Tate. Letters of fire appeared on it which spat like live coals as they were written by the burning hand of Urthamma. Tate leapt to his feet and ran from the throne while his guards jumped forward and made a ring of steel about him.

'Read!' the voice of the god thundered, and a sulphurous smell filled the room. In a ringing voice I read aloud the testimonial Urthamma had written for me:

Koschei Corbillion,
once Scholar, Priest, Soldier, Mage
and Usurper,
now Archmage and Prince

There was no need of more. Though my head swam with the after-effect of my conjuration I stepped out and ascended the throne. I, Koschei, called the governors and the guard came to me, Baptist Olburn first. Each man swore loyalty on his life.

Then, while they brought me hot wine (for I was near to fainting and the sweat, which they thought came of the supernatural fires, ran off me), I rested on my throne.

In the evening we feasted, as men will. Every fashionable lord and rich man was there. The Marshall sat on my right and Elzevir Tate on my left. The first presented me with a parchment which recited my virtues, qualifications and ancestry, and the second gave me a long cloak made of the skins of five hundred red martens. I gave them each a purse of gold and then, to amuse them while the company seated itself, I made a little strumpet appear by the Marshall's plate and a grinning elf in Tate's cup.

When we had eaten, I had a stool placed next my seat and sent for Nemione. She came veiled in white muslins and attended by the Silver Dwarf who, though he had put on a robe of yellow velvet, was clearly armed beneath it.

Nemione walked boldly up to me. I could see her contemptuous expression through the gauze.

208

'Will you be seated, Lady?' I asked her, indicating the low stool. Erchon stiffened and I saw his hand move involuntarily to his side. Nemione lifted her veil a little and smiled coldly before she let it fall again. The gauze covered her to her feet.

'Erchon thinks I should stand,' she said, 'but I, too, will sit at your feet, Koschei.'

'Will you let the company see you?' I asked as she sat down.

'I think not. They are all as drunk as satyrs.'

'I am not.'

'You, Koschei, are incapable of levity or proper repose. I know that. Life, for you, is a contest.'

'Could I have a lovelier opponent?'

'I decline to take up the gauntlet.'

The Lord Marshall, who had drunk a good deal of claret, loudly demanded music and, when the musicians had struck up (a gigue, I recall) called above its scraping and piping for more wine to make a toast; but it was the furrier from Pudding Lane, Elzevir Tate, who climbed before he could be prevented up on the seat of his chair and clapped his hands to still the clamour.

'A toast! A toast to the Lady Nemione! Salute the bride!' The carousers rose, banged their cups and glasses on the tables, and all shouted,

'Nemione! The bride! Nemione!'

'I trust you will not associate my suit with this intemperance,' I whispered.

'Oh, you would not stray publicly, Archmage,' Nemione replied. She tapped her foot impatiently and Erchon, who stood close behind her, made as if to move.

'I would prefer it if you stayed,' I said.

'Yes, my lord.'

They should have thrilled me, those three words, spoken perhaps in bridal submission or wifely admiration, but Nemione used the courtesy like cold steel.

'You said you would not fight,' I remarked, her recent

womanly timidity and yielding to me in the garden clear as Altaish diamonds in my memory.

'I have changed my mind,' she said, tart as lime. I had forgotten her insults, relished her taunts and said, with a crisp, military bow,

'Your privilege.'

Though it was mine to bend so readily to her will and bow so gallantly before her beauty.

Men at a banquet need entertainment and the music was resumed while the cupboys and stewards cleared the plates. Then came a female juggler who wore little but had much skill, given that she used her deft hands and quick eye and no magic. After her, a woman veiled like Nemione, but in scarlet and blue, stood up.

'She wears her draperies with a difference,' I said. 'Not to conceal her beauty but to reveal it.' I leaned towards Erchon. 'Your friend in Nether Pargur must have made great display for you to miss your appointment with me, and with Peklo tower and destiny.'

Erchon bowed.

'Discretion is the greater part of valour,' he said.

'But did she please, was she mistress of her craft? – surely any dwarf-wife surpasses her for refinement and conversation!'

'It pleases you to insult me, Archmage,' Erchon answered. 'I did not go to the whore for talk, nor did I remain with her because she was refined.'

'You owe me ten crowns!'

'Take it from me, lord; add it to the thousands in your coffers. You, when history has been written, will be remembered as the man who got his throne by sheer genius. I shall die a mere Silver Dwarf. Look! You are at liberty to take *her*, if you so desire.'

He looked down the hall, at the dancer. She began her tantalizing dance, slowly shedding the first veil which concealed more, six I guessed. It is an old tradition. With each successive abandonment her movements grew the more abandoned and the film of colour, which did not hide but teased her audience with glimpses of her charms, changed: a true daughter of mutable Pargur! At last, she stood naked before us. She snapped her hennaed fingers and a small grey monkey dressed in a cap and a silver jacket ran out of a corner and climbed her body as if it were a tree. It stood on her shoulder and bowed. The applause rocked the tables – many men were themselves dancing on the boards.

'The woman is without doubt a prodigy,' I said, and beckoned the seneschal. Soon, the dancer stood before me and I was able to admire her at close quarters. She had no shame. Nemione also stared at her. I could see the brilliance of her eyes beneath the white shadow which covered her face. The seneschal paid the dancer with silver and I kissed her hand.

'Will you give me something?' I asked her.

'Anything, Archmage. Whatever it is that you want, Prince,' she said.

'The monkey, the little ape if you please.'

She lifted him from her shoulder and put him on my knees.

'Keep him. I will get another.' The seneschal gave her more coins.

'Tell me his name and what you do to command him,' I said and the dancer knelt and petted the monkey and showed me how to make him bow and sit and stand and feign death.

'His name is Halfman.'

'And yours is – ?'

'Friendship.'

'A welcoming name. Good. You may go.'

She ran lightly from me across the hall, passing between the tables and the men who reached out to touch her. She easily avoided them. When she reached the doorway, where the juggler was waiting with her veils, she turned and bowed with a rare grace, letting her hair sweep the ground. I, like her monkey, could feign a lack of interest in life. I stood up, with Halfman in my hands, myself bowed to Nemione and gave her the monkey.

'Let Halfman be my embassy,' I said. 'As you can see, he has all the members of a whole man.'

'And you do not,' said Lèni, 'though you still have the best and finest member for your male purposes. Hands as you know, sensitive hands, are necessary for pleasuring a woman. Let us play a game, of seek and find, of persistence and reward. Get up now, see how far you can walk. Explore the room.'

Guy slid across the bed and slowly stood up. He felt well enough and better still, perambulating the room, bending to peer at the closed cupboards of the ornate credenza, the shut doors of the two armoires, the many unopenable drawers of the tallboy and the dressing chest. Lèni was laughing over her sewing, or at him.

'Don't be an idiot!' she said. 'The door is open, can't you see?'

He turned from his perusal of her decayed brushes and combs; indeed it was open.

He went out and found himself in a dark hall. The apartment door at first compelled him; it was certainly locked but he kicked and shoved at it, in case.

'Why are you making such a noise?' came Lèni's mocking voice from the inner room.

Some little light crept by the shutters at the far end of the hall. He passed three doors, all closed, and a mottled mirror where his ghostly reflection made him start. The open door led into a kitchen, small, filthy and close. Dirty bottles of his time were mixed with cobweb-shrouded others: absinthe, Burgundy, cognac, Champagne. He glanced at them curiously. The meat-safe was there, by the blacked-out window; a table and, on it, three rusty knives. He looked again: the tabletop was dark with old blood and marred like a chopping-block with deep cuts. A soft humming beside him made him swing wildly about – a 'fridge, incredibly an electric refrigerator, plugged in at a rickety, skewed socket. His fright had caused him to knock against the 'fridge and, as he looked at it, amazed, the door swung outwards and a brilliant light spilled from its interior. Inside, next to a packet of butter and a steak on a chipped plate, lay an open white bag with black lettering on it: *Georges Dinard, Boucherie Chevaline*. Ten bent fingers projected from it, the nails glistening in the light and the flesh and skin as white as death.

Guy stared at his hands in the bag. 'Oh empty hands, forlorn hands,' he whispered. 'What did you steal – fame was it, or obscurity? Come here!' and the nails clicked against the shelf and the fingers gradually unbent themselves and moved jerkily about inside the bag which rustled like dry twigs in a night wind. Then the hands crawled forward out of the bag and climbed down the shelving to the floor, where they hopped sideways until they found his legs. They began to climb, resting at last on his forearms – almost, indeed, in their rightful places excepting that, to hold themselves there, the fingers pointed at his elbows and gripped his sleeves. Carrying them thus, he returned triumphant to Lèni.

'Bravo – the hands of a famous lover!' Lèni cried and laid down her mending. 'Can they dance well on a woman's body, Guy? Can you dance?'

His feet tapped the floor. He was a marionette, her leaping toy; he could not stop the movement of his feet nor of his severed hands which leaped and skipped upon his arms.

'Can you dance a jig-a-jig, Guy?' Lèni bent over the sofa, showing scarred and withered breasts hanging loose in the open neck of her dress. She lifted the lid of the red opium box. Fairground music jangled from it making him leap higher and sending his fingers into a frenzied, compulsive arpeggio.

*　　*　　*

Music, Ivo told me, is the food of love. If this was so, then I had lost my taste for both though it was certain that my desire for Nemione was undimmed. Ivo engaged the best musicians to play for me and I tolerated the deep resonances of the violoncello and the shy notes of the lute at supper. But I longed for the clamour and din of a band of peasants playing on the fiddle and the drum – loud music for dancing in couples. I might thrust Nemione into such a dance, where the grasping of arms and the clutching of waists was customary, where kisses were exchanged in the round and the hay; and I wished she had been born a poor child in Nether Pargur and had grown to a calling in the oldest profession so that I might bring her from such low life up to luxurious dissipation in Castle Sehol.

Meanwhile, I knew not what Nemione did or when, for she kept to her quarters and the staircase in the White Tower which once brought me to her was cold and echoing. It led to an empty room where a dead butterfly flapped its wings in the draught from the unglazed window.

Incognito, I went to Nether Pargur again, disguised with the employment of a little magic and suitable clothing as a foreigner from the east. Again, I gave my basest instincts full rein and then, crossing the street and following an alley and a flight of steps found myself in one of the synchronicities, a Nether Pargur as vicious as the first. I visited the same whore and enjoyed the same vices. On my way from her house, as leaning and twisted a dwelling as any lodging in hell, I noticed a sign bearing the representation in paint and plaster of a pretty young demon and I went into the shop below it. It was a storehouse of ugliness, or beauty maybe since its appreciation is in the eye of the beholder. The shopkeeper was Erchon's temporary friend, the country girl, or her double. When she saw me she stepped out from her place behind the counter; in her eyes I was a plum ripe for the picking.

'Let me help you, sir,' she said. 'Perhaps you are searching for a souvenir of your visit here or even, if you have not yet tried the delights which surround us, an accommodating lady?'

'Which lady would that be?' I asked. 'Surely the only lady here is the one before me.'

'Well reasoned, sir. What would you? A little relaxation with my masseuse and then a pipe, or a vigorous interlude in my company?'

I paid her for half an hour and we went up to her bed; it annoyed me that when my intention was to uncover Erchon's tastes and deposit some token of them in the Memory Palace, I had no way of telling if this woman was the one he had enjoyed. I asked her if she had entertained a dwarf but,

'They are many,' she said.

'A silver dwarf from the Altaish?'

'It is autumn, sir. The city is full of silver dwarves with ore and ingots to sell. You will have seen their strange balloons – the canopies are shaped like loaves of bread, ugly things, and closed gondolas hang beneath. They come here every second year and their pockets are groaning to be emptied.'

In her shop I bought a dark picture, attracted by the scene it depicted. It was a portrait, I surmised, of a blindfolded and haltered young man kneeling before a beautiful witch, and cleverly painted, especially the coarse hempen rope by which the woman led him and the soft flesh of her upper arms and that portion of her breasts which showed above the neckline of her shift. I remembered that Nemione had hidden herself from me and returned to the castle where I bathed twice, first in the hot springs and then in a tub, with Ivo to attend me.

Thus cleansed of my excesses, I summoned the most fashionable architects and designers, and set them to work on my quarters from which they cast out all Valdine's arcane rubbish and installed the finest furniture and the latest appointments. I relied on their advice: my own taste was departing from me so rapidly that I had no alternative. When they were gone, I took great delight in arranging an easel in the best light and setting up the picture of the tethered youth on it. Nearby was a lacquerwork cabinet full of the rarest birds – which, on my orders, had been removed from the aviaries of the zoological gardens, skinned and stuffed. I had myself wrung their necks. I fashioned a simple spell, which made them hop upon their perches and sing with the voices of ravens.

All this work took me seven weeks. Summer was gone and the autumn in her fullest flush. I hastened out upon the ramparts after dark and, in a rising wind, removed myself to Peklo. Here I laboured hard, learning the minute particulars of my Art and passing the less arduous hours, when I was weary, in scanning my map and globe and the five mirrors which gave closer views of the secrets they revealed. I soon saw where Nemione had hidden herself. She had moved her room to the undercroft of Probity Tower. It hovered there, inside the massy vaulting, as if it were uncertain of its rightful place, and I resolved not to act upon my new knowledge lest Nemione and her room flee altogether. She was, I believed, now capable of transporting material objects a great distance, a competence almost as advanced as my removal of the Memory Palace from Espmoss to Pargur. I was content to spy upon her, most content. Like the witch in my picture, she was in dishabille. Apart from her gold chain, her nightgown and a string of corals she had forgotten to remove were her only encumbrances. Her bed was tumbled and the Child was asleep there, its slimy nakedness half-covered with a sheet. Nemione sat cuddling the little ape, Halfman, on the carpeted floor. She addressed her head of gold,

'Roszi,' she whispered. 'Roszi, wake up.'

The head arched backwards on its short neck and the pillar it stood on swayed a little. Roszi opened her eyes and the grim line of her mouth relaxed.

'What is it, Nemione?'

'I told you to call me "My Lady". The basest servant remembers that.'

'Yes, My Lady, what is your desire?'

'Oh – for a strong young lad to kiss me, or for a wise and potent man to instruct me in the art of Love and demonstrate its intricate disciplines with the utmost finesse – That is all impossible! Talk to me Roszi, of yourself; not of what I do and must do.'

'Where shall I begin, Nem – My Lady? You know every letter of my story from the gypsy witch onwards –'

'The *chov-hani*. She was a fearsome sight! Tell me about your waterfall.'

A tear, a miraculously clear drop of moisture, fell from Roszi's right eye.

'I was cold then and whole beneath my cascade. I used to wear a belt of water-borne amethysts and a long rope of palest aquamarine – my lovers swam to me whenever I called. The shining drops of air caught in their clothing made them gleam like your silver rings; but that was all the air they had, for the water they had swallowed kept them below with me and no one ever found them, deep beneath the fall. Shepherds, herd-boys, a brave swimmer, a poet, a soldier, and Diccon Flowerseller – so beautiful, with his posies in his hands and his garlands about his neck. They weighed him down when he fell in, poor boy. I let him sleep beside me.'

'How did you keep them faithful, Roszi, when the she-otters in their furs and the female sturgeon swam by?'

'I made them promises I could not keep and kept them close to me by granting small favours – a kiss, the touch of my hand, a stone from my necklace to dream on.'

'And does that suffice to hold them in captivity?'

'My lovers were dead, My Lady; yours live and the blood runs fast as greyhounds in their veins. As for the Archmage, a love of fame and a hatred of innocence drive him. Beware! His mind is keen, and his body as capable and comely as

217

my swimmer's. Where is my body – did it all dissolve in the mould?'

'I fear so. You made a deal of steam, as much as a marsh fog, when Manderel poured in the gold. We could not replicate your entire body. Manderel used all but a fragment of his magistery-stone to make the gold in the Treasury and your transformation, Coz, wasted that.'

'To treat your cousin so – you have no heart! Free me!'

'I never heard your heart beat, Roszi. You were all nivasha, but I have my father, the reeve's, heart – cold enough, I grant you. Behave yourself and I will free you when your time is up.'

'The years are long.'

'You look too closely at the minutes. Seven years is an instant in time's infinity.'

'Get me a body, Nemione, the body of a beautiful young bride. Let me have lovers again!'

'Enough! You tire me when you beg.'

Obediently, the head closed its mouth and eyes and Nemione covered it with an embroidered cloth. With a fire in my breast which consumed all reason, I watched her prepare herself for bed. It was magic of a corporeal kind. She brushed her fine hair into a gleaming aura and worked perfumes and ointments into her skin before she shed her night-gown and stepped into her bed and lay down beside the Child. After a little while, it sleepily turned and nestled close against her. It had grown, I observed, nearly as tall as Nemione. I heard her kissing it.

The excitement woken by imagined prospects roused me and I paced the room until the pain with which my magic-working had filled my head grew more intense than those troublesome sensations. I did not care into what deep chasm of iniquity my soul-less body might stray. Adventure had always been a welcome guest in my house.

I slept then, though in my curtained rooms I did not

know if it was night or day in Peklo. When I woke, I went immediately to my mirrors.

Nemione – I soon found her in the castle gardens – was playing in a quincunx of tall linden trees whose yellowing leaves dropped every now and then to earth or fell upon her hair. She had dressed herself in a velvet gown and Halfman, the monkey, wore a suit which matched her dying reds and russets, a lace collar at his hairy neck. In her left hand, she held a scarlet shuttlecock and in her right, a long-handled battledore. I applauded when she tossed her pretty missile of cork and feathers high amongst the falling leaves and stretched up to hit it as it fell. I reached for my smallest mirror, which showed me every detail of her neck and of the smooth slopes which fell away below it. The thin gold links about her neck made an anchor chain and I read the huge motto on her cross, 'Keep Faith', a tenet she had long ago abandoned. We were both deserters, cloister renegades, each hell-rakes in our individual way and meant – by all the gods! – to be a pair. I moved the glass to make examination of her intimate country, swelling mound by long ascent, and slowly climbed her neck where I found a tall stick planted beneath her chin – a single black hair – and, climbing higher, saw above her lips a meadow of like stems waving and at the dark threshold, a tooth capped with ivory. Those black caverns were her nostrils and there, on the left, another great hair. That she should have such blemishes, the female echoes of my thick beard, intoxicated me and I was forced, for the sake of my own sanity, to retreat and view her whole in a larger mirror where she appeared her customary self, a complete and perfect beauty.

I knew then how Valdine had used these mirrors for his own benefit, viewing Nemione while he was incapable, in his sickness, of any greater effort and I thought: can I devise a better way than his to enjoy her against her will?

The largest mirror showed me figures moving toward Nemione through the trees. My lady laid down her shuttlecock and bat and bade the monkey stay beside them while she hid herself behind the central tree. Such men, such prospective lovers – the youth and flower of Pargur, all six or seven years behind me in years and as many hundreds in experience! They called her name and one of them, who had a mandolin, played and sang a serenade. I considered their obliteration, my extinction of their dreams as, falling one by one dead at her feet, I relieved them of life and its anguish by the exercise of my sovereign will and supernal magic. I was too curious – and too lazy – to act. One of them crept round the tree and caught hold of Nemione, who feigned delighted surprise while I stared in hatred at his hands, bold on her waist.

'Stephan!'

'Let me steal a kiss, Lady.'

'You must earn that. Let me see you –' Here, she paused to eye him and with a smile to raise up his hopes before she dashed them. 'Let me see how Halfman likes you. Lift him from my battledore and bring it to me here.'

Though he approached it stealthily, the monkey bit him, sinking yellow teeth deep into his thumb. I laughed and so did Nemione.

'No kiss, not even one to make you better,' she said and turned her back on him. 'Randal, come here! See if you can catch the shuttlecock.'

The second suitor fared no better for she kept the shuttlecock dancing out of reach, impelled by her prestidigitatory art and her own desire to outwit such dolts. They skipped about her, trying to do her bidding, while she pirouetted in their midst, aglow in her autumn colours and with her fierce virginity – in my castle, in my gardens. I turned my mirrors face-down wishing to see no more of such intemperate folly; yet I could not but admire her for her obstinacy and the pleasure she took in exercising it.

My newly furnished apartment in Castle Sehol was my solace. I returned there and, sitting on a chair before my cabinet of birds, listened to their harsh song, which was balm to my wounded heart. I silenced them and studied next the picture on the easel where the witch and her prey played out their perpetual confrontation. He, I could see, was simply young and burdened as every youth must be by the problem of his bodily imperatives and their solving, but she, the eternal temptress, she was now the one to interest me. I was certain that her eyes, beneath the blindfold, were sapphire blue; I could see her lips, tinted a delicate pink like the newly opened petals of a camellia or like Nemione's and they were firm (especially the upper) like Nemione's. Winter came to Sehol while I stared at the picture and Urthorold, the brother of hot Urthamma, hung icicles from each machicolation and murder-hole and blew snow into every crevice of the battlements. I, Koschei, caused a tree of ice to arise in the centre of the hot pool in the garden that I might confound Nemione when she went there to bathe.

I called Ivo to me and sent him into Nether Pargur to find the dancer, Friendship. When he returned, bringing her or one of her synchronicities with him, I watched the Dance of the Seven Veils in the privacy of my apartment and afterwards kissed the naked dancer. That was all – I was my own self-limiter, happier when I spied upon Nemione unseen, a beggar crouched below the salt, a servant at a feast, the unregarded flunkey who holds the door. I flew to Peklo through the blizzard and there arranged my mirrors in order, hands trembling as I picked up the first.

She was hard to find. I searched her usual haunts: the Court of Love and its surrounding chambers, her rooms, the springs and bathing pool and, finally, the snowy gardens, yard by yard, to which – if her footprints did not give her away – she might have been carried on the back of a fancy, an ethereal griffon or a cloudy spirit of the air. At length I discovered her: she was in the kitchens (I have never ventured there) unobtrusive as a common serving wench, whose guise she wore. A marvellous change from finery! I watched her, curious to see what she would do when she left her quiet corner and her broom. As I spied on her, so she spied on the kitchen servants and waited her opportunity. Chefs in tall hats ran past her, dairymaids scurried with jugs of milk and cream, with bowls of eggs; a pair of butchers carried in the carcass of a newly slaughtered beast and at last (Nemione put down her broom) there came a little procession of chambermaids and ladysmaids bearing the tools and trappings of their trades – dusters, buckets, crystal jugs of fresh and copper jugs of hot water, scissors, fans, curling tongs. Nemione, stepping forward, joined them. Her appearance changed most subtly as she moved, from dirty drudge in sacking apron to alert and gossiping maid in clean, starched pinafore. One of the maids put a jug of drinking water in her hands.

I followed her in my mirrors. It was a strange way to get water – she had only to call for it; she might, in harder straits, make some herself, out of the snow on her window-ledge, the liquid in one of her perfume-bottles, Roszi's tears.

Nemione hurried along the corridors, crossed Garzon's random dancing floors and avoided Toricello's sudden tangles of greenery. She negotiated courtyards and halls, climbed long flights of stairs and the steeper, spiralling ascents of towers, walked the perilous, slippery rampart, her water turning all the while to ice and, at last allowing herself assistance, spoke a charm and with a cry of *Zracni vili!* was spun from my sight in the direction of Probity Tower. Hastily, I changed mirrors, selecting the circular one with the rim of spun glass. The seven colours of the rainbow dazzled me; staring through them, I saw more clearly. Nemione had undergone another shift of form and appeared as herself, most soberly dressed in the grey surplice and white scapulary she had worn in the Cloister, her cross of gold hanging bright against the linen, everything chastely covered but face, hands and hair.

She has recanted! I thought. Or does she still believe the

motto on her cross and keeps faith with the Absolute? – how, then, has she been able to work so much magic; how deceive Valdine in doing so, without his knowledge or permission? Why did she allowed herself to be used by him?

My questions distracted me and I lost concentration. The prismatic lights flowed into my mind with the force of a tidal wave and the thunderous roar of the water came with them. I cried out in pain and confusion but know not, to this day, whether my cries were the animal utterances of man who has put away his soul or were words – names – sentences – incantations. I felt a great heat at my back and, turning from the hurtful, dazzling mirror, saw fire in the doorway of my chamber and in the centre of it, Urthamma holding up his burning hands.

'Greedy Koschei!' he said. 'Why not be content with what you have already gained?'

I bowed my head briefly in acknowledgement of his presence and greater power and, daring to lift it and look him in the eye, said,

'Because I must have Nemione. I cannot fail.'

'You mortals always fail. So many centuries of civilization and yet you learn nothing and come still puzzled to your graves.'

'I am closer to immortality than you think, Urthamma. No man can kill me, or woman – but I would willingly die for Nemione. Look!'

'No one dies for love, Koschei – though he may wish to, nor do I need your petty devices to see your madonna. Behold!' and the hand of the god made a glowing arabesque which cut through air, wall, space and time so that Nemione and her room appeared in mine and I could look at her direct. It was a meeting of equals. She lifted her grey skirts a half-inch and curtsied. I bowed low.

'Nemione!'

'Koschei! Your timing is perfect. I am playing Nurse; you can be Doctor. What better part for a prospective father?'

223

She moved aside and I saw the Fish-Child grovelling at her feet, its blue hands tightly clasping the rim of a huge glass bowl. It had also changed, I saw, and grown beautiful, its entire strange and slimy body swollen with my seed. It was a curious, bloated fruit, ripe and ready to shed its children; or a stranded, pregnant sea-beast, a water-cow or manatee.

'Help her, Koschei! Help me!'

Nemione gave me the jug of water she had carried from the kitchens. 'It is the purest I can get – from Orphanswell. It must be clean water and it must be true matter, neither transformed nor illusory, drawn from the well by a human being. Hold steady and hold well!' She knelt beside the Child and spoke the secret name of the Absolute God into the waiting ether; but she spoke it backwards as became her sham fidelity. The vestments, the displayed cross, the piety: all were means to her end and she was as rotten and far gone in the way of magic as I. I waited fearfully and Urthamma, reclining at our backs and exuding a summer heat, smiled his beatific smile.

There was no thunder, no rising wind or storm but only a continued silence broken by the stamping of Nemione's bare feet upon the boards as she danced out her spell. It was terrible to behold, an ecstasy as consuming and personal as her master's, the Archmage's, when he summoned Urthamma to help him read the map, an ecstasy which should have been mine. Nemione sweated and her cloister-clothing grew stained; her hair, flying wildly about her, settled into a disorder of elf-locks and hag-curls, and her face was red as Urthamma's hot countenance, smiling on her. My love of her was complete and when the cascade of water she had created out of the little in the jug poured down upon me I was moved to speak, declaring my love. I do not think she heard, wrapped in her rite and her emotions, and when at last I looked away from her I saw that the Child had become a hen salmon which swam round and round in the glass bowl, dropping her children as she went. They were small clear droplets, like the water themselves, but they grew apace and split the bubbles apart to swim up and break the surface of the water, to breathe air and clamber with limbs of horn and gristle from the bowl. They crowded together by Nemione's feet and whimpered with the shrill voices of the new-born.

'My dearest ones,' she said, crouched down and gathered them all up in her skirt. 'And dearest one of all!' She helped the Child from the water, holding it by its fins which turned to arms and the tail to legs, the rest becoming as it was before. Nemione broke her gold chain and dropped it on the floor where the little cross, at this cross-roads in her life, was soon trampled under the hooves of the new-born. Reaching quickly down, I retrieved it and hid it in my sleeve – see, the chain is broken yet and you can read the motto quite easily. 'Keep Faith' – oh, bitter words. My Lady put off the white scapulary, pulling it eagerly over her head and dropping it likewise to the floor, opened her surplice enough to reveal one naked breast, which she held and offered to the Child.

'Though she bite me, she must have nourishment,' she said, 'and warmth and comfort after her ordeal.'

I did not know if she spoke to me or to the Child. The little creatures it had given birth to clung to her garments. While she nursed her Child and soothed her grandchildren with small chirps and sighs, she looked up at me and let me drown in the airless pools of her eyes.

'Koschei – Koschei, I shall never be your bride,' she said. 'You are married already, though there were neither bridesmaids nor groomsmen at your wedding under the green willow.'

'Take my life in return for one night of love. I have hidden my soul –'

'Hush, never tell! And what would I do with your life? Such vanity! How could I give up this, my own dear sovereignty, for the pleasures of a single night with you?'

'I shall never desert you, nor abandon my suit!' I replied.

'Then be content to spend your life yearning for the impossible. Take what is your due – one of these, your children. The rest are forfeit.'

I felt the heat increase and spread about me. Flames spurted from Urthamma's mouth and sucked the new-born in. The god smacked his smiling lips and extended his tongue to lick up every squealing, fleeing creature – all but one, which skipped away and quickly hid itself under the hem of my robe.

'Yes, keep that one Koschei,' Urthamma said. 'It will make a better servant than old Ivo. Feed it with your life's blood and it will obey you well. Remember, I do not obey you: you are wholly mine.'

His hot breath surged over me and I felt my face and hands smart cruelly; but it was a gentle breath and the god faded as a dying fire fades until he was gone. Nemione also and her Child and her room had vanished; I was alone with her cross and broken chain, and my memories. I did not shed tears (that ability left me when I hid my soul) but moaned aloud and cursed both the beautiful and the hideous, both the blessed and the damned, until a tugging by my knee awoke me from my sorrowful fit. The small creature which I had been bidden to care for was climbing up my robe. It had grown since birth, doubling its size; it was as big as my fist. I remembered Urthamma's words 'your life's blood' and cast about me, without inspiration and without sense. The creature ran along my arm and answered my dull questioning by sinking teeth of keenest ivory into my thumb and sucking there on my blood. I watched it as it fed, my child, my son – I supposed, for it bore nothing within or without its naked body that resembled the parts of man or woman. It had four limbs which it used as we do arms and legs, but inter-changeably, and a spherical body which was all head and gut. As to colour, this was at present indeterminate, but watery and somewhat yellow; later, as it grew to its full

226

size, as tall as my boots, it became as white of skin as its grandmother, Nemione. Now, ceasing to feed and satisfied, it wiped its lips with a cloven hoof and gazed at me from her sapphire eyes until I was discomfited and bade it run away.

'But Father, where am I to sleep?' it said. 'And is this calloused thumb of yours to be my dining-room?'

'I was a soldier but recently,' I answered. 'Do not expect the luxuries your mother and your granddam enjoy.'

'You are a mage and you have a conjuring-tower and a castle! Make me a castle of my own.'

'I am too weary. Find yourself some corner of the room until I am myself again. Do you think that magic-making is as easy as making wishes?'

'No, Father. I am a good child and I will wait contentedly.'

My son jumped suddenly from my hand and I saw him scuttle underneath a cushion I had left on the floor – and there he stayed till I had slept. Our next encounter came with the morning. I had woken energetic, full of eagerness for life and in the anticipation of satisfying works, for it was good to have company in the tower. I went outside on to the barren and windy promontory where the snow stayed an hour before it was whirled to perdition. Many weathered boulders rested there. I chose one and sent it before me into Peklo tower. Mine was the delight, I thought, to bring my son up in my ways, and mine the privilege to have a being I could call my own, my dear, my sweet familiar and friend. I determined to give him an honourable name, of the sort I would bestow on any human son of mine, such as Gregory, Godfrey or Cornelius.

He was waiting for me, perched on the back of one of my mirrors, and he greeted me with a skip and a bow.

'Must you feed again?' I asked him.

'If you please, Father; but give me enough of your fine scarlet liquor and I shall not ask again till this day week.' He ran sideways to me; he could run in any direction, like

227

a big cob-spider and therefore, involuntarily, I called him Cob, saying 'Come now, Cob, down to the floor. Your drinking-glass and dining table shall be the soft inside of my knee: take care you do not waste my blood,' and he never got a more majestic name. I lifted the skirt of my robe and watched him feed; it was a physical and psychic bonding for, ever after that, he was my slave. Something in his spittle closed my vein off when he had done and in time there grew a little wart or nipple in the place, which he used to suck on as a teat.

'I have brought stone for your castle,' I told him, 'and shall devote a day to fashioning it as you direct. To recommend whatever you fancy to be raised there shall be your first task for me.'

I worked with might and main on the boulder, a simple and pleasurable task but tiring to perfect. Cob was an oddity; he should have a princely palace. I imagined what my architects might have built and consulted some of Valdine's books in the Memory Palace for I still hardly dare venture among the real magic books in the tower's library. At the end of the day, a toy castle of gilded and hewn aragonite, to whose sheer faces clung a network of the crystals they call iron flowers, stood in the room, all complete with flags and cannon, portcullis and furnished rooms. Cob disappeared inside it and I heard him trying out the beds. Myself, I needed food and wine and for that, it was better to go to Sehol – where I might also have entertainments and music, perhaps also the soft touch of Friendship's hands and pleasant tales in illustrated books.

Yet in Peklo library – I went as far as its half-open door and listened there, expecting to hear Valdine shuffling about amongst the shelves. I pushed the door wide on silence and my own wildly-beating heart. The place was exactly like its memory-palace shadow. I walked more confidently. Here were books of puissant power! Though I had seen my name in it, replacing his, I avoided Valdine's Book of Souls open on its wooden eagle and lifted a grimoire of Simon Magus from its place. I lost my hunger when I opened it, assuaging my weariness and thirst on knowledge; forgot my son, forgot the passage of time, forgot Nemione who, in her room and among her dancing attendants, Stephan, Randal, Strephon, Astrophel and the rest, lived on through the winter, lived their lives elsewhere. Sometimes I felt young Cob feeding in the hollow behind my right knee and then knew nothing but signs, runes and hieroglyphics till I felt him feed again; sometimes the wind whistled in the tower-top or snow was hurled against the window-pane; once, a dragon brought a fearful darkness by sitting on the rocks outside; alien wings beat in the storm or terrible cries rent the night; once, an angel appeared before me, coldly bowed and flew away; many demons came to join me at my books, crouching under leathery wings in every corner of the room and perching, red and argumentative, on the shelves.

I came to myself in the spring. The light was strong outside and the cries of young sea-birds had replaced the weird calls which accompanied my studies. I had grown thin and hollow-eyed; Cob complained that my blood tasted thin and had lost all virtue.

'We must fly home,' I said. 'Climb inside my robe and hold fast to me lest I lose you forever in the Void.'

How I fed and feasted, glad of Ivo's tender care and the entertaining visits of Peder Drum, who brought me ice from the summit of Mount Tempest in the Altaish and told me of a winter's exhilarating and dangerous ballooning! Friendship and her companion, the juggler, were frequent visitors; Cob grew fat and noisy on my fresh, thick blood, claiming he could taste in it the salt of my renewed virility. As soon as I could look at myself in mirror or window-glass without censure, I dressed in a new-made suit of clothes and sent for Nemione, impatient to see how the winter had dealt with her. While I waited for her, I questioned one of her maids for I still believed she would desert, as she had the harsh life of the cloister, the lonely hermitage of magic to marry one of her suitors. The maid gave me welcome and unwelcome news.

'She has thrown out all her young men, my lord. No one visits her but the Marshall of Pargur, the Lord Lucas Austringer.'

A second maid came running in, she whom I marked for life with a blow from my unrestrained fist. For she said, all out of breath and tearful as she was,

'She's gone, Lord Archmage, she isn't there – the Lady Nemione has fled.'

Her companion tended her while I paced up and down, Ivo scurrying behind me and poor Cob trembling on my shoulder.

'So, the sorceress has fled away – what else could be expected of a woman who refuses love in favour of arcana, arch-chymicry, familiars, spells, the friendship of monsters?' said Ivo, his words marking time with his hurried steps.

'Her precept was once "Keep Faith",' I said.

'Not with you, Sir; never with you, Archmage.'

I knelt and shook the unconscious maid till she awoke. 'Where has she gone? Where is she – answer me that!' I shouted. The other maid replied, 'To Castle Lorne, Lord Koschei, that is certainly where. She talked of it lately. She and Lord Lucas were always looking at maps and plans.' I dropped a coin into her pocket.

'What shall I do, Ivo? Neither soldiers nor the birds will be of any use to find her.'

'You must practise the Art again, Sir. Return to Peklo, do whatever is necessary there. But Sir, they do say that if a man wears silk in this life, he forfeits the right to wear it in the next. You are better off without her. You can enjoy her in the after-life – when your time comes!'

'Why not say "hell", Ivo? As for my Lady, I have never

measured that particular piece of silk, let alone fashioned it into a garment for my use.

'Come now, pack me up a hamper of delicacies. I shall need some solace as I work.'

You, Sir, may not understand magic though it is no mystery to me. To you, it is force like the imagination, wild and unbiddable, chaos without logic external or internal. To me, its manifestations and workings are as clear and logical as the view of a knot garden on a sunny day. Why, I can see the knots unravel themselves, and how they were first tied!

In those days, I knew much but, as yet, of little – and I could not find Nemione or her stronghold, Castle Lorne. The map showed familiar territories, the globe was still, the mirrors opaque: Nemione had cast negation about herself and her environs and vanished totally, as if she were with Death, and I sent a messenger into Hell who came back with words for me from the Destiny of All Life: that he longed to welcome her to his dark dwelling but had seen neither her, nor her friends or servants. 'Nor will I soon greet you, Lord Koschei, for you have tricked me out of my due.' This sentence I wrote down on parchment and keep beneath a skull in the Memory Palace.

In Pargur, my soldiers searched for the Lord Marshall, Lucas Austringer. He, too, had gone. My jealous fears grew. Peder and his navigators searched the skies and my huntsmen and woodsmen the forest, in vain. One day, I heard Cob singing a nursery rhyme over to himself, as he sat in his little castle. I'll sing it to you though my voice is cracked these days, and gruff:

> Hush-a-bye, baby,
> On the high top,
> When the wind blows
> Thy cradle will rock,

When the rain falls,
My baby will float
Past fig tree and grey walls
In cradle and boat.

I called out to him:

'Cob, dear son – what is that verse you sing?'

'I heard it in my mother's womb,' he said, 'I heard a sweet voice sing it every time she lay down to sleep.'

To search for a single fig tree out of thousands, or tens of thousands! I ate well and then sat down before my mirrors. On the third day, I found the tree, a stunted thing with five leaves which grew in a crack on the side of Windring mountain in the Altaish. A painted canoe was tied to the tree by a seven-strand rope of finest Om Ren hair. I laughed. Nemione had kept her style of gallant mockery: a magic rope and a boat which did not sail but flew – no mean devices. As for those who stole the Om Ren's moulted hair for her, they were surely damned in her service. In combative mood, but laughing more bitterly, I went home to Castle Sehol and, to distract myself, made merry there. Peder Drum, to whom I sent orders next day, prepared Frostfeather for a long flight.

Love, its beginnings, its course, its consummation: pursuit begins it, the hunt is up and the quarry (oh, Nemione, my white doe) on the run. She enjoys the chase, having the strength to outrun her hunter; she pauses to permit him a glimpse of her beauty through the leaves; she allows him to drive her to the impasse and, casting aside her last defences, welcomes his dagger because she knows that in their first embrace he will also find his quietus.

Nemione had broken, as before in the Cloister, every rule, and still ran before me, her lawful hunter; worse, she ran with another stag. I could not excuse her. She was not to be compared with a Green Wolf roaming Malthassa in search of a battle nor was she any longer one of the gypsies, but a fair and fashionable beauty, and a Sorceress. From this knowledge, I took comfort. A woman who had given herself to her lover would have lost the power to make the simplest device; she would be incapable of negating matter and of vanishment. I hoped that she had used Lord Lucas's military skills and then disposed of him, for it would save me the trouble.

Frostfeather was my chariot and Peder my charioteer. I rode the wind and hunted the beasts of the firmament, clouds with the heads of lions and packs of sharp-fanged wolves which dissolved and re-formed as I pursued them. Windring was a small boulder on the horizon; grew in size as we approached until Peder and I could clearly see the stone circle on her summit, a natural phenomenon cut by the wind's keen knife from the living rock. We hung above the circle to admire it, floating in a round-dance in and out the mighty arches of the circle. Peder thought that giants long ago might have fashioned it.

'It is so grand – and the mountain-top within so smooth. Does the wind have a mind to imagine such a structure, and fashion it? That is where they had their feasts, the giants. Can't you picture them reclining there, with their women and their mighty flagons of wine?'

'You have become a poet, Peder. The wind has made you drunk – Nature does not require human explanation, not even the supreme answers of a poet – or a mage. Tell me, how is your breathing? Are you quite comfortable?'

'Whatever you have devised, Archmage, to bring us air, is far more ingenious than Valdine's clumsy cowls.'

'That is because I am a better conjurer, Peder. I know how to use Mother Nature and do not waste myself in admiration of her toys. Now, do you see the fig tree? Drive Frostfeather below the summit. We should find it on the sunny side.'

We sailed downwards in a shaft of light. It brought the colour out of the rock, sparkling clusters of rubies, sapphires as wonderful as Nemione's eyes, and lit up the five leaves of the fig tree to which my lady had fastened her boat: her bait.

'Put me down beside the tree, Peder Drum, and wait for me in the sky above. Do not let yourself be led away by the *zracni* – airy spirits are more devious than nivashi and impossible to hold fast. Be vigilant.'

'I will, Archmage – besides, I took my pleasure with my wife, and in Nether Pargur, before I began this journey.'

'Fare well!'

'And you, my Lord.'

I untied the rope of Om Ren hair which had no power to prevent me, his spiritual ward, and stepped into the canoe. Its prow was fashioned like the nose of a lyme-hound and it seemed to sniff its way through the air, its motion erratic. Twice, it tried to throw me out, but I was ready for it and admonished it with a whipping spell which made it yelp. I thought Nemione's combination of boat and dog endearingly eccentric. A paddle lay on the bottom-boards, but I left that well alone and, contrary to my advice to Peder, took time to admire the view – with purpose, for Castle Lorne was visible from my seat in the enchanted boat.

Shall I praise its architecture or its setting? Both call for superlatives. The castle, as castles often are, was grey, but such a soft grey like the wings of doves or the undersides of clouds. It had towers, turrets, battlements, flags, all the necessities, and stood proudly on a rock above a winding river whose banks were water-meadows starred and studded with flowers. The sun's rays were reflected by the shining wings of a weathercock on the keep and his head pointed south at the fine weather.

&c. Nemione had built herself a fair and delightful refuge. The morning song of small birds in the meadows floated up to me as the canoe approached Castle Lorne and I, leaning eagerly forward the better to see, wondered when the brazen cock would crow – as crow he did, raucously, mightily, the instant I had formed the thought. A cloud crossed the sun and extinguished all the brightness. Darkness was made visible. The castle and its pleasant meadows disappeared and I, alone in the frail boat, drifted in it without direction, the mocking crow of Nemione's watch-bird ringing in my ears. I might be crossing Styx or Lethe, might be anywhere – in limbo or in hell. I felt the boat bump against stone and a single point of light pierced the darkness. There, on a narrow quay stood a woman veiled in black, who waited patiently and held up the light.

'Tell your mistress that Koschei is here!' I called.

The woman stepped forward, bringing more light and I, when I had quit the boat, reached out and pulled aside her veil. I thought I knew her and thought I did not. She looked away from me, not coy but in embarrassment.

'Come, lady,' I said. 'You cannot hope to equal your mistress in beauty, but you look well enough. Is Nemione near? I am certain that I stand inside the walls of Castle Lorne.'

'You entered by the air gate, Koschei,' she said. 'Some would call it the most perilous, but you appear unafraid; although you seem to rely on mortal strength and not on magic, for I see your sword still at your side.'

'It is sometimes the quicker way, that is all.'

'A way you take pleasure in, if I remember aright.'

'Do I know you – perhaps you served Nemione at Castle Sehol, or before?'

'You know me well, Koschei.'

'You are not Nemione, yet you call me by my first name, like an equal.'

'Correct. I am not Nemione, who waits for you.'

'You must have a name?'

'Nemione calls me Lucasta. I dared touch her, and this is my punishment.'

I looked into the woman's eyes. She spoke the truth: I had

235

last exchanged a glance with those eyes, warm and dark with merriment at the juggler's antics, hazy with the mists of drunkenness, at my first feast in the Shield Hall: Pargur's Lord Marshall, following Nemione in hope, as I did, had indeed been brought low, his valiant manhood forced into a woman's shape.

'You want release – by magic, or in death?'

'You are still my rival, Koschei. And I still hope. Is it not possible that, some day, Nemione may admit me to her bed? She cannot fear the embraces of a woman.'

'Then I must kill you.'

Lucas, or Lucasta, watched calmly as I tried to draw my sword. 'Your efforts are in vain,' he said. 'She has locked it in the scabbard. Here, in her castle, we are both powerless unless she wills otherwise. Let us go to her and plead our separate cases.'

'As vain a hope, Lord Marshall – Lucasta – as any of mine. You helped her fortify this place – surely you remember what she did?'

'No. I have lost half my memory as well as all my valour. Take my hand, Archmage, and learn fear as I have. It is dark, where we must tread.'

I could barely see the stairs she led me up, but fear hung on them and surrounded us with a choking gloom. The chamber at the top of it was darker still, and I thought I should suffocate in its aura of despair. The sensation was strongest beside the room's only piece of furniture, a close-curtained bed which we approached cautiously, still hand in hand. Nemione's voice rang out, behind the curtains.

'You make a fine couple, Lucas, Koschei. Shall I send for a priest?'

Lucas opened sensual lips to protest, but, 'Say nothing!' I hissed and, speaking out,

'Shall I send for a body to complete you, Roszi? What would you: the legs of an estridge and the trunk of a camel, the arse of a baboon?'

I pulled the nearer curtain violently open, tearing it from top to bottom. Nemione was there, sitting on the pillows, where I had expected her head of gold – and she cradled Roszi in her arms. I looked again, and saw only Roszi; a third time, at an empty bed whose pillows were undented.

'Be patient,' I told Lucas. 'She will tire of this and show herself.' We waited, gazing at the tall pillars of the bed, at its painted canopy where cupids flew in crowds or, reclining on plump clouds, depended pink limbs and soft wings. We watched the room surge about us and finally become a bare attic high under the roof-leads. The bed, dissolving slowly, crumbled into the floor. We waited on, an hour, two perhaps. At last, Erchon came in.

'My Lady desires your attendance, Koschei,' he said. 'Lucasta is to go to her mending and the Lady Nemione reminds her that there are still twenty yards of torn hem that require stitching.'

Lucas left the room with his woman's head bowed and woman's tears on his cheeks. Erchon was brisk with me.

'This way.'

I tried my sword again as I followed him, but it would not budge. I emptied my mind, searching for my inner self, that elusive part which concentration made a subtle instrument that, ranging far, could take up and use the untamed powers which lie in all the elements; my mind filled up and over-brimmed with images of Nemione, dressed, undressed, lying, sitting, standing; running, swimming, laughing, kissing; attired for a feast, a wedding, a lovers' tryst.

Erchon left me at her chamber door. She stood alone in the room, which was furnished as a scholar's study. Stuffed birds in static flight hung from the vaulted ceiling and an owl perched on the chandelier, his feathery horns erect; the books were bound in brushed leather and lettered in gold, and a fire burned beneath a tall chimneypiece. The fire-irons had the shapes of the Gratian and the Vedrate chimeras. I walked up to her and bowed, my face level with the white kerchief she held in her hand – which I would venture to kiss. I reached out for it and saw her curtsey, her gown of golden tissue creasing into a thousand folds and, as she continued to curtsey lower and lower, shrink into itself and disappear with her. I was left holding air, bent forward before the golden head, Roszi, who smiled maliciously.

'Won't you smile sweetly for me, Roszi?' I asked. 'The body of a saint would become your lovely face.'

She smiled more gently and her beauty broke out, despite her coating of gold and the loss of every lissom part of herself. I, still leaning forward in my ridiculous position, kissed her on her hard lips, which could never part to expel a breath or admit a lover's tongue.

Then, standing straight, I turned about and saw Nemione at last, lying on a couch shaped like a cat-a-mountain, its body covered like that animal's in striped grey fur, and the open-jawed head carved out of silver chuglam wood. I started forward and the catamount's head roared at me.

'Stay where you are, Koschei!' Nemione cried. 'You may look but you may not touch. Am I not all you have dreamed of, for so long and so vainly – the crown and epitome of womanhood?'

An answer would have been superfluous. She was everything she claimed to be. Her gown, I had no doubt, was enchanted. It differed from her former attire by as great a degree as did her couch from the common, being woven from her own, living hair which flowed from her head into the neck of the garment and became a pliable second skin – she had grown a limber coat of golden hair. Again, I stepped forward, disregarding the low growl which issued from the catamount's head.

'Stay, Koschei! Do you not see my creatures about me? I have fled you so that I may be complete. A Sorceress does not need a master, or a man.'

'Poor Lucas is proof of that.'

'The presumptuous jackanapes!' Nemione stirred and her

238

creatures, which sat on cushions all around her, awoke. I saw her Child, grown blue as heart-sickness, close beside her and Halfman, the monkey, jumped from her shoulder and ran along the couch; her other familiars I had never seen before. A chattering sooterkin clung to her arm and a scaly, green imp to her ankle, while a small grey-skinned dog without fur or ears, but with crude three-fingered hands where its paws should have been, lay tightly curled against her stomach. This creature, suddenly convulsing, reached underneath its tail and produced a black egg, which it gave Nemione.

'She-mage's food, Koschei.' She bit the shell and drank the yolk which ran out of it. A trace of yellow and a chip of shell remained on her lower lip and she picked at this with her nails to remove it. 'I have become as terrible as Circe and as fearsome as the Witch at Endor. I revolt you.'

'You forget, Nemione, that I have voluntarily sundered myself from my soul. Things that were hideous are lovely to me; I am indifferent to beauty – indeed, to kiss your hard-shelled Roszi thrilled me more than the tender touch of my mistress's lips. You also, are tempted to call your soul out of your body and put it away in some remote or secret place. The signs are on you: delight in perversion, love of ugliness. We are true mates still and you cannot escape me, or your destiny.'

'Have you brought some costly or uncommon gift which will convince me of your honesty?'

'I brought nothing to Castle Lorne but myself. Only – if you will lift your ban from me, even by one iota, I will conjure a diversion for your pleasure.'

'Very well. It is lifted. Bring me lewdness, Koschei. Let me see disease and suffering, starvation and slow death.'

'I will bring you all these. Wait until the clamour of total silence has filled this room – still the crackling of the fire and the tick of the clock! I will conjure.'

I saw the spirits which live between the several worlds fly to me and felt them touch and empower me, exchanging their knowledge for my wit. I first demanded a curtain, that I might present my show with all the counterfeit emotion and pompous show of the theatre.

'Let the masque begin!' I cried.

A red curtain covered in gold-dust formed itself from the firelight and hung unsupported across the fire-place, stirred by a draught which ran suddenly along the floor.

'Raise the curtain, Koschei,' Nemione said eagerly.

'Without an overture? Listen.'

I brought music from a place outside my own space and time, loud as cannon-fire and unpredictable as a sudden thunder-clap upon a summer's day. It made Nemione's creatures scuttle under the cushions, while Halfman fled across the furniture, shitting, urinating and screaming, all at the same time – a fitter overture for my prelude than the music. Nemione herself jumped up and stood swaying her hips beside the head of the couch, which put out a red tongue and licked her thigh. I saw her from the centre of my concentration, a great way off, and marvelled at her robe of hair and at the manner in which her body moved within it. 'Soon, Koschei, soon!' I said under my breath while, with a frown of concentration and a theatrical gesture, I commanded the curtain to raise itself and my demons to come forth. A salamander crawled from the fire and, after it, a crowd of tiny demons, tusked and horned, some bearing the marks of the flames from which they were created.

'Child's play, Koschei,' said Nemione. 'Amateur theatricals.'

'But look – more nearly.'

The creatures formed a ring and danced, both facing each other and back-to-back, in pantomime of a witches' sabbat. Then, with much squealing and scratching of putrescent boils and lacerated wings, they fell to coupling one with another or with several – and with such ingenuity of organ and position that neither sage nor scholar could have classified them as fish, fowl or hermaphrodite mongrel.

Nemione leaned close and her familiars crept from their hiding-places to watch these miniature orgiasts, more adept at the niceties of nastiness than they.

'Would you choose to be this one, Nemione, or that one?'

'The second – without question. Its pleasure – or is it torture? – is the most exquisite. The other is merely crude.'

I brought the curtain down upon them. 'Then let us see a play of slow torture and utter despair, with a rousing finale – all acted by ghosts. Lights! Music!'

The curtain rose again and, now, the music was subdued and slow, the thunder rolling in it echoed by uneasy groans from the air outside the castle; the illumination, from a dozen candles, modest. The scene was close, domestic. In the decaying room which appeared beneath the chimney's hollow arch we saw two actors, a man and a woman – what others are fit to take the principal parts in life's drama? They took their ease upon a bed hung with ragged curtains and painted with cupids, he lying (as has many a lucky man and his lady-love) with his head on her breast while she reclined against a pile of tattered pillows; their clothing was as shabby as the bed. They were not solid, these figures, but moved in and out of view against the flickering background of the flames. Dusty statues and huge pieces of rotting furniture filled the room in which they acted out their lives.

Nemione, sitting on the edge of her couch to watch the play, called out, 'That is my bed!'

'Hush! They are about to begin.'

The man, lifting an arm, yawned, and moved the arm back to its resting place upon the woman's shoulder. Before Nemione could complain at the slow pace of the action, I whispered,

'This apparent peace is only to emphasise what follows –'

and, as if he heard me and recognized the truth of what I said, the man (who favoured me in looks, though not in age,

241

for then I was under thirty) again lifted his arm and looked about him with sorrowful eyes. Then, taking hold of one of the long cuffs of his jacket in his teeth, he drew it slowly back to reveal a scabby stump. Sighing deeply, he repeated his action with the other arm.

'How could he lose them both?' Nemione whispered. 'Think of it! He would be unable to scratch himself, or lift food to his lips – he could not open the smallest door!'

'It is a cruel fate,' I agreed.

'Oh, but it is superb, true comedy. He is unable to caress his lover!'

'What do you think of the lady?'

'Hideous, divine! Surely, she has used up all her beauty lotions and avoided her mirror for many years! – He, with his grey hair and without his hands, is far too handsome a mate for her!'

'But a man must seek solace where he finds it.'

'Yes, men are weak enough for that. What time and age does your play depict, Koschei?'

'Not this, but another in the past or in some imagined future time.'

'What country?'

'It is a land called Lugdon, not far from that world of Albion which we sometimes hear news of in Malthassa. I have discovered it only lately, in one of my devices, where it seems to overlay the western parts of Malthassa. Occasionally, I find it in my mind – the man is imprisoned in the room. I think he calls me out of his distress.'

'Perhaps you have imagined it.'

'Perhaps. Fancy is a wayward and fickle mistress. Like yourself, Nemione.'

'Look, the scene changes!'

The man had risen from the bed, leaving his mistress asleep. His melancholy mood had left him for he walked smiling about the room and Nemione and I saw that he was tall – as tall as I am – and that his shape, for all its deprivation

242

and confinement in the room, was fine and manly. Suddenly, he began to whistle, loud and tunelessly but could not keep to his inharmonious racket which turned to melody and soon to song. His voice was a pleasant and determined tenor.

'. . . Let me set free, with the sword of my youth,
From the castle of darkness the power of the truth,'

he sang, and, with a stirring like that of young rats in the nest, his two severed hands climbed out of his pockets. Hopping sideways as fast as my son, Cob, on his backward-bending limbs, they swiftly ascended his body and perched, two desiccated servants, on his shoulders.

Nemione clapped her hands and, high above her on the chandelier, the owl flapped silent wings, up and down, high and low, raising a draught which stirred my hair.

'He is a powerful mage!' she exclaimed.

The woman was awake, his consort, his delight (as I suppose). He sent his hands before him, love's ambassadors, and they undressed her, layer by ragged layer, while he looked on. When she lay naked on the bed, the hands returned to perform the same office for him.

'She is spoiled, too!' Nemione whispered, pointing at the woman whose stomach and breasts, we saw, were covered in a filigree of old, white scars, lace open-work from whose lattice her yellow skin sagged. 'Koschei, should we not imitate them? Come, sit on Puss's back, beside me. We will at least watch the dénouement of the play, which I think will be one common to all mankind, together.'

My pleas, my prayers, were answered! I went eagerly to her and sat close, my left arm whose hand was full of life and ambition, about her waist. So near, I was unable to concentrate, and my play disintegrated as I went, the naked limbs and sad faces of the two players becoming mere pictures in the fire until all that remained was a last, fading

243

impression of his severed hands beneath her buttocks, raising her; and the constant flames.

'All my creations dissolve before your beauty!' I said to Nemione.

'And you, Koschei, are you also clay in my warm hands?'

'Lady!'

'But, say, my Lord – your man of Lugdon surely has the means of escape from his prison, his two obedient hands. You saw how they performed his will.'

'He has not thought of that. Perhaps he will, and so gain liberty.'

'Well, it will ever be a mystery – how do you like me in this guise? I think I please you more than the old, sweet-natured Nemione.'

'Whatever you are, or become, Nemione, will never fail to delight me. I should love you even if you were as much decayed as the woman of Lugdon.'

'That is evidence of true love. I think you would have won every contest had you become a plaintiff at my Court of Love.' She lightly kissed the corner of my mouth. 'The prospect of love always makes me hunger. Strix!'

Her owl, in answer to its name, bobbed its head and flew down into a corner from which came, suddenly, the squeal of a dying mouse. With the tail hanging from its beak, the bird flew to Nemione and dropped the mouse in her hand.

'Bravo, bonny Strix. Try it, Koschei. You will find the taste agreeable – something like a ripe plum.'

'I am not hungry,' I said, mindful of my independence, for to eat the food of a sorceress is to become her slave, and that I was already because of my lust.

'Not hungry? – after such a journey from Pargur, such trials here. Taste this morsel – you will not be disappointed. See, I will season it with a kiss.' Nemione broke off the head of the mouse, put it to her lips, and kissed it. She laid the tiny, warm face, whose ears were still erect as if they listened for the hunting owl, against my lips so that I was forced to raise my hand and dash it to the ground.

'I am not hungry!'

'But you have refused my kiss. Look, it lies there on the floor, spurned – oh, cruelly rejected.'

'I will take a kiss direct from your lips.'

Nemione smiled and laid her head on my breast. 'How I torment you – poor Koschei. Very well then.' I put my other arm about her and felt the catamount-couch sink fearfully beneath me and saw her familiars back away – so, falsely convinced of the infallibility of my powers and of my supremacy, I kissed Nemione on her parted lips, tasting blood and honey and the sweet savour of herself. Her trapped hands moved against my chest, little fluttering birds or scurrying mice themselves, as they encountered the rigid cuirass beneath my coat. I pulled her closer still, devouring her and feeling her robe sunder in my puissant hands into its original yarn, a cascade of hair. But my own armour also was dissolving in our conjoined lust and even as I pushed Nemione lower and covered her more closely and more weightily, her enchanted couch opened its carved mouth and howled and Roszi on her pedestal screamed,

'Nemione! Oh my Lady – beware!'

and, looking at my half-naked love and my undone self, I saw that I had grown two woman's breasts upon my hard, well-muscled trunk. My cuirass had vanished entirely; in place of this, my armour, was women's softness and vulnerability. I moved my hands and gripped Nemione by the throat.

The couch roared, the familiars snarled and screeched, clamouring in enmity. They bit me and clawed at my eyes and pummelled me with hard fists, especially my new-grown tender orbs; and I spat in Nemione's face:

'Return my shape to me!'

'Never!'

'Traitoress!'

'Lecher!'

The owl beat its wings against my head and Erchon came running, Lucas at his heels – who could do nothing useful but rail like the woman he was; but Erchon thrust at me with his rapier so that I, to save myself, was forced to release Nemione and draw my sword. I swung it wildly, worn out with my wretchedness and the debilitation brought on by my long conjuration and the ferocity of my desire for the queen bitch, who rested on her cushions and laughed hysterically. I swung wide, missing Erchon entirely and quite unable to bring him to bay, and my blade caught Lucas's drapery and travelled on, wounding him mortally and depriving me of any hope in the outcome of the contest. Erchon knocked me to the ground and leapt on me. His small weight felt like lead on my weak and useless breast, pressing ever harder; nor could I grasp or hold him because of the familiars, which held fast to my legs and arms.

Erchon turned his silvery head to look up at Nemione.

'Shall I kill him, Mistress?'

'I must consider, Erchon. Hold him well while I deliberate – it may be more agreeable to play with him a while. The fire burns up and Puss's teeth and appetite are sharp.'

'My blade longs for his blood, Mistress.'

'I would not disappoint it, Erchon – nor you, my good and faithful servant. Why not? Yes, you may kill the Archmage – painfully, now.'

I saw her lovely long, white feet (which I would have grovelled at and kissed) draw back as she knelt up on the catamount's back for a better view; and Erchon brought his rapier down in one slow, agonizing thrust and pushed it through my left pap. I felt the tissues split and my ribs cleave apart. A terrible burning filled every horizon and my heart burst asunder. I felt it stop and saw the gates of Hell open wide to receive me. Severed heads, whose mouths stood open in lamentation and whose eyes wept tears of stone, were fixed upon its spikes, the countless heads of slothful men and women; of the proud, the gluttonous, the lecherous, the envious, the irate and the covetous. Asmodeus smiled a welcome. I reached out to take the hand he offered me and, in that eternal moment, felt a new and rapid beating beneath my shattered ribs. My heart thundered, living, exultant, strong. Satan's lieutenant faded from my sight; the iron gates vanished.

I threw the rejoicing dwarf from me and wrested my limbs from their invidious hold.

'My dear and precious Soul!' I shouted. 'Oh, Life – oh love of life!'

I laughed at Nemione, drunk with joy, swaying but on my feet. She shrank from me, clinging to her couch which, with a last roar, jumped up and fled the room with her.

Erchon came at me again; I easily cast him off to lie half-conscious across the dying Lucas. Then, trusting all to the Fates and to Urthamma on whom I called with a mighty yell, I tore the golden head, Roszi, from her column and with her wailing in my hands cast myself from the window into the rising storm.

That is how I became Koschei the Deathless.

Immediately, I dropped a thousand feet past the dark castle walls and its desolate courtyards, before the storm caught and lifted me in its airy toils and buffeted me with thunderous gusts and sturdy bolts of lightning. My body became the playground of the elements which alternately tossed me up and threw me down, while they ripped my clothing from me and beat me black and blue. Knowing I was Deathless, I laughed triumphantly and bade them do their worst, while I clutched Roszi to my breast and buried her cold face between my female paps. Soon, tiring of its vain amusement, the storm abated and a cool and soothing breeze carried me along the canyons of the Altaish until I saw the stones of Windring and Frostfeather, with Peder Drum in her basket, below me. The breeze gently wafted me down beside him.

'Master? My Lord!' The man tried to kneel before me. No doubt I was a fearsome vision with my naked and lacerated soldier's body, all its gear on show, and my fine and broad female bosom where nestled the beautiful golden head of the cruelly-used nivasha, Nemione's cousin, Roszi Baldwin.

Peder recovered himself,

'She has done her worst for you, my Lord.'

'And failed miserably, Peder. Return to Castle Sehol. I must to Peklo to repair the damage she has done.'

I spoke the charm and was swept into the firmament. My adversary the thunderstorm rolled languidly there and 'Follow me!' I cried to it. 'I will reward you with rocks to break and the endless ocean to play over.' And so, with a crown of lightning and a halo of iron grey cloud, I was whirled on the storm to my stronghold, my tower of enchantment, where my dear son, Cob, jumped crabwise from his miniature palace to greet me, not caring how my shape was changed.

Guy paused in his narrative. His two hands climbed up to scratch his back and one found a handkerchief under the pillow and tenderly wiped his nose. He had been two whole days, as far as he could judge, telling Lèni the central part of Koschei's story and she had become as close to him, during the telling, as his wife or any of his mistresses – and closer still, he thought. Not afraid to open every part of her abused body to his frank gaze.

Not afraid as he was – and had been for many months – years? Ever since he'd peered in through the window of the Old Presbytery in Coeurville and seen the shadowy Egyptian figure in Helen's dining room, the fallen petals of the roses on the polished table; ever since Alice, appearing as if by magic in the car park, had stepped into his car, his life, the life which was running now too fast, too incoherently, too out-of-control. His hands, these separated, scuttling crabs, had lives of their own and no longer wrote what was in his mind. He imagined them over there, at the credenza or at the little walnut desk, writing this new, outrageous story in which he had become a character; he peered across the room.

No hands. They lay quiet as cats on the bed. The shadows and the dim candlelight had returned Lèni's beauty to her. With bent head and loosed hair, she looked like the madonna; and Helen too, he thought, unsurprised by the exemplars his drugged and sated mind threw up, pleased only by their aptness. Lèni yawned and he sent his right hand to stroke her hair.

'Whatever the time, day, evening or night,' she said. 'Whatever the season, the people of Malthassa must perform like Guignol's puppets each time their story is told.'

'Or silently read,' he answered.

'Send me back there, Master Puppeteer. Let me dream again of Koschei and the other world I glimpsed so long ago. I am so weary now that I have told you my tale and heard so much of yours. I am exhausted without the blood, drained –'

He tried to rouse her, saying,

'Do you hear the thunder?'

'Curious!' She yawned. Her eyes closed. 'I hear it – and yet a thunderstorm is rare in winter. Perhaps it thunders in my dreams.'

'It is the storm Koschei has brought with him from the Altaish to Peklo Tower.'

'Father!'

'My son! How have you fared in my absence?'

'Well, Father, well – I have spied through the bronze mirror upon the servants and the courtiers of Castle Sehol.

I have swept the floors and dusted the furniture – and I have been sitting in my window watching for you through your window. You have brought a storm with you, Father.'

'It tried to destroy me, and it saved me. It will serve me now to conceal the magic I must work.'

My first task was to heal myself, not high magic this nor snow of the intellectual summit, but journeyman's work with herbals and chirurgeon's manuals. A few days spent and I was good as new – save for one breast, a single woman's pap upon my left side, which I could not shift. I could not shrink it, make it disappear, nor cut it off, and I tried all these means to rid myself of it. As soon as it was gone, it was in place again. I looked at it, both from my own superior viewpoint and in a mirror and, seeing it was handsome, nay, beautiful, resolved to leave it alone for the nonce. I squeezed it and a milky juice spurted forth, covering the mirror with a constellation of droplets, my own Via Lactea. My grotesque appendage pleased me, Nemione's keepsake and a singular attribute of the kind usually given to the Gods. I spent another three days with pigments and oils, taking a sketch of myself, which when it was completed to my satisfaction, I hung on a wall in the Memory Palace.

'Drink of this hermaphrodite essence, Cob,' I commanded my son, offering him the brimming breast. Obedient, he climbed to my knee and sucked; the sensation was pleasant but he complained, saying 'This stuff is weak – I want blood!' and crying and whimpering at me. So I made a spell (another week) which changed the milk to strong liquor with a taste of brimstone, black treacle and asafoetida, and this Cob delighted in, taking a good feed of it after an apéritif of blood from my leg. To conceal my odd particular I wore a padded doublet and forbade Ivo to attend me in my bath, saying I had developed an incurable impostume and feared it would infect him.

I achieved a sort of peace with the creature I fashioned from the golden head, all that remained of Roszi, and the body of a fire-demon, and I called my creation Rosalia for old times' sake. In Espmoss, my beloved birthplace, the young men and maidens hang garlands of wild- and moss-roses on the tombs of their ancestors at Soultide and this ceremony is called the Rosalia. My living puppet was a memorial too, of Roszi the head and Roszi the water-sprite, and was, besides, supremely lovely like a wreath of morn-plucked roses on whose damask petals there lie fresh drops of sparkling dew, or like a rosebud blackened by canker and hard frost which yet hangs on the mid-winter bough. The effort cost me a month in my sick-bed when Cob, faithful creature, kept watch at my mirrors, my map and my globe, and told me of the cupidity and civil pride of the Council in Pargur and how Malthassa prospered, overlaid as were its western marches by the shadows of Albion and Lugdon and dogged in the north by bad harvests.

I sat Rosalia on a chair beside my bed and gazed upon her while I convalesced. Her beauty, a blend of Roszi's and Nemione's with a touch of alien charm, encouraged my recovery. I had clothed the fire-demon whose headless body I united with the golden head in skin as pale as buttermilk. The skin had a translucent cast beneath which the demon's red veins could be seen. The creature's feet and hands, her breasts and secret parts, I modelled on Nemione's and I gave her long nails of gold, sharpened to a keen edge, and a belly in whose centre there grew (instead of a navel which she could not have, being born unnaturally and not of woman) a marvellous crystal like the blossom of a fire lily but watery and green as finest aquamarine. At the junction of the white shoulders and the golden neck, where there was a horrid scar, I placed a necklace of silver toads and water marigolds and finally, I bade Rosalia open her hard lips and replaced her stiff tongue with one which was soft and pliant, a tongue of great length, hinged at the front like a frog's. This changed her voice, which was no more the echo of Nemione's, but sibilant and bubbling, alive like falling water or a rushing stream. Her face had a melancholy expression which contrasted fittingly with her radiant smile; she was in perpetual pain, but I could do nothing about that for the demon's fire vaporized the nivasha's water and the water quenched the fire. Rosalia's body was in a constant state of flux. If one or the other had prevailed, she would have destroyed herself. Steam issued from her nostrils only to be replaced by smoke. The vapours alternately dampened and dried me when I kissed her; both warmed me and the warmth transferred itself from my lips to hers, stiff and metallic. I grew strong, looking at her, and began to give her small tasks such as the tender kissing, fetching my meals from Cob (who had taught himself to be an excellent chef), tidying my bed, turning the pages of my book as I read. She was grateful, for she had a body once more – and most desirable! On the first day of summer I drew aside the sheet which covered me and invited her to the enjoyment of my eccentric body.

Lèni slept as if she was entranced, but Guy could find no peace. Until she woke he was free of her and of the long narrative which so filled his skull that, while he told it, there was no room for other thoughts. The candles guttered and he looked to see where the draught came in. The door of the room stood open. Lèni had forgotten to close it again. His hands, which were resting on his shoulders, gently tapped his forehead. The constant soft blows annoyed him.

'Quiet!' he said, as he might to a dog; but the hands tapped on. He moved his head from side to side, attempting to avoid their touch. They moved nimbly and kept up their tattoo. He got up slowly from the bed, moving in stages so that he did not wake Lèni, noticing as he moved across the room that his hands were still again.

In the mirror which backed the credenza he saw a tattered relic of a man, pale-faced and thin, the long cuffs of his jacket giving him an aristocratic air, the two hands perching like weird epaulettes on his shoulders. The thick beard he had grown masked his chin and neck. 'A gentleman tramp,' he muttered. 'A classy hobo.' He peered at Lèni's reflection behind him, a bundle of rags in the dilapidated bed. She had not moved. A wide area of wood on the top of the credenza shone as if it had been dusted recently and there, in the polished midst of it, a photograph lay. Old and sepia-tinted, it showed two smart figures against the painted backcloth of a photographer's studio, the elaborate fashions of the 1880s before a counterfeited Temple of Diana. He recognized the chief actors of his opium dreams, those all-too-solid, passionate creatures, Paon and young Lèni herself, and bade his right hand turn the photograph over. Sure enough: printed on its back in capital letters was the legend, 'Georges et Hélène, 1882.'

Her sleeping figure in the mirror had stirred; she was sitting up. Startled, he turned about and saw her rising in the bed, her arms extended and her expression, as the bedclothes unveiled her, welcoming. She was in the fullness of her beauty, crowned by her sinuous dark hair, her fascinating snake's eyes compelling him. Obediently, he started forward, calling her by the lover's names which once delighted her,

'Beloved, Swan's Daughter, Goddess, Helen, Witch –' They were the truth, and had been spoken many times. The old words came upon him like a litany: 'She is very pleasant and will be old and young when she pleases,' and again, 'She makes any King whom she pleases and lies with any she pleases.'

Helen smiled as he reached her. He bent to kiss her and her mouth dropped open in a soundless scream. Gesturing at the shadows behind him, she fell back and became, before his appalled gaze, the scarred and drunken Lèni la Soie who, instantly ageing, shrank into her absinthe-violated body and lay still and deathly, a wasted cadaver whose yellow skin stretched tight across her bones, whose eye-sockets were empty and whose lipless mouth gaped in that final silent, hopeless scream. A shining lens winked at him from inside the skull and from its mouth crawled a snake, a lamia gaudily patterned in bands of orange, scarlet and black. It reared up before its little cave and drew back its jewelled head to strike.

There had been a time when he admired snakes. He tried to speak to the lamia to calm her but the only words which came were magical gibberish put into his mouth by the power of the thunderstorm, by his creation, the Archmage Koschei, or by his addled mind itself.

'Serpent of Evil,' he cried. 'I exorcise thee in the name of the great River Lytha and by the eternal snows of the mighty Altaish, thou snake of the tribe of basilisks, thou foul, illusory, five-sensed, variegated Lamia. O Snake, cousin of the Dragon and the Fearsome Worm, thou that art on the right side of Hell and should be prisoned by its iron walls; if thou bite me thou shalt in the names of Asmodeus and Urthamma have no power to harm me —'

— And the Lamia, which had remained upright in her deadly, striking pose, closed golden eyelids upon her glassy eyes, coiled up amongst the bones of Lèni la Soie, and vanished.

His heart was racing and his breath coming in painful gasps. He stumbled clumsily backward and fell against the hawk-headed statue. Something crashed from the hollow of its beak to the floor. His left hand ran after it; came up with a key.

He fled the room and reached the locked apartment door, which he banged and butted with his head. He kicked its scuffed panels while his hands, moving swiftly and with great dexterity and none of his panic, inserted and turned the key; opened the door. He stepped out. The stairway before him was broken and old, every window boarded up, but he rushed downward, tripping and recovering himself in the dim light. A doorway on the next floor had been closed off with a rough grey wall, another with a cross of wood. He paused for an instant, listening for the silk-looms of a century ago, but there was no sound at all. If it had been entirely dark, he would have believed himself beyond the grave. A grudging light filtered up the stairwell from below and made visible some words painted in crimson on the wall. He read them: COMME LA VIE EST LENTE ET L'ESPERANCE VIOLENTE: 'How slow is life and how violent hope.' As a clap of thunder broke the deathly silence on the stair, the sentence illuminated the long opiate night in his mind and, This is real, he thought. Outside, I shall find people, and hope, so long denied. He tried to run again, the rest of the way down, but his legs would hardly obey him, weaker agents of his escape than his detached hands.

The hallway had been reduced by the years to a grime-streaked cavern. Here were two doors, both closed. The smaller door: that, he seemed to remember – stumbling through it – some rubbish on the floor – Georges. If he were to come – now. Panic shot through him: I am still imprisoned.

The big door had no locks or bolts, but holes where they had been. A thick piece of string dangled. He lifted his arms to tug at it, expecting resistance, forgetting. The nimble hands ran down his arms, inserted their fingers between door and frame, felt around. While the useless muscles in his arms moved involuntarily the door opened. Outside, a dingy thoroughfare made darker by falling rain led away into grey-ness. Guy turned in the doorway, waiting as the hands came back to him and tucked themselves neatly away in his pockets. Daylight revealed more words, carved on a huge sheet of grey marble at the stair-foot. He made some of them out:

'*SOIERIES*' and '*G. PAON, (Appartement)*'

The street led nowhere, debouching into a rough court-yard surrounded by high buildings of seven or eight storeys. He looked up, searching the windowed façades for a clue, for some sign of life. Some of the windows were curtained, some open; nothing moved. He scanned the steep faces of the buildings again: nothing; saw, with relief, an archway. Dark beneath it, always dark. That sign, high up: Rue des Voraces – should he follow where the narrow street led? He stumbled against the kerb-stones and fell sprawling in the puddles. Another archway reared itself above his head. Slowly he crawled forward and, pushing with head and shoulders against the wall, resumed his upright position. This was the way forward, along this tunnel.

His mind led him on, through the maze. And now, he thought, I'm in a courtyard, but which one? Here is a flight of stairs and I shall climb them going up and across and up and across until at the top here's another corridor (must be high) and a last flight with – ha – another handrail and a door through which I *will* pass (Hands!) though above, the underface of the stone steps continues. These steps lead down, turn; just like those in the cathedral tower, a spiral so tread with care at the outer edge because in the centre the steps are too narrow for any but the eleven year-olds' feet. Through the window-less frame another courtyard. At the bottom another dark door but passing out of this, avoiding the old car seat and the bloody rags, I see a double row of tiny cupboards, each one painted with words in white, or black – or silver: A. Lavallé, D. Morel, Florent Navarre. Here, a door is broken, envelopes inside! Washing in this courtyard, wet as the miry ground. Hurry, wet as the washing and the dirty ground, beneath the arched doorway and begin to climb the steps. The windows on the stairs are blocked with walls of plastered stone but the arched metal frames remain. The scene is closed to view, so continue upwards into the light, dull, cold and strong. Come out – emerge in a street where a car (a Renault) is parked at the bottom of, dear God, a flight of stone steps which steps approach, avoiding a bronze lion on the kerb. His forefeet guard a tap. Climb. Ascend in the rain without slipping, fast as I can. Here at the top the street goes mercifully downhill and there are trees and a drain cover in the centre of the path, more steps but to the left. No need to go down them but pause – take in the misted view of roofs and towers far below, cars moving, two rivers. This is Lyon, the horse-butcher said. There is a Mini parked further down and I will walk that far before I rest.

The Mini, which has figures on it, 2539 JJ68. It is grey like the dusk which creeps from every doorway and arched opening and is starting to fill the street. But I must go on, down, always down.

Guy walked as quickly as he was able, veering in his course along the uneven pavement. There were a few passers-by, hurrying in winter coats or beneath umbrellas. They took him for a drunk and smiled, or crossed the street. One woman pitied him, alone and wet, night coming on; but the way was easier now he had quitted the labyrinthine *traboules* for the streets where each cross-roads presented an easy problem: which way? Downhill. And so he came into broader streets where he found rushing traffic which confounded him, a tunnel beneath the busy road and, beyond it, the public buildings and metropolitan elegance of Lyon, fountains adding their cascades of water to the falling rain, bright lights reflected, shop windows lit and, finally, a warm and sheltered doorway with a corner dark enough to hide him while he rested.

He woke, bitterly cold. The rain had got into his bed and the flapping sheet was wet. It blew against him and he read the lettering on it: GUY PARADOS, ROMANCIER, DIS-PARU AU MOIS DE JUIN A LYON. His own face smiled up at him from the paper and from a different, sunnier time. Shuffling upwards, pressed against the wall, he twisted and jerked his body to rid it of the clinging and unwanted reminder. He walked. The cold had got right inside, deep under his sodden clothes; his hands were dead weights, heavy in his pockets, immovable sinew and bone. He must get warm.

The lighted windows – chocolates, clothing, sausages, flowers – disappeared. Waste ground now, but lit. On the wall, a red mouth opened wide, screaming. Perhaps it was the source of the thunder, of the noise which rolled about him. In pain, for it was white and blue and red, torn from its column, sundered from its bodily root and neck, the head screamed. He walked past it. The street was more pleasant here, though empty of fellows and loud with the storm he was following. The yellow windows were misted over with warmth and there the people were, inside, sitting in comfort, eating, ignoring the noise. Where was its source?

The row of cars glistened. A white one, a green one, a scarlet shape he knew well, or was it Guy Parados, Chris Young maybe, who had told him about the marvellous vehicle coloured like Christ's blood, or Lèni's, or his own cascading higher than a fountain? Guy's car had Guy's name on it; this one had too many numbers, one-two-three-four, seven of them. The word was the right one though: A-u-d-i.

He paused beside the Audi, looking for more words, looking for clues. Blue again, how fond they were of electric blue neon and arabesques to make their arcane messages in the falling rain: DISCO < PHEDRE > DISCO. People here, more people – who did not turn to help him. Finding the open door, he went in on the heels of the laughing, rain-bespattered crowd and found his own face staring at him from the mirror which closed off the passage-way. Turn left. The mirrors came too, marching beside him, reflecting his new image and the already-dancing, prancing others in their tight and brightly-coloured clothes. He stumbled against them as he went, and one or two shrieked and one or two swore, but none of them stopped dancing, moving always faster as the storm increased. He slipped. The floor was glass and underneath it demons raged in a fiery pit while here the

258

lights flashed on and on now blue now green now silver like the dress of this wild girl who was falling with him and screaming louder than the thunderous music 'Gu-uy-uy-uy-uy!'

The blond boy knelt down. All down, all on the shining floor looking at themselves. All fall down. The boy spoke,

'Dad? – Dad! What the fuck are you doing here?'

'Got out – came down. All the hills.' He could not manage more. His hands had woken in his pockets and were scrambling out. The left was carrying something between first finger and thumb, running on the other three up, over his face. It scurried to his ears, left and right. A pleasant dimness succeeded the flashing lights as the sunglasses settled on the bridge of his nose and he watched both hands run in tones of brown and sepia across the girl's spread hair and over the small promontory of her chin until, reaching her slender throat round which a black ribbon was tied tight, they fastened themselves over the ribbon and squeezed. The boy shook the girl hard   her body flopped and lolled like the cloth limbs of a puppet – and, his own hands encountering the severed ones, began to scream and pull at them.

'Alice! My God! Alice, the hands! Alice!'

The music never ceased and the dancers whirled on. He was alone again, in the centre of the crowd. SORTIE, the new letters said, SORTIE, pulsing with the dimmed lights. He crawled towards them and his sunglasses fell off. The letters were red like the car, or blood or the red flush the absinthe brought to Lèni's cheeks or the roses-of-death which, spreading under Nemione's high cheek-bones so alarmed me that I snatched a feather from the wing of the sleeping owl, Strix, and held it to her nostrils to see if she breathed. The owl did not wake, head turned backward, feathery horns laid flat, but Nemione did and sneezed the feather away.

Nemione favoured me with a lingering blue gaze, but it

was an echo of her old, spirited glance. 'Koschei! I suppose you came to see if I was dead?'

'No, Lady, but to deny the rumours which abound in Pargur of your death.'

'I am ill, it is true, but they must want added tragedy if they talk of burying me.'

'That flush on your cheeks – it does not bode well.'

'Pooh, I have been asleep: that is all. Have you come in peace or to torment me?'

'I come as a friend, an old friend from the days of yore –'

'Such a friend – how I love my enemies! When we were young, Koschei, we had the sanguine tempers of the beasts. What are we now but ancient stories?'

'We are King and Queen, though we have always lived apart.'

'Well, Koschei, you would not want me now. I am Famine. Look at my hands.'

I sat on a stool beside her and took her wasted hands in mine. The blue veins showed, gnarled traceries, through transparent skin and the bones were long ivory skewers. Nemione's face and figure were similarly consumed, and her dress of grey and her grey and white furs did not help dispel my impression that she was near death. The roses in her cheeks supplied some colour – she was beautiful even so, a graceful Death or an elegant Pestilence adorned with diamond rings whose glacial stones shone in the firelight, whose sapphire eyes had grown as cold as northern winters. Her magic couch, which slumbered easily beneath her bird's weight, had also suffered from the years of famine and was white all over, save for its wooden head and feet. She closed her eyes and slept again and, softly releasing her hands, I went across to the fireplace – the same great cavern in which my demons had danced and my ghosts had played their play, so long ago – and stirred and fuelled the fire.

Fallen timber was what she burned there, dry or rotted

trees from the lands which once were forest covering the greater part of Malthassa. It burned well, fierce and hot, and was soon ashes. I piled on more – no one lacked for dead wood to burn.

This room, once the place in which she made and studied magic, was in these days of dearth and decay her Winter Parlour. Snow lay deep upon the window ledges outside, all I could see of the ravished land Malthassa had become. In summer, though there was little difference, mud and rain replacing ice and snow, she removed to her house of glass atop the keep of Castle Lorne and tried in vain to revive her orchids, creepers and flowering plants. These, which used to blossom with great vigour and stupendous colour, were dead stalks to which a clung a few twisted brown leaves and a withered fruit or two. Neither magic nor water would bring them back from the dead. In the castle, heavy furs and thick woollen cloth had replaced the silk and velvet arras and nobody wore less than three layers of clothing. The familiars had all grown dense coats, even the naked dog which was covered in trailing black hair. Only Nemione's cold-blooded Child, asleep on the couch with the rest, remained what she had always been, a creature more akin to fish than beast or fowl, her blue-green skin as chilly as the falling water of a cascade, colder than the drifted snow.

As I sat there by the fire, plaster fell from the ceiling to lie on that which had fallen before and never been swept up, for the castle servants were too busy bringing in wood to keep the place warm enough for life; some, whose parents and siblings no doubt were starving in the wasted forest, had left without leave or word. The pellets the horned owl cast up, small cartridges of mouse-skin and -bone, lay on and in the fallen pargeting. Castle Lorne's slow decay had begun with Nemione's, or Nemione's with her castle's: I was not sure. It held itself miraculously up, on its steep riverside rock – looked, from a distant vantage point, complete and strong, just as my Lady kept her skin-deep beauty though her body rotted to the core. A complete invalid, she sat all day on her couch and lay sleepless all night long in her curtained bed. Erchon, her Silver Dwarf, kept guard, lying with poison-tipped rapier in the doorway, the end of a trip-rope in his dagger-hand.

The Plague raged in many a city and market town – and there were many fatal ailments which went by this general name: the Bubonic, the Black, the Yellow, the Cachexic, the Defluxive, Felonic, Fistulous, Obstructive, Strangury and Tetterous. Malthassa's quacks and doctors made their diag-noses and sent at once for a priest. All too soon it was impossible to find a doctor. Every one of them was dead, like their patients and the priests, of whatever god. Rats swarmed where once children had played. The grimmest portent, the hungry Duschma, was seen in every corner of the land.

As for myself, Koschei Corbillion, Prince, Mage and Archmage, I was never alone, pursued as all magicians must be by the demons of Greed and Ambition and, in my unique case, Memory. I visited the Memory Palace often. Once there and snug, I dusted and re-examined all the artefacts I had brought together and puzzled over some which I could not remember collecting, two chiming silver balls and a pair of spectacles whose lenses (no use to magnify) were dark and kept out the light when they were put on. The afternoon's warmth vanished the first time I tried them. On the second occasion they caused me to see terrifying visions of a land where naked dancers wheel in perpetual motion and a lustful hag bestrides a thin young man. The third time I tried the magic eye-glasses I saw Death, who sat beneath a gallows-tree, grin at me and I knocked the cursed things from my face and trod them till they were powder. I am not easily made fearful but I went then to the book in which my soul was hid and peeped at him to be sure he was safe. And I prospered thereafter, my fragile and fastidious soul well-hidden in that poetry book. I affected a certain style familiar to those who read of magicians and know how we live – to wit, I grew my grizzled beard longer than was comfortable or fashionable, dressed always in black or dark red, carried a staff (a trifling thing which could, when I waved it, summon up a sumptuous meal, or jewels to please a lady) and stopped trimming my fingernails which grew into hard talons and curled back upon themselves, as do the tusks of potent boars. Such petty distractions helped me forget the wrong which Peder Drum did me when, using the spoken charm he had heard me utter in the balloon, he was transported to Peklo Tower. Finding me in undress and deep in the contemplation of my Art, he wrought such irreversible harm upon me that I cannot speak further of it – suffice it to say, he paid well and Baptist Olburn was the man I chose to extract his payment from him. Like Manderel Valdine, he has no grave and no memorial but the hungry maws of Pargur pye-dogs and the stinking turds they drop when they have eaten meat.

Sometimes, once or twice a month, the starving citizenry attempted to storm Castle Sehol and were driven back before they reached its walls. Their charges and the noise they made were regular diversions for me as I sat safe within the castle's impregnable defences or else worked esoteric magic in Peklo where my mirrors, globe and map kept me ahead of the mob. I grew accustomed – I had endless practise – to the cold. Roszi's fiery body warmed me at night, close against my back while on the other side, her pretty face to mine, the faithful Friendship clung, her warm brush close against my wrecked manhood – there, I speak my secret openly! – or caressed the single dug Nemione had wished on me. Sometimes the juggler (whose name was Concordis) joined us to chafe and cradle my cold feet. So, the two women and the golden-headed demon warmed me and I slept in comfort, forgetting the misfortune which had freed me from the tyranny of Love. I was eventually able, as you see, to visit

Nemione in complete composure, without one lustful thought and without rousing Erchon's ire.

The cry of the owl brought me to myself. This is what she said: 'Oh-o-o-o-o that I had never been bor-r-r-r-r-n.' Nemione did not stir, but the owl, with a twitch of her wings, slipped from her perch and those soft wings which should have borne her up never opened. She fell to the floor, dead, while her song echoed from the cold stone of the walls. I reached out to retrieve her body from the rubbish on the floor and, as I did so, saw a little transparent thing slip from it and run to the window. It was Nemione's soul, which she had hidden in the body of the owl and which, half-dead itself, now ran confusedly away. I saw it floating in the window-space before it dropped from sight below the ledge, as much a mote driven before the wind as the snow which began relentlessly to fall.

I left the fireside and crossed the room to Nemione. The owl feather lay where she had blown it, on the skirt of her gown. I picked it up and again held it to her nose knowing, even as I watched it for a sign of movement, for a scrap of hope, that it would not stir. The monkey, Halfman, crept from his warm nest under the other familiars and whimpered, scratching at Nemione's hand with his, so like a human hand. The Child awoke and gave her forlorn otter's cry. I felt the room grow colder and snowflakes whirled in from the open door which, as he crawled towards it across the endless, mirrored floor seemed more like an exit from hell than the blessedly open back door of a disco. His head was clear. Whatever he was leaving had no further place in his life here. They were all dead anyway, or transformed, Lèni and Helen, Alice and Roszi, and he was happy to be crawling, knee before stump, away from them into the snow. He wondered if it would be kinder to him than the rain.

On the threshold he paused, in case they wanted to run after and detain him. No one came so he continued his slow journey into the dark, feeling the wind rise about him as he went, almost as if he, himself, Guy Parados, had bidden it be his companion and harbinger.

PART THREE

PARADISE FOUND

What is now proved was only once imagin'd
WILLIAM BLAKE

The darkness had withdrawn; perhaps he had been all night crawling down this alley to nowhere, soaking his already-sodden clothes, chilling his already-cold feet and the mutilations which were his arms. But the snow whirling about him made it hard to distinguish anything. The faint light ahead might be no more than the inhospitable light of a street lamp at the alley's end – so it had an end – or new day. He need only crawl a little distance to find it, incapable of thinking further. The wind blew snow into his open, labouring mouth and covered his eyelids and lashes in soft, blinkering quilts; but there was something, directly ahead, a moving snowy form. What it was: impossible to tell. It took the shape of a tree and blew apart, of a mountain, of a ghost, of a bull, and again built itself up out of the half-light and the whirling snow. Whatever it was, it seemed to come no closer. Perhaps it moved before him and he, following it, would never catch up but creep for ever over the waste? A terrible weariness dragged at him, pulling him down to the ground, and he sprawled there seeing, even through his freezing tears of desperation, that the inhospitable ground was not tarmac or paving-stones but clean yellow earth across which the blown snow rolled swiftly and that there was grass growing in it, sparse stems blighted by winter but nevertheless alive. When the storm had overcome him and he lay dead upon it, the grass would continue his struggle with death and, triumphing, grow green and tall above him while its busy roots worked in his cadaver.

This thought of spring and greenness wrung him: happiness and hope had been strangers so long. He cried out loudly, 'My hands! My hands, I have lost my hands!' repeating his cry as the snow coalesced once more into that elusive, travelling indefinable shape: 'I have lost my hands!'

A voice of great warmth and felicity came to him out of the storm,

'I shall *find you*!'

The snow rose in a long plume and eddied across him. Then the man who was the source of the voice was on the ground beside him and the greater bulk, from which he had nimbly separated himself, became a huge, red-coloured horse so that, instantly, he knew where he was and who was his rescuer.

'Nandje!' he said weakly. 'It is Nandje, from the Marches of SanZu, Nandje the son of Nandje, isn't it? – did I make you Imandi? I certainly meant to.'

'"He will come crying out of the storm like a child,"' said the other, not heeding his words. 'It is you then, Parados. Do you see, the storm is already dying?'

He looked down on it from the unsteady stance to which Nandje had raised him. Indeed, the snow was light on the yellow earth and the wiry grass stems which grew in it were plentiful.

'That *is* my name,' he said, while the little man, who wore nothing beside a pair of boots and two lengths of cloth belted about his middle with linked silver discs, bent down before him and laid a cold ear on his chest.

'I am alive, if only just,' he said.

'I listen to your soul. Curious – I hear nothing. Have you lent it to someone? There is a great stillness which surely comes of suffering – a great silence.'

'I was imprisoned for some time – a long time.'

'Long enough no doubt, but no matter. I, Nandje of the

270

Ima, Rider of the Red Horse, will bring you to safety. Come now, up on the Horse with me.' He pushed Parados close against the warm bulk of the horse, which never moved but only looked backward at them with bright, intelligent eyes.

'Speak to him before I put you on his back!' said Nandje.

The correct words came from some crammed-full niche of his memory:

'Greeting, Horse. Permit me.'

He watched the long face of the horse while Nandje took firm hold of his left leg and propelled him upward, into the saddle. It seemed to nod, almost imperceptibly and then looked away from him and raised its ears, tilting them eagerly forward.

'He is keen to go – that is a wholly favourable sign,' said Nandje. 'Permit me also, Horse.' Briefly touching the heavy stirrup in his upward flight, the little man landed astride, in the gap between the saddle and the muscular hind-quarters of the horse. 'Will you pick up the reins? This is a solemn occasion.'

'How can I?'

'You can move your arms!'

The little man gave him no further help and Parados obeyed, manoeuvring the reins between his stumps. In this place, other qualities ruled. The reins, every part and piece of the bridle including the bit, were made of the hide of the last Om Ren; but he had not, when he first thought of them, made them so supple, nor imagined that the long hairs of the forest ape would still be on them, soft against his scars. The reins fell, or looped themselves perhaps (his disbelief was in total suspension) into the right places over his arms. His legs tightened round the body of the horse and the thick saddle-skirts. There was a miracle: it bounded forward into a gallop. He rode. Nandje, at his back, leaned forward and his long grey hair and the red grease on it came forward also, across his nose and mouth, and brought the scents of wood-smoke and burning oil with it.

271

'Stillness is a good quality, next to peace,' he said. 'It will redeem you, and all of us.'

'Stillness seems to hold us – though we move,' said Parados. 'Does this land of hillocks go on for ever?'

'No one knows; but we shall arrive at our destination.'

The low hills looked brown, the yellow earth becoming shadowed and mysterious by distance, the growing grasses insignificant. Had there been snow? There was no sign of it.

'The Horse out-runs the wind,' said Nandje in his ear.

'But look over your shoulder! There is no storm, no snow – only the hills.'

'Spring has come.'

'So swiftly?'

'You are here.'

As if to convince him, not only that his privation was ended but that hope had returned, some trees appeared in the near distance, a small grove or thicket of them which as they approached put out fresh, young leaves and pollen-laden catkins whose sweet perfume was a fleeting memory, sensed and gone as they rushed past.

'Praise the Absolute and all the Gods and Spirits!' said Nandje. 'Those were the mulberries we used to harvest. We shall soon be home – I must tell the young women that they flower. We have had no berries after our meat since they were babes on the breast.'

'Where is "home"? Shall I recognize it?'

Laughter, somewhat stained with a meaty breath, blew across Parados's face.

'Don't you remember? We live beneath the ground.'

There were the young women, though no time had passed, gathering round the Horse with arms outspread in welcome, pretty bare arms patterned with red grease. Young men too, dressed (or un-dressed) like Nandje, and older men and women, children, dogs, ancients, horses, more horses – so many of these, a herd, a multitude: all of them gathered about him, the Horse and Nandje.

272

One of the young women was pushed forward out of the crowd, solemn with the moment. This too, was an occasion. Parados looked down at her and felt his heart leap. She was like no woman he knew or remembered, entirely blameless. Returning his look, she said,

'The Horse has a new Rider!'

He was lifted down by sinewy, dusty arms, which pushed and shoved each other in their eagerness to touch him. He lay on a litter at her feet (bare, a silver anklet on the right) and she was giving orders to lift and carry him. The litter swayed, up and down the unceasing hillocks, level with her blue-clad hips. She smiled down at him.

'I am the Imandi's daughter,' she said. 'The youngest daughter of the Rider: I am Gry. I must care for you now you have come to us – at last, Parados.'

He smiled back. Thoughts of food and water, sleep, a comfortable bed, of her, Gry, with, beside, beneath him intervened. In his fancy, he was whole.

Gry, still smiling, shook her head.

'Care for you, Parados,' she said, 'not pander to your insanity.'

'No! I am not mad.'

'You are unclean; and you have lost your soul. How could that happen? How could you let that happen?'

The people, who still crowded after him but now at a little, respectful, distance were singing. He listened to them:

'I-o, I-ay, Spring is here!'

Men came forward to help him from the litter. A low, dark entrance waited at his feet and, looking for a moment beyond it, he saw that the brown and yellow soil had disappeared already and that the rolling hills were green with new grass and studded with small trees in flower. Birds sang. He saw some of them: pairs of turtle-doves, larks ascending, and coveys of tiny quails hurrying about their spring business of mating, laying, sitting on eggs.

Gry knelt on the ground.

'A little more crawling!' she said. 'Follow me into the house.'

The passageway was short. No more than a dip of the kneeling body was required, acknowledgement of the earth above him. He stood up slowly in the house. It was dark like all caves, and warm; dry as bone.

'I can't see much,' he said to Gry. She stood close to him, ready to support him if he failed.

'I will make light.'

He heard her moving, across an earthen floor. Her bare feet made gentle, soothing sounds. A sharper noise and flame leaped in her hands. Witchcraft? Magic?

'How did you do that?'

'I have matches – lucifers from Vonta. We buy them when we sell at the horse fair.'

'Lucifers?' The name was unwelcome here, where he felt safe.

'An old god, evil is he not? Red as fire. The mages call him Urthamma and treat him with extreme caution – like fire.' Gry bent gracefully in the darker centre of the house, bringing her flame low. He saw kindling, logs. Soon, he was seated by the fire on woven cushions and skins, a skin and sinew back-rest supporting him.

The luxury of having his filthy clothing removed and hot water squeezed over him from a sponge of dried mosses, of having red grease smelling of pine woods rubbed into his skin, and his hair and beard combed and clipped disturbed him not at all. He was content. Gry went to a big chest which stood by the wall and took a clean shirt and a suit of heather-coloured linen out of it.

'Grandfather's chest?' he asked her and was amazed when she laughed at his words and sang,

> 'She gave him a suit of the very, very best
> And the soldier put it on.'

'Am I a soldier?' he said.

'Yes. In the Lays, Parados is a mighty paladin.'

'Sing me one of your Lays.'

'Later, when you are ready to sleep. Lift yourself a little now and I will dress you. These clothes come from Pargur – they are a little out of style now, but the very best as the song tells.'

When the garments were on him, he realized that they were new. Gry set a bowl and a beaker down by the fire and knelt to spoon the contents of the bowl into his mouth. The stuff was sharp-tasting, nearly liquid: a kind of yoghurt or curd.

'Now take your kumiz, and you will sleep. Look, I have made your bed already.'

'Before I came here?'

'My father had a prophetic dream two nights ago. He got up from it immediately and began to search for you.'

At about that time, he thought, I was telling Lèni (if she ever existed) how Koschei made Rosalia – here, in this country? In my country? (If it exists.)

'Drink your milk,' said Gry. 'I have put a parsley-stem in it to help you.'

He bent over the beaker and took the hollow stem in his mouth. Though it was rougher in his mouth than a paper straw and the room was dark and firelit and Gry there fantastic in her blue skirts and silver ornaments, he felt as happy as an infant sitting on his little classroom chair. He sucked at the mare's milk, finding its taste astringent like the curds. When he had drunk it all he at once became sleepy. Gry helped him to lie comfortably on the bed, arranging the pillows, covering him with a soft fleece.

'Close your eyes,' she said, 'and I will tell you how young Parados met the Witches of Albion.'

She began to speak in a low monotone, in verse which rocked along and rhymed in couplets. It was his story after all, a part of his past history and he heard her in prose and saw the old images and pictures pass before him as he slept.

> 'Hands were strong then, strong for gripping,
> 'Strong for war and games, for loving,'

... soft, careful how and where they made contact with the other body, gentle if not yet adept. Helen moved them wherever she desired their touch. June, midsummer. The grass on the hillside was high and ready to flower – it should be cut within the week and they were spoiling part of the hay-crop under their naked bodies, not caring, past feeling how the strong stems marked them. He pulled back from her, wanting to look and unable long to bear the sight of her longing for him displayed so wantonly under the blue and open sky.

'Poor Guy,' she said. 'But I'm not sorry I kept you waiting.'

'What?' Her words had intruded where no words were necessary. He remained where he was, kneeling over her, noticing that her skin was the exact colour of oak-galls, that her black hair was tangled and stuck together in snake-locks which did not – quite – writhe but –

'You may have me now, if that is what you want,' she said.

Still he remained, drawn back from her, feeling his insatiability impossibly wane.

'Am I not your heart's desire?' said Helen.

'Yes –' but he was not certain; he questioned himself, his body reflecting each successive stage of his self-doubt. Helen knelt too, her brown arms about him.

'I am the appetizer,' she said. 'Let us say that is what I am, the choice morsel of *manrieli*, a taste of the richer cake to come! Come on – get up. We shall take a short stroll.'

'Someone will see us!'

'No. Hold your amazement tight about you. It is all the covering you need. Trust in me – there is no need for clothing, which covers up the truth.'

Then she led him upwards, following the sloping contours of the hill until they stood beside the thorns which ringed its hollow summit, naked still and closer to the sky. He stared down on the coloured fields spread out from hill-foot to horizon. A golden glaze had touched everything: the crops were all on the point of flowering.

'Look out – behind you!' said Helen suddenly. He started and swung round expecting – what? A hiker? Someone from the village out with a dog and both, either, now a witness to his folly, embarrassment, deceit. He was never (never, never, each time he relived the scene) prepared for the sight of a crowd of women naked as the day, as Helen, as himself. They stood there in a semi-circle, bare feet half-concealed in the clovers and grass which grew abundantly there and which could never be harvested because this hill of Karemarn was an ancient site, a ring-fort four or five thousand years old. Small Neolithic cattle had grazed – the women stood waiting, as it seemed, for him.

'What am I to do?' he whispered.

' "Be not afeared!" ' she quoted, smiled at him and raised her left hand. One of the women stepped forward, a young one -- quite the youngest there. Her hair was the colour the corn would turn, when it was ripe; her eyes the colour of the corn-flowers in the garden of his cottage, electric, startling. She, herself, had an air of half-maturity like a green apple only just touched with red and she held something in her hand. A sack, he saw, as she lifted it and put it in Helen's hand.

'Thank you, Maid.'

Helen lifted the sack still higher, toward his head.

'No!' he said and tried to jerk away. He could not move of course, all volition – of his will – had left him. He felt like a puppet. He would dance to their tune, he knew it.

Helen had quelled his desire with a few words and could conjure it again whenever she wished. The sack came down over his head. Strong, deft fingers tied it in place and while they worked, he tried to see through it. The hessian was coarsely-woven and lay like thick mesh across his face. He saw parts of the women, sections of sky, torn and whirling boughs on the trees for they were turning him, spinning him about till he was dizzy. He stumbled over the grass. Thorns growing in it pricked his feet and he fell at last on hands and knees, stars and fast-revolving suns illuminating the blackness in his head and a heavy warmth and smell of calf-feed from the sack filling his nose and mouth.

'Give him a drink!' called one of the women.

'Poor man!' cried another.

He tried again to dodge them, blind as he was in the sack, but their feet and legs were all about him, kicking, hemming him in. Liquid poured down over him, soaking the sack and cascading over his face, down his neck and out of the sack again, down his chest. It was beer. He breathed its suffocating, yeasty scent and licked it from his lips. The women began to call out again, one to another, their voices confident. He recognized the accents of his county and village in some.

'Is he strong?'

'Strong enough!'

'Has he come far?'

'Far enough!'

'How far?'

'Up the hill!'

'How far is that?'

'A mile and many more years!'

Something would happen now. They would release him – or destroy him. Again, though he was unprepared when it began, he recognized the rightness of it. He felt their hands on him, many fingers lightly tapping, tickling, playing, a flock of small scurrying creatures. Some climbed his arms

278

or ran down his legs: they did not discriminate. He bent, trying to shield himself, and heard their shrieks of laughter.

'He is bold,' said one ironically.

'We'll make him bolder,' another replied. Some of the hands applied themselves, with great will and perseverance to his arms, pulling him straight, forcing him to unbend. Others laid hold of his ankles. He fell on his back. His shrouded head thumped the hard ground under the turf, but no one took any notice and, as soon as he was spread for them he felt the first one mount him.

Soon, he lost count of them. He was their toy, nothing more – nor less, and in great pain with his longing for them and with his inability to bring his wonderful agony to an end. 'Helen,' he said repeatedly, 'Helen?' but got nothing in return except the howling and squeals of animals. Indeed, he heard the women addressing each other with the names of the beasts.

'You next, dear Sow.'

'It is your turn, Sister Ewe.'

'Yours now, sweet Heifer. Come to the Bull.'

Darkness seemed to come, beyond the veil of the sack. It grew cool and dew made the grass damp under him, unless it was his sweat, who still lay passive for the women and active as a ram. One of those who had the village voice spoke up,

'You now, dearest Lady. He longs to serve you.'

He heard Helen Lacey, close by him, answer her:

'Is he ready, pretty Heifer; can he endure the last and best?'

'The poor creature is in torment! Come.'

This woman was light and busy on him, crouching high, now low. The time had come, was here. He emptied himself in her, crying out with the relief, and the shame. What should have been his to give, as with his wife, with other women in his past, had been taken. His last tormentor rolled away. His hands were grasped by long, cold fingers – Helen's, without a doubt – and something feathery and warm put in them. It struggled, beating its body, its wings against his chest. He screamed and the bird screamed louder than he.

'Don't let go!' Helen's voice was urgent. 'Get up – kneel. Now pull his neck – in the old days it would have been yours!'

He felt for the thrashing head of the bird, held it; neck in the other – pulled the two apart. The neck dislocated in his hands. The wings flapped wildly against him and the bird was taken from him. He heard them rending it and sucking its blood and the raw flesh from its bones. Helen came back to him – her hands moved, tracing a spiral on his chest.

'Next time,' she said. 'You will call the tune – our king, subject no longer. You have passed the test.'

It grew quiet. He shivered. Though there had been no sound beyond a random susurration in the grass, he knew that he had been deserted, abandoned on the hill to find his own way back. His first voluntary act was to claw at the knot in the string which bound the sack over his head and then, having untied it, to remove the blind. Dark had come and the moon was up and full, yet white as the skin of the girl who had hooded him. All that remained of the cockerel were a few tail-feathers lying in the grass; of the ceremony, a dark spiral drawn, he must suppose, in the bird's blood on his chest. The initiate stood up and moved slowly down the hill to the field where his trials had begun. His clothes lay where he had dropped them in the afternoon and he collected them wearily, put them on. The familiar fields were welcome, though invaded by the moon's unvarying light. He spat on his fingers and rubbed away the bloody mark; passed his hands over his hair, smoothing it, and found a feather adhering. It glowed as brightly as a flare and he put it in his pocket to extinguish it and douse the glaring memories of this frantic, blood-spattered ceremony.

'On he wandered, hero hallow,
Bound in flesh and blood to follow
Where they led him, where they called him,
Where'er the weird sisters bade him,
Where his fated footsteps brought him.'

Gry rocked to and fro in sympathy with her verse, red lights glowing in her silver ornaments, her plaits swinging.

'That is all I have to tell and all there is to hear,' she said; but Parados was asleep and she gave him one tender and regretful look before creeping silently from the house.

He rubbed his face, which itched, slowly moving his scarred stumps over forehead, cheeks, beard. All that witchery was long ago. Now Parados lay grievously wounded in Gry's house – in the Plains – in Malthassa. He had come a long way, nearly fifty years; had never stopped travelling since that first, midsummer night. Had I truly such a wild youth? he thought. Such abandonment? Such irresponsibility? The fire burned dully, deep crimson. He sat up and looked about him: no sign of Gry. It was quiet here, too. You might hear a pin drop, a mouse breathe, a spider walk.

'Your youth was a time of discovery, I think?' said a voice at his elbow, a rich voice full of joy and good fellowship. A broad, smiling face shone beside him in the dark, spoke again. 'A time of rash deeds for your mature consideration?'

'I suppose everyone's is.'

'But yours outdid the common – how meagre, for example, were our orgies of drinking in Vonta, our little romances and our bi-annual pilgrimages to Nether Pargur, our fights at the mine, beside your exploits!'

It took a few minutes, the identification. The language, the bass voice, the coppery hue of the face –

'Githon?' Parados said. 'If I'm correct.'

'Correct! Githon of the Copper Race, poor coin beside our Silver brothers.'

'But you are Erchon's cousin, aren't you?'

'Of a kind, not kissing-cousins. My mother is the sister of the husband of Erchon's fourth uncle's second wife.'

'You take ancestry seriously in Malthassa!'

'As you well know. It is wonderfully good to see you, Parados. Your coming has been rumoured many months and, before that, was a well-loved folk-tale in many of our little nations.'

'Nations?'

'A strong, war-like word. Our tribes then, our wondrous peoples. We have as many kinds as you, more perhaps: ourselves, the Dwarves; the Giants; the Om Ren all alone – and his mate who likewise dwells alone, but in the Altaish (you would call her the *Yeti*, no doubt, though she is a fair creature and no ape); the Nivashi; the Puvushi; the *Zracni Vili*, spirits of the air; Gypsies – the wandering, secret Rom; Women (how I love them!); Men in their many kinds – and the Mages amongst them might be counted a separate race. Which brings me to my tale –'

'But tell me first how you come to be here, in the Plains.'

'I told you: rumour is abroad and, besides, I am an idle fellow who likes to roam, though never purposefully as does my belligerent cousin, Erchon. It is of Erchon – and the others – that I would speak.'

'Nemione? – Koschei?'

'Of the Lady Nemione, who died so long ago (may all the gods be generous to her soul) and the Archmage, Prince Koschei. Listen to me!'

'Great storms and plagues of rats raged in the early months of the year in which Nemione died. Many think she died of an illness associated with rat bites or from something taken of their dirt in the food on the table. Others think she died of a more sinister poison, of pride, of jealousy, of evil magic for unrequited love; that Koschei murdered her. The only certainty is that what was bad in Malthassa – I mean the

282

failed harvests and dismal summers, the cruel winters, the sudden agues and fevers, the rapid fading and death of tiny babes and sturdy children – had begun many years before she died and continued no better. Such attempts as have been made by clerks and scholars and other such delicate scum (I am a simple miner) to lay the country's misfortunes at her door are false, and scandals. She was another victim, despite her magic and her high and intricate skills. It is my belief, based on nothing but a sigh on the wind and a sight through a break in the clouds of Castle Lorne – how grey and wintry it is! – I believe she died because there was nothing more for her to do: of boredom if you will.

'Koschei built her a marble tomb, not where she would have wished in the meadows of Espmoss, where she played as a girl, nor under the greenwood tree where first she met the gypsies whose company she loved, but on a high alp above Castle Lorne – in the very centre of the Windring that the Giants raised and with a view (if one were needed in death!) of the snowy Altaish unfolding her clouds, ridge after ridge. There is gold up there if any one were brave enough to win it! And there is fool's gold and rubies and their sisters, sapphires (the colour of Nemione's eyes) and fire-opals and emeralds, carnelians as big as your fist and all the ores too, iron, antimony, nickel, mercury, chrome – we dwarves are meek and fearful fellows, Parados. Only at the mountains' feet do we dare claw our adits out.

'Enough, to the story! Well then, picture the lovely lady on her bier, at peace now and so beautiful in death. A full guard was brought up from Castle Sehol and a regiment of Navigators and their balloons. They carried her up to her resting place in a gondola specially built and laid her in her tomb – so cold in that high meadow and not a flower showing through the snow. They say that Koschei grieved so desperately he tried to clamber into the tomb with her and that his old body-servant Ivo had to restrain him. Ivo used to be a soldier and afterwards a boxer on the fairs: a strong man, though aged. He is dead now, gone to join the great company we have lost.'

Parados leaned forward, his face contorted in the flickering light.

'What is it?' said the dwarf. 'Do your hands, though they are gone, pain you? Grieve not: all shall and will be well.'

'I never meant to kill her!' Parados exclaimed.

'Koschei said something of that kind. Grief makes us witless, makes us utter wild words. He had loved her all his life, you see, and in vain too. He thought she chose to die because it was the only way she could escape him: he was mad for a while.'

'But when was this, when did it all happen?'

'Oh, years ago. It is not even a memory now but a tale. Call it fifteen years: who knows how long a year is, in Malthassa? Some years are much shorter than others. They fly by like a gale. Let us say it has been another fifteen, no – say twenty, twenty-five – since the lady died. Those years – that time has been fearful. Erchon told me how, after they had buried her, night fell in Castle Lorne and has not ended yet. The servants – those that were left, for most had fled to their homes far away – lit the lamps. Little was revealed by their dim light but the drunkenness of the funeral guests and the broken meats left from the wake. The castle, from high watchtower to deepest wine cellar, slept, except for Erchon, who in the dead of this eternal night, sat watching on the steps outside Nemione's room. It was his custom and he was not ready to give it up, though he knew it was an empty folly to guard her emptier room. He heard the night owl's silent wing, the scurrying of the cockroaches over the golden plates and the whisper of the cat to the rat: 'Take that!' He heard the terrible squeal of the dying rat, a mixture of anger and agony. It inspired him. He got up from the step he was sitting on, buckled on the rapier he had taken off and laid down in his grief and vowed to leave Castle Lorne, the Altaish, and all his past behind him, never to be re-visited. He vowed to leave Malthassa if it was possible. It was on his journey north in search of this delusive goal that he called at my house and, finding me there for once enjoying the company of my wife and children, told me this tale.'

'Where is he now? Have you heard from him?'

'Not a breath, not a shadow's shadow. Now, my friend, it is time for real dreams. Let me pull that fleece over you – I will lie down here, in the warm ashes.'

Gry, when she entered the guest-house in the morning found the two, man and dwarf, fast asleep. The house was warm and the embers of the fire glowed. She moved quietly about, waking the fire to flame, spitting steaks of dark red horse-meat, preparing bowls of washing-water, before she woke the sleepers.

'How well you look!' she told Parados. 'Clear-eyed, sweet breathed –'

'And maimed,' he finished for her.

'Fear not. All will and shall be well! Githon, I am glad to see you.'

When they had washed, and eaten the horse-meat, she bade them sit quietly and reflect upon whatever they wished, as long as it was a happy, hopeful thing.

'No sad thoughts must disturb you today,' she said, and left them. Githon smiled.

'Let us exchange our thoughts,' he proposed. 'Give me your happiest and I will tell you mine.'

Parados cast his mind into the past. It trawled the thoughts there and half-raised a few, slimy mud-coated hulks, which he quickly dropped back into the mire. The future, he thought, and saw, though it was pure fantasy, the sun rising on a pastoral landscape: pure peace.

'An abstract, I'm afraid,' he said. 'The future – not a certain hope.'

'It will do very well. Mine is no dynamite charge either – a simple prospect of my beloved Altaish on a winter's afternoon, when darkness falls swiftly from the peaks and they become one with the night sky, save that the snow capes each one wears appear to float amongst the stars.'

'Happy thoughts!' Nandje had entered the house. 'You are playing the game of Contentment,' he continued. 'It makes *me* happy to see you and it is an auspicious beginning.'

The sun had risen over the Plains and brought with its rising a warm breeze to stir the newly grown grasses. The horses of the Ima grazed them, moving outside the village in loose groups of mares and young colts. The Red Horse, meanwhile, grazed alone beyond his herd, ears cocked in case of an alarm. Of the village itself there was little to see, a public hearth built of dry turves and stones, a scaffold on which several horse-skins hung to cure, a flagstaff whose flag-less rope tapped against it in the breeze and the small hillocks, miniatures of the greater which composed the Plains, which were the house-tops. The rest was underground. Someone emerged from his house, appearing like a rabbit suddenly out of the ground. A piece of blue cloth was tied about his waist which, when he unwound it, proved to be the missing flag. The man bent it to its rope and hoisted it. His emergence brought forth others from the ground and soon a crowd had gathered which milled about one particular house-hill while individuals left it to call their horses in from the herd. Presently Nandje appeared, stood upon his house and absently whistled a tune. Far out, in the tallest grasses, the Red Horse turned his head, took one last mouthful, chewed on it and swallowed; and cantered to the village.

'You must crawl again – it is for the last time, I assure you,' Githon told Parados. 'A few yards and you will be a new man – nearly new, at least. No, not that way. That is the back door. We shall leave by the front.'

Parados tried to shuffle along the low passageway on his knees but it was not possible. He had to bend his back and so, crawled on all fours out into the daylight. The crowd, as numerous as it had been the evening before, drew back to make a space for him and immediately pressed forward when he was on his feet. People touched him, hands reaching over neighbours' heads and shoulders. Children, on a lower level, ran out to grasp his trouser-legs and the hem of his jacket, smiled up at him, and disappeared into the crowd.

'Make way, make way!' called Githon at his back and when a way was cleared and the people had stopped moving with him, Gry stepped forward with a heavy coat of sheep-skins across her out-stretched arms.

'For you, Parados,' she said. 'To keep you warm when the cold winds return, as they must, alas.' She made a show of passing the coat to him and he held up his useless arms. Then she handed the coat to Githon.

'Goodbye, Lord Parados,' Gry said, made a small bob like a bow and retreated.

Lord? He laughed wryly to himself, not liking the distinction.

'Gry!' he said; but she had vanished amongst the other blue-clad, brown-skinned women. 'Thank you, Gry!' He wished very much that he could see her.

A group of horsemen waited for him. He saw Nandje there, mounted on the Red Horse, at least a dozen others, some spare horses, a flag-bearer carrying the same sky-blue standard that flew above the village. They looked like a photograph out of the *National Geographic*, empty green steppe, un-groomed horses, barbaric jewellery, sun-burned faces, bare chests, savagery, magnificence. He blinked, but they did not go away. The men beside him conducted him to one of the riderless horses and put him in the saddle. He was not surprised that his horse was white. Nearby, Githon struggled without any help into the saddle of a smaller horse, the men of the Ima standing back to watch him, laughing at him and slapping each other's backs. Githon remained cheerful.

'It is a fact of life,' he said. 'I cannot ride – but give me a miner's pick! Nevertheless, I shall persevere and, if I fall off, do not stay to put me up again.'

Parados, confident that his white mount would display as much understanding as the Red Horse, smiled.

'Now!' said Nandje, riding up. 'What have you forgotten? Her name is Summer.'

'Permit me, Summer?'

'That form is for the Red Horse only. "By your leave" –'

'By your leave, Summer.'

'Good! Now she will treat you kindly. But I am afraid she is not such as expert with her bridle as the Horse. I will knot the reins for you. Let them lie there, on the pommel. Summer will not leave her kind.'

'Nandje, this is all very well. I have no inkling of what my future holds here – but, where are we going?'

'To SanZu, where else? It is in the wind – look, it bends the grasses eastward.' He sat tall on the Red Horse. One of the riders beat a drum. The Ima cheered, and the men and women all together. 'To SanZu!' said the Imandi again. 'SanZu! SanZu!' the crowd echoed and Gry was there again, with a flowering mulberry branch in her hand.

She held it up and presented it to her father who at once gave it back to her. Then she took it, a broad smile on her face, to Parados and, because he could not carry it, tucked it into the cheek-piece of Summer's bridle.

If, on that fortunate day, anyone had been afflicted with a sudden desire to step into the basket of a balloon and soar above the Plains or, being a competent magician, changed himself into a high-flying eagle; or, worst of choices, had been able to sit on the shoulder of the Archmage, Koschei, and stare into his magic mirrors, he would have seen a compact company of horsemen moving steadily over the low, green hills. At intervals individual riders shot forward from the rest, rode on a while and circled back. And then, if he had cast his eye, bird's or magical, on the far hills of SanZu in the east the watcher would have seen there a ring of snow-clouds hanging in the air and dense flocks of crows darkening the already-dark skies. A third look would have descried another company advancing over the Plains, an untidy line with stragglers at the rear, calves perhaps from their general outline, or goats. About five miles (as the crow flies) from the two groups, some thorny bushes spread long tentacles into the grass. It looked as though they would converge hereabouts, and meet.

The out-rider had returned again and held a muttered conversation with Nandje, who spoke in turn to the Red Horse. In a little while, it stopped and Nandje, turning in the saddle, said,

'There are other travellers abroad. We shall meet and pass them at the Nut Ground – they are carrying a branch of pilgrimage and will not be kind if we speak to them. Yet I know – it is in the wind – that their journey is ours and I will speak.'

No one replied, but long, curving swords and bows which they had concealed in their kilted clothing, appeared in the Ima's hands.

'Oh ho,' said Githon quietly, darting a glance at Parados. 'Determined men.'

It was a caravan, this other set of travellers in the Plains, a loose column of men who walked beside and kept guard on a huge, lumbering cart. It had eight wheels, Parados counted them, wooden wheels which screamed on their axles, and was drawn by a team of oxen in whose twenty horns dead twigs and small pieces of coloured cloth were twined. A large cloth woven of fibres which alternately gleamed in the sun or dully absorbed its light hung over the waggon on a frame. Two men rode on horses in front of the waggon and some boys driving a few scrawny sheep brought up the rear. One of these carried the grass-topped pole which signified a holy purpose.

The two companies journeyed parallel for a time, each ignoring the other's presence, but when the tangle of bushes Nandje called the Nut Ground appeared on the horizon, he began to make audible comments about the other procession:

'It seems they have a better purpose than ours.'

'I imagine they believe themselves to be alone under the wide sky.'

'Certainly they are foreigners crossing our Plains without leave.'

This had the desired effect. One of the riders before the waggon turned his horse and galloped straight at Nandje, drawing a knife from his saddle as he came. He flourished it and pulled his horse up cruelly, so that it canted backward on its hind legs.

'This is a poor weapon for a horseman, but I shall not hesitate to use it,' he said.

Nandje laughed openly.

'What is it you carry in your wheeled snail that requires such rashness?' he asked civilly.

'Something more precious than a flax crop; more valuable than a wain-load of mulberry leaves and far, far more delicate than the smallest silkworm,' he said. 'Yet it has no value to you. Ride on your way and leave us to our slower progress.'

'But you have made me very curious. It must be a magical device.'

They rode on, side by side, constantly exchanging these and other challenging pleasantries until they came to the bushes, where the pilgrims made a great show of halting and setting up a camp and the Ima did the same. Two fires were lit and two separate meals prepared at them. Parados, as he sat enjoying the warm wind on his face and the salty taste of the morsels of dried horse-flesh which Githon cut for him from a strip of it, noticed that the rival travellers had only hard oatcakes to eat. Githon fed him more of the jerky with a beaker of kumiz and another to follow. He grew merry and laughed heartily at Githon's jokes but, when evening came and the others lay down to rest, he could not sleep and made up his mind to cross the neutral ground between the two camps, enter the other and look into the mysterious cart. A light was burning inside it, he could see that from where he sat.

His opportunity soon came. The guards, on both sides, concentrated their watch on the outer sides from whence, he supposed, wild animals or tribesmen might attack and he walked unchallenged up to the enormous waggon where he found, set against the rear of it, steps which he climbed. The covering-cloth or awning, looking yellow in the dusk and with a light from within, hung down in front of him and he pushed it aside with his head and peered inside. A small oil-lamp burned there, on the wooden waggon-floor. Beyond it was a sort of throne: a huge stone chair. No wonder they needed such a waggon! A child-sized image hung with gold necklaces and dressed in many tattered layers of silk was seated on the throne. It was made of wax and its brown glass eyes glittered in the lamplight. He stood still for an instant while he wondered what its purpose, clearly of great significance for its escort, was: perhaps it guarded some treasure of monetary or spiritual worth. His inability to touch it was fortunate: such idols were best left to those who understood them and this one was particularly sinister, for its eyes were articulated like those of a china doll. He watched its eyelids slowly close. When the eyes were fully closed, he would dare to sneak away; but the brown eyes flicked suddenly open and the image whispered,

'I've shut my eyes and held my breath, but you are still here, Spirit. Please bless me and go.'

'I'm a man, not a ghost,' he said, staring at the image in amazement. 'And you are child!'

'Only in body,' the child said, haughtily. 'What is your name?'

'G –' he began and, remembering his new identity, corrected himself: 'Parados.'

The child jumped from her throne and came nearer, looking up at him with curiosity.

'Are you a shepherd?' she asked.

'No.'

'Are you a flax farmer?'

'No.'

'A silk-weaver?'

'No!'

'You're not a bit like my father – but perhaps you aren't a father. Have you any children?'

He racked his brains: no unhappy memories. 'Yes,' he said at last. 'I think I have.'

'"Think you have!" What a funny man you are. Are you a soldier?'

'Yes, that's what I am, a soldier.' So Gry had told him and so, he thought, he once had been – in Cyprus, that was the place. In the other life. Before.

'Have you a sword?'

'I'm afraid I haven't. I was wounded, you see.'

'Oh?' He had been afraid of this, interest. 'Where?'

'You wouldn't want to see where.'

'I would. My father at home was hurt. He lost his left leg – they cut it off after he got frostbite in the snows.'

'Well then – I have lost both hands.'

'Poor man.' She stared so hard and with such fearlessness, that he lifted his arms until the sleeves of his jacket fell back and his two stumps poked skywards like worn broom-handles. The child did not cry out or blench. 'Just like my father's stump,' she said. 'You told me your name, Parados, so I shall tell you mine; and my secret.'

'Secret?'

'It isn't a true secret, only from my enemies, and I know you are my friend. I was Livvy, from Russet Cross beyond the Plains – but that is all past. I am Polnisha, the new Living Goddess.'

'You are extraordinarily wise and mature for a child,' he said. 'I think I once knew you – perhaps you had another life before this one?'

'Of course I did – many! But no-one remembers their past lives.'

'I do.' – and perhaps I can teach her to recall hers, he thought. But, in her present state, she is so small and even more vulnerable than she was before. Too much questioning would tire her – what was she now, six years old, seven? – all swathed and decorated as she was, in her robes and ornaments. He had better treat her as a child, frame the next question suitably.

'I expect you brought a doll to keep you company?' he asked and bent low, to be on her level, but her eyes blazed so angrily and she stood so straight that he stepped back from her.

'A doll – a toy?' she said. 'You must treat me properly, Parados. My body is that of a little girl-child but, like you, I have the gift of Life. And I can also deal out Death.'

He had been aware of movement outside the waggon. Now, as she spoke the word 'death', a long knife-blade slid from behind him under his arm and remained there, pressing against his ribs.

'Like this?' he said. 'By setting a trap for me?'

'No.' The child smiled suddenly. 'Put down the knife, Master Finder. This man is not an enemy.'

'You must prove it to me, Goddess. I did not leave Flaxberry all those months ago to fail in my task. I did not journey to Russet Cross to bring back another dead child.' The knife moved slowly up and down against the cloth of Parados's jacket, shaving wisps of fibre from it.

'He has a kindly look on his face,' said Polnisha.

'So may a murderer.'

'He wears linen clothing.'

'Anyone may buy that.'

'He has no hands!'

'Now that, Goddess, interests me. Step down from the waggon, Master Anonymous, and let us see what we shall see.'

The knife compelled him and Parados turned and jumped from the waggon, stumbling as he landed on the dark ground and unable to save himself from falling on his face.

'Stay there!' The knife kept him down. 'Now, Sir Stealthy – who are you?'

'Guy Parados.' The two words, spoken into the ground, were lost but the child, somewhere above him, had also answered,

'Parados! That is his name. He is a soldier but, I told you! he has lost his hands – he can't fight you.'

'He might be a magician. You didn't think of that, did you?'

'Is that the way to speak to Me? Let him get up and prove he is what he says he is.'

He was raised from the dirt. Hands dusted him down, wiped his face and gently touched his bruises: Nandje was there, with Githon and two others of the Ima, Leal and Thidma, whose names he had learned as they rode. The lamplight, spilling from beneath the awning of the waggon, patterned their faces with yellow shadows. Nandje muttered some words which, half-heard, sounded like prayers, turned to him and tucked the branch of flowering mulberry beneath his arm. He looked wonderingly at it: there was no sign on it of withering or decay and the green and gold catkins were as fresh as they had been when Gry brought the branch to him. His assailant was now the one upon the ground, fallen there in astonishment and awe, while the child, Polnisha, styled the Living Goddess, clapped her hands joyfully. He looked away from them – they were all mad as hatters. He must also be, or asleep and dreaming. The stars winked at him, colluding in the dream, their constellations as unfamiliar as the wild inventions of a story-teller.

I saw and admired my foe, the story-teller. He had troubled me a long time, appearing with regular inevitability in my dreams and conjurations. Leaving aside the matter of his maiming – and that was not obvious while he rode the white mare, her idle, knotted reins seeming disregarded by an expert horseman – he looked strong and fit. Torture and privation are good teachers. I moved the mirror so that I might see his face which was lined, but with the experiences of life not sickness or despair. A firm mouth was buried in a beard luxuriantly thick and grey. He had blue eyes, not speedwell bright as were Nemione's (mourn her!), but likewise keen and I wondered idly whether such eyes are common in Albion – Helen, of course is a Romany chi, dark as her witchcraft and possessed of almost as much beauty as was Nemione (rest her!). Her peculiar practices with blood keep her young. Indeed, when first I spied her in that extraordinary prism which is hidden in the back of my smallest mirror, she stood naked – a remarkable work of bronze! – in a cold, winter garden, a bowl of crimson blood on a bench beside her. I watched her anoint herself with it, as a woman customarily uses a perfumed oil.

I wished I might welcome Parados as a brother. Finding significant numbers of his possessions there, I had recently set up in my Memory Palace a new table dedicated to him. The first objects I laid on it were the chiming silver balls which, on closer examination, I found were incised with a grinning silver dragon each. A dragon, to the commonalty, is the sign for fertility: well enough, for Parados has fathered many children. Their musical chiming pleased me. I opened the window to compare it with the striking from all quarters of Pargur's unsynchronized clocks and thought, as I stood there listening, that the dragon in his awesome pride is a cosmic force, the ultimate of dangerous beasts. The shattered eye-glasses were another potent matter. I had ceased, now they were powder, to fear them; nevertheless, I took a chirurgeon's care in sweeping their remains into a dust-pan and depositing the gritty pile on the new table. Then there was the cock's feather, an everyday object – my neighbour of the old days in Midnight Street kept a loud and colourful rooster to master and tread his hens. It looked dull under our dull skies and its meaning eluded me; I wished for an opportunity to question Parados about it and discover what tide of memory it would release.

The bedroom furniture of his infancy, the birthplace bed with its blue coverlet and worn toy bear, encumbered the palace so much that, each time I passed through the brazen doors, I felt I entered the dark shop of a dealer in second-hand goods, or the attic of my grandfather's house in dear Espmoss. His staircase also took up a deal of room but I made use of that, for a good staircase always has more than one ending. I resolved to construct a new room to house his belongings.

Why did I not simply cast out this clutter of his, perhaps by flinging it into some convenient void in the ether or by consuming it with preternatural fire? 'Let it remain!' I said to myself and Cob. 'The care of it will teach me caution and besides remind me Parados is here, walking the cursed earth of Malthassa. Its constant presence will sustain me while I wait.' – For I had already decided to bide my time in the matter of Parados. I had felt a new vigour since he came into the land. Each night I slept deeply; each morning woke rested and, surveying my face in the pier-glass between the westward windows, saw that it had more colour and solidity than for many a year – long devotion to the art of magic wastes the flesh as well as the mind. The fingernails of my left hand were magnificent, five foot-long ram's horns, all

gilded but that of the middle finger which was encrusted
with the detritus of my alchymical and chymical creations
for I used it as a rod to stir my crucibles. My woman's pap
was firm, my wind sound, my mind agile. I felt a dozen years
younger, near my true age. Vanity! All -- and nothing. I was
not a man and the deficiency I concealed with much padding
and decorated cod-pieces kept me sombre-hearted. He was
whole, entire. I envied him. There can be no disputing which
was the greater, my deficiency or his. With utmost concentration I watched him riding his white mare over the Plains,
curious – nay, fascinated – for soon he would realize that
all was not right in the world and his first inkling, at the
border of SanZu, lay only three or fours hours ahead.

The province of SanZu, marked by its permanent cloud-
cover, grew ever closer as they rode across the spring grass.
New flowers opened and the sun shone down.

The two companies had mingled, one with the other. Ima
guarded the rear and flanks while the people of the Goddess
marched in front of her waggon and Parados rode beside
her on his white horse and taught her nursery rhymes and
songs. The awning which had covered her was turned back,
so that she might be seen by the mass of her people when
she came to SanZu and because she demanded to be no
longer in the hot half-dark beneath it but where she might
see the wondrous Spring. She sang,

> Here we go round the mulberry bush,
> The mulberry bush, the mulberry bush,
> Here we go round the mulberry bush
> On a cold and frosty morning,

and 'Teach me more,' she said, 'for I will see nobody but
my nuns when I am in my own house in Flaxberry. I shall
sing your rhymes over in my solitude.'

297

'Your life is in that rhyme. Mine is in this,' said Parados, and recited,

> If all the world were paper,
> And all the sea were ink,
> And all the trees were bread and cheese
> What should we have to drink?

'Stories!' cried the Living Goddess.

'It isn't a riddle,' he said and turned his head to greet Githon, who had ridden up beside him.

'You haven't fallen off!'

'So far,' said the dwarf. 'There is still time. Do you see the black birds flying over SanZu?'

'Why are there so many of them?'

'Ride on a way. We don't want the little one to hear. Now: crows feast on the dead and there has been no harvest in SanZu since the last Goddess died. Two girl-children, before this one, were found and brought back from afar, but they died before they got ten miles inside the border – who can conjure food out of the bare earth? No doubt they were not the true Goddess but I am afraid the same fate waits for this one.'

'I won't let her die, Githon. She is like a daughter to me because, once I had daughters, and sons too ... but never mind it. Our happiness was an illusion caused by the fine weather. Thoughts as black as those crows come to me –'

'From SanZu. Be thankful they are not sown in your mind by Koschei.'

'He has a powerful reputation. You all speak of him with awe.'

'We have good reason. We thought Valdine evil in his day: we knew nothing, supposing that his love of gold and finery and his courtship of the Lady Nemione were terrible sins. That was a passing fancy beside Koschei's obsession.

298

He has destroyed the country with his lustfulness.'

'You were more sympathetic when you told me of his grief at Nemione's death.'

'That's a legend now, tells well, and he was noble once like yourself. These days, he is old and envious, devious – and inventive.'

'Then he has one redeeming quality. You speak of him as if he has a place in my story.'

'That is for you to tell us, Parados. At present, we devote ourselves to the search for your happiness.'

'But Koschei is a very skilful magician?'

'The best. He has and has had no equal. Now that Nemione is dead, the study and the practise of his Art is food, drink and religion to him. Love.'

The honeyed scent of the mulberry catkins was strong, filling the air for yards around the white horse, Summer. Parados lost himself in it, recalling the past from which memories reached out to him like dreadful ghosts. If he were to be made happy – had he ever been so? Possibly, he thought, but those times had no value now, as far-off and unreachable as Nemione in her glass tomb on Windring. Glass? Had Githon told him that? – he could not remember because his picture of Nemione, white hands folded about an everlasting flower of diamonds and amethysts, dominated everything, the sunshine, the mulberry-scent and his old and worn-out memories.

A breath of cold broke his dream open and he struggled out of it, convinced that he was crawling in the alley, eternally without a destination. The horse snorted. She was alive and moving beneath him; the saddle creaked. He looked ahead and saw a dark division across the land, straight as a ruled line. On the near side, the renewed turf of the Plains flourished. Birds flew up from it and a hare ran swiftly away. On the far side were many small fields, bleak with perpetual winter; nothing grew in them and the road which wound between the fields was filthy with black mud and pools of stagnant water. No animal walked there and no birds flew save the black crows.

'Take me forward, Summer,' he said to the horse, which broke at once into a canter and carried him to the front of the company. A murmur of voices followed him. He rode across the line into the cold and empty land. The mulberry branch in Summer's bridle turned instantly black, and died. The voices called more loudly and he turned in the saddle to see the Ima and the people of the Goddess shouting at each other and gesticulating angrily as they rode.

'He is no Redeemer!' someone cried. They were galloping now, after him.

'Let us wait for them, Summer,' he said and the horse slowed her pace and stopped obediently, her white coat already splashed and soiled by the mud on the road. The man Polnisha had called the Finder reached him first, plucked the stricken branch roughly from Summer's head, and flourished it. Two others seized the reins. Behind him, Nandje was shouting orders at his men and Leal had already laid an arrow in his bow and was lowering it and sighting. In the waggon, the Living Goddess screamed as if she were a mere child.

Githon rode unhurriedly into the midst of the turmoil.

'Gentlemen, gentlemen,' he said, his ungainly presence and his deep voice so arresting he had no need to shout. 'Sirs, Masters, Lords – whatever you be: a fight will cure nothing. Let the Imandi deal with his shaman – whose capabilities are not your concern. The Goddess is your charge. Have you journeyed so far to find her and will yet desert her at the very margin of SanZu?'

The Finder flung the dead branch into a pool, where it sank and surfaced amongst stinking bubbles of gas.

'That for your Saviour!' he said. 'Follow us to Flaxberry if you will, but expect no welcome.'

'Except from me. Let them be brought to my nunnery.' Polnisha, small and bright, shamed them with her childish voice and smiles. Like a lark amongst vultures, like a frail hurdle holding back a flood, thought Parados. So they rode on with abashed faces, avoiding the water where they could and where they could not, when it covered the road and the sodden earth of the fields, splashing through. Summer's head was freed but the two men still rode close by Parados and the new friendship between the Ima and the men of SanZu dissolved in mistrust. Only Githon and the Goddess herself seemed unaffected.

The place offered no comfort to body or spirit. Every farmstead, thatched roofs black and rotten from the rains, had its grove of mulberries, many of them close by the house and all leafless and dead. Viciousness and crime were all the crops SanZu grew, evidence of their flowering unmistakable, unavoidable by the road: gallows with their swinging burdens stood beside it and, at each cross-roads, grew a forest of them, different kinds shaped like door-frames, sign-posts and Ts, or plain poles surmounted by old cart-wheels on which notorious thieves had been stretched to die. It was a landscape for all and every time, common throughout history, a landscape of death.

Githon rode beside Parados.

'They keep the best food for the nuns and their oxen,' he said. 'This may seem perverse to you, but they have still not lost their faith in Polnisha. It has been a hard race, as you see, a long and dreadful famine of rotting food, foul water and gangrenous diseases. The children die first, before the old, and those few that are reborn (as they believe) last scarcely a week. Their mothers have no milk, for the puvushi put their slimy offspring to human breasts in the night, or the cold nivashi swim into the houses and carry the babes away. I have seen the Duschma walk through Flaxberry, laden with a mighty burden of the dead – but fear not, Parados, hope and better fortune will prevail and that little mite come into her own.

'The Finder and his men went to look for her more than

five years since. It is a hard task, exacting. There are certain tests. She must know her rightful name as soon as the Finder addresses her and know and recite, besides this and while a dry twig burns, the nine names of Zernebock, proof she understands the power of her eternal foe. She must be able to tell him in what phase the moon is when the flax is planted and, again, harvested, how many silkworms must die to make a mile of thread and how many flax-plants, and show him the right way to wind a shuttle of silk and a shuttle of linen thread. Lastly, she must not be above seven years of age, have hair as dark or darker than her last incarnation and a violet-coloured birthmark on the left side of her body. They made two false choices (for some ambitious parents coach their children). Hope that this time they have done their work well. The truest test must be Polnisha's infallibility.'

'She is courageous and determined,' said Parados. 'Look at her now – staring at that spread-eagled corpse without flinching. A perspicacious child and a – what place is that?'

He inclined his head north-east, toward the darkest part of sky where night waited to make the dismal day wholly black. A monstrous rock lay across the horizon, resting its massive weight on the gloomy land.

'The Rock,' said Githon.

'I see that, a huge rock – a young mountain.'

'That is its name: the Rock.'

'I have seen it before.'

'In your dreams?'

'In reality; but I have never been here, in SanZu – in the flesh, that is.'

Githon looked fearfully at him, as if he were a ghost or fetch from Hell.

'Fear not, Githon. All I mean is that I have seen a rock like that one in my past, which you may describe as a dream if you like.'

'I understand you now, Parados. It was in your other world of mystery and shadows which apes ours – but I daresay the rivers there, all sweet water the colour of bluebells as I've heard tell, don't overflow like that one.'

'Why not, Githon? Do you think Malthassa holds the only patent on disaster? This was once a fair land, as you told me, till Koschei made it die.'

'True. Once upon a time it was paradise enough.'

Flaxberry was isolated on its knoll above the river, the floodwater lying all around it as if it had always been there, a huge lake.

'Can we get through?' Parados asked Nandje.

'The Finder says we must dismount – there comes the boat for us, now.'

'It looks shallow – there is the bottom and there some tufts that were once the flax crop. Will you follow me?'

Nandje hesitated.

'It should be enough that you –' he began while Githon, interrupting, said,

'Yes! Follow Parados. He has seen such floods before.'

Still, Nandje hesitated: 'It is not the water I fear, but the nivashi. There must be a swarm of them out there,' and the two, man and dwarf continued to argue as though they were alone.

'Do you think they will dare touch us when Parados is with us?' said Githon loudly.

'Maybe not; maybe – they are seductive creatures. I once lost a dozen men to them.'

'Parados is proof against them – "The most perfect, virtuous knight there ever was or ever will be".'

'You are very sure of him.'

'We were discussing things, the world, philosophy, before you came up.'

'If it were safe to ride through the water, do you think Polnisha would wait for the boat?'

'Polnisha is not herself yet – she may after all be the child she appears to be.'

While they disputed and Parados sat quiet on the white mare, staring across the floodwater to Flaxberry town, the Living Goddess jumped from her waggon and, shaking off two of her escort with little cries and blows of her small fists, ran across the mud and pulled at Summer's mane. The horse bent down her head and Polnisha whispered in her soft ear and fed her a fragment of dry oatcake.

'You are here, Polnisha,' said Parados. 'What do you think – Nandje and Githon argue, but is it safe to ride to Flaxberry?'

'Ask them, "Is it safe to ride anywhere with me?" Or, better, I will climb up before you and show Summer where to tread.' She reached up for the stirrup and then for his sleeve while Summer bent her foreleg backward to make a step. When she was safely up, astride the mare's neck, she picked up and unknotted the reins and, gathering them, called out 'Off we go, Summer.' It was only when the mare had waded a yard from the shore that her men missed her. Shouting did not bring her back. Those that had horses were forced to follow her into the flood and the rest waded, the Ima riding cautiously at the rear. Only the oxen, their waggon with its heavy stone seat, and the sheep and their boy remained behind.

Soon, Summer was abreast of the boat, which had turned in its course to come up with her. The men rowing it shouted warnings and prayers.

'I hope you are praying to Me!' called Polnisha.

'It is very deep. You will be swept away!'

'We find it shallow,' Parados replied; and indeed, it was so.

Flaxberry had once been a pretty town, he thought, as they rode into it. The houses were decaying, stained with damp and with the water which had risen through the soil and the drains. It reminded him of somewhere; he could not place his thought and let it go, looking sadly at cold hearths and bare tables behind the townspeople gathered in their doorways. The first people had hostile expressions but, quickly, as they rode along the street, news spread and expectation, if not hope, awoke. The crowd murmured busily and many individuals cheered. Polnisha smiled at everyone. He could not. The place was still so grim, the people thin and starved and their children yellow-skinned and wasted. What dogs there were, and he supposed that many had been eaten, ranged the gutters looking vainly for scraps or a dead rat, their ribs more prominent than Famine's skeletal horse. He heard a cry,

'The blue flag!'

'The Ima!' someone else shouted in alarm.

'With Polnisha!' cried another.

Polnisha of the Silk and Linen, the Living Goddess, was lifted carefully from her place in front of Parados. Her sudden mutinous expression was taken by the crowd to be solemnity. She allowed the Finder to carry her to the nunnery door and knocked on it with her fists, making so soft a sound that the Finder also knocked, with an empty shuttle. No doubt it was part of the Mystery. Nandje helped Parados down and they stood with Githon in front of the crowd. A long silence succeeded the knocking of the door, extending itself across the street and along it to the nearest cross-roads. This, the Finder broke with a howl. His body shook with tremor after tremor and the sullen expression of Polnisha, in his arms, turned to one of fear, then awe. She began to howl herself, in a high-pitched whine, lifting her head and thrashing her hands in the air. She could not stop. Grief, or madness, possessed her and first one and then another of the crowd imitated her while the dogs, beginning with a dirty white hound which loitered at the street corner, barked.

The nunnery door opened suddenly. An old woman, robed

like Polnisha in a mix of linen and silk but bent and almost hairless except for some white wisps on the crown of her head, stood on the top step. The Finder carried Polnisha to her and put the child in her bony arms. She was so hideous that Parados wished for the strength and means to run forward and wrest the child from her; then, carried up in the air on a magic wind, they would fly far off, beyond the crone's reach. The door banged shut behind them. In his mind, he could hear the child's screams – perhaps hear them in reality echoing down the cold corridors of the nunnery as she was carried to her bed of stone. When, after a short pause, the door re-opened, he was bewildered for Polnisha stood there smiling at him, bright as the Plains flowers in her rags of silk. The old Abbess loitered behind her like a fossilized thorn-branch.

'You are to come as well,' said the Living Goddess.

He exchanged a look with Githon, but Nandje prodded him in the back and he stepped forward and up the steps. As he reached the topmost, he saw that his right sleeve was caught up and his disability on show to all. He tried to smooth the cloth down against his body but while he struggled, his stump brushed against a dead potted plant which once had graced the entrance. Something colourful, he thought, something gaudy and scented to welcome pilgrims on a sunny day; but the green plant which rapidly unfolded against his scars, all its spent life revived, its missed seasons telescoped into a single moment, was flax, the mother of linen, a crowd of blue flowers nodding on its stems. The Abbess darted out of the shadows and Polnisha jumped in the air and clapped her hands together. Both knelt down beside the flax plant and he felt obliged to kneel with them.

The Abbess laid her claws on his stump and turned his arm back and forth. She touched the leaves of the flax plant.

'You have brought us Life,' she said.

Something stirred in the crowding leaves and they drew

back from the plant fearing that the little miracle was about to turn sour. The leaves rustled as whatever was beneath them struggled free. A yellow head showed and after it the body of the unknown creature. It pushed upwards and was free, a small yellow manikin some two inches high, which jumped from the pot-rim into Polnisha's hands. The goddess and the Abbess sighed aloud.

'You have brought us the Harvest,' said the Abbess. 'Hold up your hands, Polnisha. Let our people see the Thread Man.'

As Polnisha held the manikin on high and the people cheered and wept, a ray of sunshine as thin as a silk thread pierced the dark cloud overhead. He shone and glistened in it, turning himself about in cartwheels and somersaults on her hand.

'Let us give thanks,' the Abbess said and led the people in prayer. Then she and the goddess and Parados and the Thread Man, who was the soul of SanZu's harvest, went into the nunnery, leaving the door wide open behind them as a sign.

In a long line of townsfolk Nandje, Githon, Leal, Thidma and the other Ima climbed the nunnery steps to see the marvel of the flax plant. It flourished even as they looked at it, growing sturdy and tall. The dusty floor inside the nunnery stretched away from Githon's feet as he stood in the doorway, but he saw the polished boards beneath the dust and the new sunlight warming them and making them respond to its yellow touch. A breeze blew lightly past him, driving away the fevers and stenches which haunted the town. He turned about and saw the Finder of the Living Goddess nearby.

'It seems to me that the fates of the people of SanZu and the Ima were never so closely bound together,' he said loudly. 'What do you think, sir?'

307

The Finder, trapped by the surging crowd of worshippers on the steps, looked about for a means of escape and, finding none, said

'It was and is an old and bitter feud.'

'Did it not begin with Koschei?'

'It is said he was an agent of the Imandi – who gave him orders to destroy the Goddess.'

'Have you not learned, after all this –' and Githon made a gesture which encompassed the whole of famine-stricken Malthassa '– that Koschei is nobody's agent, unless his own?'

'That's as maybe. The fact is that the harvests began to fail after Koschei crossed the Plains in Nandje's company and, pretending that he was an ambassador of the Archmage Valdine, came with his henchman into SanZu, into Flaxberry and the Nunnery itself! Nandje was not Imandi then; we have only permitted him to enter Flaxberry today because of his status.'

'Ear-wax! Because the Goddess told you to. Look, Master Finder, at the blue flag of the Ima – it is the colour of a flax flower and is made of silk woven here, in the town. Let it be a symbol! I believe that Koschei stole your harvests and sent the plague amongst you. Let the blue flag be a symbol of new unity – Parados will be downhearted to see our quarrel continue.'

'Well – it is no thanks to you Dwarves or the Ima that we stand here marvelling at this living plant. It is all the doing of Parados.'

In the heart of the nunnery the same sunlight and breeze worked to clear away the ghosts and shadows the famine had left there. The Abbess showed Parados the trays of dead silkworms and the cocoons which had rotted before the silk could be taken from them. The sight of the Thread Man leaning eagerly from Polnisha's hand to see his new home brought them comfort and they watched him run about over the idle looms and leave his footprints in the dust.

'Soon,' Polnisha warned him, 'you must go to your rest. Then, at harvest time, we will unwind you and the nuns will weave a square of silk from your skin and another of linen from your bones and you will be born again, good as new.'

They sat at table in the refectory and a nun brought them oatcakes smeared with a thin coating of lard and tea without any milk.

'I must also rest,' Polnisha said. 'I am tired, Abbess. I have had a long journey and need the quiet of my house.' She unwound a piece of the linen which was tied about her waist and took a red box from it. 'This is your house, Thread Man. Please step in.' She lifted the lid and the soul of the harvest stepped lightly into the box and lay down there, still as a stone. Polnisha closed the lid on him. It was decorated with a silver bird whose tail of gold shone brilliantly in the sunlight which fell on it.

'That is the Firebird,' Polnisha said, 'who lives in the Forest.'

Parados was troubled once more by his past.

'Where did you get the box?' he said.

'Get?' Polnisha smiled. 'It is mine. It has always been mine. The last one, which Koschei stole, was made of alabaster.'

'I know. It had a design of fish and octopus on it and the words "Prospero's Book". Koschei took the Thread Man out of it and hung him in his own silk,' said Parados miserably.

The child reached out to him, taking hold of his two stumps as though they were not hideous incompletenesses but ordinary, workaday hands.

'You will soon see, Parados, for you are as great a magician – if only you would believe it! – as Koschei, that all will and shall be well,' she said and, turning from him, followed the Abbess from the room. They will walk along the corridor, he thought, and come to the two carved doors which the Abbess will open. Then she will lead Polnisha to her bed and help her lie down beneath her mask and her special coverlet of linen and silk, the same kind of cloth they used

309

to shield her from view in the ox-waggon. While she lies there Polnisha will keep the box which contains the Thread Man safe and she will lie as still as he does unless the moon shines into her house – on those nights, she will rise to eat and bathe and change her clothes.

He did not need to follow Polnisha and the Abbess: he could see it all in his mind.

'And she won't be bored,' he said aloud, 'because she will be singing to herself,

> Here we go round the mulberry bush,
> The mulberry bush, the mulberry bush,
> Here we go round the mulberry bush.'

He got up from the table and left the nunnery in search of Githon.

Nandje sat amongst the willow trees on the muddy ground outside Flaxberry to smoke the clay pipe which he always turned to when there was something to be considered. He was oblivious of the dirt beneath and about him as he watched the waters recede and flow away in a swift tide as if they were eager to be back between the banks of the river. There would be floods lower down – but what matter? The world was turned upside down. He welcomed the strange reversal, thought once of Gry and how her love of the new-comer must be disappointed, and returned to his problem: what next? Meditating on uncertainty he fell into a deep trance, so that when Parados found him at sunset he looked as still and grey as the trees which surrounded him.

'Look,' said Githon who, with Thidma, had accompanied Parados. 'There are catkins on the trees.'

The Imandi woke at once and jumped to his feet.

'We must consult the shaman at Hijafoot,' he said.

'For what?' said Githon. 'I might just as well go up into

the Altaish and seek out one of our wise men. Look how the willows flower!'

'We must call a divining-woman with her crystals and birch twigs,' said Thidma. 'But meanwhile, let us all go in to Flaxberry and enjoy whatever meagre meal the Finder is able to set before us.'

'No.' Parados spoke quietly so that, at first, they did not hear him and went on talking amongst themselves. 'No,' he said, more loudly. 'I must go alone. I know the direction, that way, about north-west.'

'Back into the Plains,' said Thidma. 'I will guide you.'

'No, it is not the Plains, but another country. I do not know what it is called.'

'There is no other land in that direction!'

'Hush,' Nandje interjected. 'He knows much more than we do.'

'Of the Plains – where we have lived all our lives in the embrace of our forefathers?'

'He did not say he was going to the Plains. What place is it, Parados, where you must go?'

'A new land, very old – that neither you nor I have seen before. I must have no companions and I must go to it now.'

'Go tomorrow,' Githon said, laying a hand on Parados's shoulder. 'Go in the morning after rest and a meal.'

Parados moved, so that Githon was forced to let his hand fall.

'Good-bye Githon,' he said, 'Nandje, Thidma. Sleep well and may there be enough to eat.'

Again, Githon attempted to detain him but Nandje pushed him aside and, without another word, they watched Parados walk away from them and wade out into the racing floodwater. Soon, it reached his waist.

'Stop him!' Githon cried.

'He is well. Look – the water is already shallower. He is making for the alders over there, beyond the dark line that is the bank. Now, I have lost him – you are younger, Thidma, do you see him still?'

'He walks into the sun – it is hard to make him out. There he goes, between the alder and the crooked willow and – I cannot see him.'

Githon continued to protest, 'We must find a boat and go after him,' and Nandje and Thidma who had as much strength as the dwarf between them held his arms.

'Come in, Githon,' Nandje said. 'In the morning, if need be, you shall have your boat. There are no wild beasts out there except the hares and the foxes which prey on them. He is not going to the Plains where the wolf-mother roams at night – I believe in him. So should you.'

'I believe, Nandje; but I have seen the Duschma and you have not. Pray she has other business tonight.'

'I must.' The search had become imperative. He was becoming Parados, man of action not of words, and knew that when the apotheosis was complete, so he would be. He walked a long way, weaving between the wetland trees, the ground sucking and bubbling under him as the enthusiastic waters rushed back to the riverbed; he almost glided, his boots sinking only an inch or two into the boggy ground. Always, the light was red, that fading colour intermixed with the gold which fills the sky and senses as the sun goes down and, though there is warmth in it, prepares the body for the chill of night; but the sun did not go down, remaining balanced on the horizon close beyond the wood. He was travelling uphill. The ground dried out and the willows and alders gave way to hazel and then to open country. The skyline and its poised sun moved back as he advanced and he blinked rapidly to clear his eyes and mind of the strong red light. A wild beast howled not far away. He felt the fear of awful possibilities crawl along his spine and stopped to listen, not able to identify the animal; but what dread creature hunts at sunset in the peaceful fields of home, he thought? My England – Albion – has nothing more terrible than vixens wailing in the torments of desire. Here – what was that ahead, the untidy bush with wings? Surprised into immobility, he stood beside it in the unearthly glow and looked about him. Was it possible that one of these had howled?

The grass of the hillside was covered in listening animals and birds. Some stood up on boulders, others crouched on fallen logs and they were made, every one, from sticks and odd-shaped pieces of wood and carefully arranged bundles of straw. If he moved again, they would surely come to life and start up from their watchful poses. Here was a wild cat, a cat-a-mountain with a mottled head of bark; there an eagle, wings spread wide, and there a rearing crocodile. That one, with its ridged and scaly back, had no original in life and there – narrow and straight, arms rigid by their sides – stood two men, much smaller than the surrounding beasts. Their eyes glistened but, he saw, were only glossy pebbles. Cautiously, he shifted a foot, pushing it softly forward through the grass. Nothing else moved and he continued across the grass and further up the hill, giving each creature a wide berth as he came to it and passed it. A ditch made horizontal lines across the slope, a wavy-backed serpent lying on its nearer bank, head down as if it drank and watched by a crowd of skeletal birds with wings upraised. When he reached the snake and stood by it, he saw that the ditch was no shallow trench but a rocky crevasse perhaps twenty or thirty feet deep, perhaps unplummable with lurking monsters far below, invisible in the shadowy depths. His fear grew and he held it tight so that it should not escape and overwhelm him.

A plank bridge crossed the ravine. It was guarded by another of the strange animals. This one, though it had the jutting features of a huge gorilla, was less frightening for it seemed entirely made of straw and had toppled over into a bush grown up beside it. The guardians, he supposed, were powerless now, old tutelary spirits fallen into disuse but, since the bridge was there, he must cross it – or how would he know what lay beyond? And he must cross without a thought of the drop below: a man without hands would find it impossible to climb up once he had fallen, or if he broke a leg – The bush rustled under the straw gorilla. He thought of mice and then of serpents. The straw head moved, a great, dark head with a yellow mane, and then the legs, unfolding and projecting from the bush. Bunches of green leaves were stuck at random into the hairy body and a dense beard of them, thick as an ivy clump, grew about a terrible mouth which opened to show two rows of sharp, yellow teeth.

'There are greater perils than the bridge,' the beast said and stood up on its hind legs like a tower brought to life. 'You are late, but I have enjoyed the long rest in my rustic bivouac.'

Parados, poised in the moment between grovelling fear and flight, swallowed his panic but could not speak. He recognized the creature. Its mane was a straw rope wound round its neck and shoulders.

'Am I such a shocking invention?' the Om Ren continued. 'Come, Master Storyteller, you know me. I am wearing my wedding-clothes, dressed all in leaves like Jack-in-the-Green for I am ready to seek my mate.'

'Was it you who roared as I came up the hill?'

'I? I am a gentle fellow, unless roused.' His hairy cheeks twitched in imitation of a smile. 'And all for the general good. You should have come into Malthassa many months ago, before the Archmage – whom I admire, for he is an ambitious, fearless fellow – well before Koschei's pain had bred so many terrors and apparitions.'

'I could not get out of the place in which I was imprisoned.'

'You let it detain you – loss is something to be overcome, not enjoyed. No matter, here you are. I will guide you over the bridge and up to the hilltop. But walk in the centre of the bridge, along the line where the two planks meet – who knows what trolls lurk beneath it? And do not heed the animals when you are on the bridge.'

They crossed the bridge, which swayed and was much longer than it appeared from the safety of firm ground, Parados walking behind the Om Ren who paused now and then, reared up to his full and dreadful height, looked down into the chasm and growled. Parados did not look. He had an impression of coils, of tongues and teeth, but the din of the wooden creatures behind him and his perilous position itself made him unsteady. The animals rushed forward after him but could not, it seemed, venture on to the bridge, though the wooden eagle soared above him and the smaller birds flew close with angry shrieks.

Parados walked up the hill beside the Om Ren certain he had not been here before although the place seemed familiar, the hills of his imagination and reality being, in this respect, much the same. It was a universal hill, well-shaped and not too steep. Sometimes a leafy twig dropped from the Om Ren's hairy body and he paused to retrieve it and put it back in its place in his fantastic green garment.

'She will expect nothing less of her groom than perfect sartorial elegance,' he said, 'when I have climbed the Altaish to find her. She is not like me, Parados, a gross, unlovely beast (albeit with a silver tongue and the mind of a philosopher). She is – but I do not know. I have not seen her yet. Perhaps she is a slender human she, the sort Nemione once was. Or she may look like a bear, or an ice-bird or yet a dancing spirit of the snow.'

'I heard someone tell – it was Githon the Copper Dwarf. He said your bride is fair.'

'I hope so, I trust. What will she make of me, the Wild Man of the Forest?'

'She will love you, Om Ren, and make your climb to find her worthwhile.'

315

'Then I will start my journey as soon as I have attended you. You will need all my strength and yours too, Parados, when we come to the top of the hill. We are nearly there. Already, I hear them singing.'

Airy voices which might have been those of nightingales, or the wind plucking at a golden wire, sang and threads of vapour drifted towards Parados and the Om Ren, torn shreds of the mist which covered the hilltop and was at once grey and dense and lit eerily from afar by the ever-setting sun.

'Do not open your mouth,' said the Om Ren, 'or you may suck one in. They are *zracni vili*, spirits of the air. I shall not speak again till we have passed them.'

The spirits swirled about them, continuously shifting shape and beckoning with hands which dissolved to become eyes and lovely mouths open in song. The Om Ren held Parados's shoulders in his iron grip and propelled him forward into the mist until the sun's light was blotted out. There were no more *zracni vili* but, beneath their feet, the grass thinned out until they were walking over barren, rocky earth.

'I can also help you here,' the Om Ren said, 'but put your arm through the crook of mine – just so. I have hold of you.' He crushed Parados's left arm against his body and pulled him close, so close that he appeared a shambling mat of black hair and green leaves. Huge whiskery lice crawled incuriously over his hide and the greenery. 'Hush now, Silver Glance; sleep Adamantine, rest there Sulphur Eye!' he said. 'These are puvushi beneath our feet, the spirits of the earth. Tread carefully or they will trip you and, if one catches hold of your ankle, she will pull you under.'

The earth looked like a roughly-ploughed field. Large stones lay trembling on its surface and some of them moved aside, pushed by knotty grey fingers which waved in the soil and groped for a foot to hold. They were hideous, carnivorous weeds, Parados thought. Avoiding one set, he staggered and trod on another, feeling them scrabble and try to grip before he forced up his foot and crushed them under the sole of his boot.

'Have a care!' the Om Ren cried, pulling him upright. 'They can turn a man to metal. Do you want to be dug out by a prospecting dwarf?'

The mist lifted, gradually at first but soon faster and higher as the sun broke through. They left the puvushi behind them and came to the edge of a wide land of lakes and interlacing streams whose waters were dark mirrors which reflected the setting sun.

'Are you a strong man?' the Om Ren asked Parados.

'No more than most,' he replied. 'Especially since I lost my hands.'

'Not strong in sinew and muscle, but in will: that is my meaning. The nivashi, which lie ahead and lie indeed in wait beneath the water there, will tempt and weaken you ere we pass. They are beautiful, sinuous creatures.'

'More beautiful than Nemione?'

'That is not possible – but lovely enough. You will see; or shall I bind a cloth about your eyes?'

'I should like to see them.'

'Many a man has died after saying that. I will tie my rope about you and keep you on dry land; then you can look your fill on each nivasha.'

He fastened his rope of straw about Parados's waist. The path wound between the glassy lakes, a thread of green turf, and nothing stirred but the Om Ren and Parados on his leash, who looked about him and wondered how this infinity of water could fit on the top of a hill. He did not believe that the rope would hold him, but was reluctant to test it with a wrench or pull since it appeared to be a thing the Om Ren valued.

'Your rope is a curious object,' he said. 'I suppose the ply holds it together?'

'I suppose blind men see visions,' the Om Ren replied. 'Be

content, you will soon be given an opportunity to try its strength.'

They walked a little further along the shore of the first lake. Reeds grew in thick clusters and there were kingcups in the muddy shallows; beyond them swam a woman whose wet hair trailed behind her in the water. She was a human, of Parados's kind, who as he watched stopped swimming and rolled over to float in the very centre of the sun's red reflection. He stepped forward.

'She does not fear the nivashi: she has come here to swim in the warm evening,' he said.

'Look again! You see what you wish to see.' The Om Ren spoke gently, like a patient teacher.

'A woman who – ah!' Her skin, which had been white and rose-coloured in the evening light, was the colour of lichen, or verdigris, and the long hair had grown and split into filaments like water weed. Her hands, which she raised to beckon him, had webbed fingers and the even teeth her ill-boding smile showed him were tiny, very white and sharp as an otter's fangs. She had become herself, a nivasha, at once the negation and the archetype of womanliness, alike alluring and loathsome.

'Let me go!' he said.

'That is not your true desire. But I give you a little rope so that you can discover what it is like to hang yourself.' The Om Ren paid out two coils. Parados moved quickly away from him, splashing into the water, and the nivasha, which had waited for a sign from him, swam closer. When she was a yard away, she rested in the water and looked at him with eyes as luminous and overflowing as a seal's but cold and dead as fish-scales on a marble slab. Her necklaces were made of finger-bones and knucklestones and her voice, when she spoke, hissed and coiled across the water to entrap him:

'Come down to my garden, Knight. I have planted some new flowers there, those pretty goldicups from the bank.

Their colour, underwater, is far finer than the gaudy yellow you see there.'

'What will you give me if I come with you?'

'My everlasting love, even when you are no more than bones and clay.'

'I am afraid you already have a lover.'

'I do, but neither of you will mind the other when you are both at peace. He is here with me, see. His name is Corydon. You do not need to fear him.' She reached into the water and her fingers, when she brought her hand up again, were interlaced with the bony digits of a skeleton. It lay just under the surface, clearly to be seen, and the empty sockets where its eyes had been stared upwards in mute contentment.

'I am afraid you will devour me.'

'I? Oh no, gentle Knight, the fish will do that and my friend the otter bitch. I will only nibble at your sweet flesh and I will keep you by me a long time before I begin.' She laughed and again showed him her sharp teeth. He imagined them biting into him and was surprised to find the prospect pleasurable. It would be worth any amount of riches or fame to swim beside her and kiss her once.

'Let me kiss you first,' he said, and the Om Ren tightened his hold on the rope.

'That is a hard forfeit. What will you give me in return?'

'Myself and the pictures that are in my head.'

'Very well.' She dropped the hand of the skeleton and swam to him, standing up when she reached the shallows. He leaned out until the rope was tight. Her skirt was woven of rushes and the feathers of drowned white birds; she had the breasts of a woman and a long red fin grew out of her breastbone and fell in spiny folds towards her waist. Wanting to touch her strangeness, he lamented the loss of his hands and contented himself with studying her for a long moment before he leaned still further forward against the pull of the rope and kissed her bloodless lips. They were wet

319

and very cold but they did not taste of fish. She parted them and he felt an overwhelming desire to kiss her again and put his tongue into her mouth so that she could take a piece of it between her pointed teeth and bite. He had inhaled her muddy breath and opened his own mouth before the Om Ren's rope jerked him violently backward and sent him spinning face-down on the bank. He got up at once, ready to fight the Om Ren, and saw the nivasha collapse into the water in a cascade of silver and vanish. A huge pike rose and broke the surface, clashed its teeth in its bony jaw, and was gone. He looked at his soaked and muddy legs and, sheepishly, at the Om Ren.

'Did you see?' the great ape whispered. 'You turned her into a great luce!'

Parados laughed, seeking relief from his embarrassment. 'Must I kiss them all?' he asked.

'I do not think you will be troubled again. The place has a new and desolate feeling and the sun is setting.'

'It has been setting ever since I came here!'

'No, it dips below the horizon, see! We have less time now than I expected.'

'Where are we going?'

'Forward!'

'And?'

'What will, will be.' He would say no more about their destination but untied the rope from Parados and, taking his arm in a hairy hand, led him past the myriad lakes until they came to a stone pillar whose wide foot was buried in the grass.

'Here we are,' said the Om Ren.

'Where?'

'At the start of the maze. Can't you see it?'

'The bank there?'

'That is only the first.' The ape sat on the ground and arranged his rope in coils about his neck.

'Go on,' said Parados.

'I am tired now. You must lead me – begin, there is a good light from the stars.'

Parados looked up at them. They had become familiar and he could name their constellations: the seven stars of Bail's Sword in the north, the Swan, the Hoopoe and the Dancing Crane. He took a step forward, past the beginning of the high bank and found another which ran parallel with it. The path between them led away round a curve.

'Watch how you go,' the Om Ren said. 'You must not walk the maze, but dance.' He picked some white flowers which were opening their petals to the night and tucked them into his coat amongst the leaves.

Parados, feeling like a bull at the ball, lifted his arms and skipped a step. The stars pricked the dark cloth of the night sky with their pulsating light and woke his imagination: he would dance like a crane, flapping his incomplete arms as the bird does its wings. He leaped, and sprang in the air and heard the Om Ren's heavy tread behind him. The path divided continually as he danced on, taking now a left and now a right turn until he lost his way. He could not climb the steep turf banks without hands and, thinking again of the crane, whose dance he imitated, he raised his arms high and soared up into the night sky to fly below the starry Crane and above the maze. It was made of seven spirals, each one linked to the rest. The Om Ren looked small, far below, an animal in the night. He had lain down on the path and was asleep. There was the centre of the maze, a shadowy boulder at the heart of the central spiral. He flew down and alighted on it, his beautiful snowy wings turning back at once to mutilated arms, his short space of freedom over, his terrible disability come back. The wonderful lightness of body and spirit had fled with the wings whose long, primary feathers had been so much like fingers. But there! His severed hands were lying on the rock, a few steps away. They looked like hungry spiders crouched in wait for a careless fly, and the left one clasped the right. Once, he had been able to

321

animate them. He had used them to make love to Lèni, to eat and drink and perform a thousand personal actions; he had hoped to teach them to write. And before, when they had been parts of his whole, they had written millions of words; been immersed in the waters of the Pacific, the Atlantic, the Indian Ocean, the Thames; tended a garden, stroked animals, caressed a host of women, his wife, Helen and the witches, his mistresses; touched his dead grandfather and his new-born children. He did not wonder how they came here into Malthassa but knelt down close beside them and looked at them with love.

'If I could only touch you,' he said and smiled at the impossibility of his wish.

This Ima coat had no long cuffs like the ones Lèni had sewn. The sleeves hardly concealed his stumps but there were deep pockets into which the hands might climb as they had done before. He felt in the pockets: there was ample room. The right one contained a clasp-knife and in the left was a handkerchief. He remembered beautiful Gry, who must have put them there, and took out knife and handkerchief to examine. The knife was heavy and had two blades. He opened and closed the blades. The handkerchief was clean and made of white linen. He blew his nose on it, bent his fingers and unbent them, pushed back his sleeves so that he could see his wrists: there were no scabs, no scars or any sign that there had been a wound and nothing on the rock where the hands had lain but ten fingerprints, two sets of hollows in the stone. He clapped his hands together and shouted until the hilltop rang and echoed with his joy. The Om Ren must hear!

'Wake!' he shouted, 'W-a-a-ake!'

He climbed down quickly from the boulder, his hands finding the necessary ledges and holding him steady while he moved his feet. The way out was clear in his mind. He careered along it until he found the Om Ren standing with head and ears upraised, but did not stop until he had run into the ape and let his hands experience the rough, criss-cross pile of his hairy coat, the hard flexibility of the twigs, the ridged leaves and the smooth flower-petals of the greenstuff which adorned it. 'Look; look at my hands,' he said tearfully, incoherent with happiness and realized dreams, and the Om Ren took them both in his and held them for a moment.

'All is well,' he said. 'And I must take the road. Follow your nose Parados and, remember, the animals cannot cross the bridge: I am certain you will find your way home.'

'I have no home – I have become a wanderer like a gypsy,' Parados replied.

'Home to Flaxberry, where you will find that the people call you a knight-venturer – and perhaps they wait for you to earn your spurs.'

'And my horse! The one I ride belongs to the Imandi.'

'Summer, the white mare? Farewell, Parados and do not concern yourself about horses. Time solves every problem. A horse would be a handicap where you must journey. But you will find a good rope made of my hair. I had it woven as a gift for the Lady Nemione.' He let go of Parados and took several paces along the way he had come. Parados ran at his heels.

'Am I going into the Altaish, like you?'

'The Altaish, as you know yourself, is an immeasurable mountain range.'

'Shall I meet you there?'

The Om Ren only raised one hand in a salute and did not turn back.

'Then, goodbye!' Parados called after him, 'Farewell.'

The night, for all the beauty of its stars, seemed darker. Being alone in it with the nivashi, the animals and whatever other supernatural creatures might be abroad was a daunting prospect. Parados climbed the nearest bank and looked down on the sevenfold maze. He could not be sure its curving pathways were empty of dread and danger. Thinking that he might fly over all the perils he expected, he lifted his arms and beat the air with them; but whatever magic had helped him find the heartstone and his hands had departed. The path across the lakeland was a maze itself and the way between the guardian animals its beginning, each stage leading to the next like a many-coloured ball of wool. But wool could be unravelled and to delay was vain. Thoughts would not carry him back to Flaxberry and the ford across the River Morus. You may lead a horse to water but a man must walk there by himself, he thought illogically and, scrambling from the bank-top, strode out along the path. He felt his boots sink in mud and then in water and looked intently about in case the nivashi were abroad. The sun's rays broke suddenly above the horizon and all the stars vanished into a pale, early-morning sky. He saw the ford at Flaxberry in front of him and, on the far side of the little river Morus, the rejuvenated town awakening, smoke rising from its chimneys and a wonderful smell of new bread wafting out toward him. At his back, the level fields of SanZu stretched out, green and flourishing with new crops and the prow-shaped Rock on the horizon was sunlit and studded with bushes. The leaves on the trees were well out and the bleating of lambs and joyous bursts of birdsong filled the air. He splashed hurriedly through the clear water, delighting in the fish he could see there, for Githon had appeared on the far side and was shouting greetings at the top of his voice.

When he took hold of Githon's outstretched hands he felt the callouses the miner's pick had raised and the wonderful warmth of the hands. He reached down and embraced the dwarf: the cloth of his brown coat was soft and a tear on the right shoulder had been repaired with large, hard stitches of horse-hair.

'Let me look at your hands,' said Githon. 'Are they the same, with fate etched in the left and reason in the right? Look about you – you have brought life back to SanZu, and the Goddess and the Thread Man between them have given the people food. The people found their granaries had filled with corn overnight and discovered living silkworms where there had been only dry, dead skins. And the trees are in leaf, the flax grows. It is a happy morning and the Finder, the Mayor of Flaxberry and the Abbess wait to welcome you.'

'Polnisha?'

'The child? – she has demanded fireworks, a procession and seven nights of celebrations. It is not difficult to welcome excess!'

Parados flew, but without wings. His balloon was pale blue and grey, the colours of the sky before dawn, with a resplendent sun blazoned on its convex walls. It rose softly and he, leaning against the basket's side, had plenty of time to gaze his fill upon the roofs and environs of Flaxberry as they receded from him and the town, lying comfortably amongst its green fields and leafy groves, became no bigger than a model settlement.

Before he left, the Abbess, restored to vigorous middle age and with a fine head of iron-grey hair, had taken him about the countryside and shown him the mulberry set, multitudes of green berries on every tree: there would be a bumper crop. The flax was being harvested and they had ridden into the fields and watched the tall stems being cut and carted to the retting pits where they would lie in water and rot until their strong fibres could be drawn out. At each homestead he had received a royal welcome and been surprised when children ran up and begged him for a piece of his coat to keep, or shy girls blushed and asked for a lock of his hair.

'Humour them: you are not an ordinary man,' the Abbess said.

He had asked her about the Rock, which he saw lying

asleep on the skyline every day as he went about the business of balloon-making in Flaxberry.

'Surely they go out from the town to climb it and spy out the land – or take their wives and families for the day?'

'Not there, we have balloons for that, and the people make excursions to the river or to the forest-edge.'

'What about the farmers whose land reaches to its foot?'

'They are busy men. Ask no more questions, Parados. It is not in our country but falls under the Imandi's rule; it is Ima territory in the heart of SanZu.'

Three balloons had been ready when he returned to Flaxberry. He watched impatiently while the other two were assembled and sewn. There was plenty of silk, bales of it, barns-ful. As the Mayor told him, 'No one eats silk,' and the Finder, 'No one buys silk when Malthassa starves.' Some had been used for shrouds; the rest had lain, gathering dust, until he came and Githon proposed that the expedition into the Altaish should be undertaken by balloon. Nandje and Leal had returned home to the Plains and taken the horses with them, but Thidma remained with him, a sturdy and somewhat morose lieutenant. The other men, who would navigate the balloons and fight if need be, were sought in the town and, further afield, in the villages of SanZu.

Here they were, a flight of five balloons, sailing slowly up into the bright blue summer sky. His navigator, a young man from Flaxberry called Aurel, worked hard at the furnace. It was necessary to carry the fuel for the balloon, dry stuff and dead stalks collected from the forest, and the calculation to raise it loaded was fine. He had thought of lifting them all by thought but the power worked randomly and he, growing used to its vagaries, was content to lean on the wickerwork and admire the fruitful garden he had made of SanZu. About them the other balloons of the flight, Githon's copper-coloured, Thidma's bronze like the Plains in autumn, and the two which carried the soldiers a workmanlike dull green, rose silently.

326

At last Aurel turned from the fire, smiled at and saluted him and brought packets of ham and cheese-and-pickle sandwiches from the hamper.

'She rises like a lark,' he said. 'What will you call her?'

'Perhaps Summer, after the horse I rode across the Plains – or Lèni for a courageous woman I once knew – But I think, yes, I will call her Esperance, for I always journey in hope.'

'A good name. It reminds me of my sister who went singing through the darkest days and died last year when the grain ran out. She is buried in the nunnery garden. Look, there's the old Rock! My mother used to tell such a tale of it.'

Parados looked eagerly out as Esperance approached and passed over the huge outcrop. From above it looked flat, a lumpy contour map, and the windcut trees and low bushes were hastily-drawn-in details. A group of small white clouds of the kind which pass across the sun and make a hot day chilly rushed together below the balloon, obscuring his view. They reminded him of a herd of galloping Plains horses as they streamed below him in the wind. He did not speak because Aurel continued to talk of his childhood and, after following many side-roads and diversions through his earliest years, began his mother's story of the Rock:

In Riverside, they call the Rock a cat-a-mountain and in Linum and Bombyxius a lion. They say that those two long ledges which overhang Ringan's plot are its front paws, it rests its hind feet in Aldwyn's highest fields and its tail stretches out a half-mile until the tassel at the end of it stirs the loose stones above Forcat's land.

But we of Flaxberry know a better tale. Look at it, my son! It is the great ox-cart which brought us the first Polnisha who floated with her waggon and ten oxen over the sea and drove through the ever-shifting forest until she came to SanZu. The name means Homeland, Aurel, and it is not one of our words. She met the magician Garzon, who built Castle Sehol, walking with his Firebird on a crest of land above the quiet fields.

'I hear that you are an architect,' Polnisha said to Garzon. 'Would you make me a castle out of my ox-cart, for I do not need it now that I have come home?'

'That is like asking for a feather from the Firebird,' said Garzon. 'What will you give me in return?'

'My body, to enjoy for ever,' said Polnisha and, good as her word, she stepped into Garzon's embrace and submitted to his will there, on the hillside. So, when he had loved her for seven nights, he built the Rock from her cart and sent her oxen into the forest where they bred and became the herds of wild cattle which are there today. Polnisha was happy but, knowing she had work to do in SanZu, on the eighth night stepped out of her body and left it, a beautiful, witless shell, for Garzon to kiss and whisper words of love to as long as he should live. Polnisha wandered for a while, in SanZu and out of it, until she found a girl-child who would take her in and give her human shape.

And that, my dearest son, is why each new Polnisha comes to us in the shape of a little girl and why her Cart stands mute and petrified above us as we work the silk and linen.

As Aurel finished speaking, they left the Rock behind them and floated on.

'Thank you. It is a good story well told,' said Parados. 'But why does the Rock belong to the Ima?'

'They say it is their most sacred ground and that their shamans have released evil puvushi from their prisons in the shifting sands of the Far Plains to live there (sometimes a boulder tumbles down into the fields and that is their doing) – and worse things I dare not name. So, the Ima keep the Rock for themselves. To question their right would only cause another war and, besides, we keep the living Polnisha and her waggon in Flaxberry.'

The wind blew them south-west toward the forest and the Altaish, and played on the struts and cords of the balloon like a mad harper. When SanZu was far behind, it seemed to Parados that the land was too empty, nothing but scrubland in which the trees became ever more dense but were not yet forest. He wondered where the deer drank and, looking down, saw a gushing spring, which quickly became a stream and flowed swiftly away between the birch trees.

'There!' he said. 'Look there, Aurel. That is the source of the River Sigla.'

'Which flows into the Lytha? A sight to cheer us – I have heard men say that its headwaters are impossible to reach, yet here we are sailing above it and the way to it through the trees looks easy enough.'

'The water should be sweet,' said Parados. 'It is as clean and bright as our new weapons.' He gestured at them, two swords and a heavy pistol; all of them wrapped snugly in oiled cloth and leather to keep out the cold and the damp, deadly yet comforting presences which might one day save his life. He had tried and was sure of them; but of his ability to put rivers in the landscape he was less certain, and the Sigla had surely been there amongst the grey birches and the blue-leaved junipers all along? Githon was shouting from his copper-coloured balloon,

'Drop down! Drop! Room by the stream!'

They descended and were camped near the spring before sunset. Aurel and Hadrian, one of the soldiers from Flaxberry, collected wood and lit a fire. They sat a long time round it, eating the bread they had brought with them and drinking the clear water of the Sigla. Beyond the circle at the fire the balloon-baskets lay idle, their neatly-folded silks stowed out of sight inside them, and Hadrian walked constantly in a wide circle, keeping the watch. When it changed and Vaurien took over, Hadrian went to his basket and brought from it a tin flask which he offered Parados.

'It is sulphur-water of Hijafoot. The shamans drink it before they leave their bodies to journey with the dead but, in ordinary folk, a tot will keep out the night's cold.'

Parados unscrewed the lid and took a sip before passing the flask on. It circled the fire and, when it came back to him, he drank again and again sent the flask round the fire. The liquor, despite its terrible smell, was good and warmed his stomach. They drank a third tot and emptied the flask, talking with loosened tongues. The men exchanged tales of nightlong duels with giant fish, of food, drink and capacious bellies, of tavern fights and brawls, hard work, starvation and the long famine; in return, Parados, who found his storyteller's tongue fit and wagging, told them the story of the loss and recovery of his hands.

'You told me that you journey in hope,' said Aurel, when the tale was finished, 'but what is its purpose: where are we going? – oh, I know "into the Altaish" but to view what towering peak, to stay in what upland settlement, talk with which race of men? The Altaish is a vast and hostile wilderness, all except a few of its nearer valleys unvisited and unknown.'

'I have been told that the Altaish should be my next objective.'

'By the Abbess, by Polnisha herself?'

'By the Om Ren.'

'You have been entranced, day-dreaming. The Om Ren is a creature of fable.'

'I told you – he was there when I found my hands.'

'That was a *story*!'

'Then, if I tell you that I hope to rediscover Castle Lorne, you will not believe me?'

Hadrian spoke before Aurel could frame a reply,

'Forgive Aurel before he speaks again, Parados. He is quiet, even meek, by day, on water. He takes the liberty to over-exercise his tongue: it is the sulphur-water speaking.'

'We have emptied your flask, Hadrian; but let Aurel speak. I would rather no one is uncertain, or kills his fear as the basilisk slays her enemy – by staring it full in the face.'

'I should like to believe you, Parados, for I have often dreamed about Castle Lorne and in my dreams it is a place to wonder at,' said Aurel, flushed with the liquor and with embarrassment. 'If we find it, we may discover other wonders which we thought were merely verses in the Lays of the Ima.'

'Do you know Gry, the Imandi's daughter?' Parados asked him. 'She recited one of the Lays to me when I stayed in her house.'

'I once saw her pass by at the Horse Fair in Vonta, a pensive child, eight or nine years old, more like the daughter of a shaman than a lord. I was a child myself.'

'She has grown, Aurel. She is a lovely woman who should be wooed and wed.' He rolled over and lay down on his back to sleep with his memories of Gry, seeing the starry Swan, Bail's Sword, the Hoopoe and the Dancing Crane float above him before his eyes closed. Gry kissed him in his sleep, but it was the kiss of a sister and saddened him. I will give her something to remember me by, he thought, and placed a single bright star in the dark emptiness above the head of the Crane. Later in the night, he woke and heard the wind blowing from the Plains far west of them, where Nandje's village was. The balloon baskets creaked softly and Githon snored while Aurel, taking his turn at the watch, walked about them on silent feet. In the sky, his star burned where he had placed it in his dream, a fiery pentangle of great clarity and beauty. He smiled happily and fell asleep again. Aurel, when he brought hot linseed tea and warm bread in the morning, told him of it, eyes and voice full of wonderment.

'There is a new star in the sky,' he said. 'It appeared just before dawn, huge and glowing, directly above the head of the Crane. It has five points – you can count them easily – and I think it is a sign that our journey will be blessed.'

'I pray that it will,' said Parados. 'We will reach the foot-hills tomorrow and begin today to rise up into the mountains, and danger. Enjoy the last of the holidays!'

All morning, as they sailed, he was possessed with love of his creation, the pentagonal star. When night came and it appeared, they were camped in rough ground where the forest met the bare foothills. Rocky formations had built themselves into towers and crazy buttresses amongst the cypresses and pines, unsure whether they were children of the mountains or older outcrops which preceded them. He asked the men what the star was called.

'It has not found its name,' Hadrian said. 'Such a new and glorious star, soaring over the high peaks like a sign from heaven, must not have a common name – perhaps we should give it some name such as Harun, which means portent and also mountaineer.'

'Or Polnisha!' another soldier offered.

'Or Parados,' said Aurel quietly. 'What would you call it, Githon?'

'I would give it a simple name,' said the dwarf. 'A plain name which is easy to understand, but meaningful. So I would call the star Guardian, but would dignify the name and give it gravity by saying, in the old scholar's tongue, Custos.'

'Custos!' Aurel echoed. 'Yes – our helpful guardian!'

Looking up at the star, the men spoke its name aloud and it climbed higher in the sky and waited for them above the first peak of the Altaish.

'That is the way we must go tomorrow,' said Parados. 'After Custos. Following the star.'

They were all asleep, except the soldier Vaurien who kept watch. The cold was intense and the men of SanZu and the dwarf were dreaming of the famine; but Parados dreamt of a fair woman. They made a romantic picture lying there between their folded balloons and the fire, each back covered with the hoar-frost which crept out of the foothills and touched them as they slept.

I laid down the mirror. One can have too much meat at a banquet and, if I may continue in metaphor, I was tired of being the spider waiting on the wall. I was hungry for so much: to meet Parados, to stand before him and be seen, to look into his face and tell him my name. Also, I hungered in the common sense for, though I had fed Cob his red and white nourishment, I had not myself eaten for twenty-five hours. Accordingly, I bade my son goodnight and conveyed myself to Sehol, where I sat at the head of the long table in the Shield Hall, keeping my feet warm in the lap of the lissom juggler, Concordis, and suffering Friendship's kisses and caresses for she was glad to see me at home. Rosalia, I had sent to air my bed with her fiery body. My chief councillor sat on my left – Strephon, who had once courted Nemione – and next to him, the Lord Marshall, Elzevir Tate, whom I had promoted to flatter and secure. Others of Nemione's suitors sat at table, all of them mine and all of them corrupted and corrupt. They were no longer pretty fellows. Stephan and Randal were coarse-faced, sweaty and fat from good living, while Astrophel, who had caught the plague and recovered from it by my will, was left with red pustules on his handsome face and painful and permanent swellings in his joints. He walked with the aid of two sticks. Strephon had the clap and Corinel (the brother of Corydon who, preferring the cold charms of the nivashi to women's parts, had drowned somewhere – I relate a rumour, for he was not worth the searching) – Corinel, the dolt, was perfect, manly, hard of muscle, mellifluous of voice, a poet, a swordsman, a good dancer, and loved only dogs. His favourite bitch sat by him on a chair, his jewellery round her four legs, shaggy neck and tail, her nose in a gold dish heaped with steak and marrow bones. The bitches belonging to my other councillors (Astrophel had two) leaned on the backs of their master's chairs, fanning themselves with estridge feathers and gossiping in shrill voices. When I looked at them I wondered how in all creation I had ever come to love a woman. Stephanie and Randelle wore patches on their greasy cheeks, Stella had powdered her face too well and forgotten her neck and the vast ledges of her bosom; Ophelia had black teeth, Corinna the pox to go with Corinel's affliction, while Strephonita farted continually, filling the room with a stench the finest perfumes could not disguise. My tastes are inventive and unusual but, I think, not gross. The dog, by the by, was called Cora.

The tastes of Parados were clean and pure. He had reinvented himself, and this creation, of the gentleman and knight, was as fine as his others, his clever tricks with his hands, with travel and renewal, the River Sigla and the star Githon had named Custos. Though I tried with wine and conversation to banish him, he would not depart and remained like a phantom with me. I was haunted by his valorous spirit. He would float, an innocent mayfly, eventually into my web, despite his powers, in spite of his honourable deeds. I saw his face even before I closed my eyes. He stared at and seemed to acknowledge my presence before, like a ghost again, he drifted away.

The magician, who seemed to lean forward out of a confused background of candle-light and coloured brocades, was staring fixedly – almost as if he slept with open eyes. Parados met the unwavering gaze. Koschei's hollow pupils were dark as death and the brown irises which surrounded them as glossy and repellent as the pebble-eyes of the wooden animals on the hill. Once, those eyes had welcomed others, sparkled with glee, with life and the love of it. Parados was sorry, seeing to what a deep abyss Koschei had been brought, and looked away. Opening his eyelids, he saw the balloons upon their sides, furnaces roaring and canopies inflating slowly like giant, landfast squid. Aurel handed him a mug of tea.

Wrapped like their weapons, but in fur beneath leather, the balloonists ascended from cold into greater cold. The foothills mounted up, height upon steep rise, until they became mountains. They passed over the peak the star had guarded for them and saw the highest lands, inaccessible to man but not to beast (for the Om Ren's mate, whatever she was, lived there and there he must climb) and coated all over in deep drifts and tottering overhangs of crusted snow.

'Soon we must land,' said Aurel, 'to bring ourselves below the height at which we should cease to breathe. There is no air for we mortals – even so, it may be that the mountain-tops are also without the blest stuff which fills our lungs so effortlessly. Do you think there is a village, Parados, where we can get pack-animals to carry our kit over the crest?'

'There is Excelsior Pass,' said Parados diffidently. 'If we keep Esperance ahead and low, we should cross it safely.'

'Is that where the star leads?'

'Yes. Custos has gone this way – we shall see him watching over Castle Lorne tonight. We must use all the advantage we have been given while Koschei sleeps off his excesses of body and mind.'

The sun, which had been tardy, rose to accompany them and touch the summit snows with rose and gold. Its glow rebounded from the walls of the pass and dazzled them as they crossed, one balloon after another, grey-blue, copper, bronze and green, until they all hung on the far side, between the light and the darkness which covered Castle Lorne. Its turrets only were visible, conical white caps rising out of the night, each one topped with snow. On the furthest, the brazen cockerel, Vifnir, lifted his enamelled wings towards the sun.

'What food is left in the hamper?' Parados asked urgently. 'Quickly, find some small and tasty morsels.'

Aurel, wondering who would choose to eat at such a sublime moment, obeyed and found a handful of sweet raisins, which he offered Parados.

'No, hold them up in your outstretched hand. If we do not act speedily, the cockerel will crow and warn whatever waits in the darkness below; or it will wake Koschei in Pargur – it is a noisy bird.'

Aurel, though he shook his head from side to side, held up the raisins. Minutes passed and the cock shook out his wings and smoothed them in his beak. He winked a golden eye and suddenly was aloft, flying fast and direct on his multi-coloured wings. As he landed on the rim of Esperance's basket and stretched out his neck to take the bait, Parados seized him and muffled his head in a scarf.

'We will have him for dinner! He is fleshy and heavy and he can't turn back to brass while we have him.'

Aurel, who felt sorry for the magnificent bird, stroked its green back and pulled out one of its golden breast-feathers.

'Now you have a powerful charm,' said Parados. 'Keep it safe and it will guard you from ambush. I will tie Vifnir's beak and his legs so that he can neither move nor crow. Back to the furnace and the sandbags, Aurel. We must find the magic canoe which is the entry into Castle Lorne.'

'Is there a river down there beneath the dark?'

'Yes, but the boat we must find is not a craft for sailing on water. It travels, like this balloon, through the air. Nemione kept it moored to a fig-tree close under Windring.'

All day, they flew on the edge of darkness in search of the fig tree and the canoe. Once, Parados attempted to fly across the gloom but it was so cold that his balloon dropped suddenly, plummeting into the dark, and only Aurel's skill saved them. Githon wanted to try, but Parados forbade him. They shone the light of their lanterns and of brands lit from the balloon furnaces below them and the light was swallowed up. Not until the sky, which had covered them throughout the daylight hours like a grey shroud, also grew dark and the stars came out, did they find a way. Custos rose and hung below Windring, illuminating the rocky arches on its summit and the fig tree, frost-covered and alone, clinging to the cliff. The canoe was missing but the Om Rem's rope was tied fast to the tree and depended into the invisible valley.

'I shall climb down it,' said Parados.

'And I! You will need a torch-bearer,' said Githon.

The navigators fastened the five balloons to the fig tree. Githon and Hadrian scrambled from their own baskets into Esperance's, which dipped with the extra weight. They armed themselves, Parados buckling on his new sword for the first time in earnest. He was the first on the rope. As he took hold of it, he remembered how he had touched the Om Ren's hair with his new-found old and beloved hands. The rope was rough and easy to cling to: tufts at intervals along its length made foot- and hand-holds and, though he was wary of dropping into negation, it did not end but was always there, however far he climbed down it. He thought that, if he opened his mouth, he would drink in the darkness and become part of it. Githon, just above him, had a lantern tied to his leg but it was no more use than water to the dead. Darkness should be comforting, a warm place to sleep, but this was colder than the Poles and threatened his hands; it was too late now to adjust his hold and put on gloves. His left foot touched a solid – the bottom, a projecting stone? – and at the same time, the rope began to shake and twist. He heard Aurel cry out in alarm as he clung to the bucking rope.

'Hold tight,' said the Om Ren in his mind. 'This is Koschei's doing, a small, annoying spell. Trust me: count three and let go.'

Again, Parados felt stone, then it was gone and he had counted three. There was no time to pray or consider his fate: he dropped from the rope and found stability, the ground beneath his feet. He stepped forward, an inch, a foot: he stood on something larger than an isolated rock. The others called out from the rope; but soon, they were all with him and Githon was unfastening the lamp from his leg and holding it up. Here, the dark was less invincible: they could see the ledge on which they stood and, with the aid of a second lamp which Hadrian lit, the castle wall and a sally port.

'That way!' said Aurel. 'It must be the entrance to Castle Lorne – will it be like the castle in the Ima's tales?'

Hadrian went first to take what he claimed should be his due, the harm from any snare or trap in the gateway; but all was quiet and inside the arch they found a stone stairway to which, as they began to climb it, their lamps brought a fresh light, as of early morning. Still, the stair was grim and Parados for a moment saw it as the terrible staircase of his recurrent dream before a new light, falling from an arrow-slit, showed him spiralling steps like any in a church or ancient ruin. In front of him, Hadrian paused.

'There are footprints – here, in the thick of the dust!'

They went before, up the stairs, the footprints of a man for they were large and regular, of someone who knew his way. A curious fan in the dust beside the left print was, Githon said, caused by a tassel or fringe come loose to flop in the dust. So, following in Koschei's steps (for who else would, or could, come willingly to Castle Lorne?) they entered Nemione's bedchamber where there was nothing but more dust and the trail of footprints leading on. A light seeped reluctantly into the room, around the edge of closed shutters, and Parados ran forward and flung them open.

'We have brought the day!' he cried. Outside, the snow-bound castle walls and towers came slowly into focus as the light increased and the air began to move from its stasis. Nemione's flag, on which three golden hinds were worked, lifted on its cord. The darkness ran before the breeze and

338

full day was imminent, yet waited to be called as if it had forgotten it should illuminate the works of Man and the Beasts.

Her cell, or study, lay beyond the bedchamber. Parados went fearlessly into it and crossed to the window. Here, where there were no shutters and the snow had blown into the room were many sets of Koschei's footprints, overlaying each other and telling a tale of misery and devotion.

'Koschei's sleep is fathomless,' whispered the Om Ren's bodiless voice. 'He has not been here for a month but, as you see, he made his visits in great agony of mind.'

A great heap of fallen plaster lay on the floor in front of a cavernous fireplace, some stuffed birds decaying on the top of it beside the rotted body of a great horned owl. Nemione's desk and bookshelves were in similar disarray, her writing materials and grimoires tumbled and mildewed, her crystals and petrified flowers sullied with cobwebs and grime. Her drinking water had frozen in its glass. A sagging curtain, weighed down with the damp, its woven scenes of Arcadian life a garden now for mosses and ugly growths of toadstools, hung across a corner of the room. While Githon and Hadrian stood by with drawn swords and Aurel held the lamp to augment the slow new-born light, Parados lifted it aside. It crumbled where he touched it and the toadstools covered his hand with slime but, though he involuntarily wiped his hand on his coat, he did not notice the filth: Nemione's cat-a-mountain couch stood there at bay, a tangled nest of creatures curled up in its long, white hair.

The couch-head roared. Its carved eyes were sunken and the ivory teeth it bared decayed but it took a pace forward and lashed its moth-eaten tail. Hadrian ran forward and would have thrust his sword into the cat's open mouth but Parados, smiling and shaking his head, said,

'That's no way to treat Nemione's guardian,' and stroked the angry, wooden head and the furry back of the couch which was its neck. The familiars hissed and spat, uncurling and separating from the warm squalor in which they slept. Halfman sat up on the Child's knee.

'Come,' said Parados and held out a friendly hand. At once, the monkey jumped up and swung from it, turning a somersault round the resurrected wrist and running up to Parados's shoulder where he sat and chittered comfortably. The Child, scarred by her untimely knowledge of magicians and men, was more reluctant, but she touched Parados hesitantly, knelt and said, in her fish's voice,

'You are not the Archmage. Have you come to lead us away? – we cannot leave our home, though it is a cold castle. This was my mother's realm.'

'I shall not take you anywhere, unless you wish to go. I am Parados, journeying in hope.'

'That is an unknown commodity here. Koschei has none of it and we gave ours up when my mother died.'

Parados gazed at her glistening blue nakedness and wondered why she had not frozen like the water in the glass. Her presence woke fear in him: she, the daughter of an archmage and an enchantress was too much like a nivasha to please him.

'Have you no dress, or cloak?' he asked.

'They have all rotted in the time we have been here.'

Parados removed his outer coat of furs and draped it over her thin shoulder. Thus dressed, she was more hideous but smiled. Her face showed gentleness and trust.

'Thank you. It is soft. The others grew their own warm coats, but I cannot – all I can grow are scales and spines. See, my fingers all have their own separate fins.'

She held out her hand and raised the transparent fins which grew along the backs of her fingers.

'I should live in water,' she said. 'Here, Leo, we will stay with Parados and see what he will do – quietly, Beasts, or this man-magician will send you back to Beelzebub's pit and the fires of Asmodeus, where you belong.'

'How do you know what I am?' He was astonished: he hardly knew it himself.

'No one but a magician could enter Castle Lorne, especially in the steps of Koschei. Such a one must be of equal standing and ability.'

The earless dog, Leo, which had obeyed her call and stood close by her, licked her hand and held it in its curious three fingered grip.

'You are no better than your fellow-familiars,' she said. 'Beware! Now I will show you Castle Lorne. That way, you will avoid Koschei's magical snares, for I know every one. He is a careful keeper of other people's treasures.'

Aurel, who had taken shelter at the back behind Hadrian and Githon, crept forward.

'Are you not afraid of these brutes, or are they your lap-dogs?' he asked, fear and loathing loud in his voice. The imp spoke up from its long coat of hair,

'Neminies, Neminies,' it squealed.

'They are Nemione's familiars,' said the Child. 'I am her only daughter, got from the seed of the Archmage Valdine and conceived in my virgin mother's bath. Do not be afraid – I am old but still a child. Treat me as one and your tolerance will be rewarded with good fortune.'

The four men followed her about the castle. Decay was everywhere, and everywhere they went the heavy darkness in which the castle had slumbered retreated to let in the light. It seemed to Hadrian that the further they went into the castle's most secret places, the quicker its recovery was and the more magnificent, a fine grandeur of tapestries like gardens and of white marble basins full of mysterious green water which, as Parados came near, turned crystal clear. A fountain shot up from one and played over the dirt on the floor, washing it clean and revealing red and white tiles in the shapes of roses and lilies. Another was surrounded by stone beasts from whose open mouths fresh water suddenly poured. They stood by these animals and Aurel cupped his

341

hands and took a drink of the water. He was certain its eyes moved in its head and that it licked its dripping lips when he had drunk. Some of the castle's peculiarities they never noticed, too slow of eye to see that the mirrors often reflected faraway places, or how the statues turned on their plinths to stare after them as they passed. In a small room near an open court where the growing light discovered mock-oranges in bud, they found a table set for six, but dared not go near it and did not see the disembodied hand which set napkins by the plates when they had turned their backs. Beyond this room, in a wide hall furnished with cushioned benches and a harpsichord, Parados stood still and held up a warning hand.

'Something follows after us,' he said.

'Koschei!' said Githon. 'The footprints must be fresh after all.'

'He sleeps in Castle Sehol. I know it.'

'It is the couch!' The Child burst into bubbling laughter as Nemione's couch bounded into the room, the Imp, the Sooterkin and Leo riding on its back and Halfman on its head. It had grown young again and stripes and spots appeared in its fur. Its eyes were full and bright and it hung out a red tongue and panted before lying down and purring with a thunderous note. A tremor ran suddenly along the keyboard of the harpsichord and it began to play a galliard. The Child capered and Halfman clapped his paws together.

Then nothing could stop their joyous progress through the halls and courtyards, the cellars and towers of Castle Lorne. The walls renewed themselves about them, the snow on the sills melted away and, when they looked out of the windows, they saw a pretty valley, a sparkling river and peaceful fields planted with wheat and groves of birch. Githon ran outside and looked up at Windring. Far above, on the steep cliffside, he saw the balloons tethered to a green fig tree and he called loudly up to Vaurien and the soldiers and navigators.

'Wake up! Wake, lazy dolts!'

When the balloons had been brought down and the castle shown to all, with its gardens crowded with flowering lilac and laburnum, its sparkling white walls and towers and its curios, curiosa and curiosities, they took possession of it in the name of Hope and, finding the stores and wine-cellars as full as those of happy Flaxberry, they set about preparing meals and sleeping quarters; but Nemione's Child was quiet and sat beside the fire with her head in her hands until Parados, thinking she was tired of the new company and diversions, bent over to ask her why she wept.

'We have forgotten my mother,' she said. 'We ran about the castle joking, laughing and making merry as if she was alive and we only waited on her pleasure till she chose to put on her finest dress and come down to the feast.'

'But look what I have found you.' He held out a white dress. 'Is it Nemione's? Put it on for memory's sake and, tomorrow, we will carry flowers to her tomb, kneel there and remember.'

Parados, though he was exhausted, for he did not know that magic saps strength and eventually wastes the body unless remedies are taken, slept uneasily. He had chosen to lie down in a room on the floor below Nemione's study where he had found her bed, pushed into a corner and forgotten. Githon, imitating his kinsman Erchon, lay with drawn sword across the threshold of the room to protect him.

If the bed were haunted, Parados thought, it could not be by a sweeter ghost. He drew aside the curtain, expecting moth-holes and decay, but found a pristine bedspread covering lavender-scented blankets and linen sheets. Not until he had climbed into the bed and lain down did he see that the bed-canopy was a painted swathe of silk exactly like the ceiling of the bed in which he had been imprisoned; but these cupids were whole and smiled down on him. He watched them and soon, convinced they were watched by no one but a friend, they began to frolic and play, chasing each other about the Rococo sky and swinging from the garlands which hung between the clouds.

'There he is,' said one. 'Parados himself.'

'And in a better state than when we saw him last,' another replied. 'Like ourselves.'

'Cupidon, this *is* Arcadia.'

'Don't you think, brother, that Parados lacks something, though he has got his hands back and looks to me the sort of well-appointed man a whole-hearted woman would adore?'

The first cupid hung upside down and fluttered his wings to keep aloft. Parados laughed: he looked absurd, suspended there like a pink and white bird of prey, all pitiless innocence and childish raillery; and then Parados, before another minute had passed, lay groaning softly like a man in a dream, so quickly had the cupid's arrow been fitted to the golden string and fired. It had hit him in the heart. Gritting his teeth, so he would not make more noise and alert Githon, he pulled the arrow out. Three drops of his heart's blood trickled from his chest and stained the sheet before the wound closed up and disappeared. But he knew he was stricken and turned the arrow over in his hands, examining it. It was small and wickedly sharp.

The cupid called out to him,

'Can I have my arrow back?'

'Certainly not,' Parados replied gruffly, and leaned across the bed to stow the arrow safely in the pocket of his discarded coat. Now, he was free to dream. He looked up. The cupids had had their fun and lay asleep upon their clouds. A warm breeze drifted down from the azure sky and it seemed that the sun shone on him, quietly, gently, as on an afternoon in spring. He saw Nemione walking across an empty street. The doorways of the houses were in shadow and looked inviting, some doors standing open to the breeze; but she passed them all and, coming to an arched gateway, went in.

He followed her. He was in the cloister, walking swiftly after Nemione: he must catch her up, declare himself, kneel to her, swear eternal love. When she only was twenty paces away, he saw Koschei walking in the opposite direction, towards him. There was a spring in his step and his dark hair and youthful beard were neatly combed and oiled although he wore the habit of the Order. His eyes shone with anger and amazement.

'What is the matter, Little Corbillion?' said Nemione pertly, and swished the skirt of her white robe aside to show her ankles and her high-heeled shoes.

Koschei was distracted at once. 'Nothing,' he muttered, 'Nothing – I thought I saw a ghost, a trick of the light and shadows under the colonnade.'

Parados woke with two things in his mind, Koschei's astonished gaze and his own abiding love of Nemione. The second soon obliterated the first. He was, he reflected, in exactly Koschei's case, desperate for love of a dead enchantress. So it was that he lay wakeful when the cockerel Vifnir, which he had saved from the oven and released the evening before to serve as his watchbird, crowed to welcome the dawn. He had no more time for pensiveness: the Child came to call him to breakfast, making her noisy entrance in the lost canoe which carried her along three feet above the floor and barked at him with its dog's head.

'Hush, Sirius,' said the Child. 'You have slept, Parados – you look refreshed and strong, like some old traveller gazing on a new-discovered land or a man in love! Come, ride in my boat. When we have eaten, remember, we are going to pray at Nemione's tomb.'

Pray, he thought: for deliverance, release, escape? Paradise has its own consuming fires.

He travelled in the Child's boat, Aurel and Githon in Esperance: there was no hope for him. The rest remained behind to guard Castle Lorne. He nursed a sheaf of white flowers and Nemione's familiars crowded about his feet. Windring bore its stone arches lightly, they and its wide top thick with snow. They landed outside the circle and approached on foot but, before they had passed under the arches, saw three shepherds standing forlornly in the snow. The skins and fur they wore did not seem to protect them from the cold, for they leaned on their crooks and shivered miserably.

'We have lost our sheep,' said one of the shepherds, grey-bearded and older than the rest.

'You should get a dog,' Aurel told him. 'What use is a shepherd to his sheep without a trusty dog?'

'Lend us yours – ours have perished in the snow.'

'Our dog? The wild brute with the werewolf's hair? He would make a fine, bloodthirsty sheepdog.'

The Child snapped her finny fingers. 'His name is Leo,' she said. 'He is skilled at finding whatever is lost – he has found many things for me, my comb, this boat; but he cannot find my mother. That is her tomb in the circle.'

'You may call yourself her daughter,' the shepherd said. 'The lady who lies was never married, in church or out of it.'

The Child snapped her fingers again and Leo bounded up. 'What I am is not your concern,' she said. 'But take the dog. He is so small he walks, as you see, on the snow and will soon find your sheep.' She smiled to see the dog, which ran about like a visible whirlwind, barking in a high, shrill voice and sniffing with all the gusto of a bloodhound at the snow. Eventually he lay down and wagged his tasselled tail.

'Now dig!' the Child commanded. 'If, that is, you have brought spades which I doubt, since you are so careless as to lose both your sheep and your dogs.'

The shepherds were humble and grateful.

'We have spades, lady,' they said and dug where Leo had shown them. The sheep were snug below, a flock of thirty, each with a lamb. Their warmth had melted the snow

beneath them, exposing the grass which they had been crop-
ping in their snowy cave. As they ran out and forward the
snow melted under their feet and the same was happening
wherever Parados trod. They all followed him to the tomb.
Snow covered it and the ground immediately about, except
in his track. He stood quiet for a moment (Githon thought
he prayed), lifted his right hand and dusted the snow from
one side of the tomb. It was made of glass. He could see
Nemione's long skirt and the white cloth which lay under
her; but there were words engraved in the glass.

'*Et in Arcadia ego*,' he read. The shepherds crowded round
him and peered at the words as if they were a sacred text.
One of them exclaimed 'So He is!' Parados swept the snow
from the top of the tomb and looked in on Nemione's lovely
face. Her eyes were closed and some colour lingered in her
lips so that she seemed not dead, but sleeping. More words
were cut into the glass above her shrouded breast:

> Cease now your suits, and sigh no more,
> I mean to lead a virgin's life,
> In this of pleasure find I store,
> In doubtful suits but care and strife.

'I must kiss her,' he thought. 'Just once, though she is in
another Paradise.'

He laid his flowers down carelessly: such tributes did not
matter now that he could see her. Githon and Aurel dropped
to their knees and the Child and all the familiars wept silently
but the shepherds helped him clear the last of the snow, even
as it melted to nothing. The tomb had no seam or join in
any of its clear, transparent surfaces and he could see no
way to open it.

'Smash it!' someone whispered in his ear and he turned
about fearing a supernatural visit from Koschei and saw, as
in a dream or vision, the Om Ren toiling up a distant peak,
so far away he seemed an ant on a sugar cone. Hardly

knowing what he did, he drew his maiden sword and, expecting it to shatter or rebound, brought it down on the glass: it was the glass which shattered, and the sword vibrated with a single ringing note as if he played on the world's wine glass.

The mirror cracked in two and doubled my picture of him: I saw two men, two swords, a double tomb in which twin Nemiones lay cold as marble effigies and then the crack multiplied itself by four and eight and swiftly doubling increments until the mirror and the image were in a thousand, nay ten thousand fragments, and a hail of glittering shards surrounded me, a storm in which there was no sound but the staccato lament of breaking glass. My flasks and retorts burst open, my wine goblet exploded, my Actinidion paperweight returned itself to scattered millefiori; I felt my pocket looking-glass rupture in its case and the lenses shot from my telescopes and broke upon the stone floor; the quicksilver poured from my thermometers and barometers, every one of my mirrors and the beautiful spun glass which framed the perfect circle was devastated and my private and clandestine view of Malthassa, its people and the doughty adventurer, Parados, lost.

Now, I had no doubt of his power. He, who could move through space and time and change the geography of my country at will, the very rivers and mountains, had also turned the beautiful sarcophagus Oliver had carved for me – of sardonyx and serpentine it was and finished on the outside with a representation of my only love, Nemione – he who had come wanting into Malthassa was now so strong that, merely by imagining it, he had turned the polished stone to glass so that he might break into Nemione's last and final sleep and, in so doing, smash all the glass in Peklo tower. He must, I thought, and was afraid for the first time, know of these mirrors; and he must also know that by destroying them he weakens me. I wished I had interrupted his glorious career before he got his hands back, or killed him at the start when he first crawled, weak as a babe, through the storm. My own curiosity (to see what he would do) and my cynicism (as he made his crazy progress at the head of these witless child-worshippers of SanZu) were handicaps I had myself strapped on.

I brushed aside the spun glass which lay in a rainbow veil of finest gossamer across my table. I took up the mirrors one by one and shook the broken glass from their delicate frames. It fell like noisy raindrops, like hard frost disturbed from a branch, upon the broken vessels of my alchymy and chymistry, the sherds which had been my poison-jars. I watched the acids eat pits in the floor and mingle, hissing, with the oils which spurted from my fractured aryballuses. More glass was falling, the shattered window-panes in Cob's small palace as he pushed them out. He brought his convex countenance to the one of the empty casements.

'Have you failed in an experiment, Father?' he asked.

'You may say so,' I answered. 'Though not with saltpetre, nitre and sulphur but in my patient study of the phenomenon of Parados. He has plucked out my far-seeing eyes – shattered my mirrors with thaumaturgics and telekinesis. Come with me, my dear, and hold fast. We must away to Pargur and to Castle Sehol and prepare our defences there with artistry and consummate care. It will be a heavy struggle.'

'Father, can you not see him crawling over your map and on your turning globe?'

'Can you see him there, Cob? There is Windring, certes, but the scale is too vast. Those representations of our world are kinetic devices: they are not meant for scrying.'

I caught him to me and he clung in the bosom of my robe like the greedy leech he was. We shot into the seething vat of negation, he squealing with joy for he loved the disorienting sensations and the speed, I shouting out in grief at my loss and with anger at the presumption of the alien. And so, alighting from the maelstrom, we walked into the Bower where Toricello's random vegetation was, at that moment, bursting into riotous flower. I sat down by the fountain and listened to the play and splash of the water; I let it cascade upon my left hand, for I had cut myself on the glass. Paloma flew from her perch in the dovecot and settled her self on my other hand. She preened and, turning about, drew her long, white tail feathers through her beak until they were smooth and neat as an officer's cockade.

'How are you today, my little dove?' I asked her. She had not been given the power of speech and nodded her head and looked at me sideways from a red eye. I called the flock about me and watched the cushats strut on the fountain's rim and dip up water from its edge. They were mirrored for an instant before ripples broke the picture up: the sight reminded me of my blindness and recalled primitive techniques. I calmed myself with even breathing and stared into the fountain. The water ran across blue and green tesserae and I tried to forget them and interpose the scene on Windring as last I saw it. Once or twice the motion stayed: I saw flat, reflective water and a dark background; but nothing moved there and I let my concentration lapse, seeing the mosaic again and the wavering images of the doves. What use is a third eye if it sees nothing? What might Parados have done with Nemione since he took away my glass eyes? Why should I not sweep down upon Windring or storm Castle Lorne and take her? To remove myself there was a simple task. (I had myself moved the Memory Palace, if not mountains, countless times, stones, boulders, cannon, storms, waters, snow, ice, nivashi, puvushi, demons –) Yet, patience Koschei! I exhorted myself. There is much pleasure to be gained in anticipation and inventing. Set a trap, tempt them, see them walk in and fall the harder. Take them both, he to Asmodeus, she for yourself.

I spent my anger and frustration in Baptist Olburn's company, watching him ply his uncharitable trade and myself trying out his apparatus on those who had the mischance to have wronged me. He has a mort (an apt term!) of ingenious devices in the anterooms of his dungeon, a Screw-Rack, Pincers, Pliers, a Pressing Plane, a Tantalus Engine, a Vertiginous Hoist, and a very fine Iron Maiden whose embrace is agonizing death – eventually – as well as hot fires, consuming acids, boiling oil, sand, thorns, molten lead &c &c. The everyday practice of the black art of torture is his kingdom, as mine is Peklo, my books and those indefinable regions beyond the upper firmament which none but an archmage can gain.

The broken glass lay in pieces on Nemione's face and ashen hair. Parados brushed it away with trembling fingertips. The shepherds were picking the splinters from her winding sheet. One them licked his finger,

'Not blood,' he said. 'This is water – see, it was ice, not glass.' Indeed, the pieces Parados had brushed away were turning into perfect drops. One trembled like a bubble on the back of his hand, but another was stuck fast, unmelted, to the nail of his forefinger. He tried to shake it off and it stood up and bowed to him, a tiny clear figure which he knew at once was female and was Nemione's soul, a little homunculus like the yellow Thread Man.

'I have waited here an age,' it complained. 'I was asleep on the tomb, as close as could get to my mistress. You might have killed me!'

'I would not knowingly harm anything of Nemione's,' he said, 'but I am wounded in the heart and I must kiss her even if it means that I, too, must die.'

'Everything must die. You might have met her beyond the grave,' said the soul pettishly, and climbed to a safe vantage point halfway up his arm, where it clung and drummed its minute feet.

He turned back to the tomb. The sheaves of roses, Koschei's tributes, which were heaped about Nemione crumbled into dust. She was neither a beautiful relic nor a noble effigy, not asleep but a corpse, quite dead. Hesitantly, he drew back her shroud. Her hands, just as he had dreamed, were folded about a posy of flowers made of amethysts and diamonds. He touched one hard petal and the gaudy posy became a bunch of simple violets on which the dew was fresh; he beheld Nemione's white shoulders rising from the gown they had dressed her in to be entombed. A banded snake was coiled about her neck, an ugly, unexpected ornament. It opened fathomless, bejewelled eyes and looked knowingly at him. He shook with fear.

'Helen!' he breathed, so quietly that none of his companions heard him. The snake, as soon as he had spoken the name, began to fade away, disappearing as he looked at it. When it was gone and the long neck was as white and pure as he desired it, 'Nemione!' he said in firmer tones, and bent closer, wondering at the exactness of his vision: she was all he had imagined when he built her out of memories and hopes. 'Now I should kiss her,' he thought, bending lower, but her soul reached her first, jumping from his arm where he had forgotten it, and nestling beneath her chin. He blinked, and it had gone. Nemione opened her sapphire eyes, pleasure in them, and amazement. But she did not speak to him. Instead, she raised herself on one elbow and called out to her Child.

'Daughter, be the first to greet me.'

The cold, scaly creature, an apparition in her draggled gown, sprang up. Nemione reached out to touch her wild seaweed hair, embraced her. She murmured lullabies to the Child which, as she sang, her voice hardly audible, lost the unnatural colour, the scales and fishy form which made it outwardly a monster and smiled up at her, a fair, fair-headed seven-year old child, made in her image, whose eyes were green as the water in a tidal race and sparkled mischievously.

'Now that you are a proper child, and fit to be my daughter, I shall give you a name,' Nemione said playfully. 'What shall it be? – Grace, for your transformation from deformity; Patience, for what you have been; Charmian, since you are charming and no longer maladroit; Chloe, which means green shoot; Zillah, shade, Verity, truth, Tabitha, gazelle, Barbara, Delilah, Cassandra? I have it! Your name is Lilith, Child, and here is a kiss to sanctify it. Lilith was mother of the Gypsies, you know, and it is best to make friends with them, or beware!' She looked about her, smiling. 'You are all here, my faithfuls! Halfman, let me stroke your soft fur and Leo, sit by me!' They jumped up to her, the dog becoming, as he leaped, a real lion-dog with bronze hair, wrinkled face and pendant ears. The monkey, being already fixed in his destined form, remained as he was. As for the ugly sooter-kin and the imp: Nemione looked at them and sighed. 'I cannot keep you now,' she said. 'Go – you are released. Return whence you came and never trouble Malthassa again!'

The creatures wailed and cried in vain as they shrank into the ground, vanishing Hellwards with a double thud. The new grass closed over them.

Nemione held up her hands to Parados.

'I am weak, sir,' she said. 'Lend me your strength.'

He took her hands (which his encircled as strong shoots entwine tender stalks) and helped her rise. He had to lift her from the slab on which she had lain so long but, as she stood and he supported her, she felt the new blood flowing in her veins and a delicate blush spread over her cheeks. She spread her arms and yawned, stretched and smiled at them all.

'The shepherds, too,' she said. 'How wonderful. Githon – how do you? This, Sir, must be your man?'

As Aurel saluted, Parados bowed low. It was time to speak.

'Love, not Death, lives in Arcadia,' he said. He knelt at Nemione's feet.

She looked down as if she saw him clearly for the first time.

'And requires its reward,' she said, bent a neck as white and slender as the marble columns which hold up Toricello's folly at Sehol, inclined her perfect face and kissed him. 'Stand up, Lord Parados, beside me. I see my stronghold, clear and bright in the sunshine beyond the mountain's shoulder, and I know you have already been there and lit a fire to warm it. Parados, my new love, Lilith, Aurel, Githon – let us go in to Castle Lorne. I am sure the table is laid for supper.'

Beyond Malthassa's forest lies a tract of salt-marsh, too large for anyone to compass; but Erchon had been there. There is a place where a traveller may cross it and it is marked by a line of sea-worn poles, so bent and eccentrically-shaped they look like mute and headless statues guarding a sanctuary. Erchon had followed their course and come to an island where sea-mews sang and where the wild swans gathered to let the wind drum through the pinions of their up-raised wings. A hermit lived here, all alone with his prayers and mantras. He had no possessions and no memories of his past, having discarded them all, but he told Erchon that he had reached the end of the world.

'How can that be?' said Erchon, 'when I see the marshes stretching their waters and their shining mudbanks to the sky on every side and the way is marked beyond this island?'

'Have you considered that the end may be the beginning?' the hermit replied.

'I will go on and see,' said the dwarf. He followed the crazy markers and arrived, in time, at the forest edge. Deer were grazing on the salty grass where the trees began. The dwarf crept silently through the herd and under the forest canopy; but he did not know where he was. He made a fire to cook on and to sleep by and a meal of the dried fish he carried and the wild garlic which sent out its pungent scent wherever he trod. Satisfied with the food and his own company he slept lightly, dreaming of the swans, and awoke in the small hours. His fire had burned away, but the light from the new star filtered through the tree-tops and silvered the ground. He heard the woodmice rustling about their business in the leafy litter of the forest floor and the stoat which was hunting them. Then, 'She lives!' A mighty shout drove away the quiet and there came a thunderous tattoo on the kettle-drums, the tapping of the snares and rolling waves of reverberation as the great culverin of Castle Lorne fired – nine times, nine again; nine times nine. His head echoed with it. The peace of the forest and the small sounds of its intricate night life returned slowly, but he was unable to sleep. He had no doubt that he was many marches from the Altaish, knelt in the ashes and covered up the last warm remnants of his fire with earth; then, taking up his rapier and buckling it on and hoisting his bast-bag to his shoulder, he set out towards the day and Castle Lorne.

I also heard the commotion, from my throne in Castle Sehol: the rejoicing of the rebels who must be gathering at Castle Lorne in that wondrous courtyard guarded by the statue of Princess Persimmon and the griffon-prince. Nemione's army would be encamped there, renegades, market traders, farmers and peasants, mercenaries and mountebanks, the northern gypsy tribes and their raggle-taggle kings and queens. Then this new nobility would embark to float in the swaying baskets of their many-coloured balloons which, gently rising up, would travel forward in the changeable airs of the Altaish. I was pleased to await them. These so-elegant lords and their peerless Lady, when they had crossed the forest, might take Pargur, walk its streets and rediscover its elegant squares and mutable pleasure-grounds but, save Her, would never lord it over me in Castle Sehol. I had laid my plans. I lifted my glass of blood-red Myrish and drank to the future. Vive Nemione! Vivat Koschei!

The leaves changed from fresh to dull green, from green to yellow and from yellow to red and gold as Erchon journeyed. His ardent heart was already in Castle Lorne and he urged his body on to catch up with it. A pedlar gave him a ride in his tilt-cart for nothing and a fine lady carried him on the step of her carriage; he paid her by opening the door for her and handing her down. He worked a passage along ten leagues of the Sigla in a barge carrying horse-skins and was brought another ten leagues by a merchant balloonist ferrying spices in his fleet of patched balloons. The temptation to draw his rapier and seize one of the balloons was strong but the worn-out craft, he reasoned, could not rise into the Altaish. They set him down in a glade where there was a spring and, when he had filled his water-bottle, he set out. He walked a month or more, setting his course by the sun and stars, marvelling as did everyone he met at the beautiful new star. He called it Nemione's Jewel, but it had been given many other names. One old fellow, a wood-cutter living alone with his axe, his adze and his lame, blind dog called it his Dear Departed and another man, a women's quack who claimed to cure all monthly pains, milk-fevers and distempers of the heart, My Beloved.

It was clear to Erchon as he journeyed that the famine had abated and the long-lasting winter withdrawn. There had been a summer and now the nuts and apples were ripe and hunger satisfied. Hope lived everywhere. He came upon the gypsies in a village by the Lytha. Dark women and hawk-eyed men were stalking the streets, interfering with no one but causing much concern. The villagers offered them wine, which they drank, and cakes, which they disdained. A truce developed and the gypsy women went about from door to door to sell their curious flowers made of wood-shavings and their tin-bound pegs. Their men and their dogs gathered in the square before the chapel. When Erchon walked by them, the men were wagering gold coins on a match between a big brown cur with torn ears and a small, yapping terrier.

The armed Silver Dwarf, carrying his simple bag of woven grass, and dressed in his shining breastplate and cuisses and fine, feathered hat was a novel sight even to the gypsies and some of them turned to stare at him. Erchon smiled to himself: this was what he desired for he hoped to persuade the Rom to let him travel for a while in their company, as once his mistress had done. One of the men, a grizzled ruffian with a patch over his left eye, called out to him,

'Is that skin of yours your own, or did you borrow it from a cock-salmon, Dwarf?'

'It is old grease-paint. He comes from a travelling show,' said another gypsy.

Erchon eased back the sleeve of his leather jerkin and undid the cord at its neck.

'Take a look,' he said. 'You may care to bet on your proposals and I will take one fifth from the winner.'

The gypsy men surrounded him and some of them rubbed at his skin with handkerchiefs and neckerchiefs to see if the silver would come off. One removed his hat to examine the skin of his scalp and the gleaming hair itself.

'I'll lay out three coins,' he said. 'The dwarf has one of those gorgio illnesses like the yellow-touch, only it has turned him silver.'

'It is his clown's camouflage,' another said. 'Five coins.'

And so they piled bet on bet until many gold coins had been promised and were ranged in heaps along the graveyard wall. A gypsy chieftain was called as referee and the village sexton brought from his dinner to judge. He consulted the doctor and an encyclopaedia before he came and was satisfied with the explanation Erchon whispered in his ear, that the unnatural colour of his skin was the penalty all Silver Dwarves paid for their mining.

'But are there Gold Dwarves?' he wanted to know.

'Of course,' said Erchon, ' – and priceless as that metal.'

The dog-fight forgotten, the gypsies bet on, wild explanations succeeding fantastic as their gold-fever grew. They made so much noise and commotion that only when she had struck the biggest of them with her cane and cleared herself a passage did anyone notice the old gypsy woman who walked into the fray.

'Hear me, by Lilith and Gana!' she screeched, beating the ground with her cane. 'I have the explanation here, under my scarf.' She tapped her head. 'I will wager this bauble –' and here she drew a red handkerchief from the pocket of her skirt and opened it to disclose a huge, translucent stone which shone in the afternoon sunlight and caused the men to fall silent and their eyes to gleam with greed. 'This against all your money, my lads. He who guesses right shall take it to his rawnie. Agreed?'

'Agreed,' said some and, 'Aye, Lurania,' said others.

'Will you have my explanation? Are you sure?'

'Yes!'

'Then who has laid out most?'

'Muldobriar!'

'Taiso!'

'No, it is Danku!'

Danku who wore a purple sash and a sprig of rosemary in his buttonhole, cleared his throat and spat into the churchyard. 'This is my explanation,' he said. 'This dwarf, as we all suppose him, is *not what he seems*, and we should be wary. This so-called dwarf is a trap laid for one, or more, of us. We have a shape-shifting puvush among us, lads – who, now she is discovered, will vanish as you see!' He raised his arm and the gypsy-men all took one step forward with their fists and sticks up. Erchon laughed loudly and waved his hat in the air.

'Peace!' he said. 'I am not worth your trouble.'

'So Danku is the cleverest man of our tribe? You are all witless, or drunk,' the old woman said. 'The dwarf hails from the Altaish where he used to mine silver – the metal is in his skin until he dies and he will go shining to the grave, proud of it. Am I correct, Sir?'

'That is what I am,' Erchon said. 'A miner with silver dross ingrained in his hide and love of the bright metal in my soul.'

'And so says Doctor Scrimshaw and my *All the World's Wonders in Six Volumes*, that you may know a Silver Dwarf by the argent glister of his skin – which does not diminish with age nor in sickness – and by his love of all things made of silver and silver in colour,' said the sexton.

Erchon flourished his hat and bowed to the sexton. Turning back to the gypsies he bowed again, low to the ground, and replaced his hat.

'Mistress Lurania is right to say that I used to mine silver,' he said, 'for I have left that far behind me and am bound in the service of a fair lady, once Nemione Baldwin from Espmoss and now the Lady of Castle Lorne.'

The old woman made the sign of a crescent moon on her breast. 'I hear she has recovered from her long sleep,' she said.

'And I!' said Erchon eagerly. 'There has been high magic or a miracle, for I heard the great culverin of Castle Lorne and the drums of the Watch beating a tattoo when I was many leagues away to the west with the hermit of the salt marsh.'

'I told his fortune once, but he would not believe it. How does the beadsman? Well, or does he tire of his lonely meditation and the everlasting chorus of the sea-mews?'

'Hale, hearty and full of good jests. He has plenty of practice, telling them to the birds.'

'Perhaps I will pay him a call if we travel that way – but you must take your reward, Sir Silvercoat. Now, my boys:

I won and therefore all your money is mine. But I shall not be hard on you. I'll tax you, no more than two coins from each pile and half of them I'll give the dwarf – who has come here as an innocent traveller and made you a fine afternoon's entertainment and a subject for talk for a good twelvemonth.'

Lurania took her coins and counted half into Erchon's hat, pocketing her share with the brilliant-cut diamond which, Erchon had seen at once, was a piece of moulded glass.

'Now hold the end of my cane,' she said, 'and I'll take you to my sister who will assist you more than I, a mere white witch, can. My dear sister is a witch of every colour, red, black, green, white, silver, gold. She has all the talents at her command, a true chov-hani.'

The chov-hani sat in the low doorway of a tent made of bent willow-sticks and red and black checked blankets, old like Lurania but with round and wrinkled cheeks which were brown as a russet apple taken from the loft in the dead of winter. Lurania, when she had presented Erchon, withdrew, tapping the ground with her white cane as she went.

'She is blind,' said Erchon, 'yet she knew what was taking place at the chapel.'

'Blind as the day she was born,' the chov-hani replied. 'The sun never rose that day and she cried from the moment of her birth until the next day week. That inauspicious beginning, and her blindness, is the reason she can never be more than a homespun witch. For scrying and spells and earth-turning a woman needs her sight and her other five senses besides. And you, little man-cousin, your sight is better than excellent and your hearing too. The Lady Nemione left her stronghold in the summer and nears Pargur with her knight and her company of soldiers and navigators. You who were beyond the forest have covered the greatest part of the ground which lies between this place and her train.'

'That is because I sent my heart before me as a messenger,' said Erchon. 'But who brings Nemione to a contest of arms with Koschei – one of the suitors is it, Lord Randal or Lord Astrophel?'

'Do chicks hatch from bad eggs? They are all bought and belong to the Archmage. It is the Paladin from the Lays, Parados of the Ima of the Plains – that is where he first discovered himself, appearing to Nandje out of the heart of the storm and ever after working wonders as he journeyed in SanZu and the Altaish. It is he we must thank for waking the sun and the wind, for calling up the green shoots from the earth, and for Nemione's return from the halls of the puvushi.'

'Will you help me, chov-hani? I must go quickly to my Lady and help her fortunes forward.'

'Is that enough for you, Silver Dwarf?'

'More than enough!'

'What of Koschei? He drew you to him as the star does the moth.'

'My long and lonely journey has shown me that he is a dark star.'

'Will you be content to let things be whatever they will and to bring me what I ask from Pargur?'

'I am content and I will bring what you ask, even if it is my heart's desire.'

'Too much, Erchon! Dwarves are over-ready to promise any fool the moon. You will never get your heart's desire now, but I must have what you will bring me. Fetch me the golden nivasha, Roszi (which he calls Rosalia), from Koschei's bed. He has joined her lovely head to the body of a fire-demon and both must be destroyed.'

'It will be a sad day when that happens.'

'Roszi was born to sadness. I knew her when she lived under the waterfall: she was a miserable, tearful thing in those days, doting on the men she drowned and sighing over their bones. And when Nemione had befriended her and persuaded Valdine to give her all that was left of the nivasha (I suppose she felt responsible for one of her kith and kin) after his experiments with molten gold, she was a whining ninny whose only use was as a watch-goose, and a goose is what she was and is. Nowadays, she warms the Archmage's bed and serves his unnatural lusts. It will be easy for you to persuade her of a better future once you are inside Castle Sehol. She will remember you from the old days when, at least, she could complain to her cousin.'

'Inside Castle Sehol?' said Erchon wonderingly, 'Inside the castle which is unseizable and unslightable? It would take Koschei himself to perform such a feat.'

'Tilly-vally! I shall convey you into the very heart of Koschei's stronghold. If you are fearful, say your prayers, then come with me.'

Erchon muttered a charm of the Mountain Dwarves and followed her. She moved quickly for a woman of advanced years, scurrying along the village street as if she had a gale behind her. Soon, they came to the Lytha between whose steep banks the water flowed swiftly down by purple heathlands known only to the curlew and the windhover and through the uncharted forest to Pargur.

'Lie down here, Dwarf,' said the witch.

He obeyed at once: he had spoken all the prayers he knew. She looked at him with her knowing, gypsy eyes and kicked him hard and expertly into the river.

' – Duped!' was all he had the time to think before he hit the water and sank beneath its swirling tide, swallowing the mud and rubbish which the river carried with it and sending up a broad stream of bubbles as the air rushed from his lungs.

Esperance flew high and swift, its flight unimpeded by the burden of an extra passenger: Nemione travelled with Parados in the guise of a young knight. A crested helmet hid her face and hair and an engraved breastplate made her trunk as straight and solid as a man's, cuisses covered her thighs and greaves her slender lower legs, a tasset removed the curve of her hips from view. The armour was light and shone brightly: it would have served her better at a tournament. On her belt of dragon's leather she carried a golden-hilted sword. The belt was fastened with a buckle made from the cupid's arrow Parados had given her and the device on her shield was *argent* on a chevron *vert* between three hinds *or*; but all this only added to the show and dazzlement. Nemione's weapons and her armoury were in her head where the years of magic had amassed a library of spells and put a steel barrier between her lovers and herself. She had kissed Parados many times in Castle Lorne and they had reclined side by side on her couch to talk or listen to music, and to embrace each other. He had given her the golden arrow on one of these sweet, frustrating occasions and she had told him what she vowed so many years ago, in the cloister at Espmoss.

'I was determined even then to make magic,' she said, 'and my vow seemed a small price to pay for a lifetime filled with everything I desired, except union with a man. But I love you, and, when we have prevailed, there will be such a wedding! Till then, Beloved, you must enjoy me in your dreams.'

Parados kissed her, resolving to be worthy of such untainted love, and filled his days and many of his nights with preparations for Nemione's assault on Castle Sehol. He drew up plans and maps, made lists and issued orders to his officers and sergeants. The halls and yards of Castle Lorne echoed to the blows of smiths' and armourers' hammers; Iron Dwarves forged chains and cast cannon balls; gunsmiths proofed muskets and tested powder while soldiers, navigators, new balloons and supplies were brought up through Excelsior Pass from SanZu. He was often lonely, though one or many more of his men accompanied him and his tasks were carried out in fellowship. He no longer heard the Om Ren's helpful voice and must rely on his own judgement; concluding that the Wild Man had found his bride, he thought enviously of their joyous and mighty coupling somewhere high in the snows and silent peaks of the Altaish. He watched his craftsmen and wondered why Nemione did not employ magic instead of these heavy and time-consuming skills.

Nemione prepared herself and her arcane weaponry, all, even the Child, Lilith, excluded from her room. So Lilith, with Leo and Halfman always at her heels or riding on her shoulders, ran about from undercroft to battlement with messages for Parados, with food and drink for him or the books and tools of coppersmithing for Githon, who was making bullets for a new gun he had invented. He called it his Shrike, because he hoped it would make many corpses as does the butcher-bird. Sometimes Lilith rode Sirius, the dog-headed canoe, along the corridors and swooped back and forth below the kitchen rafters, her nurse trying vainly to tempt her down with sweets and promises, her governess trailing after them both, and all the chefs and scullions shouting encouragement to the Child.

The Lady of the castle and her lover spent such time together as was meet in the face of war, an hour each day of companionship to which he looked forward with a mix of hope and impatience and she with calm fortitude. They walked often in the gardens or climbed to the top of Gyronny keep where Nemione's circular glasshouse gave her tenderest plants shelter. The house, when first they went there, was neglected and full of holes from which the dry tendrils of dead plants hung out and tapped forlornly in the wind. Parados touched a vine which immediately quickened and sent out new leaves and flowerbuds.

'It is like our love, grown out of death,' he said. 'Touch this, Nemione, and these. You, who have seen Beelzebub parade before his court and Asmodeus walking in his pride, are the one with best claim, of the two of us, to bring your mandrakes, night-orchids and sleep-cusks back to life.'

'No, my Love, I have only seen the Queen of the Night who danced among her pale vili. There are no colours underneath the ground but black and white,' said Nemione softly, but she went from pot to pot, touching the dry earth here and whispering to a bare stalk there until the glasshouse had filled up with green leaves and shoots, the broken glass healed itself and the split and warped woodwork grown strong and straight.

'This is the last part of Castle Lorne to be healed,' she told Parados. 'Everything that has happened in the castle followed your wish to see my tomb and everything you have ever done, or been, or wished to be has brought you here – from your salad days when you were green in judgement to this, your splendid maturity.'

'I did nothing in my youth to prepare me for it,' he said. 'Nothing edifying or noble; and when I had more years than I cared to admit to myself, I was a fool.'

'No, it was all groundwork,' she insisted. 'Don't you see, without the least of them you would not be here beside me?'

'I loved intemperately, randomly.'

Nemione laughed. 'I,' she said, 'thought I loved Koschei and I did love a gypsy –'

'So did I!'

'Yours was quite as beautiful and fascinating as mine, I am certain,' she said. 'He was a forest Rom that I met when I was travelling to Pargur between the pure life and the self-denying. His hair was black as ivy-berries, his white teeth even and stained at the gums with the honeyed tobacco he chewed and his name was Ladislas, after one of their kings. He praised my beauty and called me his rikkeni rawnie – though I had dyed my hair and darkened my skin and wore gaudy garb and brass jewellery to look like a Rom. Ladislas brought me new-laid eggs and a young hare to make a pet of, and the pale flowers of the wood-anemone which the gypsies call blushing maidens: because its name and nature were mine in any language, he said. I left him with the promise that if I returned, I would wed him.

'In those days I was ambitious, Love, and wanted silk and satin, precious jewels and a grand house and to be renowned for my beauty as much as for my Art; nor was Ladislas my true-love. Men have died for want of me, Parados, but you will not.'

She smiled and kissed him.

'My gypsy was called Helen,' he said. 'She was a witch – should I say "is"? – and had the hair of a gypsy-witch, which falls down straight from the head and curls upon the shoulders – and dark, too, black as the coat of a panther.'

'A witch?' said Nemione, and stiffened, as if she sensed a rival. 'A witch called Helen – I have read of her, have I not? Something in my mind, ah! – "bitter suffering once came from you, Helen".'

'What you say is true enough.' Although that was another Helen, he thought, of Troy. He did not correct Nemione, reflecting that she had her origins in the same vast, abstract world of words. Nemione sighed and laid her head against his chest.

'Let us invent a Malthassan history for you, my love. You are tall and fair (though grizzled as a good soldier should be, who has fought in many wars) and your blue eyes, which are nothing like my sapphires but lucent as a blue-stained goblet of pure water, are those of a kristnik. Your father was Stanko and you have eleven strong brothers, all knights like yourself, and a hatred of witches. Also, as a proper kristnik, you have won the love of a spirit, for I am more than half nivasha through my mother and my father's mother. Am I not beautiful, dear one, am I not all you desire and all you ever have desired?' and she ran across the room and into the stair-turret, Parados following swiftly after and catching her for seven sweet kisses halfway down the stair.

Side by side with her in Esperance, while Aurel drove the

balloon on high and fast, he knew contentment, happiness and joyous expectation. Nor was he afraid, neither of the coming battle, nor of being wounded; but he thought of Koschei with a secret hope that the Archmage and he would never meet.

'Why do you not use magic against Castle Sehol' he asked Nemione, 'instead of transporting the cannon and pot-guns in pieces to be reassembled outside Pargur? And all our folk?'

'Magic is a weapon that turns easily against its user,' she replied. 'It is better to keep such fickle strength for desperate situations and do what can be done with engineering and the soldiers' skills of sapping, mining and bombarding. Also, the men need an occupation: what sorts of creature would they be if everything they asked for came to them on a golden plate?'

She leaned over the side of the basket and shaded her eyes with a hand. 'But I miss my Dwarf, Erchon. We have not finished crossing the forest, Parados, and there is nothing to be seen but the tops of the trees. They look soft like a great green bed – I should like to play in it with you! Where is Erchon, do you think? Githon says he went away in despair. I hope he does not still.'

Erchon, as Nemione spoke, was formless and liquid, a single drop of water rushing towards Pargur in the River Lytha. He retained the consciousness of a dwarf and saw the water he was part of, the broken flotsam, fish, weeds, stones and swimming and reclining nivashi about their deadly under-water business all anyhow about him as the current tumbled him on. He was swept into a mill-leat and thrown up and over a mill-wheel; he lingered in an eddy and travelled on. The river widened and bent itself round rocks, created islands, brought down trees. Reeds and fallen willows slowed its pace; it entered a long tunnel and emerged between banks of cut stone. Pleasure barges ruffled its smooth waters and Erchon was lifted on the blade of an oar and fell, glittering twice as much as did his usual, silver self. He drifted up against the bank and was sucked into a drain. Darkness took him, held him and cast him forth in a spray of shining droplets like himself. He dropped into the tiled bowl of a fountain, floated to its polished rim and climbed out, himself, dry, silver-coloured, clothed, with all his gypsy gold in his purse and his feathered hat clapped jauntily on his head. His rapier rang against the fountain-bowl as he emerged.

He was in Decimus Toricello's pleasaunce, the Bower, where columns dressed with climbing roses and arches smothered in white clematis rose out of a mosaic floor. There was no time to hide, for Roszi and two more of Koschei's playthings, the dancer, Friendship and the juggler, Concordis, were a yard away. They had been playing with a coloured ball, tossing it from one to another; now, all three had turned and were staring at him while the ball bobbed in the fountain.

'It is *Erchon*!' Roszi cried while Friendship laughed delightedly and Concordis stood on her head.

'He was hiding there to catch us out,' she said, and swung to her feet.

'He missed us,' said Friendship. 'It is a long time since he went away with the Lady Nemione and poor Lucas. Isn't he handsome, and neat?'

Erchon removed his hat and bowed to her.

'If I had been hiding, Concordis,' he said, 'I should have chosen a better place – under your bed, perhaps. I have come from Lythabridge in the forest – no, do not trouble your bonny heads about it. I stand here, inside Castle Sehol. That is enough.'

'Stand?' said Concordis and knelt in front of him. She rubbed her pretty nose in his beard and kissed him on the lips.

'This seems to be a more perilous place than the battlements,' Erchon said lightly.

'For goat-footed dwarfs, yes. Have you come to bed us, Silver Dwarf?'

'If you like.'

'All three?'

'Only three? – I have come to speak with Roszi, no one else. A message from her mistress, Nemione.'

'Not now,' said Roszi sulkily. 'I belong to Koschei these days – can't you see? He gave me a body and calls me Rosalia, so I am not even the same creature.'

'You look like Roszi to me, except that your wonderful head has a gained body every bit its equal in beauty. My lady, Nemione, used to talk to you of your waterfall, of Diccon and the others that you loved. I saw some of your sisters in the Lytha today, singing and playing with their lovers' bones.'

'Do not make me sad. I am half fire – it is what Koschei made me. Oh, Erchon, I am tormented.'

'Come into the fountain with me. It will cool you; soothe you.'

'Erchon, I dare not.'

'Koschei is not here; besides, he is occupied with Nemione's invasion. Come with me.' Erchon took her hot hand and led her to the edge of the fountain. 'Look, the water dances over the mosaic! Dip your hand.' He drew down her hand until it met the water, which hissed and turned to steam. 'Step in.'

Roszi entered the fountain.

The water bubbled in the bowl and rose in a cloud of vapour, which hid Erchon and Roszi.

'He has his way with her, in there,' smiled Friendship.

'Small as he is,' Concordis added. 'Soon, she will step out, flushed and delighted with her watery games.'

The steam drifted up into the roof, hiding the rambling roses and the doves which perched amongst them. The cool waters of the fountain played on, but Erchon and Roszi were nowhere to be seen. Twice they had mounted, water drops, to the summit of the spouting cascade and twice been cast into the fall; they slid to the bottom of the pool and so, by a grating, back into the pipework, the conduit and the River Lytha. Erchon bobbed to the surface. I hope I shall be dry when I reach the bank, he thought, and squeezed Roszi's hand. She was wet and delightful, her cast-gold hair streaming with water, her metal smile fixed and her hot, soaked, silk-clad body wholly desirable, even to the necklace of miniature toads and water marigolds which marked the seam Koschei had made to join her head and body. Erchon read Koschei's mind and saw what his intention had been when he reconstructed Roszi. The dwarf drew her close to him and kissed her hard lips, amazed when they parted to let out a long and supple tongue, which licked him and wrapped itself tenderly about his neck.

'We must land,' he said, and disengaged himself. No ordinary woman waited for him to deliver his prize, but a witch. He should be afraid. They clambered up the riverbank and Erchon looked about him. There was no sign of Pargur.

'We have been swept a long way downstream,' he said and Roszi laughed triumphantly.

'He has succeeded!' she said. 'Koschei has moved Castle Sehol in all its versions and synchronicities. Only yesterday he told me he would hide it from Nemione, and while you dallied with us in the Bower, he has made good his boast. He is a great magician.'

'And a heartless,' said Erchon.

'I suppose your heart is very small – how could it be other in that body?' Roszi teased.

'I thought I had sent Nemione my heart,' answered the dwarf, 'but I feel it beating strongly. It is a foolish, fervent heart, Roszi and you are driving it with spur and lash.'

'Then I have not lost all my beauty?'

'Lost! You have gained colour and warmth – why, you are as hot as a salamander and heat in a woman means only one thing.'

'And you, Erchon, speak pretty compliments. You are considerate and have rescued me from a long and tedious life acting as Koschei's warming pan and rag doll. I don't doubt that you have all your proper parts and no more.'

'What do you mean, Roszi?'

'Do you not know? Are Friendship, Concordis and I, Koschei's bed-fellows, the only living souls beside himself to know? Well, I will tell you and we'll see how the sparks fly.'

'They will Roszi, they will when we come together.'

'Be quiet, Erchon. You are nothing but a philanderer in little, I can see. Koschei is not a man, you know – at least, he no longer has that which distinguishes him from a woman. I do not know why, if it is magic gone wrong or because of some malady. Also, he has one female pap, at which he nourishes his misbegotten son.'

'What can I do with this knowledge, Roszi? It does not disqualify him from his magician's calling.'

'Keep it in your heart with me. You may find a use for it by and by.' Roszi's clothing was drying on her and Erchon looked her up and down and took her hand.

'Dry me, Roszi.'

'I shall set you on fire!'

'Then touch me just a little, here and there.' Roszi caressed him, withdrawing her hands when his jerkin began to smoke and smoulder and his silver breastplate to burn him through the leather. 'Less!' he cried.

'Be patient, I shall learn in no time.' The grass flared where she stood and she breathed deeply in and stamped out the little fire. 'That's better. Now feel, I am quite cool, no hotter than a sun-warmed wall.'

'Are you hot all through: inside?' he asked her.

'I can be as temperate as a summer's day.'

He looked at her again. It was useless, he could not do the witch's bidding; he was lost, his heart and body burning for her with a fire as hot as her infernal, internal flames. His will had melted. One course was open to them: flight.

'We might make our home in the mountains, where the silver lies deep in the rock,' he said. 'I can mine it by night and bring it to the surface to work into long chains and intricate filigrees to adorn your gold; and by day we can lie abed and please ourselves and each other. Come with me – be my love. Your talents will not go to waste when the cold comes to cover the Altaish with snow and turns their grey peaks into death-white fields.'

'And never see Nemione?'

'I, her faithful dwarf who only left because he believed her dead – I, Erchon, will never see Nemione again.'

'We agree. Let us begin our journey then, my Silver Love, and you shall sleep tonight in the forest, beside my fire or in it if you will!'

Hand in hand, they ran across the narrow strip of scrub-land which lay between the river and the forest and vanished beneath the trees. Nothing was seen of them again in Sehol or Pargur and, fearing the wrath of the chov-hani, they left no clue or message to show which way they took. Only this is sure: that Erchon, when night fell, saw the fiery veins which glowed beneath Roszi's buttermilk skin, the crystal flower which grew, in place of a navel, out of her belly; and that he felt the keen edges of her golden nails.

The insurgents fired their culverin regularly. One could have set the clocks in Pargur by it if the city's time had been subject to the ordinary laws of motion and mechanics. I could see the gun clearly from the north wall, a giant cannon many yards in length. It took near an hour to cool to a safe temperature and, when the culverineer's gobbet of spit merely steamed instead of vaporizing in an instant, he loaded it with toothed chains and iron balls, whose circumference was equal to or greater than my magic globe, and tamped down the charge. The breached wall had been patched with pieces of its own, shattered body and the largest gaps filled with gabions. I stood tall and hallooed the perseverant rebel gunners, heard one of the Copper Dwarf's shot whistle by me and felt his second missile, a barbed bullet of lead, plunge through the right wall of my chest and come to rest into my busy lungs. I bowed to the force of Githon's shot and to Asmodeus and withdrew quickly from his halls. The kerchief I laid on my new wound was quickly soaked in blood; I watched it flow out of the sodden cloth, darkening my robe and dripping to the battlement, where it formed a pool. Cob should be here to feast, I thought (for, tired of his apish jests, I had sent him back to Peklo); or, had I time enough before the coming confrontation, I should collect this life-ichor and study it to see what I was made of. I breathed evenly. Knowledge of my invulnerability had made me care-less of taking risks. Like one addicted to the juice of the sleep-poppy or to gross women, say, or female dwarfs, I sought violent sensation and this, of cheating Death, was the finest. I hailed my assailant,

'A good shot, Githon, or a lucky one!' For he and his fellows could not see, most likely, at what they aimed. The fragments of wall dazzled more than the original undivided crystal and, besides, the city quivers and moves in time as did my new illusions of Sehol inviolate. But folly or its sister, hope, directed them and they continued to bombard the walls with their culverin, and their pelicans, shrikes, onagers, mangonels and trebuchets while the balls from their pot-guns soared over the walls and, falling steeply to earth, buried themselves without harming my men. Under cover of the noise and dust their sappers and miners dug out trenches and began to undermine the wall near the gate.

Their tents, many of them brilliant-hued, stood in the lee of the forest and were pitched within a bow-shot of the walls; but Nemione had raised an airy and steel-hard barrier in front of them. I saw it with my inner eye and it was a lovely, numinous thing which ordinary folk might liken to a veil of spider's silk or an insubstantial dew-covered curtain

like that which hangs athwart the eastern sky in certain
auspicious seasons and seems to touch the highest rock of
the utmost peak of the Altaish with one thread of its hem.
I could have dispersed it there and then, but let it depend
and shimmer prettily while my heart leaped without my
willing it toward Nemione's white tent. The new star which,
in Pargur, they called Corbillion or Vengeance, stood high
above that tent, lately visible by day as well as night; and
Nemione's flag, with its green chevron and golden hinds,
flew stiffly. I imagined Nemione (for it would have been
unwise to alert her by using obvious means) seated on her
camp-stool within, her armour burnished and well-suited to
her willowy form. And Parados there also, strong beside her
and leaning on his sword while he softly discussed with his
commander (in love – alas – as well as war) the implacable
tactic of siege-warfare. She well knew where I was – I had
no doubt of it – and I prayed Urthamma that some subtle
tincture of regret coloured her knowledge. Sympathy was
too much to hope for from Nemione-Militant; and she had
always been that, for all her decorative speech and the succulent female flesh she revealed or else concealed with silk,
feathers, fur, lace – she had scalded, scolded and baited me in
our childhood and since. When night came, for she believed
herself as safe as a cooped hen behind her magic barrier, she
would doff her showy helmet and unbuckle her intricate,
interlocking plates of silvered steel, untie the padded coat
she wore beneath them and reveal her undefiled body to the
servile eyes of her maid and the bold and sparkling glances
of her emeralds and diamonds. The maid (I did not care to
imagine her so closely) would lift her night rail, extend it on
careful arms, another snow-white tent, another frail balloon,
and put it on her so that she became no Amazon but a Venus
in reverse, an Aphrodite reversed, sinking in the abundant
foam – and poor Parados was not in the tent nor anywhere
close by, exiled from her tent and made to patrol the camp
or drink with his subordinates and the Copper Dwarf. Was

he, though banished, yet within call? I thought so. Without her maidenhead Nemione's strong magic was impossible and with it she was a worthy prize. I did not pity, though I envied Parados his yearning exclusion. I did not jealously crave; but I coveted the force of his desire.

Evening had come and was darkening into night. All was quiet now, the cannon and the lesser guns put to bed beneath tarpaulins. I climbed down a ladder into the gabionage. Corinel was with me. He made a useful soldier despite his canine predilections. We found a squad of my engineers below, all gathered round a big bald-pated man from Sink Street – his name was Fuller. He was standing over one of those wide, open-backed drums the mummers use on May Day. It lay on the ground like the full moon sunk to earth or a mighty cheese. Another man placed a dried pea on it and everyone stood still. The pea jumped and bounded on the flat surface of the drum as if it were a hungry flea.

'Still digging, My Lord Archmage,' said Fuller gravely.

'Can you tell the direction?' Corinel asked.

'Aye – watch the pea! Toward the Shambles, passing directly under us and nowhere near the gate as we thought. There must be dwarves among them – they've dug so far so quick.'

'Can we not dig down and surprise them? I've always fancied myself a terrier!'

Fuller grinned. 'Have you indeed – Sir?' he said. 'Well then, if you have the proper claws and teeth, begin. They have dug beneath the rock and we are standing on it. 'Twould take many charges to blast them out.'

'My Lord?' Corinel turned to me, stupid hope and a begging question on his handsome face.

'Let our enemies dig, Corinel,' I said and, addressing the engineers, 'Let them dig, for we will catch them inside and cut them to pieces amongst the beast-carcasses in the Shambles. Any weapon greater than a sword is wasted on such cattle.' I turned away, as if to study the packed gabions and, indeed, they had caught my eye for they made me think of traps and webs, their wickerwork stuffed as it was with gleaming lumps of shattered crystal and those sparkling toys of the nivashi, water-worn pebbles of fool's gold from the bed of the Lytha. All that glisters – thought I; and nothing beckons greedy men so strongly as the promise of gold, the prospect of power. Parados would come willingly enough, but Nemione was proof against such enchantments.

I took her at dead of night, blowing away her gossamer gabionage – it was a female thing and weaker than my will – and making her guard as drunk on moonshine as a fiddler's bitch. I occupied him further with a nubile illusion. (Curious to see a grown man tup a phantom.) And Nemione? So, once, would I – enough, Koschei! She was the only one who recognized how great I was and how vulnerable. She alone knew how extraordinary was the place I had reserved for her in my grand design.

The roar of the enemy's shot woke Parados and he lay still, waiting for it to be rebuffed by the bulwark Nemione had made of thistledown, cobwebs and a few whispered words; but the ball passed on and felled an oak in the forest. Her magic must have failed. The air was rent by the agonized screaming of the sundered trunk and splintered boughs for many minutes before its fellows closed around the fallen tree. Then came many long sighs and crisp, leafy whispers before the bombardment resumed and slingshots and arrows began to fly across the greensward which lay between the forest and the walls of Pargur and patter against the palisades. By then, Parados had his boots on and was armed. He called Githon and Aurel to him and ran into the forest without waiting for them. There lay the oak, in line with the broken tower and a yard to the right of Nemione's tent. He calculated the time which would pass before their cannon cooled down – enough to move Nemione to other quarters.

The trees were rustling loudly though there was no wind. And maybe they feel as much as we do in their fixed innocence and seasonable beauty, he thought. Words sighed about him. He leaned sideways to catch them in his ear,

'Koschei is no man becaussse, Koschei iss noo maan becaussssss . . .'

and, remembering the danger and Nemione's mortal peril, ran back to the encampment. Aurel stood on guard outside her tent, a drunk and unbuttoned soldier face-down in the grass at his feet. The navigator glanced nervously at him and, gesturing at the drunkard, said,

'A fine watch!'

'Githon?' Parados asked.

'Within. Hurry, my lord.'

She was not there. Her maid stood by her bed in tears, cradling the shining helmet which, only yesterday, Nemione had worn to walk about the encampment and review the progress of the attack. Nothing else was disturbed and the imprint of Nemione's body was still to be seen in the bed, the pillow dinted and the sheet flung neatly back without haste or panic, its lace edge just touching the lambskin on the ground.

'Nemione?' he said, fearing that the word would stick in his throat, overtaken by the tears and panic which threatened to well up.

Another single word sufficed to answer him.

'Koschei,' said Githon.

Parados knelt, as if he would pray. He raised both hands and beat them on the foot of the bed until they were bruised. Then, turning to the maid, he said,

'How was she taken – was Koschei here himself?'

Her tears, he thought, were enough for them both. Sarai blew her nose and dabbed at her eyes with her kerchief.

'Gone, Sir; gone when I came in to call her.'

'Why did you not remain here with her all night?'

'She forbade me, Sir. She said that soon she would be

unable to pass any night alone – she meant when you were wed, Sir.'

Though the honestly reported words wrung him, he remained outwardly unruffled. Other words were dancing in his mind, that unfinished phrase the trees had whispered, 'Koschei is no man because . . .' He was besieged himself, under assault by magic. How was it possible to find out the truth about Nemione's disappearance or any other matter?

'Githon,' he said wearily, 'what on earth – if that is where I am – should I do now?'

'Use your head,' said the dwarf brusquely. It sounded like censure and Parados replied in kind,

'We are here because I used my head.'

'Thought can move mountains,' said Githon more kindly. 'Remember the headwaters of the Sigla, Excelsior Pass –'

Remember. Memory, good servant, solace of the solitary, creator and director of history, present action, future resolution. The Memory Palace. That would be the perfect place to hide, disguised as a memory. Seeing the little building and the ornate additions Koschei had made to it, the steps of grey-green porphyry, the brass double doors, he bowed his head and rested it on the bed-rail so that Githon, pitying him in his indecision and grief, reached out to raise him to his feet, felt the steel of his cuirass and then nothing. Like Nemione, Parados had vanished.

Koschei was waiting for him. The magician bowed and, straightening his velvet-robed body, drew the long nails of his right hand down through his beard.

'You have caught up with me at last. Welcome, Sir,' he said, with all the courteous ceremony of the Saracen he resembled. 'It is a beautiful day, so sunny – the song of the honey-birds is quite charming!' Parados bowed in return.

'I am delighted to be here, Archmage,' he said. 'And to find you at home.'

Koschei raised both arms in a gesture which encompassed the palace and its garden.

'The making of the Memory Palace and its transportation from Espmoss were the greatest achievements of my young adulthood,' he said. 'Nowadays of course I can move anything anywhere and conceal and reveal whatever I will. I began building the year the Sacred Ibis left the marsh. The foundations were soon dug and the footings laid. It was, after all, a small building. Many years passed before my spiritual troubles began, coinciding with the first extensions.

'A new building for a new decade (my third).'

He began to relate the story of his early years in the cloister at Espmoss. When he spoke Nemione's name, or described her in those years, his strong voice (which contrasted oddly with his decadent appearance and with his elaborate way of speaking) became reflective and tender, almost melancholy. He spoke vigorously of his desire to join the roving band of sanctioned outlaws, the Brotherhood of the Green Wolf, and of the orderly, box-hedged garden of the Memory Palace with its wild, untended opposite, the zone where Nature was allowed to sow and reap as she pleased in memory of the original garden at Espmoss. Parados watched him closely as he talked: the man looked old, true, but had a vigour which belied his greying beard and his bent back; indeed, he seemed to grow younger and stronger as he spoke.

'Notwithstanding these outside imperfections,' said Koschei, 'the interior of the building is, as you will see, in perfect order. We will climb the staircase (genuine porphyry – but mind the broken step! Segno did that – a servant of mine. He was a careless fellow: I put him in the dungeon for Olburn to instruct.) We will climb the staircase and enter by the brazen doors which, yes, resemble more than a little the Gates of Paradise.'

The old man took a key from the leather wallet he wore

on his sword belt, fitted it to the lock and turned it. Parados followed him through the left-hand fold of the doubled doors.

'I love to entertain my visitors (few enough) with such speeches,' said Koschei. 'They are props to the ailing structures of my mind. As for the palace – here it is. I cannot escape from it. It has swallowed me whole, mind and body, hates and loves, possessions, beliefs, gold – that which glisters and is my fool's reward and grail attained.

'Since I am the one you never forget, it will be easier if I show you round. I'll make you regret your memories of me! The grand tour I think, the one that takes in all the sights, leaves not a stone unturned. I do not have the resilience of some, not now. I lack the boldness of those outside.

'Here we are. I'll close the door – it lets in too much light, and also dirt, from outside. This is the chamber in which I was born. You must begin at the beginning, you see, if you are to make sense of my memory palace.'

His guest craned his head forward as he tried to distinguish the heavy pieces of furniture with which the room was furnished from the general gloom.

'Could we have a little light?' he asked.

'A glimmer!' His guide struck a match and lit a small bull's-eye lantern. But even with this it was hard to make anything out – the furniture seemed very big and also far away, the sort of dim and massive wooden giants he remembered from early childhood, of bottomless chests, cavernous wardrobes and tables as big as houses. He stepped gingerly forward.

There was a bed. The covers were partly thrown back, white sheets, blue blankets and a patchwork quilt. He could just about manage to climb up. His teddy bear lay on the quilt; the smell was right – Castile soap and Eau de Cologne, a faint overlay of sweat.

'Mummy?' he said and heard the dry laugh of the old man with the lantern.

'Forgive me, Parados. I cannot preserve *your* memories.'

'But this is my mother's bed; where *I* was born, not you.'

Koschei laughed again. He held the lantern high so that its light fell on both their bearded faces.

'Curious. We are the same height, the same build: we might be brothers,' he said. 'But as to the question about this room and the objects in it: it may be yours, it may be mine. That remains to be seen. The case as yet is unproven.'

'No,' said Parados. 'We have proved it time and time again. These are my memories.'

'But don't you remember our discussion in the room I built for these disputed memories? We had, each of us, a different explanation for them – the notebooks, the pomander, the shells; and the objects which appeared here more recently, I mean the cock's feather, those pretty silver balls which imitate the chiming of Pargur's clocks and your shattered eye-glasses, doubtless has, one and all, an explanation and a story. Hold the lantern, here is something else.'

Parados took it and the magician plunged his hand deep in his wallet and drew out a gold cross hanging from a broken chain. He lifted the chain on the end of a cork-screw nail and let the cross swing from it.

'That is Helen's cross,' said Parados. 'I saw it once amongst the glittering trinkets which covered the bosom of her gown.'

'Protecting her deep and comely bosom, her heart and soul themselves? Well enough, she was always one for talismans and charms – but I salvaged it from the floor of Nemione's room on the day she played midwife to my son!'

'Then are they one and the same, Helen and Nemione?'

'The gods must judge – you know what is inscribed on the cross: "Keep Faith". We have both done that. But it may only be that your memories and mine have coincided yet again. One thing, certain, amusing, diverting: we both lust after the same kind of headstrong, heart-wrecking woman.'

'Lust? You, Koschei, after what Peder Drum did to you?'

381

'And what is that?'

'Come, Archmage, why dissemble? We both know how much Peder enjoyed cutting flesh and making blood flow. The land is humming with rumours; the very trees whisper to each other and to anyone with ears keen enough to hear that Koschei is no man – but they can give no explanation for their strange words.'

'I have heard them – not an hour ago, in the garden. They speak with Erchon's voice. He got himself into Castle Sehol with the help of the gypsy witch and has stolen away my Rosalia, my lovely bedfellow born of the golden head, Roszi, and a fire-demon I took, in my turn, from Urthamma's kitchen. Erchon and Roszi have fled and, doubt it not, he now has all her superstitious fear of me and my supposed habits in his dull, dwarfish head. His new knowledge burdens him and, imitating the Phrygian king, Midas, he has whispered his secret abroad; the first tree told another and so you heard the false rumour. You must not believe everything you hear in the forest. What do they say about me in Malthassa? – tell me! I can at least derive some amusement from the inaccuracy and marvellous variety of their guesses.'

'I left as the rumours were beginning. They have surely grown by now, but before this, as I travelled in SanZu and the Altaish, I heard nothing said about you that was not tinged with fear.'

'Good.'

'Some were kinder than they should have been.'

'Most members of the human race have an over-developed capacity for sympathy, women and dwarves especially. I am disappointed in you, Parados. I thought to hear inventive splendours and wild, weird theories.'

'I could invent some, Koschei, as I invented the whole tale and you.'

'I do not discount that possibility. But, as with our disputed memories, the case is not proved and you are, at the moment, in my Memory Palace. If you want to see more than this nursery of genius you must climb the stairs. There is the door to them, look – over there. Hold the lamp carefully or you will douse the wick in the oil and put it out.'

Parados opened the terrible door, pressing the latch down boldly. He stepped into the cupboard behind it, saw that it was not a cupboard and that the infinity of wooden stairs to which it was the beginning reached up into the dark. His little light gave no more comfort than a glow-worm. I can't, his old, remembered selves protested. I can't! Don't make me!

'Do you hesitate? Are you afraid?' Koschei's voice thundered out of the room beyond the little door.

He did not speak an answer but began to climb the stairs. They were more precipitous and rickety than ever before; if he looked down, he saw them in perspective and in plan, both at the same time, the spiral winding tighter and tighter below in a well as deep as the one which was Goldenbeard's prison and home. Each time he reached the door and opened it he found the same endless ascent waiting for him, and quailed. The lamp burned low. When it goes out, he thought, I shall fall over the edge. How long before I hit the ground? Where is the ground?

'Hurry!' Koschei called and his voice lingered on every turn of the stair; but the stairs and the door were always there to be climbed, to be opened, to be climbed.

Again, Parados thought of the failing lantern and the fall and, with jolting inspiration, of his goal, the little room whose window gave a view of the cloister. He opened the door and stepped into the dusty, steep-ceiled room. A small table stood near the window, with a box on it, a plain box with a brass lock-plate and keyhole from which a key projected. He turned the key. The lid of the box flew open and a severed head rose suddenly up. He recognized it: it was his own but of long ago, when he had been the artless choirboy, Chris Young. The fair hair was neatly cut and the mouth as soft and tender as a girl's. The eyelids opened to show the grey-blue eyes Nemione had likened to water in a stained-glass goblet and the lips parted. The boy sang:

> When a knight won his spurs, in the stories of old,
> He was gentle and brave, he was gallant and bold;
> With a shield on his arm and a lance in his hand
> For God and for valour he rode through the land.

> No charger have I, and no sword by my side.
> Yet still to adventure and battle I ride,
> Though back into storyland giants have fled,
> And the knights are no more and the dragons are
>   dead.

The voice was pure and the notes exact, without strain. That was water, the melodious fountain soaring upward out of the child's mouth. When he had sung the hymn in school – at the Christmas concert, he was eight or nine? – he had pictured the knight riding in his shiny armour, white surcoat over it, lance in its rest and ready; the dragon roaring from his cave; the maiden in distress an ill-drawn, scarce-defined picture compared with the fiery dragon. The head began again,

'"When a knight ..."'

'Another of your selves?' said Koschei sarcastically, coming into the room behind him. 'Another memory? It is a pretty toy. I made it one winter's afternoon when the storm beat against the walls of Peklo tower; and that is your land he sings of, the place the giants have fled.'

'"... and the dragons are dead.",' sang the boy in the box and immediately began at the beginning,

'"When a knight ..."'

'Asmodeé!' said Koschei irritably. 'Zernebock! I should have given it more verses.'

'I never sung the last,' Parados told him. 'An epidemic of scarlet fever had broken out in the school and while I trilled "dead" and my mother got out her handkerchief (she was proud of me), I fainted dead away and they had to carry me off the stage and put me to bed in the sanatorium.'

'You have a solution for every problem and a ready answer in every situation. Listen to the wretch!'

Parados reached out and closed the lid of the box.

'There, he's gone; good as dead. He *is* dead. I am not he.'

'You are the paladin from the Plains, that is what the people say. The man who follows the star.'

'The man who is watched over by the star.'

'Look out of the window.' Koschei approached the open casement and stood beside it with one hand extended like a conjurer exhibiting a trick on stage. Parados looked out. It was night, and this surprised him, but there was the cloister, in every other respect exactly as he imagined it should be, Nemione's small, arched window above the north arcade. She stood there musing, her green and white gown as fresh as the flowers which spilled from the bunch in her hands, the whole picture gilded by the light of the single candle which burned on her windowsill. Parados leaned from his window and called softly to her, 'Nemione! Love!' but she did not answer or even turn her gaze toward him.

'She is fixed for ever in that attitude, and in memory,' said Koschei.

The stars were bright above the steep roofs of the buildings which abutted on the cloister. Parados did not recognize them: they were neither those remembered far-off stars which shone over his garden in the other world, nor were they the newly-familiar constellations of Malthassa, the Swan, the Hoopoe, the Crane and the rest; Custos did not shine.

'What have you done to the stars?' he asked Koschei.

'You should know: that is the night sky of Belgard,' said the Archmage.

Parados looked at the strange stars once more. They were like a glimpse of the dream-world whose after-image haunts every moment of the following day. He asked no more questions about them, for he had no way of telling whether Koschei had merely borrowed and displayed a facsimile of Belgard's sky or if he had moved Castle Sehol there. In either case, Koschei would lie.

'You are cheating,' he accused the magician. 'This is a Memory Palace.'

'May I not have memories of Belgard?'

'I know nothing of them.'

'Nor should you, for you do not know if Belgard exists outside my mind. Beware, Parados: the you and I who stand here and discourse with uneasy courtesy are not memories either – we are men who act and re-act and will soon resume our mutual hostilities. We shall be as Gogmagog and Alexander, as Fenris and Odin at Ragnarok – our minds are labyrinths which can hold an Armageddon, a world or two, the universe, comfortably within their narrow bounds; but if I strike you lightly – so! – you feel my blow. Leave that superseded Nemione to her eternal musings and I will show you a different sort of maze.'

Koschei led the way into the library of the Memory Palace, opening the grey banewood door which was the replica of the library door in Peklo. He passed through with a swirl of his crimson robe, grown in strength and apparently another half-dozen years younger. The broken tassel on his slipper tapped the floor as he went. He strode up to the lectern and pointed to the complicated prayer of dedication and ownership visible on the first page of his Book of Souls.

'Read here!' he commanded and Parados read the nine names of Zernebock and Koschei's own to which was now appended the title, 'the Deathless'.

'That is my style throughout Malthassa,' Koschei said proudly. 'A name I travelled beyond the Gates of Hell to win. Turn the pages. See – there is your name and Nemione's upon the white left-hand page which signifies Malthassa. These names, and these, known to one or other of us here

386

or in your Albion or Lugdon, are written on the red. Sometimes the red and white correspond: "Father Renard" and "Brother Fox"; "Olivia" and the little Polnisha, "Livvy". But they are all written in ink, not blood.'

'Subject to change?'

'Subject surely, to the vagaries of the continually-revising mind?'

'Find me another name, Koschei. It is "Helen".'

'Of Troy? Of Jerusalem? Of Myrah? The milliner of Espmoss, the cartomancer of Actinidion?'

'Plain "Helen Lacey".'

'There, behold! Her name has been a long time in the book, since Valdine's day. You loved her once, I think?'

'Before I knew Nemione.'

'"Since", Sir, "since". Nemione has been with us both far longer, if only as ideal or ghost. And remember always, writ in ink.'

The names danced before Parados's eyes and seemed to make new combinations. Weariness overtook him and he grasped the book and closed it feeling, as he did so, the soft hairs still fixed in the cover which had once been the skin of a parricide's back.

'I have tired you, Parados, strong as you are, for you are not used to the toll magic demands. It is easier to travel a hundred leagues through the forest than to cross one room of the Memory Palace. Let us eat.' Koschei reached up, above his head, and pulled a basket from the air. The basket, which had been nothing, was a sound and solid chip and, being opened, was found to contain two stone bottles of beer and a great pie.

'Do not fear to eat my enchanted food: I shall also partake,' said Koschei. He drew a dagger and sliced the pie in two. 'Thus have you divided Malthassa: half for Koschei, half for Parados, and interfered with my design. See, the pie is stuffed with chickens, squabs and larks, all headless, not knowing what has become of them.'

387

He lifted half the pie from the basket and gave it to Parados. A rich, savoury jelly oozed from it and some fell to the floor.

'But if Malthassa is an invention, a tale as unreal as a vision, the case is altered,' said Parados. 'For instance, your very identity and name may be stolen. There is a great magician in the storybook of Mother Russia: "Ko-sh-ch-ei" – that is how they spell his name. I omitted an "h" when I borrowed it.'

'Are you certain, Parados, that your Koshchei of the North is not myself with the addition of an "h"? Have you proof that I am not he and that those folk-tales are not records of my appearance in your world?'

'I have no proof that anything is what it seems to be – that door, for instance. It is not the one we entered by.'

'No, it is the one by which we shall leave.'

The door was made of dark wood which, in the blinking of an eye, changed to a billowing curtain of muslin. Shelves of books could be seen beyond it.

'What is there?' Parados asked.

'Some other rooms of this library. It has a great many and we shall visit some of them when we have eaten the last crumbs of this excellent pie. Truly, the cooks of Hell exceed my hand-picked chefs of Castle Sehol in pastry-making and the art of combining spices and meats! Nor is their brewing indifferent – you are replete? Come then, through the changeable doorway.'

If these endless shelves of books and comfortable groupings of overstuffed chairs, sofas and small tables, were in the library of the Memory Palace, it was vast, thought Parados. Galleries loomed overhead, one atop the other and all iron-railed and reached by open-backed stairs; niches and alcoves were filled with books on stands and in neat piles on desks and tables; doorways opened into other book-lined halls.

'Browse at leisure if you will,' said Koschei and left Parados beside a shelf labelled 'A'. He wandered as a traveller lost, attracted now by this book, now by that. The books were in every language, neatly and alphabetically ordered but without reference to subject. He needed only to walk past 'Altaish', 'Andersen' and 'Arboles' to realize the contents of the library were infinite and, deciding to seek proof, left his course beside the first letter and struck out at right-angles until he came to 'P'. There they were! – the three books of short stories and all fifteen novels including his last, the unpublished *Making of Koschei*. He took one down, *Koschei's Marvellous Library*, and put it hastily back, unable to face the chaos into which his mind would be thrown by reading one line of it. Hurriedly, he walked away until he came to 'Q', that weird cousin of the perfect circle, 'O', an eccentric even to Koschei's twisted mind, Malthassa and this library. *Quaquaversal Dance*, he read. *A Quatch-buttock's View of Nether Pargur, Quinquagesima and Quasimodo, How to Rid Your Pleasure-grounds of Quitch, Quodlibets for Students of Bibliomancy* and *The Art of the Quipu in Mnemonics*. So, turning once again from the incomprehensible, he came to 'K' and immediately recognized his old, green-backed poetry book, the Keats anthology he had been given as a prize (for boxing) at school.

He took it from the shelf and lovingly stroked its stains and scars, unsurprised when it fell open at the ode which had possessed him in those turbulent, adolescent days, *To A Nightingale*. Someone, obviously himself, had left a marker there, a small scrap of blue paper and he picked it up and held it while he read rapidly down the page; but there was no time to read further than 'And with thee fade away into the forest dim' for the bookmark moved in his fingers, of itself, and when he parted them fluttered erect and danced lightly on his palm. My soul! he thought, That's why Nandje could not hear it – I left it in these pages all those years ago –

But two pale blue souls were skipping on his hand, two small identical figures like a child's cut-out chain of paper men, joined at hands and feet. As he watched them they separated, the creased joins tearing softly, until they were two individuals who danced in mirror-image, each exactly mimicking the other. The two souls bowed to each other and, spinning on their tiny feet, to him and the one nearest his thumb ran suddenly forward and up his arm as fast as a mouse pursued by a cat. He felt it step up on his chin, wriggle between his lips and under and over his teeth. It lay like a communion wafer on his tongue; and was gone, for it had tickled his throat with fingers as fine as hair to make him swallow.

He looked down at the other soul on his hand.

'What have I swallowed?' he whispered to it.

'Your rightful property,' it replied. 'Do you think my brother and I would make the elementary mistake of confusing our identities?'

'Your brother?'

'In spirit, in imagination, taste, preference, quality. We souls cannot have blood-ties since we are without the organs which manufacture blood; indeed we have no organs in the common sense of the word – you could say "we are all soul" if you liked.' It emitted a queer, high-pitched squeal which was clearly meant to be laughter and Parados was comforted, for in speech and attitude it was so like Koschei. He turned and looked behind him, seeking the owner of this strayed soul. The library displayed its sunlit silences for him, its rows of speechless book. Koschei was not there but, when he turned again, Koschei was quietly waiting by the shelf, an amused smile on his lips. The soul had gone and the green poetry book was no longer in his hands but in Koschei's.

'Do you read much verse?' said Koschei urbanely. 'I find that the smallest dose distracts me from my real purpose and pre-disposes me to melancholy and thoughts of doomed love.' He closed the green book and returned it to its place on the shelf.

'Once, I read it. These days, as you know, I make up

my own fantasies,' answered Parados. 'Did you see –' but Koschei interrupted him,

'See? Look there, Sir, if you want something other than dry text to occupy your eyes.'

Parados looked where he pointed and suppressed a gasp.

Helen had come into the library, walking with graceful, dreamy steps along a line of dark wood in the inlaid floor. She paused, raised her head and smiled gloriously; her dress was one of the fantastic gypsy costumes she had always favoured, a yellow and orange tiered and layered thing from which a low-necked bodice rose like a spirit from the cupped flower of a summer rose. Her bronzed neck and breasts and her black cascade of hair were stronger magic than these feeble dreams of Malthassa and Koschei. She pulled the embroidered shawl from her shoulders and, raising it to her lips, kissed its golden fringe and flung it at his feet. He bent to retrieve it and to accept her flirtatious challenge. Nothing beside a sunbeam lay on the floor; nor was Helen there. The memory was gone, and so had Koschei.

Parados walked quickly to a window and looked out for a clue to his whereabouts. He saw the shattered crystal towers and ivory roofs of Pargur beyond a wide and sun-filled park. Where was the exit, a door, the way out? He ran swiftly back the way he thought Koschei had brought him but found three painted statues, Odin, Ulysses and Thor – simple, a true mnemonic device! – and a flight of stone steps leading down. The brazen doors stood open at the foot of the stair and, emerging into the garden of the Memory Palace, he looked up at the great keep of Castle Sehol. He listened to the chimes of Pargur's random clocks which told him the hour was noon, or nine, or six, or seven. He heard the booming of the great culverin and its lesser sisters, the ona-gers and pelicans, begin as they pounded the walls of the castle's outermost bailey. It was most likely, then, that the tide ran in his favour. His men had gained Pargur while he stood safe in Sehol, confounded for the moment by the disappearance of his quarry but in good heart, clear-headed and ready to resume the chase.

Aurel Wayfarer, promoted Captain, stood beside the culverin watching its propulsive glow fade and the dullness of the cooling iron re-appear. He could feel the gun's heat through his armour though he stood two feet away. He turned and addressed the culverineer.

'Good! A fine attempt. But tell me, Gunner, and forgive me for expressing myself so honestly – do you think you have hit one solid target in the entire assault?'

'It is hard to tell, Sir,' the culverineer said. 'Very hard. The target isn't stable, you see. Moves all the time.'

'It seems to me that the city moves – the walls, though they were already in bad case, appeared to draw back. Perhaps Pargur wants to welcome and assist Parados.'

'Where is he, Sir? He's been gone near a week.'

'With Koschei, I am sure of it. Parados left on a spell when he found the Lady gone. There can be no other explanation – Githon and Sarai saw him vanish.'

'I hope he is not entrapped, Master Wayfarer. Koschei is better than a genius, though they are saying he is no man but is a demon or the fiend himself from Hell.'

'I hope *we* shall not be trapped, Master Gunner, in this fine changeable city. The gun is cooler – carry on.'

'Sir!'

Aurel walked quickly across the broken ground of the riverbank to the officers' table. Maps, plans and orders were spread out on it and Githon was studying a sheet of paper on which one of the sapper-commanders had drawn a scheme to undermine the western walls of Castle Sehol.

'It would be rape, don't you think so Aurel?' he said. 'Look at the castle! That misty otherworld appearance it had this morning is gone. It appears quite solid and the towers are beginning to flush red. I saw it years ago of course and know of its colour-changing powers – who does not? In my youth it was grey, as I remember, and sometimes flushed with gold; nothing like this! To see it once more in the stone, so to speak – why, as wonderful a sight to a dwarf as the sheer rockfaces of the Altaish.'

'Garzon was a great visionary. I wonder, Githon, if we ever gain the inside, whether we shall find that Koschei too has made his own elegant changes to the castle's fabric? Privately – repeat this to no man, or dwarf! – I believe Sehol's reputation of impregnability and I do not think we will ever be in a position to satisfy our curiosity about the wonders inside it.'

'We shall see, Aurel. Do you doubt Custos there, shining by day now as well as night?'

'Then where is the Lady Nemione? How can the star shine so while she is missing?'

'It has faith, Aurel. It is not a man, to trouble itself with doubt and speculation.'

That night, as the guns and gunners rested and the officers and sergeants sat in council, the star Custos moved into a new position over Castle Sehol, between the twin towers of Vanity and Probity. Its light shone on both and it seemed to pose a question by its presence mid-way between folly and temperance. The council broke in indecision and confusion and the men slept, worn out by the labour of continuing the assault. About dawn, as Aurel was waking, two men entered his tent with a plea. He propped himself on one elbow to hear them. One of the men was his fellow officer, the ballistics captain, Hadrian, but the other was a stranger, a man of middle-age, sturdy and plain of looks and dressed in the uniform of the Castle Guard. Hadrian held the end of the chain which fastened this man's fetters.

'We found him walking about by the guns, Captain Wayfarer. A spy!'

'Is that what you are, Guard?' said Aurel as sternly as he could and sat up straight.

'I am not, Sir. I am a sergeant of the First Watch. It is my job to guard the gates of Castle Sehol.'

'Then why are you here and in such a position of ignominy? An interest in guns?'

'I was looking for the Commander, sir, for Lord Parados.'

'To murder, no doubt,' said Hadrian.

'No, not murder but help. I was born in the Castle, Sir, and I know a good thing when I see one. This Parados brought the Plains and SanZu out of winter and the Lady from the dead. Now all Malthassa wakes. He may yet restore the fortunes of Sehol and Pargur. Besides, they are all saying – the guard and Captain Olburn himself and all the servants and many of the gentlemen and their ladies too – that Koschei is no man. Some fear he is Beelzebub and some say he is Asmodeus or even him whose name begins with a Z. That, beside the fact that my strong gateway is no longer what it was, is another reason for my leaving the castle and risking my life here.'

Aurel got out of bed and pulled on his boots.

'Call for water and some breakfast, Hadrian, if you please. We must pay this man better attention. What is your name, master?'

'I am Estragon, sir, Guard-Sergeant Estragon Fairweather at your command,' and Estragon who had debated the rights and wrongs of his defection for a long time with himself, clicked his shackled heels together and saluted smartly.

Parados had annoyed and incommoded me by disturbing my soul. I had narrowly avoided its passionate attempts to rejoin itself with me and forced it back into the book, where it lay trapped between 'O Chatterton! how very sad thy fate,' and 'O Solitude! if I must with thee dwell.' To have it with me, in me, would have been true folly for, in that circumstance, I should have become my old and vulnerable, mortal self, no longer deserving of my style 'the Deathless'. But there was no permanent harm. When I appeared beside the shelf, Parados had looked at me with as vacant an expression as a mooncalf. I did not think he had noticed my little blue soul.

I was at Peklo, in my tower. Nemione also. I had brought her there immediately after her capture from the rebels' encampment and imprisoned her in the oubliette at the bottom of the tower – in darkness, cold and damp and chains. This cruel, uncalculated abuse was the abyss to which my great love of her had brought me. Jealousy gnawed like vitriol at my vitals, consuming them and any pity I may once have been weak enough to acknowledge.

'Father dear,' whined Cob, when I entered my wrecked room and beheld the floor and furniture still covered with a false frost of ten thousand thousand fragments of glass. 'Feed me, father, I am very hungry.'

He looked thin, his rotund body shrunk like a withered orange into itself; but I had other, pressing business and though my pap was full and tender with his bitter nourishment and the teat on my vein sore, 'No!' I said and closed the door on him. I hurried down the stair. Nemione had been seven days in her durance and must be humble, tearful; full of plaintive, sad pleas. I should listen to and humour her before I shut her up again. Not until I chose, should she walk free, but then! – I had built myself a male member out of a mandrake and a devil's thunderbolt, a fine new pillicock. It wanted ten more hours in its bath of blood before it was full grown and ready to be united with my truncated root – all the pride the traitor, Peder Drum, had left me.

I had a saffron cake in my hand, to taunt Nemione with and, setting down my lantern and kneeling by the grating in the store room floor, I called her,

'Lady Lorne, show yourself. I have a pretty toy to sweeten your mouth. See –' (and I dropped a piece of the cake into the dungeon) '– it is made of fine manchet flour, butter, honey and eggs. It will satisfy your hunger – if it is not poisoned. And if it is, well, it will release you from your duty.'

I lifted the lantern and looked into the dark well beneath the grating. Nothing moved. She must be sitting still and pressing her lips together for fear of answering me or of taking my bait; and pressing together her thighs also, for she did not know I was incomplete. I saw the chains running from their anchor in the wall; but they hung slack, encircling nothing. Nemione had gone.

A moment passed. Panic filled me, rage – and then understanding. She had not been rescued; Parados had not prevailed. Above my head, in the angle where the ceiling of the store room met the wall, was perched a dark brown butterfly with wings folded close. It was almost invisible in the dark.

'Better for you if you had made yourself invisible,' I whispered, stood up and cupped my hand to capture the trembling insect.

Peklo tower pointed an angry and accusing finger at the grey skies. It knew, thought Parados, how far from piety and honour Koschei had departed. His view of it was clear and as he moved towards it, or the headland came to him, the tower grew darker and the skies more lowering. Certainly this was the place in which Nemione was held captive. Soon the tower was below him, very close. His feet brushed the pointed roof and he found himself standing on the walk which ringed it, the door of the small, projecting bartizan wide open before him. The stairway was narrow and the steps steep and close together but he ran down them, his hand on the outer wall and, arriving outside a closed door, shook his head to dispel a wave of giddiness. He felt as though he walked on cat-ice or across a quicksand which would quickly suck and swallow him up. He put out an unsteady hand and lifted the door-latch.

Inside was Koschei's room, his cell and laboratory, the

heart of his darkness. It looked as though the storms which were gathering over the sea outside had ventured here; or else Koschei himself had suffered a berserker's rage, for the table, shelves and floor were littered with broken and powdered glass. A doll's house shaped like an ornate castle stood in a corner and a large, pallid ball, half-deflated, lay on one of its towers. It had legs, he saw, a mouth and eyes, and recognized it as Koschei's misborn son, Cob. The creature was quite dead.

Parados turned away and continued down the stairs, past the library which was the original of the one in the Memory Palace. A single glimpse of it shocked and disoriented him still more and he hurried on. In Koschei's living quarters, below, the bed was tumbled and unmade and on a gilt table close beside the head of the bed was a statuette of Nemione, naked. Jealously, he lifted it: who had made it? did it represent a wish or reality? had Koschei seen Nemione in this raw and touching state? The statuette was made of ivory, warm to the touch. Parados stroked its hair and, taking the scarf from his neck, attempted to dress it and preserve its modesty. He left the room and, suddenly returning, picked up the image and spoke to it.

'Is this what he has made of you?' he said aloud; but the carving remained motionless in his hand and he remembered that Valdine had caused it to be sculpted. He set it down again.

The stair was dark. A lancet window should have brought him light, but there was none to give. Seeing only shadows where the steps should be, he stumbled and, tottering there and trying to grasp the smooth stones of the wall, realized that he had fallen against a body.

It was Koschei, magnificent in death. A small and eerie light crept from beneath one arm of his corpse. Cautiously, Parados touched the arm and, nothing stirring, moved it aside. The magician had fallen on his lantern and it burned still, inside its case of horn. Parados pulled on it and the dead fingers which grasped it let go and rattled their long nails against the lantern before the hand fell back. Parados opened the door in the lantern and lifted it high.

The body was that of a man his own age; there was no outward sign to show how Koschei had met his death. Slowly at first, impeded by the lantern which he put down on the step above Koschei's head, then faster and more boldly Parados unclasped the red robe the magician wore and saw his broad chest and, swelling on the left side of it like a gall on a fine oak, a single woman's breast. The wound which surely was the cause of Koschei's death pierced the chest on the right. He bent closer and saw that the wound was closed, with a thick scab over it. The magician's loins were girded with a white cloth: he did not dare untie it and find out the truth but examined the legs, the right wedged against the wall and the left against a stair and fallen sideways – on it, in the soft skin at the back of the knee-joint was a small, red papilla or teat. The body bore many other marks and evidences of a dangerous and active life, criss-cross scars from slashing swords, old bullet-wounds and, in the single breast, the deep scar of Erchon's accurate rapier-thrust.

Terror and excitement rose side by side in Parados; he wanted to flee unsatisfed and to remain, knowing all. He wished to punish and to feel pity and he drew the pistol from his pocket, primed it and emptied it into the corpse, drinking in the smell of the powder and admiring the rents the bullets made in the dead flesh. He threw the gun away, out of the window. The pocket of Koschei's gown was better reward. He took the leather wallet from it and, opening it, found many pockets, each one filled. There were amulets and talismans, a knotted cord and a paper of black powder, matches, a half-burned purple candle, bills and receipts, paper money of many strange denominations, gold coins and a minute book – but this was only a collection of sayings and proverbs. In the last pocket he found Helen Lacey's cross and Nemione's broken chain. 'Keep Faith' he read again. With them was a lock of black and gypsy hair. To touch it concentrated his emotions and he felt the ghost of old and shameless desire. This, surely, was a lock cut from Helen's head? Ashamed of his inquisitiveness, he replaced everything he had found and put the wallet back in the pocket. To mutilate, to poke and pry about a dead, unhallowed body was the black reverse of all he had become, an action befitting Koschei himself and not the kristnik Parados, twelfth son of Stanko of Belgard.

Yet his need to know the whole truth was paramount. It directed his hand. Roughly, he pulled apart the knot in Koschei's loincloth and exposed his inmost secret to the light. It was true, this rumour which was sweeping the land. Koschei was no man because every essential part of him which had been male was gone, sliced off long ago by Peder's jealous and intemperate blade. Enough remained for fulfilment of the lower bodily functions; but that was all. Neither the anticipation, pleasures, or satisfaction of desire could be got from what remained. The Prince and Archmage of Malthassa had a grievous wound.

Parados dropped the fold of cloth to cover Koschei. The end had come, had passed and been endured; the uncharted future lay ahead. He stepped over the magician's corpse and went on down the stairs. In the storeroom he found boxes and barrels of biscuit, raisins and flour and casks and bottles of wine and, set in the floor, the grating which was the sole entrance to and exit from that close and fearful dungeon, the deep oubliette beneath Peklo tower. He knelt, as Koschei had, and peered in. The dreadful place was empty though a set of chains, some straw and a clay beaker half full of water showed that a prisoner had recently languished there. So, Koschei and Nemione having in their different ways departed, he must climb the stairs again. He pushed past the body on the stairs and, safe above it, paused to make the sign he knew from childhood, a cross. Here, in Malthassa, it had a different meaning of choice and the best path through life, but to him it was still the sign of those who would be charitable and blessed.

Koschei's study kept its power to terrify. In a corner by the miniature castle and its still and wasted tenant was a work-bench on which were several china flasks and a brass alembic on a tripod. Beside this stood a lead tank full of bubbling blood. Something seethed in it and a pale, fleshy thing like the leg of a foetus in a devil's stew rose up, broke the excited surface and sank out of sight. Parados looked away along the shelves, glanced at the titles of the books on the revolving stand: alchemy, arch-chymistry, mages, magi, magic, mechanics – A glassy object glinted underneath the bookstand and he bent and picked it up. It was a small prism which reflected the yellow beam of the lantern and sent it forth in seven rainbow colours. The blood boiled audibly in the tank and, without warning, the big globe in the centre of the room began to turn, creaking upon its spindle; and as abruptly ceased. Malthassa, the world he thought he knew, was displayed there, the forest tilted toward him. Nothing distinguished one part of it from another, all vast and green except the hollow squares which marked towns, the blue threads of the rivers and some red lettering. He read it: 'terra incognita'. The 'o' was a well or vortex. He felt it draw him in and looked away. The same dark green covered the map on the tower wall; but the 'o' was larger and, looking closer, he saw that the painted surface was composed of individual trees, oak distinguished from ash, elm from pine and pine in all its thousand varieties from spruce. He did not look further: to do so made him feel the forest's unknowable extent. Instead, he turned the pretty prism over in his hand. The rainbow colours had left it, all but one. A single ray of green lay across his palm and, fascinated, he held the prism to his eye. He saw the forest captured there and, a shadow between the evergreens, a white deer – a hind, for she had no antlers and was neatly-made and graceful as a sapling. A second deer stalked her, lingering in concealment beneath the trees, his wide show of antlers brushing the lowest branches. Parados thought the hind was oblivious of the other's presence, grazing quietly on the little tufts of weed which grew where the trees were thinnest; but then, for she delicately turned her head and stood alert, ready to run, he saw that she was most aware. The hart came from his hiding-place and the hind, instead of fleeing, opened her long and slender jaw and spoke, her voice a soft and drawn-out bleat which nevertheless shaped itself to the words she used,

'You know the rules, Koschei. They are ancient and hallowed. You are required to show yourself in your proper form before you shift your shape again.'

'I no longer have my body, Lady. It was a worthless thing and I think the frame of an animal will better serve my turn. For the present, I enjoy the fleet limbs and taut senses of this hart.'

'Then you are handicapped indeed!'

'I think not. Contrariwise, I have the advantage.' As he spoke, the hart began to change, his antlers and proud muzzle fading and reforming as a keen-eyed hook-beaked head, his legs dissolving into wings, his tails and body into talons and feathers. The hind, who had begun her own transformation, melted briefly through and into the lissom and unclothed shape of a young and beautiful woman whose fair hair, even as it appeared, was changing into white wings. She flew, a dove, into the fir tree above her while the hawk, hopping awkwardly over the ground, worked his wings hard to gain the air.

'I will fall on you as you fly,' he called.

'Will you, Koschei?' The dove lifted her wings and, where there had been only she perched on the tufted branch, appeared a flock of doves all alike and like her. 'Come, my little hunted sisters,' she said, 'Paloma, Barbary, Berthe – let us fear not but fly up and confound the sorcerer.'

Parados watched her with love in his heart and on his

lips. He felt his soul dance deep inside him. 'Nemione!' he said. 'My brave love!'

As for Koschei who had lain, as he thought, dead a little while before, his shifts of shape were bold and rapacious. Parados lifted a hand and saluted his adversary.

The hawk dashed out of the sun and struck one of the swiftly-flying doves. Gripping it fiercely he bore it down and they tumbled together into the raft of the tree-tops. A single white feather drifted after them and all was still. The forest held its breath. Then the white wings rose again, but they had grown into angel's wings and carried a dark and full-grown girl aloft. She wore a long silk dress and an absurd feathered hat, the height of someone's fashion somewhere long ago. A fur stole dangled from her left arm but she, ascending as smoothly and effortlessly as the sun itself, seemed not to notice these peculiarities for her hands were clasped in prayer and her eyes turned heavenwards. Parados heard one word of her prayer, 'bliss'. It drifted down and lay like a blessing on the tops of the trees, settled about him; for he was there, flying carelessly without wings, buoyant with exhilaration and joy.

Paloma rose into the sun. He could not see her and the other doves had flown; the hawk was nowhere to be seen. He smiled happily and floated down amongst the trees until he stood in dappled shadow on the forest floor.

There seemed no course for the moment but to walk. Which way? There was no path, no track but only endless crooked rows of fir trees and the soft floor, carpeted with old, brown needles, underfoot. He spat on a finger, held it up: he would walk with the cool prevailing wind of Malthassa in his face, westward, the friendliest direction. There was no wind. He tried to see where the sun stood but its face was hidden by the trees. Perhaps he could judge by the intensity of light – or the prism still in his hand! He held it up and looked deep into its heart. There was nothing in it now to aid him. A host of rainbows dazzled him. He blinked and saw them copied in the air. Opening his hand he made to toss the useless thing away, then closed his fingers round and pocketed it. So, he was lost. He walked forward, ducking between the trees, thinking only of the glimpse he had been granted of Nemione. How fast could a dove fly? How soon would she judge it necessary to take another shape?

He walked far. Once, he saw a cow and calf, two of the wild herd descended from Polnisha's oxen; he thought he saw the Firebird pecking at the pine cones underneath the trees. He knew that the tall birds which gravely bowed to him were silver pheasants; he recognized the tiny baskets hanging from the boughs as nests. Here, the trees were different, graceful larches whose supple trunks and arched, depending branches made him think more intensely of Nemione. He stopped to admire one, gently touching its short needles and unripe cones, smooth and firm as tiny breasts. He stretched out his arms. The girl he held in them was lissom, very tall. Rags of green and blue stuff which were like fabric and yet were part of her hung from her shoulders, wrists and waist; were wound about her legs. Her head was covered in green bristles.

'How fortunate I am,' she sighed. Her breath ran sweetly, resin-scented, over his face. She stretched her woody neck and leaned forward to be kissed on lips which were studded with golden beads of sap. He felt her branches close about him and her needles dig into his neck, and into his left leg – sharp thorns which scratched. A thick bramble stem was caught about the leg. He shook it, stamped; felt himself pulled from the larch-girl and roughly thrown aside. A terrible scream and a wild crackling filled the air and the larch tree was engulfed in flame. He lay bruised and panting in a bramble thicket.

'Foolish man-child!' The voice came from the air above him, seven or eight feet up, and an ice-cold hand sprung out of nothing and slapped him hard across the ear, once, twice, hard cuffs which made his head sing. He lay defeated, looking fearfully up at the creature which had rescued him. It was huge, but not as great as the Om Ren, and seemed to have no form or, at least, a form which constantly changed. He saw a foot, large but comely; a strand of hair like the stem of a wild rose and roses of the palest pink flowering on it; the hand again, frosty and cold, vapour rising from it and the bramble loop which had snared and saved him in its fingers; a merry brown eye. He put his hands together, raised them in a reverent salute and said,

'Thank you, Forest God.'

The invisible creature laughed and showed another piece of herself, dense fur as white as any snow-drift and thick enough to keep out the harshest cold. A furry baby, pale gold, clung there and he heard it sucking.

'Thank you, Lady of the Forest,' he said.

'Good! That is good,' she said. 'I am the Forest Mother, the Weshni Dy. *She* was one of my samovili, wicked girl – they are difficult things, larch vili, shallow-rooted and keen to take whatever tasty man-morsel comes their way. Had you been a cruel woodcutter I would have let her appetite take its course. Tell truly, Sir Parados – did you not learn wisdom with my husband and the nivasha?'

'The Om Ren?'

'Himself. He has married me and brought me down from my Altaish to rule his realm. This is his son, the Om Ren.'

The Weshni Dy showed a little more of herself, a long leg draped in oak-leaves. She bent it and sat her child on it and the baby stared at Parados with dark, wise eyes.

'You will be such a great and dreadful beast!' his mother chirruped. 'Look at him, all milky warmth and gentleness of spirit.' She nuzzled her baby and kissed him.

'He is a true son of his father,' said Parados.

'Oh, Parados; you would not say that if you had seen the Om Ren lately. Death approaches and he is no longer what he was when you journeyed together in the enchanted place beside SanZu. Will you come with me? I must build my sleeping-nest and rest the night. In the morning, I will show you the way you should follow.'

Parados woke in the night and was conscious of great inner peace which the moon's light shining in the glade emphasized. Beside him in the nest of leafy and sweet-scented linden-branches, the Weshni Dy slept quietly, her young Wild Man curled on her stomach. He wondered if she dreamed and of what those strange dreams might consist – the snowy Altaish perhaps or her own fluctuating female form which was not quite woman and not exactly ape, sometimes white and icy and sometimes green and fruitful as the forest itself; occasionally as lovely and alluring as one of her samovili and irresistible to man and ape. He closed his eyes and slept soundly in his own nest of dreams.

The Om Ren's wife had set him on his way. A wide track divided limes from oak trees on the far side of the glade and there she had bade him walk, facing north.

'When you hear it,' she had said, 'you will know what you have been seeking.'

He walked for many miles and hours until the sun was high in the sky and, hungry, he stopped to eat the fistful of nuts and seeds the Weshni Dy had given him and to drink rainwater from the hollow of an oak. He did not know that such water, suffused as it is with the sap of the oak, confers strength but only that after drinking it he felt courageous and bold. Soon, he heard the steady beat of horses' hooves behind him on the track and turned to see an old and rickety cart approaching. It was drawn by two horses harnessed one before the other and, as it came near, Parados saw the driver, a heavy red-faced man who was sleeping as he drove. An

405

old garland of willow-boughs and dead flowers swayed above his nodding head.

The pair of horses stopped abruptly when they reached Parados. He patted the leader on its neck and recoiled, seeing the dead and wasted bay horse which was tied with fraying and dirty bits of rope to the body of the cart. The driver belched and woke.

'Who-aaa!' he roared and, seeing Parados, 'Why, Sir, good-morrow! Many years have passed since we met and I see that you have indeed advanced out of your Green Wolf's calling. Your cuirass now – what splendour, what exquisite metalwork. It is by Sardon of Pargur, am I right?'

'I know not – my Lady gave it me.'

'Gained a lady too! Rich? Beautiful? You have succeeded.'

'Remind me, Master Butcher – where have we met before?' said Parados uncertainly.

'In that mean village, Sir, how could you forget? Where the heathen corn-growers dwell. You won yourself a scrawny sacramental bride. And afterwards I carried you, *on this very cart* – I never took the garlands off it, see – into the forest and set you down by a big chestnut tree where you had an appointment with a dwarf. Did he come, Sir? I hope he did. It was a lonely spot. And before we parted you gave me a silver thrupny, there it is. I keep it for a good-luck because I saw what you were beneath your disguise – one of the Brotherhood, a Green Wolf running after blood.'

'My name, then? I must have given it.'

'No Sir, you didn't. I've wondered to this day.'

'The man you carried on your cart was Koschei Corbillion. Do you know the name now?'

'By the Dark Lord and all his devilish crew – you are the Archmage! Don't harm me, my Lord, I am only a poor horse-butcher.'

'I am not Koschei but, let us say, his brother – that is good enough. I am Parados.'

'The man they worship in SanZu! Get up, Sir, here beside me. I will carry you wherever you want.'

'Once,' said Parados quietly, 'you carried me where I most devoutly did not wish to go; but you were kind enough. What is your name, Master Butcher – does it begin with a "G" or a "P"?' He climbed up and sat beside the butcher on the narrow and slippery seat of the cart. The man hawked and spat into the undergrowth and smiled at him, showing a row of decaying stumps.

'Clever of you, Sir Parados, when you might have picked any letter. Yes, my name is Georg which, as you rightly guess, begins with the seventh letter of the alphabet. And the one that follows after it, the one whose initial you also struck on, canny Sir, is Peacock, though I am a poor crow. It was my grandam's name. My last, that my wife is proud to bear and my ten children too, is Deaner – which means "shilling", sir, and those are what I hope to make a mint of.'

'Your wife? Let me guess her name   is it "Helen"?'

'Not nearly, sir! It is Martha; but she has a cousin named Helen who makes all the hats in Espmoss where we live these days. We lived a while in Tanter and before that and expensively in Pargur. The country air is better and the country living cheaper.' He shook out the bunched reins and clucked to the horses which, after nodding their heads and snorting loudly, moved off. 'We do well in Espmoss,' he continued. 'I have two horses now, had to get new harness, too, and a china dinner service.'

Parados was content to sit in the warm sun on the jolting cart and doze while the horse-butcher talked as if he had important tales to tell and never a good listener to hear them; but both the world of action and its shadow, the contemplative world of fiction were, he thought, like this stoical butcher, better inclined to tragedy and the dogged acceptance of fate and circumstance than to comedy. Soon, as they drove, the track grew narrow and the trees which had been in proud summer foliage began to drop brown leaves.

'Have a care, now,' said Georg. 'There are puvushi here so keep your eyes on the road ahead – and hold tight!'

He took his whip from its socket on the dashboard and cracked it loudly in the air.

'Whahaw!' he cried. 'Haw! Haw!' and the horses lumbered into a trot, a canter and at last, as they felt his fear, a headlong gallop.

'There's one!' the butcher yelled. 'Close your eyes!'

Blind, trusting in the horses, they sped on. The cart shook and rattled, the axles screamed in the wheel-hubs and, beneath the bare trees where the ground was soft and friable, the puvushi rose, rested their elbows on the edges of their holes and gazed hungrily after the two men on their speeding cart.

Parados opened his eyes. The trees had thinned and, ahead, the forest was turning to scrubland where grass and low bushes grew into each other and the track veered off to the left.

'I must set you down here,' said Georg. 'I have business with a sick mare in Zelkova but the Plains are close, that way. You will be glad to get out of the wood!'

'Indeed, for I cannot see what I seek when I am beneath the trees,' said Parados. 'I have no silver threepenny bit to give you but take this to remember me by.' He cut one of the gilt buttons from his coat and handed it up to the butcher.

'A sun resplendent, and a "P" for Parados,' said the butcher, examining the button. 'I'll keep it with the coin I had from Koschei, here in my weskit pocket. The Archmage *and* Lord Parados, well, well, what tales I'll tell! – but fare you well, Sir, and do not fear to walk over the grass of the Plains. There's too much light there and too much wind for the zracni-kind!'

'Adieu,' said Parados and strode out at once without lingering to see the cart drive off. There was a track of sorts in front of him, a wide trail of flattened grass, and whistling 'When a knight won his spurs', he followed it.

The rebel party followed Estragon into the deserted Court of Love. There was no one now to set the statues playing their drums and bells nor any lady fit to hold court.

'This is a melancholy place,' said Aurel. 'I wish I had a mistress to enthrone there, on the dais!'

'The castle is unsettled,' said Estragon. 'It does not know what rooms to show you, nor who you are yet – but it perceives you are honourable and kindly. Let us try that door.'

A long, white shoot sprouted from the floor when they had gone, turned green, grew into a sapling and a tree and burst into blossom which, falling, left red apples on the tree.

Estragon led Aurel and his men along a short passage, the artery between two painted doors and, stepping back, allowed Githon to push open the door.

'So this is how the castle treats us!' the dwarf exclaimed. The room beyond, equipped with chairs and sofas and tables for chess and backgammon, with harpsichords, spinets and a forte-piano, also contained twenty or more men. Young fops dressed in silk and lace, they lounged gossiping on the furniture. Some were smoking and others drank champagne from pewter tankards because all the glass, like Pargur's crystal walls and Sehol's magic, rainbow gate, had been shattered by Parados's blow. Half a dozen of the gallants looked idly at the rebels as they entered and one drew a scimitar quickly from the piano, for he had seen the naked sword which Githon, who was not deceived, had raised.

'They are Green Wolves!' the dwarf cried. 'The Brotherhood!'

Then hats and lace collars were thrown aside and the Green Wolves emerged from their disguise to fight. It was the first fight for Castle Sehol and Aurel only won it because he preferred to negotiate. The second fight, in which the Brotherhood joined on the rebels' side was with the Castle Guard, Baptist Olburn at their head; and Aurel won this after twenty minutes. Most of the Guard were killed and Olburn badly wounded but not gravely enough to prevent him being locked in his own dungeon.

Now Castle Sehol showed itself. More of Toricello's crazily beautiful flowers and trees grew up from pavements, staircases and turret-tops. Friendship and Concordis came from the cellar in which they had hidden themselves and welcomed Aurel and Githon especially and all the rebels generally. The Lord Marshall, Elzevir Tate, and his Council thought it expedient to visit quiet, country places, and went away. Many tales were told and, with a roll on the timpani, a fifty-gun salute and all the bells of Pargur chiming, Aurel, Captain Wayfarer, was named Regent of Castle Sehol and Hadrian and Thidma his Chiefs of Council. Aurel's flag, *gules*, a mulberry leaf *argent*, flew beside the golden sun of Parados on the top of Probity tower and a standard with his canting arms, *argent*, a wayfaring tree *vert*, was planted on the Devil's Bastion. Custos, no longer wandering but a fixed star in the firmament, watched over them and its five points, on which all the world had hung, were keen and bright.

Without instruction or direction from anything other than its mysterious, alert self, the great globe of Peklo tower spun once more upon its axis and the green extent of the Plains above its northern tropic turned the colour of dry straw. The same faded yellow covered every inch of Koschei's Mappa Mundi on the tower wall while, between the 'a' and the 'i' of 'Plains', there appeared the tiny, finely-detailed image of thirty pine-trees standing on a low knoll.

Parados emerged from the long, ripe grass and stood at the foot of the hillock. The wind was blowing softly, to cool

410

him and stir the grasses and the pine-tops languidly. This, surely, was a pleasant place in which to rest and eat the bread the horse-butcher had given him. He walked up the incline before him and, sitting down beneath the nearest tree, unbuckled and shed his heavy cuirass. There, in the sea of grass below him, his route out of the forest was clearly marked – and that of the other who had gone before him and trodden down the stems. Of the forest itself, there was no sign. It had vanished, or retreated into another dimension, and he and the piny hillock were deep in the Plains where other low hills rose, one succeeding the other to the limits of sight, and all yellow with high summer.

Not caring how coarse and gritty it was he ate his ravel-bread and, shading his eyes with tired, sweaty hands, lay down to sleep.

First the left hand, then the right, were lifted and opened to be read. The left was strongly marked, especially with Love and Life, but the lines etched deep as gold-lodes in the right disappeared as the palmist stroked them until the hand was as smooth and soft as a baby's and all Reason fled. Lastly, the Om Ren (for the palmist was he, huge, mighty and grey with life fulfilled) examined the strong wrists and the veins and sinews which showed their pliant selves beneath the grimy skin.

'Good,' he muttered. 'Excellent – not a mark or a join to be seen and a great grip too, by the look of them. A hard journey, too, to reach this place – how peacefully he sleeps! Now, Sir –' and he opened up the cavern of his mouth to show his fangs, '– awake, Sir Parados, wake up!'

The roar and the hot animal breath coming together like a gale in his face woke Parados at once. He sprang up with drawn sword.

'Splendid! Magnificent – a new Galahad, a Roland reborn!' cried the Om Ren. 'And I – what am I, but an animated cadaver, dead meat walking, a tough hide waiting to be flayed? You shall bear witness to the last hour of

411

the Forest's Father, Parados – a fitting culmination to your journey.'

Parados sheathed his sword.

'I have seen the Weshni Dy and your son, Om Ren,' he said. 'She is a wonder and he is another. I am here because she showed me the way.'

'So!' The Om Ren drew his lips back from his teeth and bared them. 'To see me die, to make a mock! – but I am not bitter. My life has run its course. I am not bitter but my soul is angry; soon the rage will take me.

'So!' he said again. 'My wife directed you – she knows which way the wind blows. I am lighter than a mayfly when Fate exhales.' He spoke more kindly so that Parados dared approach and stand beside him, child-sized beside the towering ape.

'Can I help you?' he asked.

'Would that you could. The only thing, alas, that you could do for me, is plunge your keen sword into my heart; but that is not permitted. I must submit. Look, the first sign – the horses! They know!'

The herd had come up silently, to the foot of the knoll. Parados, staring down at them, thought that time itself had taken charge and overridden sense. There had been no warning of the horses' presence, no sounds, no scents; and the tall grass he had walked through was gone, replaced by short, green turf on which the horses nervously waited, ears pricked and nostrils flaring wide.

'They await the last act,' the Om Ren said. 'My final feat. Stand aside, Parados – you and I must part in friendship. Go!'

He unwound his straw rope from his shoulders and tied it to one of the pines. 'Away, Parados, away!' he roared, terrifying the herd which neighed and reared as one horse, and sending Parados running. The Om Ren, still bellowing out his passion and agony of mind pulled on the rope so that the pine tree screamed and one of its boughs broke off

412

with a loud crack; but still the Om Ren pulled until the tree bent and tottered and came up from the ground, its roots tearing from their anchorage in the soil with a great sigh. It lay dying on the ground, fallen outwards, its green head at the bottom of the bank. The Om Ren gave one last tug upon his rope which separated into a cloud of stalks and chaff and blew away.

'You must make another of those, my son,' he said.

He loped down the bank and bent to pick up the tree.

The horses were silent now and perfectly still, their muzzles all pointing in his direction, the colts and stallions in a rough circle behind the mares and fifty or a hundred yards away, on the far perimeter of the herd, the Red Horse himself, alert, eager. He carried Nandje on his back, crouched low and red in his grease and dye and other riders of the Ima sat their horses close about.

'Come Little Man, Brave Imandi, Ape-Killer, Slaughterer, Flayer, Butcher!' the Om Ren taunted. 'Ride closer if you dare!' He raised his hairy arms and shook both fists at Nandje, roared once and swung the pine tree by its top. He whirled it up and round until it spun above his head, its earth-covered roots the head of a great club; and ran forward, scattering the herd. Like a rumour or a plague the excitement of the new danger swept through the herd. Even the tame horses were affected and two threw their riders and galloped off. The Red Horse snorted and pawed the ground. Nandje fought him for mastery. The mares fidgeted; some neighed and some put back their ears and snapped at one another. A bunch of colts reared and suddenly were off, galloping blindly. The rest, their panic mounting to full pitch, wheeled and followed them, the Red Horse first.

The herd circled the knoll and Parados, standing amazed on its bank, watched them pass by, circling the mound continually, building up their combined speed and strength and moving as inexorably as a river in full spate to sweep up and over the Om Ren standing his ground in their midst. Colts rushed by, and mares with foals, fillies, more mares. A white mare was running with them. Parados recognized her – his old mount, Summer. Close behind her came one of the stallions, as dark and grey as Death himself, or Winter stripping the last leaves from the cold and naked trees. She is lovely like Nemione, he thought, and he as baleful and jealous as Koschei.

The horses were leaving him, galloping away and carrying the raging Om Ren with them. Parados strained to see what was taking place out there, in the stampede. He attempted to rise into the air, but there was too much noise and commotion rushing by: it was impossible to think. He tried to see a crane, a lark, a falcon, himself riding in it, part of its flexible body and buoyant wings; but he could not leave the ground. The horses passed again. Nandje was still in the saddle, crouched low along the back of the Red Horse. A third time they circled the hill and Parados looked for the white mare and the grey horse; and for the Red Horse in his pride and strength, head and neck at full stretch, hooves pounding, heart pumping and mane flying up and out on the wind as if he were a part of that eternal current which coursed unceasingly across the Plains and was bred and instilled in him, through his mother's milk, the clear streams of water which flowed through the Plains and the rich and juicy waving grass itself.

The Red Horse broke from the herd, out of control. Nandje was a passenger on his back, vainly tugging on the reins. The Horse came on, beating the turf underfoot into a pulp, huge, unstoppable. Parados glimpsed his wild eye, his open jaw and the foam which spilled from his lips across his shoulders. He put up his arms, bent, and dodged, but the bank was steep below him and slippery with loose pine needles. He tripped and went down and, lying there defence-less, was able at last dispatch his body into Limbo, tear his

414

soul free and send it soaring upwards to fuse with the spirit of the Red Horse.

Parados heard his own ritual question, 'Greeting Horse. Permit me,' with long, horse's ears and answered it with a loud neigh; he felt Nandje's heels in his ribs and his knees tight about his girth; he felt, and fought, the bit with which Nandje lorded it over him and longed to shake it off – but it was too cruel and tight, wedged in the gap of his teeth and lying like an awful bony punishment across his tongue. Nandje was making him run straight, on towards the ape who, wielding his pine tree stood up in the grass and yelled defiance. He veered to avoid the club, swung round and back at the Om Ren. The herd was milling and wheeling about him, driven tighter, close-pressed by the riders on its boundary. Horse to terrify horse, he thought. Ultimate cruelty, Man's abominable depravity. He felt the pine roots sweep his neck and his rider bent sideways. A young foal went down beside him and disappeared beneath the pounding hooves. He was angry; he wanted this to end. He wanted to punish this presumptuous ape whose father's finger-bone and skin kept him in check. He wanted blood; he wanted to kill.

A second blow of the tree swept Nandje from his back. He went the way of the foal and was overwhelmed, flesh to grass, as the herd trod him into the ground. The Red Horse neighed and reared in triumph. The Om Ren roared and brandished his tree.

They met in the centre of the herd, at the still heart of the hurricane. It was at first a duel between equals, a simple matter of horn meeting wood, of two strong sets of teeth except that, as the horse and ape fought, the dejection that had entered the Om Ren's soul prevailed and he grew weary. Raising the club above his head, he made to bring it down upon the Red Horse to break his back; but the Horse was swift and struck first, his hooves raking the ape's chest and belly, ripping open rib-cage, muscle and hide. The Om Ren fell to the ground, writhed and died, his pine-tree striking a by-standing colt as dead as himself.

So I have won; I have triumphed, Parados and the Red Horse thought, killing the creature who was most good to me and the friend of all animals.

He saw Gry in the distance, shrieking and wailing over Nandje's body and tearing her plaits open till the tangled hair flew away in her clawing fingers. There were blue flags all about her, raised in the hands of the mounted Ima, a wave of silk to hold the horses back. The blue tide turned, rolling towards him, menacing the herd. He neighed and pawed at his head and rolled on the ground until he was free of bridle and saddle. He called the herd, his voice like thunder: Ha! Ha!

The madness of the horses was in the Ima too. They urged their mounts toward him, trying to cut him from the herd. He would have none of that but, finding the white mare and grey stallion near him, shoved them both in turn with his mighty neck and began a new stampede. He did not want to run; he wanted peace and sweet grazing, a long draught of water and to roll in clean grass; but the men had made a brute of him. He would out-run them and escape. His desire for freedom gripped the herd. He galloped and his horses swept after him. The Ima, riding with flags high and flying, came last and believed they drove the herd.

On, beneath a burning midday sun they galloped; east across the undulating surface of the Plains. Yards became miles and miles leagues as they fled, so fast they overset time and ran through morning into red dawn. Wolves, lying down to sleep after the hunt, raised weary heads to stare at them and the wolf-mother howled. Cold night and the chill waters of the streams they splashed through soothed them. The sweat

416

dried on them and they took new heart, galloping on beneath the stars which were huge, bright and close. The Swan, the Hoopoe and the Dancing Crane raised their wings and flew above the horses. Bail's Sword swung over them and the warrior Bail appeared to grasp and lift it. He stepped down from the sky to run with the herd.

Then, from the skies and myths and tales of Albion, which was so far in distance from Malthassa and yet so close in spirit, other star-beasts came leaping to join the stampede: the Great Bear, growling deep in his throat, the stalking, spotted Lynx, and great Taurus, the bull. Pegasus heard them and lifted his dripping muzzle from the well of Hippocrene which he had made with one stamp of his moon-shaped hind feet. His folded wings quivered and he suddenly unfurled them and flew with the herd. In far Thule the Kelpie which pulls men to their deaths in water swam from his loch into the air and, swift and blue as lightning, crossed heath and heather until he reached the Plains. Sleipnir galloped faster than the wind on his four pairs of legs and Ambarr, Mannanan's magic horse, ran over the seven seas. In Emain Macha Cuchulainn's chariot-horses, which could weep and speak like men, broke free. The first was slight and slender of hoof and limb with a flowing mane and a shining coat and the second lithe and swift-leaping, powerful and long-bodied. His hooves were the size of bucklers. The Mari Lwyd, put out of the stable to make room for the Virgin and Child, left her ceaseless, lonely wandering and turned towards the Plains, her yellow teeth clacking in her bony skull and her ragged shroud flying behind her. In the heavenly pastures of Hy Brasil Mancha and Gato pricked their ears and began to run; the White Horse raised himself from his bed in the chalk Downs and the Four Horses of the Apocalypse, the White which carries a Conqueror, the Red which brings War, the Black which bears Justice and the Pale Horse whose rider is Death, roused and ran.

Next came the war-horses, swift Veillantif, Gryngolet in

his gold-bedecked harness, Charlemagne's Tencender whose name means 'Strife', and the bright and lofty-crested bay Ruksh. A host of horses followed them: first and running neck and neck in line, the Godolphin and the Darley Arabians and the Byerley Turk, Nijinsky a short head behind them; Nearco, Dante, Melpomene and Lord Polo galloped close while Flick, Schlutter, Nelusko, Zorah and Jack, the father of Shetland ponies, and Janus the original Quarter Horse kept pace with Justin Morgan and the poet's little Morgan which was nervous and jumpy as a flea, still flecked with the snow of the storm from which the herd had called him. Nimble Spot and Synon, the Wooden Horse of Troy, galloped side by side while Janus ran with the brass Fairy horse, which was shown as a wonder to Cambinskan, and wily Hogarth with the Green Knight's great Green Horse. Finally there came a string of stragglers, Rosinante creaking her old bones, Black Beauty, The Piebald which won the National under Velvet, Tom Pearce's Grey Mare, Trigger and, all together in a bunch, Arkite, Choru and Spooky, Canis Major yapping at their heels.

The motley herd passed into yesterday's translucent evening and the sun rose backwards in a glowing arc. Larks shot downward from their airy stages, their songs sinking in a thin stream back into their beaks; the flowers in the grass, which were closed up, stretched their petals wide; and the motley herd of living, dead, and imaginary horses galloped on, the flag-flourishing Ima hard behind. Gry's brothers called to Leal,

'The Horse leads us where we want to go!' and Leal shouted back,

'He knows what he must do!'

The Ima had no leader themselves, unless it was the Red Horse, far in front with the grey stallion and white mare. Fathers and sons rode as if in a race and brothers and cousins looked challengingly at each other, wondering to whom would fall the title of Imandi; yet they, while anticipating contest, worked together and still believed it was they who kept the herd on course. Sunlight, hot and high, beat down upon them so that they began to sweat, great drops, which they dashed away, appearing on their painted faces. The lather built up on the horses' necks and shot from them into the wind where it fountained up and filled the clear air with cloud. The herd ran into a fog of its own making and rocks and areas of stony ground passed under it like old memories as it penetrated the new night.

The enticing smell of the white mare filled the nostrils of the Red Horse. He nuzzled her crest and the long slope of her neck as he ran and, feeling a sharp pain in his side, turned his head from these pleasurable delights and saw Winter, teeth bared and eyes malicious, closing in for a second bite. The Red Horse snaked out his long and muscled neck and let his teeth sink into the grey's tender ear until they met; the grey squealed defiantly but he dropped back out of sight. Mud and water surged up under the hooves of the red. Deepening water slowed his pace. They were afloat and swimming, his steaming wet flank bumping against Summer's streaming shoulder. The effort to swim was huge: he would have rolled upon his back and floated, cradling Nemione in his arms. He would have drowned Koschei in the water and in his keen and puissant mind; except that they were horses all. He plunged from the river and the fog into a warm morning. The town of Flaxberry lay before him, its empty streets calling out to be invaded. He looked behind: the herd, brown, bay, dun and black, was pressing on behind him, each horse a sudden, sparkling fountain as it shook the river from its coat; but the star-beasts, the birds and starry horses were gone and the equine figments of his imagination fled, extinguished perhaps in the water; there were no dead but only living horses and the Ima shouting at their backs and cracking the air with their huge sheets of blue silk. The Red Horse and Summer led them into the town.

The herd swept clattering through Flaxberry and brought its citizens running to their doors where they cowered, amazed. The Abbess screamed a prayer from her abbey steps; but her words were lost in the storm of noise. Polnisha leapt, too late, from her bed of stone. The herd was in the fields trampling the blue-flowered crop. It swept through groves of mulberry trees and brought the green fruit down in showers. Nothing could stop it and the people of SanZu stood by and watched the Ima and their wild horses wreck their quiet farmlands.

The Red Horse saw and recognized the Rock which, though it reared steeply up from the gentle fields, was the place he sought. He turned towards it and his herd followed. Up there was perspective, knowledge and fulfilment. It had the shape of a great, safe haven, a huge cart which might soar up and away with him and the white mare its only passengers, forsaking all others and leaving Winter behind in shame and want.

The long back of the Rock sloped upwards to the far horizon. The Red Horse hardly felt the greedy fingers of the puvushi he broke under his tread and his herd, hastening behind, crushed them to a fine powder which drifted up between the furious hooves and reformed into attenuated, grasping hands which beat and pinched the horses and made them mad. The wide body of the Rock was hardly able to contain half the herd; yet still the Ima gave chase, dividing their ranks to ring the Rock and to pursue. The horses crowded, faster, wilder. Winter reared in the mêlée and brought sharp horn down on the Red Horse's back; hot blood spurted from the wound. The grey closed, seizing his advantage. He harried Summer, nipping her to make her turn with him; and the Red Horse stumbled.

Winter swung and reared again. Every good spirit held its breath and every evil screamed in triumph. The Storyteller was fast in his own snare; but so, as the two worlds lay motionless in conjunction, the Red Horse saw the precipice and halted above the terrible drop, his four legs braced. Nimbly, he pushed the mare aside and she staggered and stood safe in his protection, her beautiful white head low. Crest firm and proud neck arched, he shielded her from the force of the oncoming herd. Winter could not stop. His legs made hopeless bounds in the air before the weight of his body carried him down and, mane and tail streaming, he fell from the Rock. A group of Ima stood amongst the mass of tumbled rocks beneath, Leal and Gry's brothers amongst them. Unsheathed knives and butchers' cleavers glinted in their hands.

PART FOUR

PARADISE LOST

I have come forth alive from the land of purple and poison and glamour

G. K. CHESTERTON

The brown limestone of the Rock of Solutré was warm in the afternoon sunshine and the entire outcrop a playground for tourists, holidaymakers and climbers. Some were in the underground museum looking at the model of the site in prehistory or reading the legend of the Rock that, fifteen thousand years before this summer afternoon and maybe on exactly such a sunny day, hunters used to drive the wild horse herds from the rock to death, butchery and the spit. Other visitors picnicked or admired the view; still others, roped together, climbed the south face of the Rock. Past these fell a scatter of dark shapes which might have been the memory of a dying horse-herd, rocks, a man – or just the drifting shadows of the small white clouds which occasionally interrupted the steady shining of the sun. One climber called out involuntarily, '*Avalanche!*' and, laughing at himself, listened happily to the derisive shouts of his companions, for there was nothing there.

Koschei picked himself up from the bushes into which he had fallen and looked up, back at the Rock. It was so like the Rock of SanZu that he suffered a pang of fear and longing but, collecting himself straight away, bent to rub some dry dirt from the knees of his jeans. His legs, inside the tough cloth tubes, were firm and ready to walk or run wherever he desired; his body was lithe and limber, likewise good for any challenge or activity. It was a fine, complete body and he was pleased with it and with his skill at summoning it from the Fifth Circle of Limbo, that many-coloured, timeless dimension on which Parados had so carelessly abandoned it. Ha! Koschei snorted as forcefully as the Red Horse, and laughed. It was a strong, fit body and would serve him well.

These strange garments which he had conjured to clothe the body – economical and practical, excellent! No need of chafing breastplates, dragging robes or the encumbrance of tasselled shoon. Koschei laughed again, more softly, and looked out across the rolling Burgundian landscape. The sky was a gentle shade of azure and the distant hills a darker hue; a river, mountains (not as high as the Altaish) far away; closer and below were crowded fields of vines, all in heavy leaf, and small villages of stone houses. A tall tower rose from the nearest – it had no aura of magic or of alchemy, but a golden tissue of peace and veneration lay over it and he supposed it was the dwelling of some god of seasons or other agricultural deity. The god of wine perhaps. He brushed his legs again and stretched as if he had just woken from a nap beneath the sweet-scented myrtles. These, glossy green and white-flowered, he knew, for their like grew in the cruciform garden of the Memory Palace and he had used their black berries not to perfume meat or bring a subtle savour to game but to distil a strong and aromatic liqueur in which to disguise and administer his poisons. He broke off a sprig for old times' sake and, after crushing it between avid fingers and inhaling its scent, dropped it to the ground. In Malthassa the breaking of myrtle wood was said to mark a new epoch.

The sprig had fallen amongst the roots of an older myrtle, whose trunk was grey and split. There, beside it, almost touching one of its bruised flowers, the lamia lay, resplendent in her scaly, banded coat of scarlet, orange and black, the jewels on her head gleaming dully in the broken light beneath the tree. Her tongue flickered out to touch the myrtle twig

426

and she turned the full force of her mirrored eyes on him. Equably, he returned her gaze.

'So, my Lady,' he said. 'You cannot resist me – after all.'

The snake uncoiled herself and rippled forward, nearly to the toe of his shoe; but she did not touch it, nor fawn on him nor otherwise abase herself, but only passed her agile tongue once over her bony lips and began to swell and bloat as if she were full of eggs or live, writhing young, and let her colours slip, one into another, until they all were faded and her skin was dry and papery and hung from her long body in rags and tatters. Koschei himself stepped back a pace. The lamia reared up and moved her head about in agony while diamonds, emeralds and rubies showered from it. Koschei was not deceived: he recognized the scattered wealth for what it was, Illusion – and that the transformation was not. Aghast and sickened, he nevertheless kept his eyes upon the lamia's belly and so witnessed (with an oath: 'Asmodeé!') a terrible birth. The hard belly-flesh tore slowly open with a soft noise like that of a cook's hand grasping the heart of a fowl and, first, a brown forefinger whose nail was a perfect, lustrous oval and then five brown toes were extended from the red intestines of the snake; next two elbows, two slender knees, the belly and the dark pudendum, the heavy breasts, the neck, the face, and finally the drenched and stinking hair, the entire bloodstained body of Helen Lacey, the gypsy witch. Her hair flew out, was clean and glossy, settled in wave after wave on her drying shoulders, thick black hair exactly like the lock of dyed hair he used to keep by him at all times. The witch exhaled, seven tiny tails and gobbets of mouse-skin and flesh flew from her mouth; she retched and hawked and spat and wiped her mouth on her hand, lifted both naked arms in the air and instantly was clothed, her familiar and extravagant skirts flying about her in a red and orange typhoon and disposing themselves correctly, her rings and beads and bangles clashing into place. She also, Koschei observed, summoned a plain

427

white vest of the kind he had appropriated, and he watched it arrange itself to cover the deep and glorious breasts he had seen naked but an atomy's breath before. Anticipation of the love of which he had so long been deprived ('Nay, starved!' he whispered) awoke in him and filled him with delight and lust for her newborn, comely body.

Helen looked at him, her snake's eyes shallow, capricious waters.

'Guy!' she said and laughed. Then, flourishing her skirts as if they were a fan and dropping Koschei half a delighted and flirtatious curtsy, 'Master!' she said, 'Koschei.'

The magician laughed with her and bowed in return. Their conjoined laughter billowed about the trees and swept the wooded hillside and the blue skies like a sudden squall; it was surely heard in stone-faced, secretive Lyon and glittering, mutable Pargur. They were quiet and the vines and all the summer vegetation settled with them into a happy stillness. Koschei spoke. His voice was not the even and melodious tenor of Parados, but deeper and shadowed with malevolence.

'Lady,' he said, and laid his healed and borrowed hands possessively on Helen's shoulders. 'My Lady – what will you and I not do together?'

Helen did not answer but stepped closer to him, laid a brown forefinger on her lips first and then, caressingly, on his.

'Where shall we go, my Love?' she said. 'Look, on the road there – beyond Solutré village. Dominic speeds to greet us.' She gestured towards the valley below, which was as full of roads as of vines, narrow grey ribbons which climbed among the fields and wound between village and village. The glass of a windscreen flashed briefly in the sun and the vehicle itself could be seen, a bright and swiftly-moving blur which, as it came rapidly nearer resolved itself into a shiny, blood-red car which halted at the roadside below.

'Your chariot of fire!' said Helen triumphantly and bent

to retrieve her lamia-skin from the myrtle-root at which their gale of laughter had deposited it. She rolled it carefully into a tight and rustling ball and tucked it under her tongue which, Koschei was intrigued to see, had retained its snaky, cloven shape.

One field of vines lay between them and their earthbound car. Quickly, Koschei straddled its wire fence and catching Helen up in his arms held her there, between heaven and earth. The cross, false earnest of fidelity, which she and Nemione had both worn first as an honourable badge and then as unregarded trinket, had undergone a final transmutation and become flesh, a small but obvious scar beneath the septum of her nose. Its southernmost arm almost touched her upper lip and made her supernatural beauty all the more compelling.

'*Chov-hani*, Witch-woman,' Koschei murmured and kissed the witch-mark first and then the curving, sensual mouth itself. Time, by his will, was suspended while they kissed and Dominic, standing in the road beside the car and looking up at the sun-haunted rock, the trees and the enchanter and enchantress frozen on the margin of the wood and field, saw the high, drifting clouds come to a standstill and heard the rustle of the leaves and the insect-hum cease. Then Koschei set Helen down in the vineyard and life and living started up again as they strolled hand-in-hand down the hill towards him. Koschei, as they approached, surveyed the boy eagerly and he stood up, straight and tall, his fair head shining in the sun, his brown gypsy eyes unfathomable.

'Dominic, my son and his,' said Helen. 'Or ours, perhaps, since you have his body, blood and mannerisms all.'

The familiar stranger gave a broad and charming smile. He made a figure in the air with his hand, as if he removed a hat, and bowed.

'Koschei Corbillion at your service, Dominic,' he said. 'A fine substitute for my own dear son. Dominic – the name means "Sunday", does it not? – was that the day on which you were born to serve Zernebock?'

'Or Satan – he has many names and titles,' said the boy. 'Where will you travel, Koschei? Where shall I drive you?'

'But I shall drive!' the magician exclaimed. 'I have the body, mark you, and no doubt it will remember all that in the past has made it what it is today.' He turned to Helen and repeated her words on the hill: 'Where shall we go, my Love? You know your world better than I. Shall it be to his place, the old priest's house in Albion?'

'You are premature, Koschei; do not let immediate ambition get in the way of prudence – besides, do you want a wedded wife (who waits for him there) and six more children to go with this one? Accusations, recriminations, grief?'

'I do not fear any of these.'

'Let me be your guide. As you say, I know this world and its ways. Let us follow my spirit which goes, like the *traboules* of the Croix Rousse or the twisting streets of Nether Pargur, in as many directions as the compass needle. As for my heart which also has its yearnings, for my past incarnations and my future selves, but most of all for the Unknown Paradise – I will give it in charge of blind Fate and take the road. We'll go where this *drom* leads us, my fine *rai* – eastwards first, for I am tired of this great and civilized country. Let us travel to older, wilder places and retrace my people's long journey, back into the night of their birth.

'Come, Master, step into your chariot!'

Footnote, Koschei to his Journal

I write this sitting at the cedar-wood table in the small white temple with the gilded roof which is the satellite of my Memory Palace locked in Malthassa. It is a fair room and I

430

can see the pink siris and the smaller Tree of Heaven from my seat. Beyond, in the 'real' world (as some say) it is a Holy Day, the day for the propitiation of the great Naga or cobra snake, and the people have laid food and water at the round doorways of the snakes' houses. My Lady smiles and says nothing; she has kept her human form since we first met on the slopes of the Rock at Solutré; she has been Helen and Hélène for two whole world-years. I travel gladly with her, my knowing Mistress, dark shadow of my older Love, whose brown body and lustrous witch's hair, whose forked tongue and pitch-mirk eyes are the counter of Nemione's fair pallor and golden showers, soft corals and sapphires set in pearl. How does he find her, pure white mare? – is she slender, fast and willing? Has she borne him a filly or a colt to bless their thunderous union? Does it favour her, ethereal, tender, or him, solid, red-coated, vigorous? His discarded body works hard for me, by day and by night. I have a fount of brute energy! New life, new landfalls and horizons, new mistress; but the same misspelt name, Koschei, which he – or I – trawled from the infinite world of the imagination, collective memory, universe of tales.

Here they think it is a gypsy name and that is what they take me for, one of themselves, dark-skinned from the hot sun of this land, a Rom colourful and canny.

Our lives are simple, Helen's and mine. Our angel-haired son left us a while ago in a cold country, in winter, the snows and the mountains calling him – he drove away in the wheeled firebird to whatever dissolute or physically punishing pastime best amuses him and we travel on. Our conveyance now is a creaking cart with a canvas tilt for the rains or worldly privacy; once it was painted in gold and red and black and decorated with suns and moons. A few streaks, weather-ravaged, of this old coat remain, for we fashioned it together (one starlit night in the Yellow Desert) out of the material of her *vardo*, her gypsy caravan. From the skewbald horse we made a brown and white ox to draw it. We love and laugh and live as gypsies, the last of the true vagrants, and tell fortunes when we are asked. Helen reads hands while I pretend to scry in my little prism – I found it lying in Limbo beside Parados's abandoned body. It is a useless, shiny bauble now, the only souvenir I have of Malthassa, its compound, magnifying eye fixed firmly on the last thing it saw, the dove-woman Paloma flying (in her second apotheosis at my, or should I say 'the cruel hawk's' talons?) into Malthassa's sun.

My divine Helen, for her rich clients, uses her magic Cup, the King's Goblet upon whose surface passes not only What is Gone but What Will Be, here on Earth. It is not hers, this wondrous Cup but stolen like my body – and I think we are both scented by an ambitious pursuit for I have seen (one dawn in Suleiman's Mountains) an eagle fly up hastily from the rock beside our camping-place and (in the hot afternoon when the red dust rises over the Thar) a camel wake from deep sleep to stare after me.

We have wandered through the warm, wine-loving countries which crowd around the shores of the Mediterranean Sea; we have crossed the driest deserts and the highest mountains to reach this, our temporary home. Its people, who are god-fearing and industrious, call it Sind; but we belong to a smaller nation, my Lady's Tribe of Romanies which history, legend and themselves name the Gypsies of the Gypsies. They crowd about and protect us with their noise and numbers while we make our grail-less, idyllic odyssey. In time, we shall journey to Albion, or England – as I have learned latterly to say – that old land full of loose, unharnessed magic which jealously guards its ancient secrets and its long-held reputation for perfidy. He showed himself perfidious after all, that son of Albion, the Englishman Guy Parados, in moving my mountains and causing new rivers to run through my lands. Once there, in his birth-place, I shall easily reclaim my throne, that of the true author of Koschei the Deathless. Unless the Red Horse of the Plains

432

can open the book in my memory and find my sleeping soul I have eternity in which to make my mark and Helen Lacey and her people to aid me for

Ki shan i Romani
Adoi san' i chov-hani.

Wherever gypsies go
There the witches are, we know.

City of the Iron Fish
Simon Ings

'Simon Ings goes into orbit as a science fiction master'
Daily Mail

Only a fool would ask what strange providence, amid an inferno of scorching heat and splintered rock, saw to the care of the cool, well-watered municipality which is the City of the Iron Fish. The seafaring traditions of the City, the tang of salt in the air, are sustained by powerful magic, and by the bizarre ceremony of the Iron Fish.

But young Thomas Kemp is enraged by the City's contradictions – and, like a fool, sets out in search of an answer to the conundrum. Turning his back on the City, Thomas strides towards the limits of reality armed only with curiosity. It may kill him. Worse, it may not be enough. Worst of all, his companion Blythe, who is as carefree as her name, might be the one to discover the meaning of the City's isolation.

In this riveting gothic adventure Simon Ings probes the very fabric of existence and tears it open . . . to reveal an amazing, sometimes horrifying, world within.

'Simon Ings is a bright light on an otherwise dim horizon . . . a rosy glow announcing the dawn of a new era of excitement in sf'
The New York Review of Science Fiction

ISBN 0 00 647653 8

The Time Ships

Stephen Baxter

The sequel to H.G. Wells's *THE TIME MACHINE*

The Traveller promptly embarks on a second journey to the year A.D. 802,701, firmly pledged to rescue Weena, his charming and helpless Eloi friend whom he abandoned to the cannibal appetites of the Morlocks. But what Stephen Baxter knows that Wells did not is that, by making his first trip into the future, the Traveller has changed the future ... and he will change it again.

Stephen Baxter undertakes a radical – and amazing – reinterpretation of Wells's ideas in the light of cosmological insights gained from outer space and quantum mechanics. The Time Traveller is hurled towards infinity. But he is not a man to abandon his intention to rescue Weena. He must resolve the paradoxes building around him.

'Stephen Baxter has a stunning talent.'   *Locus*
'Arthur C. Clarke, Isaac Asimov and Robert Heinlein succeeded in doing it, but very few others. Now Stephen Baxter joins their exclusive ranks.'   *New Scientist*

ISBN 0 00 648012 8

Beauty
Sheri S. Tepper

Brilliant, unique and unforgettable. The first great fantasy achievement of the 1990s.

Winner of the Locus Award for Best Fantasy Novel.

On her sixteenth birthday, Beauty, daughter of the Duke of Westfaire, sidesteps the sleeping-curse placed upon her by her wicked aunt – only to be kidnapped by voyeurs from another time and place, far from the picturesque castle in 14th century England. She is taken to the world of the future, a savage society where, even among the teeming billions, she is utterly alone. Here her adventures begin. As she travels magically through time to visit places both imaginary and real she eventually comes to understand her special place in humanity's destiny. As captivating as it is uncompromising, *Beauty* will carve its own unique place in the hearts and minds of readers.

'*Beauty* lives up to its name in all ways. It is a story of mankind and magic, fairies and fairytales, future and fantasy all intertwined into a complex collage about the downfall of Earth . . . It is a story you can float away in. The writing is beautiful and the storytelling immaculate, so get it' *Time Out*

ISBN 0 586 21305 8